Absolute Flanigan

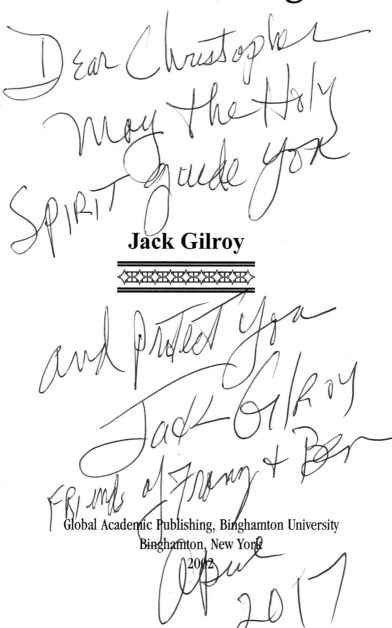

Jack Gilroy

Dear Christopher
May the Holy
Spirit guide you
and protect you

Jack Gilroy
Friends of Franz + Ben

April 2017

Global Academic Publishing, Binghamton University
Binghamton, New York
2002

Library of Congress Cataloging-in-Publication Data
Gilroy, Jack, 1935-
    Absolute Flanigan / Jack Gilroy.
        p.cm
    ISBN 1-58684-233-1 (pbk. : alk. paper)
        1. World War, 1939-1945--Pennsylvania--Fiction.   2. Human experimentation in medicine--Fiction.   3. Illegitimate children--Fiction.   4. Draft resisters--Fiction.   5. Smokejumpers--Fiction. 6. Pennsylvania--Fiction.   7. Prisoners--Fiction.   I. Title.
PS3607.I455A63 2002
813'.6--dc21

Cover illustration by Linda King <jkjaking@att.net>
Cover design by Shalahudin Kafrawi

Published by Global Academic Publishing
Binghamton University

Distributed by
www.jackgilroy.com

Acknowledgments

The suggestion to write fiction to illustrate the truth and power of nonviolence came from my peace activist friend, Charlie Schultze, a WWII combat veteran. My debts to all those friends who read this manuscript, suggested changes, and pointed out typos. My appreciation to my wife Helene who read each chapter immediately after I wrote it and let me know just what she thought. Maureen, my daughter who gave encouragement and advice and commented on every page of this book. To Jerry Berrigan (big brother of Dan & Phil) for his skill in finding and correcting so many of my errors. To Karen Bernardo, my editor and writing advisor. To Mary Heyman who read and reread, made suggestions, and then pushed for the publication of both this novel and my second novel. To Stu Naismith for his suggestions (another WWII combat veteran who became a Quaker after the war) and Roland Austin a WWII conscientious objector who helped me with factual information. To Lori Vandermark of Binghamton University for her keen insight and corrections. To Parviz Morewedge who had the courage and grace to say this book should be published. Thanks to James Bennett and his *Peace Hope* writing committee for the Peace Hope International Award.

Contents

Prologue

The Lt. Colonel gazed from the hospital window but paid little attention to the blue-green vista of the Tennessee hills. Behind him, on the edge of his hospital bed, sat a young man adjusting his leg prosthesis. The young man was smiling as he talked.

"Dr. Lark, I didn't ask to be put in a military hospital. I don't want to be here and I shouldn't be here. The least you could do is to tell me what your medical staff has been pumping into my body."

The LT. Colonel turned from the window and faced the young man.

"I'm a pathologist, not a psychiatrist. You need to think out your past to deal with why you're at Oak Ridge Army Hospital. I wouldn't be of much help on that score. My job is to study human tissue, not emotions and reason.

"True, you're not in the military, but keep in mind that a war is going on. A lot of questions are left unanswered. I don't know what the injected substance is. I do know it's termed 'the product' by my superiors. That, and the fact that you're an HP, is the extent of my knowledge."

"HP?" said the young man.

"Correct. Human Product." Responded the pathologist.

The young man rose from the hospital bed, and adjusted his stance. Face to face with Dr. Lark, he said: "Yeah doc, I must be a good product – better than a rat."

The pathologist paused at the door, "One other thing I do know is 'the product' was already tested on rats. Apparently, it's time to move up the chain."

The young man took the pathologist's place at the window. I'm only 21, he thought, but here I am, in and out of prison, dodging death, testing my moral and religious convictions, and now the government is testing me like a lab rat.

He laughed and said out loud, "I sure do manage to get myself into some strange situations. Maybe it all started with the good nuns. Got to blame somebody!"

He reached into his pocket and fished out a letter he'd received earlier but could not get himself to open. He knew by the handwriting it was from Anna Maria. He bit down hard on his lower lip as he slowly began to open the letter. His premonition of the contents sent his thoughts whirling back to Wurtsville, and the school where he first met her.

Chapter 1
If Good People Said No

"Please, p-l-ease open the door. Someone, please open it. I can't stand the odor."

Sister Hildegarde could be heard only if one happened to be on the bottom floor of St. Catherine's Academy — far removed from the classrooms. Peter Flanigan and his friend, Smacks Paulson, pushed their backs against the boys room door, and Sister Hildegarde had a slim chance of budging the door against the combined weight of the boys. Smacks lit a cigarette and whispered to Peter, "After we share this butt, we better run like hell or we'll be missed in study hall."

"Relax, Smacks. Let old Hildegarde inhale the sweet smells of that stink hole. She treats us like shit. Now it's payback time."

Sister Hildegarde held her nose as she usually did when she went looking for smokers in the boy's room. She was familiar with the stench of the place, but her greater concern was for the boys who said that they were going to the lavatory and came back smelling like tobacco. On many occasions she'd sneaked down to the boys' room entrance, held her hand over her mouth and nose and ordered all boys out. She caught more than one lad with his pants down, but no smokers. It had never occurred to her that old Pat Burke, the convent handyman and fireman, loved company. Pat's attitude was that if the boys wanted to talk and smoke in the boiler room, so be it; let them. Pat simply gave them the usual admonishment, "Ye lads shouldn't be inhaling those terrible gases in the tilet room. If it's a little smoke you want, smoke in here and then be gone with ye."

Just two weeks had passed since school opened, but the lavatory reeked. The toilets were blocked for over a week, and Mr. Burke made no effort to clear them. "Plumbing isn't me favorite chore," was his usual response to those few nuns who pleaded with him to take action. Old Pat found it easier to simply hose out the toilet area whenever the spirit moved him. Not able to use the toilets, the boys took their bowel movements wherever they found a bare spot to stand. A single sixty watt bulb hung loosely from a rafter and threw off barely enough light to enable one to avoid stepping into previously laid piles. Most boys, having only to urinate, would stand at the door, hold their noses, and shoot out to the drain in the center of the concrete floor. The urine would then pass down the sewer pipe and into the Lackawanna River.

"Geez, Pete, if Hildegarde sneaks around through the toilet room and up the back steps, someone will probably open the door for her in the first floor hallway."

"Smacks, did you ever try to go up those stairs? There's enough shit on those steps to grease a battleship. Old Hildegarde may be determined, but she's too prissy to stomp through those loads."

"Peter, don't you think we ought to let her out? If Mother Superior finds out, it's 'Good-bye-St. Catherine's' for both of us."

"Relax, Smacks. You hold the door. I'll run over to the boiler room and get Mr. Burke. We'll tell him that we heard someone screaming in here but that we couldn't get the door open."

Peter bolted into the boiler room. Pat Burke was rocking away, pipe in mouth, one hand rubbing his three day old stubble beard.

"Quick, Mr. Burke, someone is locked in the boys lav. You'll need a key to open up."

"Key? Bejesus, lad, there's no lock on the door."

"Well come anyway, Mr. Burke. Quick!"

The old man hobbled out to the boy's room door, gave the door a push and it opened easily. He walked in, twitched his nose a few times, and hollered out, "Anyone in here?"

Sister Hildegarde screamed, "Thanks be to God." She rushed past Mr. Burke and vomited before reaching the open door. Hanging onto the doorway, she eased herself into the fresh air and bright light, and then she leaned back against the wood frame building. Taking several breaths, she said: "I could not have lasted much longer in there. If you have any idea who locked me in that ghastly place, please tell me."

Peter, silent until now, promised that he would try to find out and report back to her. As he made his way to study hall, he murmured to himself, "Isn't that something? The good Sister Hildegarde thanking a bastard like me."

Earlier in the day, Peter had been humiliated by Sister Hildegarde during one of her tedious readings of Shakespeare. The class had just recovered from a grueling week of listening to her monotone rendition of Julius Caesar. Now she was locked in on King Lear, and the kids were resigned to hear words while their minds drifted far from the topic.

In Act I, Scene II, the entire class had perked up when they heard Sister Hildegarde say, "Bastard." Sensing the group's reaction to Edmund, the illegitimate son of Gloucester, Sister stopped after reading Edmund's chant: "Now, gods, stand up for bastards." Elizabethan English was a drag, but everyone knew the word "bastard." Looking down at their raised heads and smiling faces and hearing a few chuckles, Sister Hildegarde slammed the text on her desk, jammed her palms onto her hips and tore into the class.

"If you think that being a b-a-s-t-a-r-d is funny, then let me tell you just how funny. A rose by any other name is a rose, and a bastard is a bastard. Does anyone want to define it for me? Speak up if you think it all so funny."

Fuming, Sister Hildegarde paced the open area between chalkboard and student desks. "Two weeks of Shakespeare and the only real reaction from you wretched lamebrains is when there is reference to a bastard. You don't even know what the word means. You've heard it used and some of you probably use it not knowing what in God's name you're saying."

All smiles and chuckles had stopped. Peter Flanigan sat in the middle of the room. He knew what the word meant. He also knew that his classmates knew. He felt as though he were on stage. As he sensed all eyes focusing on him, Peter's ears began to tingle.

Making eye contact with everyone, Sister Hildegarde continued, "Bastard means that you don't use your father's name because no marriage between your mother and father ever existed. Of all the lowly creatures in the human race, bastards stand out as the most pitiful."

Although Sister Hildegarde shifted her eyes from person to person, Peter felt the sting in her look when she came to him. He had always been able to shrug off most of what she said. He had ignored her frequent lectures about impure thoughts and how such thoughts would send one to hell as surely as impure acts would. Even her 'boys only' talks were a breeze. The girls in the class were often told to report to Sister St. Stephen, and, once the door was closed, Hildegarde would lay sexual guilt on the boys. Before the period was over, most boys saw themselves as budding rapists, perverts or simply, as hell bound sinners.

The reference to 'bastard' and Sister Hildegarde's obvious glare directed toward him, embittered Peter. Everyone knew he was a bastard. He didn't need Shakespeare or Hildegarde or his friends to remind him. To be told in special sessions several times a year that you were perverted because of your thoughts was something he learned to suffer through. He had lots of company on that one. "All my pals have

to be perverted if that's the case," he thought. But Hildegarde's words
kept ringing in his ear: "Of all the lowly creatures in the human race,
bastards are the most pitiful."

Peter sank in his chair. "To be singled out so crudely," he thought,
"demands vengeance." The doodles he had been scribbling soon were
pushed aside, and on a crisp, clear piece of note paper, he carefully
printed a message.

Sister Hildegarde:

Two boys (I won't tell you who) are smoking in the boy's lavatory.
They are behind the second stall. You will probably have to go right in
to get them.

I know what they are doing is wrong, and my conscience tells me
that it is my duty to report them.

From a student who cares

Peter folded the note in half, neatly creased it, quartered it and
tucked it into the inside pocket of his sport coat.

Sister Hildegarde had stopped talking and was staring at Tom
O'Reiley. She was in one of her fixation stares and Tom, unaware that
she was looking at him, continued to gaze out the window.

Hildegarde, in a near whisper, told the girls to report to Sister St.
Stephen. When the last girl had left, Hildegarde walked swiftly to Tom's
desk, stood over him and said, "Mr. O'Reiley, you have been playing
pocket pool for the past several minutes. Now take your hands out of
your trousers, fold them on your desk and listen to why the likes of you
has a fiery future."

Peter closed his eyes when Sister Hildegarde began her boys-only
lecture. As she rambled, Peter's vision was not of Sister Hildegarde but
of Anna Maria Machelli and her lovely body swaying past his desk as
she moved so sweetly up the classroom aisle. Peter could feel the slight

smile on his face as he traced in his mind the narrow waist, full breasts and lovely legs. In the shadow of his thoughts, he watched Anna Maria as she walked toward the cloakroom. He saw her turn and flutter her long eyelashes in a sexy tease. Then she was gone.

Peter opened his eyes hoping to catch sight of the real Anna Maria, but Sister Hildegarde seemed to read his thoughts. Or was it that Peter knew her speech? "Some of you glare at the girls. I've watched you as your eyes move up and down their bodies. Let me remind you, gentlemen, that their bodies are temples of the Holy Ghost. Your thoughts and blatant desires are not only deadly sinful in themselves but you are also violating a child of God. Your looks and thoughts are as sinful as your deeds. Remember what our Christian faith teaches: If your eye scandalize you, pluck it out! "

Peter shut his eyes again and sure enough, there was Anna Maria. Only this time Peter's smile widened. Anna Maria exited the cloakroom minus her woolen uniform and white blouse. Delightfully to Peter, only he could see her as she paraded past several classmates in her pink panties and bulging bra. She stopped in front of Peter, pursed her scarlet lips and teasingly said, "Peter, honey, will you please help little me by unhooking this dumb old bra?" She wiggled around, pushed out her pretty backside and cinched up her shoulders as she waited for Peter to do his chore. Peter reached up to undo the bra and felt a stinging slap across his face. His eyes popped open and Anna Maria was gone. Sister Hildegarde was in one of her tirades.

"Mr. Flanigan, if you think that waving your fingers and closing your eyes is suitable behavior when the word of God is being spoken, then you don't belong in a Catholic school. Your irreverence is sacrilegious. Either you sit up with your eyes open or go out that door forever!"

Back stepping away from Peter, Hildegarde picked up the tempo. "Last week a girl from the public school was sexually ravished over at the colliery. There is reason to believe that a boy from St. Catherine's was the rapist."

Looking into the eyes of each boy, Sister Hildegarde slowly walked across the front of the room. "I also have information that one of you in this room is responsible."

As she approached each boy, she stopped, and with her hands hidden under her robe, she rattled her rosary beads and waited for a response. Peter could clearly hear O'Reiley whisper, "She wants us to say, 'Is it I, Lord?'"

Peter had not heard of the incident and he wondered what Sister Hildegarde really knew. Whatever the case, it opened up a detailed explanation of the vileness of the human sex act as evidenced by the alleged rape.

The noon heat mixed with the steamy atmosphere created by Sister Hildegarde. Smacks Paulson felt beads of sweat dripping down his neck as Sister Hildegarde recreated the graphic details of the "disgusting use of genitals forced on an unsuspecting and decent young woman." Smacks loosened his necktie and unbuttoned his collar. Peter Flanigan leaned toward Smacks and said, "Hey, Smacks, are you O.K.?" Paulson rolled his eyes and began to gag.

Sister Hildegarde stopped her story line and shouted, "Out! Out! Both of you get out of my classroom immediately! Don't you dare interrupt God's teaching."

Peter grabbed Smacks by the elbow and lifted him to his feet. Hildegarde, oblivious to the plight of Smacks, continued to ramble on as Peter helped him shuffle his way to the door. As he passed by Hildegarde's desk, Peter dropped his note on her grade book.

"What happened to you in there, Smacks?" said Peter.

"That old son-of-a-bitch had my head in a swim, Peter. I was hot and dizzy; I thought I was going to pass out or puke."

"Geez, Smacks, you mean that sex talk made you feel faint?"

"I don't know if that was it, Peter. All I know is that I never felt so terrible about being a guy as I did in there. That lady thinks that guys are as low as whale shit, and that's at the bottom of the ocean."

"We're not as nasty as that old fart has us pegged to be," Peter said, as he put his arm around Smacks. "Let's go down to Dirty Freddie's and shoot some eight ball."

Several days later Peter was called out of study hall and told to report to Mother Rachel, the principal of the school and the mother superior of the convent.

Sitting only a few feet from Mother Rachel, Peter was mesmerized by her attractiveness. Her radiant beauty, in contrast to the appearance of the other nuns, was startling to Peter. "Yet there is so little to look at," he thought. The Sisters of Mary were packaged in a Medieval costume. The only skin showing, other than that of the hands, was an oval of facial flesh which was encased by a ring of hard, white starched linen that pinched the chin, forehead and cheeks. The starched linen head gear looped over the forehead and squeezed the temples. Thus it became a set of blinders which prevented peripheral vision. Shoulders, breasts, waist, hips and legs were draped in straight blue and black cloth, leaving only the very tip of the nun's shoes exposed. In order to hide ample breasts that might bulge, a heavily starched half moon plate of white linen was stretched across each sister's chest. Behind all the garb, Peter saw in Mother Rachel that which he failed to recognize in the other sisters: femininity and beauty. She smiled easily and her soft green eyes seemed to enhance the sincerity and pleasantness of her voice.

The warmth that the mother superior conveyed to Peter quickly disappeared when she addressed him as "Mr. Flanigan". Peter knew immediately that his reason for being there was not social.

"Mr. Flanigan, two recent events have been reported to me, and I demand an honest, open response from you. Can I count on that?"

"Yes," replied Flanigan.

"All right then, Peter, look at this note and tell me if you recognize it."

Peter took the note, examined it, and said, "Yes, I wrote it."

"Did you tell Sister Hildegarde about the smokers because you wanted the boys to stop smoking in the lavatory?"

"Boys don't smoke in the boy's room, Mother Rachel."

"Then why did you write that note, Peter?"

"I guess I wanted Sister Hildegarde to feel low and wretched, and the boy's room seemed the ideal place."

"Peter, what occurred between you and Sister Hildegarde that led you to plan such a punishment?"

Peter lowered his gaze for the first time and was silent. Mother Rachel shifted forward in her chair and said, "Tell me, Peter."

"Mother, every day that I come in contact with that woman, I feel rotten. She's made all of us boys think that we're low life. She implies that we're either sex maniacs or perverts and that the only thoughts we ever have are evil. A lot of the guys are saying, `If we're going to hell because of the thoughts we have, why not go out and really do something bad? At least we'll have some fun in the meantime.'"

Mother Rachel sat upright again and said, "Peter, many of the people you will meet in life will tell you things that they believe to be true but that you do not have to believe. Our religion is based on faith in God, belief in the divinity of Jesus Christ and doing good works. What thoughts flash across one's mind during the course of a minute, a day or a year or even of a lifetime are inconsequential. How one acts toward another and the sense of justice that a person develops is the measure of one's worth - whether he be Christian, Jew, Hindu, Moslem or Atheist. We have to keep things in perspective, Peter.

"Everyone makes mistakes, but central to all of our teaching is human dignity. It seems that, if what you say is true, Sister Hildegarde has deviated from that central point. What any boy or girl, man or woman thinks is unrelated to how one acts. Man is known by his actions, Peter. Good is the absence of evil. Evil cannot exist simply in the mind. It must be activated; it must be performed. Do you understand?"

"I like what you say but after being told just the opposite many times, I find it pretty hard to understand."

"The church is imperfect, Peter. The church is not just pope, cardinals, bishops, priests, brothers and nuns. The church is all of us - all who profess a belief in the divinity of Jesus Christ. As Roman Catholics, we believe that the bishop of Rome, who is the pope, is directly inspired by God. He may sin, make mistakes and act as any human might, but, we believe that when he speaks from his official position as the pope, he cannot err."

Peter listened carefully. He couldn't accept that line about a human not being able to make an error. It was of those frequent multiple choice questions found on religion tests. Match "pope" with ex cathedra. But although bored, he listened. The whole issue of a person not making a mistake was bogus to Flanigan. His only reason for not objecting was fear of alienating the nun he most admired.

Mother Rachel went on, "Peter, no pope, no official doctrine of the Roman Catholic church has ever taught what one thinks is in itself sinful. Some people, including priests and nuns have misinterpreted the teachings of the church. Quite often, even blind faith has led some of our clergy into deep error. For example, the central teachings of Jesus Christ on unconditional love have often been ignored by priests, bishops and popes who have encouraged and supported violent actions. What you have experienced here at St. Catherine's is perhaps, an example of one's misinterpretation of Christ's teaching."

Peter leaned forward, "Like Father Goodman's joyous smiles when he teaches how good Americans are at killing enemies? Have you seen that sadistic smile on his face when he explains how we eliminated savages from the Great Plains to extend our frontier to the Pacific. Lately, he drools over events happening in Europe. He claims we're going to be drawn into another war with Germany. He hopes that Russia can be our enemy too — he wants to see the United States at war with the Godless Bolsheviks."

"Peter, I am aware of Father Goodman's enthusiasm for the military might of our country, but I am saddened to hear of Sister

Hildegarde's preaching on bad thoughts. All that I can say is that you should think carefully about the central teachings of the New Testament. The message of Christ is a message of love, not violence. Perhaps Father Goodman is caught up in the violence portrayed in the Old Testament. We are people of the New Testament, Peter. You will not find Christ promoting violence of any kind."

"I have to speak out against anyone praising bloody conflict. Father Goodman is not the only one who seems anxious to send our young blood to another European war. Peter, imagine what would happen to the lust for power if good people said no? Imagine what would happen if parents of children in the German Youth Movement refused to send their children to war preparation camps? If priests, ministers, bishops, school teachers, lawyers, doctors, and workers in general refused to cooperate with the violent plans of military-political leaders? It seems people in Europe are acting like sheep instead of Christians. I wonder where the true followers of Christ are? Where are the people of faith standing up to violent leaders?"

"I know Father Goodman's answer to that," said Flanigan. "Father Goodman would say that people must follow government decrees. That Jesus said to render to Caesar that which is Caesar's, and to God that which is God's."

"Peter, do you think that young Germans recently involved in the bloody Blitzkrieg of Poland were doing God's work?"

"I suppose some of them think so. Especially if they had teachers and parents who told them they had a duty to God and country," said Flanigan.

"Peter, people around the world need to think out the relationship of their own conscience to the power of violent leadership. You are a very mature young man. Few people — even people older than you — question the power of government and the claim that because you live within a man-made geographic border, you must kill others to protect that border, or to expand that border into other areas. My only advice to you is to continue to question and think of non-violent options. That would include non-cooperation in the face of violent actions.

"Peter, I am not unhappy that your observations have detoured us from the central reason for your being here. However, our meeting is not to discuss Father Goodman but your actions this afternoon. We have not finished with the boys' room incident.

"Locking Sister Hildegarde in the boy's lavatory was cruel and unjust punishment for what you considered to be errors on her part. If you had only come to me, this whole situation would not have occurred. I shall tend to Sister Hildegarde, and, in the meantime, you and the other boys must stop your vindictiveness. I shall have some general sessions with all of the sisters and bring up the problem you have explained to me. As punishment for your acts — not for your thoughts — you may spend the next two weeks hosing out the boy's lavatory every day. I have already ordered Mr. Burke to clean up the mess. You and your associates can help the old man and at the same time do restitution for your wrongs."

Peter, smiling sheepishly, rose slowly, and, with his head half bowed, said, in an nearly inaudible whisper, "Thank you, Mother Rachel."

Chapter 2
A Messy Introduction

Peter Flanigan was reflective on the long walk home from school. He told himself that he needed to get over his sensitivity about his absent father. But when he approached the railroad trestle, he stopped and smiled. The railroad trestle that he walked under each day brought back memories of Eddie Brosnan and himself over five years ago. He looked up and could almost see himself and Eddie, leaning precariously over the trestle on a warm spring day.

"The deep, black puddles near the coal pile will be best for filling up the rubbers, Eddie."

The boys weren't really looking for the rubbers, but they were just waiting to be picked up and filled with the nice watery soot that drained down from the massive coal pile on the far side of the trestle. A gallon or so of soot made a bulging bomb in search of a target. The only question the boys would ask was, "Who will the unlucky receivers be?"

Peter Flanigan didn't really care who got nailed with the muddy condom. Anyone dumb enough to walk under the trestle was fair game, but cars were more fun — choice cars, big Packards, fancy Cadillacs and Mrs. Rowe's Rolls Royce (the only one in town).

Peter and Eddie began scooping up the water and muck; Eddie was forced to stretch the condom's opening. Each receptacle took one #2 soup can to fill to the brim. Peter gingerly poured the mucky concoction, while Eddie quickly knotted the opening of each missile.

"Wouldn't it be great if that old fart would come cruising by in her Rolls, Peter?"

"Naw, I don't care about fat ass Mrs. Rowe, Eddie. Wait till you see who's going to get these beauties."

Each boy now had two bouncing sacks of mud, and getting to the top of the trestle became a balancing act as they pushed upward along the coarse blocks of granite. Once on top, they marched coolie style, backs bent, partly from the weight of the rubber bombs, mostly out of fear of being seen. The street was now directly under them and Peter cautioned Eddie to keep down until they spotted their target.

"Who ya aimin' to hit, Peter?"

"You'll see. Just wait. He comes this way every Wednesday at nine o'clock. To the links is where the bastard is goin'."

Eddie's mind was whirling. He knew that Monsignor Golden went golfing every Wednesday morning, and today was Wednesday.

"Jeez, Peter, ya aren't gonna hit a priest with that rubber, are ya?"

"Just shut up, Eddie. You don't have to drop yours. Take them home to your old lady and tell her to wash them out for your pa."

Eddie was silenced; Peter didn't usually talk that way to him. To others, he did, but Peter was his friend. Even though Peter was three years older, Eddie knew that Peter didn't mind his hanging around. If anyone minded, it was Eddie's father, Mr. Bradley. Mr. Bradley was always making comments about the fact that Peter didn't have a father. Eddie thought that not having a father was pretty bad, but Tom Connors' father had been killed in the mines, as had Rats Boland's dad. Besides, a lot of kids' fathers were away working or looking for work. Not having fathers around was kind of normal.

"Get ready, Eddie. Here comes the son-of-a-bitch."

Eddie tightened his hold on the rubbers and stretched his neck over the iron guard rails.

"It's a big convertible, Peter. It's the Stutz Bearcat, Peter. Holy Moses, we can't bomb the mayor, Peter."

"Like shit, we can't. Watch this."

***

Just a half hour before Peter's caper, the Mayor was preparing for a leisure afternoon of golf. Mayor Mahoney looked real snazzy. He had an expansive wardrobe in his little dressing room off his office at city hall. There were frequent functions for him to attend, and a quick change of clothing, to suit the occasion, was necessary to maintain the appropriate image. So he had changed from his double breasted pin-striped suit to a sporty Hawaiian style shirt and white cotton pants. This morning he had only one appointment and that was with Monsignor Golden. Mahoney knew what the good father wanted. In a town of twenty-five thousand souls, few scandals were secret. Now, Mahoney wanted to think golf, but the old priest occupied his mind.

"Mr. Mayor," the monsignor began, "It has come to my attention that you are opposed to pressing charges against the Susquehanna and Hudson Coal Company. Is that so, Mr. Mayor?"

Mahoney twitched his jowls. He hadn't expected a man of the collar to weasel into civil matters. "This foxy old bastard is up to something," thought Mahoney.

"Monsignor, that is an absolute untruth. Why, anyone would agree that opposing that Protestant company would drive them out of the valley. I'm not against seeing the whole lot of them go to jail, but what judge or jury would convict them? Not only would our tax structure suffer, but our people would be on the dole and our businesses would be teetering on economic disaster. Needless to say, Monsignor, your

Sunday collection would not be the grand sum you are used to; now would it?"

The old man tried not to sneer at Mahoney. He knew the power of the man and the popularity he had with the electorate. Mahoney was a crook, but a jolly crook. He was fun to be with and he always delivered when a favor was asked. However, a favor, once granted, demanded repayment and Mahoney had a fantastic memory. The old priest stroked his chin and tried a new ploy.

"Mr. Mayor, the loss of the Susquehanna & Hudson to our people would be devastating, agreed. But, what of the existing loss of our people on the west side? The mine 'cave-ins' are destroying homes throughout that area. You have seen the houses, Mayor; tipped and tilted they are. Why, a lad can't eat his oatmeal without having it slide off the table. People would gladly move out of the homes they so dearly love, but they have nowhere to go.

"If the Susquehanna & Hudson Company didn't rob the pillars of coal beneath those houses, the caves would not have occurred. But rob them they did, and now they must face up to their responsibility and fix the houses or provide new homes for the victims of capitalistic greed. You know as well as I, Mayor, that unless you and the courts force the company's hand, nothing will happen. Our people need the jobs, but no company has the right to destroy a man's home and hide behind archaic mineral rights' contracts."

Mahoney couldn't help himself any longer. His chuckle, suppressed for the last minute or two of the old priest's monologue, intensified, turned into a laugh, and then, an uncontrollable roar.

Father Golden was red with rage. His emotions told him to slam the door in Mahoney's fat Irish face. Instead, he slowly moved toward the door, grasped the brass knob, and while stiffening his grip and his demeanor, slowly turned to the mayor.

Before the monsignor could speak, Mahoney, over his laughing spell, shifted his thumbs into his weskit pockets, poised himself and made eye contact with the old man.

"Father, you have spent the past thirty years at St. Catherine's, and in all of those days and months, you have been a compassionate, bright, but naive man. How, in God's name, can I or the courts fight an organization that owns all the underground mining rights to this anthracite region, controls every railroad track and steam engine, box car and caboose, machine shop and even the goddam coal mines themselves. Taking on the Susquehanna & Hudson has about as much probability of succeeding as the Jews taking on the Nazi party. Use your common sense, Monsignor; the S & H is in control, and won't be put down by politician or priest."

Monsignor's grip on the doorknob hardened again; rope like veins of blue rose above his whitened knuckles. With his free hand, he snapped on his wide brimmed, black felt hat, swung open the tall walnut door; then, turned to Mahoney.

"May your day at the country club be filled with gaiety, and may you enjoy the charm of all your fucking coal mining friends, Mr. Mayor."

The slam of the door jolted Mahoney. He thought he felt his teeth rattle. Within the hour, he would be jarred again.

***

Dropped from a height of thirty feet, the hitting force of several pounds of muck in a thin rubber container split the spent condom and sent the watery mess in all directions. Mahoney's driver quickly hit the brakes and sent the mayor toward the windshield. The mayor's immense abdomen acted like an inflated balloon, and simply took the shock as the paunch squeezed against the dashboard.

For a moment, driver and passenger sat dazed as they tried to figure out what happened. Overhead, on the trestle, a boy had one hand on his stomach and the other pressed against his mouth, but the laughter was too much to muffle.

Eddie had already cut out. Crouched low on the track bed, he had managed to pick up speed as he scampered along the railroad ties toward the coal strippings which formed a man - made canyon on the west side of town. Once off the trestle and around the bend, it was easy to lose sight of a person in the strippings. There were no trees, plants, grass or animals – it was a moonscape scene with huge boulders randomly dropped by steam shovels in their search for coal veins close to the surface. A heavy snow could hide the ugliness, but now, in July, these great hills of dirt, lined with eroded furrows, were an embarrassment to the people who remembered the greenness and the little brooks that laced the ridges above the town. Picking his way along the rocks, Eddie found the concealment he wanted. The trestle was clearly visible, and Eddie, when he saw what was happening, wanted to holler to Peter. Mayor Mahoney's driver, wiry old Pat Walsh, was climbing the terraced stone abutment, and if Peter didn't get moving fast, the mayor would have him for sure.

Walsh was in good shape for a man of sixty, but the excitement of the bombing and the climb up the tiered foundation left him panting on the last stone before the bridge. Catching his breath, he heard giggles break into laughter, then drift back to giggles. Walsh eased himself up, peered around the iron fencing and saw Peter Flanigan. The boy had his eyes closed, his back to the guard rails. When the giggles turned into laughter, he clamped his hand over his mouth and turned the joy back to muffled laughter. Walsh cautiously stepped up and tip-toed across a dozen ties. When he grabbed Peter by the neck, he expected a scuffle from the little scamp. Instead, Peter popped his eyes open and said, "I wish I coulda run, but this was just too much fun."

Walsh had been a dedicated go-fer and yes-man and body-guard since 1932, the year his boss was elected mayor of Wurtzville. There'd been threats against his leader in the past and many bad words, but no one had ever accosted the mayor. He wanted to whip the boy.

"I ought to beat the living shit out of you," said Walsh as he twisted the boy's arm, grabbed a handful of red hair and led him down to the mayor's car.

Mahoney was sitting in the car, still cleaning himself with his golfing towel, when Walsh and his prisoner marched up to the convertible. One contraceptive was still on the hood of the car, black streaks streaming to left and right. The mayor's hair was plastered along his forehead, and although he cleaned his face, it was evident he'd taken the full shot of the water missile.

The mayor unlatched the door, stepped out and, before Peter Flanigan could say a word, Mahoney unleashed the back of his hand across Peter's face, tumbling him to the ground.

"You little freckled face son-of-a-bitch," yelled Mahoney. "What's your name and where do you live?"

It was the moment that Peter wanted. He could have avoided capture. "Old man Walsh would have been lost in my dust," thought Peter, "but what a great way to meet Mr. Mahoney."

"Well speak up you little shit and get your skinny ass off the ground."

Peter defiantly sat on the road and, knowing full well that the salty taste in his mouth was blood, smiled broadly at Mahoney.

"My ma says I look a lot like you, Mr. Mayor, but I always said, 'Naw, Ma, he's too fat for me to look like him.' But, you know what, Mr. Mayor, up close — jeez, there is a resemblance."

Peter rose slowly, dusting off his corduroy trousers. Mahoney, taken off balance by the boy's absence of fear, forced a sardonic smile, and gesturing to his assistant with his foot, suggested that the boy should get "a swift kick in the arse to get him talking."

"Hold on, don't get your dander up, Mr. Mayor. I live in that little unpainted house on the corner of Boland and Clune Court. My mother's name is Flanigan, Eleanor Flanigan. You remember her, don't you, Mr. Mayor? Remember about twelve years ago-when you used to screw her every Friday night after Bingo? Well, one of those nights, you helped make me, Mr. Mayor, and bingo — here I am, Peter Flanigan Mahoney. I'm a real prize; ain't I, Mayor? Or maybe I should be callin' you, 'Dad.' What do you think?"

The blood drained from Mahoney's usual ruddy complexion. Walsh, recognizing that his verbose boss wanted to speak but couldn't, stepped in front of the mayor, and grabbing Peter by the ear, said in a near whisper, "If you ever make such a comment to the mayor or anyone again, I'll take you to your mother and have her whip your ass raw. Now get on with you and don't ever let me see you around the mayor again." Walsh released his grip on Peter's ear, and, simultaneously kicked the boy in the backside sending him reeling into the fender of the Stutz. Peter lost no time in putting distance between himself and Walsh, but at twenty yards, he turned and hollered, "Nice meetin' you, Dad."

Walsh reached for a rock to throw at the boy, but since Peter was swiftly out of hurling range, he dropped the missile and went over to Mahoney. The mayor, immobile and glassy-eyed, stared down the empty street. Peter had already darted off to an alley and was halfway home.

"Don't pay any mind to that little shanty Irish bastard, Mayor. We'll not see or hear from him again."

Mahoney with a broad smile across his flushed face unstuck his tongue and said: "Mr. Walsh, no blood of mine would back off that easily. I'm sure we'll be hearing from Peter Flanigan."

Chapter 3
Scheming For Boom Times

As years passed and the decade of the '30's came to an end, Peter Flanigan matured as Mayor Mahoney tightened his political grip on Wurtzville. Monsignor Golden continued his role as a city hall gadfly and spokesman of his parishioners. The only change that occurred was more mine caves and more home destruction.

The mayor made his trip to Wurtzville Country Club every Wednesday, always with an eye on the trestle above and always with the convertible top up. The drive to the Wurtzville Country Club took Mahoney up and out of the soot and smoke of the town. Once he was over the ridge, the scarred side hills and black culm piles were but a gray blur in his rear view mirror.

An undulating plateau of farms and green forests stretched out to the horizon. It was late August and wheat and oats, plump from a warm summer, were ready for the reaper. The glaciated lakes and reed-rimmed ponds were visual feasts for the people from the valley. Down in Wurtzville, the Lackawanna River flowed black. Collieries, the huge buildings where chunks of coal were smashed into burnable pieces, washed out black powdery waste and flushed it into the Lackawanna. Recently, a new method of coal excavation, called stripping, was tearing away grass, bushes, trees, rock and dirt to reach coal veins close to the earth's surface. With every heavy rainfall, the stripping piles developed deeper fissures, and the runoff transposed the river from ugly black to ugly brown. Trout once thrived in the river, but now no living thing, neither plant nor animal, lived in or on its banks.

People accepted the Lackawanna as it was. Only the very old knew what it once had been. Now the river pollution was simply a price that had to be paid for jobs created by the coal companies.

As Walsh drove through the farmlands, Mahoney's thoughts were on Peter Flanigan and his mother, Ella. The mayor hadn't thought of Ella for years. Occasionally, he saw her in town, spoke to her in a courteous fashion and usually asked, "How are you?" It was always, "Fine, Billy, and you?" and off she would go.

"God, what a beautiful woman she was," thought Mahoney. As he daydreamed, he realized that he was trying to recreate that period of time when his political career was gaining momentum. Ella, bright but uneducated, and with no financial connections, had little to offer Mahoney.

Analyzing why he and Ella had moved apart, Mahoney shifted his thoughts to Sally Caufield. He remembered dating Sally. She wasn't bad looking. In fact, she was cute in a plump, pretty way. She had a college education, and her family lived on the east side of town, the Protestant side. Her father, George Caufield, was president of the Lackawanna Miners' Bank. For a young Irish lad on the move, Mahoney was instinctive enough to smell success when Sally Caufield gave him some flirty come-on's.

Old man Caufield, fully aware of his daughter's intellectual shortcomings, wanted Sally to go away to a nice little college in North Carolina. Graduating would be no problem down there, and the chance of meeting a fine young Baptist would be considerably greater in the south than in the Wurtzville area. The two local colleges for girls were Catholic institutions, and George Caufield was determined that his Sally would go to neither school. However, Sally was adamant in resisting her father's plan. When she insisted that she would not go away, Caufield, grudgingly compromising, performed some minor financial miracles for the expansion of Ellenwood College. In return, his daughter was admitted there without reference to high school performance or to admission test scores. Ellenwood was considered to be a first class Catholic college for girls. Most of its students were wealthy Catholic kids whose homes were far removed from the lovely campus setting just a few miles from Wurtzville. A limited number of middle income girls commuted to Ellenwood from Wurtzville, but they were the best academic students from the area. The same sisters who ran Ellenwood also maintained an extensive parochial school system, making it an easy chore to select the most capable students for scholarships.

Mahoney met Sally shortly after she finished her four years at Ellenwood. By that time, Mahoney was gearing up for the mayoralty after having served his apprenticeship on the Board of Education. He had tucked away a few thousand dollars during his four years on the board. There were always anxious young men and women who wanted teaching jobs and the under-the-table going rate was five hundred dollars a position. As the president of the board, Mahoney met privately with candidates, and if he requested a second meeting, the person knew he had a job; that is, if he brought Mahoney five hundred dollars in a plain envelope.

When George Caufield called Mahoney about an appointment for his daughter, Mahoney was smart enough to understand that not only would Caufield's daughter get a teaching position, but also that Mahoney would be without the usual required five hundred dollars.

"Fair enough," Mahoney remembered saying to his political cronies, "but remember, Boys, there is no such thing as a free teach."

Mahoney smiled to himself as they motored through the lacy

wrought iron gates and past the velvety practice greens of the Wurtzville
Country Club. "Sally has been mine for years now, and she hasn't pressured me to marry her, but I have yet to collect from old George,"
thought Mahoney. That thought pleased the mayor for he knew that
George Caufield would be at the club today. Wednesday was contact day
for businessmen and every good businessman gave a friendly greeting
to Caufield and Mahoney.

As the Stutz Bearcat came to a stop at the edge of the flagstone
steps, it was quickly attended to by half a dozen boys who had spotted
its arrival from their perch on the caddy shack railing. Each boy pushed
and struggled in his effort to be the one who would open the door for
the mayor. Mahoney was a very good tipper, and the boy selected to be
his caddy would be the one who had opened the car door. Tony Faldo
happened to be the fastest boy in the group, and a pat on Tony's head
from the mayor assured the lad of a one dollar tip for just nine holes of
golf.

Mahoney, nodding and waving to busboys, waiters and bartend-
ers, made his way to the locker room. All smiled and gave their "Hi,
Mayor" greeting.

After quickly changing into shirt and slacks and slipping on his
golf shoes, Mahoney admired his fresh look in the wall mirror, and he
then set off for the pro shop.

Willie Cooligan, the caddy master, had the mayor's set of clubs all
washed and shining. "Your foursome is ready to go, Mayor. The other
three gentlemen are out on the first tee warming up," said Willie.

The caddy who had been selected by the mayor tugged at the
huge bag, lifted it up and slipped the rough leather strap over his right
shoulder. Tony Faldo weighed ninety-five pounds, and the mayor's bag
weighed in at around sixty.

Mahoney was known to lose his temper on the course after each
of his many bad shots, and a faulty club or two often made it into the
lake or was banged into a tree for its misperformance. To compensate

for his tantrums, Mahoney carried a double set of clubs. The bag's side pockets were often stuffed with shiny Titalists or Wilson K-28's at the start of the game, but Mahoney's slice assured the caddy that ball weight would be reduced before the nine holes of weekly torture was up.

Tony, listing to starboard side, made his way through the tall spruces to the tee. As he and the mayor emerged from the shade to the sun, there was a chorus of, "Hi, Mayor."

"Hi, Boys. Hang on to your dollars, Gentlemen, the Ben Hogan of Wurtzville is on the scene."

"Hi, Partner," said George Caufield as he grasped the mayor's hand and swung his left arm over Mahoney's shoulder. Caufield walked the mayor over to Mark Chaddock and Liam Barrett, the opposition for the afternoon. Chaddock and Barrett acted as if they were old pals of Mayor Mahoney. They knew that if the golf wasn't good, then either the mayor's humor or his temper tantrums would add a touch of theatre to the day.

"Mayor, tell these lads what is going to happen to them this fine afternoon," said Caufield.

Mahoney pushed his moon shaped face close to Chaddock and Barrett and said, "Hang onto your balls, boys; you'll need some security after we whip your asses and pinch your wallets."

Chaddock and Barrett chuckled, but Barrett, the club champion and Chaddock, a four handicapper, knew that Mahoney couldn't beat his caddy.

Barrett had known Mahoney since grammar school. Unlike Mahoney, Barrett had gone to college, finished law school, and quickly rose to the position of District Attorney before being elected Judge of the Superior Court of Pennsylvania in]937. Now everyone knew him simply as "Judge," and Barrett loved the title.

Mark Chaddock was an outsider. He had come to Wurtzville during the railroad strike of 1922. As a strike breaker, Chaddock was hated by the loyal union men who'd been without work for over a year. Scabs were a pox on the community in this labor oriented town. Yet, Chaddock survived the threats, glares and snubs by the workers. The company rewarded him with a job as a foreman after the strike was over. Now, eighteen years later, Chaddock held the title of Superintendent of the Susquehanna & Hudson.

"You're up, Billy. If you and George are going to tan our hides, get on with it," said Barrett.

Mahoney, his bulky driver tucked under his arm, was in the process of extracting his ball from the ball washer. "Me good muther, God bless her soul, always told me to wash me balls before I go out to play. Now you byes keep your eagle eyes on the middle of the fairway, and I'll give you a lesson in clean Irish livin'."

Mahoney took a practice swing and prepared to trash the ball soundly. The club head swung far around the mayor's shoulders and his narrow tongue snaked out of his determined mouth; nearly touching his nose. At the top of the swing, the club head wobbled about for a second, then wildly whipped around until it met turf first. A divot went hurdling into the rough and the shiny clean K-28 sat untouched.

"Maybe Billy should take a job as a dragline operator in my coal stripping operation," whispered Chaddock to Barrett.

"Notice he didn't replace the divot, Mark? Shades of the Susquehanna & Hudson. When was the last time that you filled in one of those coal pits you boys have been gouging?"

"Let's talk golf, Liam. I hear enough bullshit about that from the whiners and troublemakers in Wurtzville."

Billy didn't let himself get ruffled by the poor practice swing. He stepped toward the ball, wound up and smacked it dead center. The ball sizzled out over two hundred yards as teammate and challengers shouted, "Good shot, Billy."

The first five holes went smoothly. Mahoney and Caufield were down by only two after Billy's handicap was calculated. The conversation gradually drifted from golf to business.

"Billy, I'm glad we have an opportunity to discuss the letter you sent me last week. I have to admit that the whole tenor of the note took me by surprise. Surely you haven't taken up sides with the good monsignor on the mine cave issue. Have you, Billy?"

"Mark, let's look at the issue from my point of view. Monsignor Golden is my parish priest, and basically, he's a good fellow and has the interests of the parishioners always on his mind. The cave-in on the west side of town has everyone concerned, and the old man believes that I have a finger in the pie with you on this one. I've been able to wave off a few cracked foundations and tilted houses as normal subsidence in a mining town. But, goddamn it, Mark, he's on to the pillar robbing that your men have been doing over the years. He knows that the pine timber props which are being used to replace the tons of coal pillars are rotting, and once they fall, the goddamn roofs start falling too. It's got fucking disaster written all over it, Mark, and we both know it."

"I can sympathize with you, Billy, but I know a hell of a lot more about mining techniques than you. My engineers suggested that we start taking out the coal pillars in 1928. Since then there have been only a handful of subsidence problems, but do you know the high grade of anthracite we have taken out? It's hundreds of thousands of tons. Goddamn it, Billy, you haven't been neglected. We have taken good care of you, and the house in Palm Beach is yours to keep. What more can I say?"

"You can say that we are both dancing on egg shells, Mark. I don't buy that shit about just a few subsidences. Wurtzville has been mined for over a hundred years. The subsurface of the town is honeycombed with tunnels; virtual rivers flow through many of them. Those treated pine props which your smart ass engineers stuffed throughout the mines aren't going to last forever, and when they go, the whole fucking town will start sinking."

"Billy Boy, this town wouldn't even exist if it weren't for the mines and railroad. Our work has problems and disadvantages just like any other industry. Down in Pittsburgh, a few newspaper quacks are getting worked up about smoky skies and soot. Across the Atlantic, the English were beginning to think that the industrial dirt of Leeds and Manchester and the mining problems of Newcastle were first rate problems. The Nazi Luftwaffe has silenced those people. No one complains about mining and industry during times of crisis. Anyone with an ounce of sense knows that a strong industrial power has to have some smoke, some accidents and unfortunately, some holier-than-thou preaching panic. Tell the good father to come up with a plan that will keep his people working; I'd like to hear it. Remember, Billy, if it weren't for the pillar profit, your country club life and sporty cars would have to come out of your own pocket. Billy, this country is going to be at war before the year is out. Mark my words, and if it happens, coal cars will be backed up from the Port of New York to Wurtzville. Boom times, Billy! The coal won't come from the few bloody pillars left to rob."

Mahoney frowned at Chaddock's last comment and raised his thick dark eyebrows. "Tell me," the mayor said, "just where the hell you'll be getting the coal? You know damn well that your company can't afford to go down to the deep veins."

"Draglines, Billy. Big fucking steam shovels gouge tons of dirt, rock, slate and finally, good, black, money-making anthracite. Those little shovels over on the west and south mountains are thimbles compared to the monsters which the Susquehanna & Hudson have on order."

"Mark, those shovels you have in operation now may be small, but the complaints against them are growing. Two Italian families came into my office yesterday. They 'donna lika dat noise a clang, a clang, a clang'. They 'donna lika dat-a light from a steam-a-shovel on their housa all a-nighta'. Goddamn it, Mark, if those guineas are starting to complain about noise, and all night spot lights swinging across their windows, can't you just picture the protest when those fucking iron jaws start chomping away at Wurtzville's mountains? What are you going to say to the people then?"

"Look, Billy, every day London or some other Limey town is shown on the front pages of American newspapers. What do people see? They see buildings in ruin, broken bodies, burning industries. So what do we tell the assholes who complain about a few torn up hills and a little extra noise? We tell them that we are already on war production; and we are, Billy. You have no idea what the federal government is ordering in coal. They have got to be stockpiling for some reason and my bet is that war is in the making."

Mahoney's game, so loose and easy for the first five holes tightened on him during his conversation with the S & H mining boss. "Chaddock," he thought, "has my ass in a sling. If I break with him now, all my other contacts will be in jeopardy." The mayor knew that Chaddock had the good judge in one pocket and Caufield, the banker, in the other. The Lackawanna Miners' Bank was publicized as the Independent Bank of the Anthracite Valley. In actual fact, the Susquehanna & Hudson held thirty per cent of the shares in the bank, and several subsidiaries held another thirty per cent. Caufield was beholden to Chaddock in a very discreet manner. No mention of the power of the S & H over the Lackawanna Bank was ever made by either man. They just knew.

As the foursome approached the ninth tee, Mahoney and Caufield were five down, and the game was all but conceded. Slicing into the woods, hitting some divots further than the ball and, for the last two holes, using the caddy as a whipping boy; the mayor had obviously lost his new found touch with his clubs, and was back in old form. Tony, the caddy, was willing to take abuse because he knew that, whatever the outcome of the match, he would get his dollar tip plus thirty-five cents for carrying the bag for nine holes. For Tony, the sweat and strain was almost over. He could see the ninth green and the bamboo hole pin and red flag quivering in the wind. A few years back, Peter Flanigan had told Tony how to make some extra cash on the notorious non-tippers or, as Peter called that group, the "obnoxious assholes." Tony knew that a good caddy always kept the ball in view and marked it well if it came down in the rough or woods. Peter told Tony to forget the "old crap" about finding balls. "If you're carrying for a prick, heel his balls," said Peter as he showed Tony how to hide a ball by standing on it and ramming it into the turf. "After you collect your caddy money, go back to the woods or rough and dig out the balls. Then take them down by the lake hole tee and sell them to the duffers who knock their shots into the lake."

Tony didn't expect to do that, especially to the mayor. His parents had great respect for the mayor and his title. They had voted for him, and Tony's father, who hadn't worked for years, was confident that a job with the city road crew was soon to come. After hearing the mayor's caustic talk about Italians, Tony quickly changed his mind. He heeled balls on holes six, seven and eight, and now, at the ninth tee, he smiled when he saw the rough on the right side of the fairway.

Chaddock's ostensibly threatening comments to the mayor threw Mahoney's game into a tailspin and turned his jolly manner grim. Mahoney learned over the years that delegating authority was an easy way of getting out of work, and projecting blame for his own failures to underlings became common policy.

"O.K. my little grease ball, get your tail over into the woods, and keep your eye on the ball," hollered Mahoney. "If that little Dago loses one of my balls, I'll castrate him," mumbled the mayor as he orchestrated his wiggling tongue with his dancing club head and lashed out at the ball. The unorthodox swing slid the ball off the end of the clubhead and over Tony's head into the trees beyond the fairway boundary. Tony was there in seconds; he spotted the ball immediately and stomped down hard on it. The K-28 slid into the soft soil, and Tony neatly tapped the mulch which surrounded the ball. In one quick motion, he looked back at the tee, stretched out his arms and empty hands and shrugged his shoulders.

Mahoney stood fuming. When Tony's no-found signal hit him, he could restrain himself no longer. In grand ballerina fashion, Mahoney did two complete spins while swinging the driver over his head. At the top of the third body turn, he let go of the club. It was an amazing throw; it traveled farther than many of his golf shots and landed, with a gentle splash, in the lake below. The mayor declined to play out the last hole. In fact, the driver was still in flight when Mahoney started his long quick strides toward the clubhouse.

After Barrett, Chaddock and Caufield holed out, they went into the club lounge and were instantly greeted with a cheery, "Great game, boys. Come over and sit down; the drinks are on the way."

Mahoney, once off the tortuous course, washed out the frustrations of the game and prepared himself for a session of politicking. It was mid-September, 1940 and less than two months before election day. Getting elected was no real worry to the mayor; Lou Lewis, his opponent, posed no threat. Mahoney liked to tell his cronies, "Lewis has about as much chance of beating me as Wendell Wilkie has of beating F.D.R." However, Chaddock had just injected something that compounded the existing cave-in problem—his plan to strip mine the town.

While the mayor took a long draught of his gin and tonic, the waiter served three more for Mahoney's friends. Before Barrett could bring the tonic away from his lips, Mahoney leaned into him and said, "Liam, from a strictly legal point of view, what rights do property owners have in lawsuits against Mr. Chaddock's company?"

"What sort of lawsuits, Billy?"

"Well," said the mayor, "a growing number of West side residents have been trekking into my office and raising hell about broken water mains and cracked foundations. Whole houses have tipped because of underground mine settlings. They are challenging me to do something about it, but what the hell can I do? Isn't it Mark's responsibility? The S & H controls the mines; the city doesn't."

Chaddock leaped into the discussion before the judge had a chance to answer. "Billy, some of those tunnels are a hundred years old. The S & H has no responsibility for mine shafts and tunnels it never dug."

"Wait just a minute before you get yourselves confused about responsibility," said the judge. "As Mark probably knows, property owners have no rights to minerals found under their homes and/or land. All mineral rights in this valley were legally claimed by the S & H in 1852. Mark's company has documents to prove that, and the county clerk has the original documents on file."

"But that doesn't absolve the S & H from responsibility if a claim is made against them, does it?" said the mayor.

Chaddock again jumped the judge's reply. "Gentlemen, the S & H has already established a repair crew to attend to complaints from the people. Our masons have replaced bricks and patched cement walls, sidewalks and foundations. Our plasterers and carpenters have worked overtime, and, in most cases, the houses are left in better condition than they were before the physical damage caused by the mine caving in."

The judge finished his drink and asked, "All well and good, Mark, but what are your thoughts about a major cave-in? I mean, a real disaster. I worry about that myself because I have relatives living over the cave zone. Can you imagine the horror of it all if people are buried alive? Think of the legal hassles that would follow? I've heard rumor that your company has been taking out the coal pillars that have held up the mine roofs for years. Is that true, Mark?"

Chaddock glared at Mahoney. Then he quickly smiled and caught Judge Barrett's eye. "I'm no fool, Judge. My company would not put itself in a situation that would do harm to people or to our business."

Caufield, well aware of the pillar robbing and uneasy with the direction of the conversation, excused himself saying, "I'd like to stay for lunch, boys, but that line about banker's hours doesn't apply to the Lackawanna Miners' Bank. I've got a lot of work waiting on me, fellows."

Judge Barrett, citing a court case which he needed to discuss with state attorneys, took his opportunity to leave as well. Chaddock and Mahoney were left facing each other and managed nervous smiles until Mahoney broke into a broad grin and commented, "Mark, I've known Liam Barrett for over thirty years; he hasn't changed much. That little shot he threw you about pillar robbing is just a signal. He knows damn well that his judicial power could make or break a case. What do you say we invite the good judge and his family to Palm Beach for Christmas?"

"Billy, you're a marvelous bastard. That head of yours swims in creative schemes."

"Just the devious Mick in me, Mark. Let's have another tonic before we head down to the hall."

Chapter 4
Twenty-Three Years
Of Taps

The autumn of 1941 passed swiftly for Peter Flanigan. In the past, St. Catherine's had always been able to field a good football team. This fall was no exception. With only eighty boys in the high school, it was considered a minor miracle that they were able to field a team at all. Some of the neighboring schools were beginning to experiment with the two-platoon system, but having both an offensive and defensive team was out of the question for St. Catherine's. With only sixteen boys on the team, the coach was happy to have a few reserves who could fill in for injured players.

Peter started the season as a scrub. His weight of one hundred twenty-five pounds was on the low side for St. Catherine's. In fact, the team coach, Hal Linnen, tried to discourage boys of Flanigan's size and, instead, concentrated on out of town recruitments. Most of the big fellows were high school drop-outs that Linnen classified as post-graduates. They rarely even showed their faces at school.

Just to be on the team was a supreme thrill for Flanigan. Known for his swiftness, Peter took greater joy in tackling and blocking than he did in offensive play. He had played sandlot tackle football for as long as he could remember, but never used protective equipment. As one of the youngest and smallest in his gang, Peter had learned that speed and maneuverability were more important than size. Tackling high, even waist high, could hurt. The big guys ran over him or dragged him along. If a runner was to be put down, he had to be nailed low. Ankles to knees was the target area. Flanigan loved to surprise the one-hundred-sixty pounders as they charged his position.

Spikes, padded pants, hip and shoulder pads, and a helmet were new to Flanigan. The practice uniforms were worn and torn, but while putting his on, Peter felt like a knight donning a suit of armor. Thrilling, absolutely titillating, was the feeling that Flanigan had the first time he tugged on his gear. Now, as he walked out toward the field, he couldn't resist stopping for a moment to look at himself in the locker room mirror. Admiringly, he said aloud, "You may be a bastard, Flanigan, but my, my, you do look tough."

Alley Oop Rozer, the veteran half-back, was listening. He stood up and said, "Tough? You got to be shittin' me, kid. You look like a reject from the Ethiopian Army."

Flanigan twirled around, half embarrassed and bitterly annoyed at Rozer's cutdown. Wanting to be equally caustic, Flanigan tried to think of a sharp retort, but common sense prevailed and he smiled at Rozer. "You're right, Oop, but my appearance is not the whole story. Out on the field, I'll look better than that mirror image."

Rozer tapped his finger on Flanigan's chest and said, "Tell you what, little twit, take one more look at yourself in that mirror." Rozer picked Flanigan up and swung him around so that he was once again facing the mirror.

"Now take a good look, Twit, don't you look pretty? See how nice and clean and fresh you look now. When we come off the field, we'll check you again to see how tough you are. O.K. little twit?"

Peter didn't respond. He turned the corner of his mouth into a half-smile and walked out onto the turf.

After running the boys through a series of calisthenics, Linnen ordered the boys out on the field and into their offensive and defensive positions. As usual, the coach was short of two full squads, but knowing Peter's speed, it made sense to him to put Flanigan in the safety position. Peter went into action when Rozer smashed through the line on the first play, cut to the left sidelines and blazed away for ten yards before he felt his legs go out from under him. When he descended from his flight, Flanigan was still holding onto Rozer's shins.

"O.K. kid, you can get your fuckin' little paws off now," snarled Alley Oop Rozer.

Flanigan got up without looking at Rozer. The skirmish lasted for over an hour with frequent interruptions from Coach Linnen who pointed out both the weak spots and the glaring mistakes. Halfway through the session, Linnen stopped the action and took the ball away from Rozer.

"Rozer, you're busting up the defensive line just fine, but why can't you get by this skinny kid? If your blockers miss their hits or are wiped out, then, damn it, use your stiff arm downfield."

Three plays later, Rozer came charging through the right tackle, stiff-armed the line backer and headed straight at Flanigan. Peter had been repeating to himself at every play, "Hit knees-to-ankles." However, when Rozer stuck his arm toward Flanigan's face, Peter went for the arm instead of the lower leg. Surprising Rozer, he grabbed his arm, side-stepped and used leverage to slam him to the turf. The egg shaped ball bounced into Flanigan's arms and Peter shot across the field to follow the sideline strip to the end zone. Rozer was still lying on the turf when Coach Linnen blew the whistle and motioned for everyone to go to the locker room.

Peter finished his shower, quickly dressed and made his way out through the gate of Stephen's Park. It was a two mile walk home, and he didn't want to waste time because he had promised his mother that he would take her out to dinner. It was Ella Flanigan's birthday, and Peter had saved some caddy money for the occasion. He was exhausted but didn't give a second thought to the long walk as he took measured strides down the brick road. He would be home by five thirty and, within a few minutes, he and his mother would be headed back to town to Bivoni's Italian Restaurant. Thoughts of lasagna and hot garlic bread made Peter forget about the soreness already setting in from the workout.

Flanigan jumped over the curb onto the slate sidewalk when a horn sounded, "a-googa, a-googa" in several rapid sequences.

A model A Ford pulled aside of the curb and Flanigan saw Alley Oop Rozer behind the wheel.

"Come on in, Crusher, I'll give you a ride home."

Peter hopped in and Rozer Proceeded to compliment him for his afternoon of football.

When Rozer pulled up to Flanigan's apartment house, he switched off the ignition and said, "Tell me, Crusher, do you know how to make any good bucks other than by carrying golf bags for the assholes at the links?"

"No, Oop, not big dollars, but enough to help. I've sold wood, coal and collected and sold scrap iron, peddled papers, sold lottery tickets and even made money selling berries during the summer. No big bucks."

Rozer sat back, took out a Lucky Strike from a pack tucked in his shirt, scratched a long wooden match on his corduroy pants and lit the cigarette which was dangling from the corner of his thin mouth. On his second drag, Alley Oop broke the silence and said to Peter, "You know, Kid, you could help your mother and yourself if you earned a few good bucks each week. My old man hasn't been around for years, but look at me. Do I need the old fart? Look at what I got: nice little car, good clothes, smokes when I want them and ..."

Rozer reached into his back pocket, yanked out his wallet and thumbed it open. Holding it under Flanigan's nose, Rozer said softly, "Crusher, this kind of dough could be yours if you're as gutsy as I think you are. Tell you what. If you want to help your mother have a better life and have some fun yourself, see me after the game tomorrow."

Alley Oop turned the ignition key and moved the long handle stick shift into low gear as Peter hopped out. Rozer stuck his head out of the window on the driver's side as Peter made his way across the street.

"Hey, Crusher, come here a minute."

Peter walked over to the car and Rozer poked his head out of window and said softly, "Kid, don't mention anything about our little talk. O.K.? I think that you'll be happy to find out that after a few weeks work with me, you and your ma won't just be going out to dinner once a year. You'll be enjoying that wop-o food every week."

"See ya, Crusher," called Oop as he pulled away.

Peter took the back stairs to his third floor apartment. The building was in an advanced state of disrepair. Several strips of unpainted clapboard siding that had worked loose over the years hung in vertical suspension, clinging to a rusty nail or two. Eaves and troughs had long ago buckled under the weight of snow and ice. One pitted piece rested in a windswept position on the roof as it waited for another storm to blow it onto the street.

Peter's mother stepped out through the kitchen door to the back porch as Peter was just beginning the second flight of stairs. "Hi, Peter, I hope I don't appear too anxious."

"Not at all, Mom, I'm as eager to eat out as you are. I'll stash this gym bag in my bedroom, and then we'll be off."

It was a twenty minute walk back to town. Once they were over the railroad viaduct and past Levine's junk yard, the city hall building was in sight along with the town's only other prominent feature: the Lackawanna Miner's Bank. Tucked between the bank and the city hall was the tiny Bivoni restaurant. The smell of the restaurant was intoxicating to the Flanigans who ate out so seldom.

Ella Flanigan pretended to be very interested in her pasta, but after a few sips of Chianti, she rested her fork on the edge of the plate and said, "I was talking to Mother Rachel today."

Peter suddenly raised his eyes, but said calmly, "Oh, and what did she have to say?"

"She talked about you, mostly."

"Did she say anything good?"

"As a matter of fact, just about everything she said was positive. She thinks you are a very mature person and that you should go to college. I told her that we needed to talk more about that. I suspect she knows our financial situation."

Peter grinned. "Yeah! Like usually broke."

"Oh, it's not all that bad, Peter. We have neighbors on the dole. That has never been a worry for us. I'm healthy and have a steady job."

"And I have to soon get my act together and start making some cash."

"Peter, you are only seventeen and not even out of high school yet. There is plenty of time to make money. You could commute to St. Thomas College, get a part-time job to help pay expenses, and I could probably get more hours of work at my job — between the two of us we could manage just fine."

"Well, most of the guys in my senior class aren't talking college. It's army, navy, or marines — or off to New Jersey or Philadelphia to get work."

"Peter, the money being made working in the war industry isn't at all impressive to me. But that is your business. By next May, you will be finishing high school and ready for a very important life decision. I pray every day that your decision will be based on justice and peace — not on money or trumped-up patriotism."

"I haven't discounted the military. Not the navy — all that water and sky doesn't appeal to me. But I guess the infantry would suit my craving for adventure."

"Yes. Very adventurous, Peter. I remember young men like you in 1917 who went off to the Great War and the great adventure devoured them. We Americans have the same adventurous lust for bloodshed as our European cousins."

Flanigan raised his eyebrows in thought and looked away from his mother's eyes. "All I know is that next June 1st, I turn eighteen and I hand my body over to the government."

"It's not handing your body over, Peter. It's simply registration for the draft."

"Same difference. I sign a piece of paper and they get a piece of my life."

"You can sign and not serve. People have done that before. Maybe you should re-read some of your uncle Frank's letters that he sent you from Bethesda Army Hospital."

"I've thought about that but it makes me uncomfortable. Fact is, I'm confused. I wish I had more time with Uncle Frank. I bet if he lived around here I would have been his pal."

The war didn't kill him instantly, Peter. It just made him suffer for another lifetime. He was gassed at age twenty and existed in misery for twenty-three more years. The only good thing about his funeral was his request to not have the starts and stripes on his coffin and his note to tell the Army and the Veterans of Foreign Wars to stuff their bugles. 'I've had twenty three years of taps', he said. I made sure his wishes were granted."

Peter Flanigan didn't speak. But as they rose to leave, she murmured: "I don't want you to think you have to serve."

Chapter 5
Having The Law
On Your Side

"Flanigan, you really are a tough little shit, aren't you? I never thought we'd beat Jessup. Their halfbacks knocked the crap out of our defensive line, but you didn't fail on a single tackle in your safety position. Your cash award comes tonight, my friend. See you over at Coalbrook about eight, O.K.?"

Peter didn't walk to the shower room; he hobbled. Practice sessions were pain producers, but playing against twenty-two and twenty-three-year-olds was brutal. Every team in the valley cheated on age. "Post-graduate" was the title given to any guy who had talent, could use brute force, and wanted to play football. The Jessup team was known for its dirty play, and no one could hereafter convince Flanigan that they didn't deserve the distinction.

Flanigan could deal with the physical pain but Rozer's money-making plan worried him. "Should I back out," he thought, "or make a few fast bucks on Rozer's scheme?"

Alley Oop Rozer was approaching the locker room door when he heard his name being called. Turning, he saw Flanigan slowly jogging toward him.

"Roz, let's talk for a minute."

Reading Flanigan's concern, Rozer said, "O.K. Let's get away from the door."

Moving a few feet away, Peter began, "Roz, I'm a bit worried about tonight. I'm not a goody-two-shoes, but the plan you have is simply too mysterious for me. I've got to know what I'm getting into."

"All right, Peter, I'll give it to you in one brief sentence. We're gonna' steal from the fuckin' rich to help poor bastards like you and your old lady. Now if that is too fuckin' mysterious, then forget about our conversation and keep your mouth shut."

"Look, Roz, I've swiped stuff before, who hasn't around here? But the circumstances and who we are taking it from and the risks involved are all important to me. I'm all my mother has, and I can't afford to get into anything that would make life difficult for her."

"Okay, Crusher, let me give it to you straight. If you decide that you want no part of the action, fair enough." Roz continued, "What we talk about doesn't go beyond the two of us, understand?"

Flanigan tightened his lips while staring Rozer in the eye, and he nodded his head affirmatively.

"What we will do is very simple and very profitable. At eleven P.M. tonight and on every Saturday night, the last shift at the breaker is finished for the week. A new crew doesn't come on until Monday morning at seven A.M. Do you know how the breaker operates?"

"I just know that the sound of coal being smashed into burnable pieces is the worst damn noise in town."

"Exactly, and that fact helps our little caper, Peter. When the coal is crushed and washed, it's sent down chutes to hoppers that hold thousands of tons of coal. Most of the hoppers are built along side of the railroad tracks so that coal can be poured into individual rail cars. Three of the hoppers are set up to accommodate trucks. The chutes and release gate are on the road-side."

Peter listened quietly as Roz continued, "Our job is simple. We pull up a coal truck to one of the road-side hoppers. You stand on the truck cab and release the hopper chute lever. Out comes the coal! When you see that the truck is full, push the lever upwards and the chute will close. You jump down onto the pile of coal, and I ease out of the hopper area with twenty, shiny clean tons of top quality anthracite."

"Slow down, Roz, a few questions. First, where does the truck come from? What about people seeing and hearing us, especially the bulls? And who the hell buys twenty tons of coal at one shot?"

Alley Oop smiled, wiped some dirt and sweat from his nose and said, "I was waitin' for tonight to educate you, Crusher, but why not here and now? The truck and the coal sale come in a package deal. I sort of borrow a truck for a couple of hours, and we sell the coal to a nice old fart with ready cash. No one is going to hear us, Crusher. The noise of the breaker drowns out all other sounds. The flow of coal coming down one chute will simply join in the thunder of the breaker. Our only problem is to get our job done before the breaker stops at eleven P.M."

Peter was still a little worried. "The bulls."

"That is where you come in, Crusher; you're the reconnaissance man. Your job will be to scout the hopper area before I pull the truck in. You'll have a flashlight to signal me if no bulls are in the area. Two short hits on the light will mean that all is clear. Three short hits followed by one long hit will mean 'stay away, trouble'."

Flanigan was fascinated by the idea now. It was adventurous. It was a way to put it to the coal company, and that made him smile. He couldn't suppress the desire to be vindictive—to get even with a coal company that was destroying the valley and get bucks back in cash.

"Roz, why are you dealing me in on this?"

"Flanigan, we heard a rumor that the S & H is increasing the number of bulls on duty. If so, there is a slight chance that they might spot us. If you patrol the hopper area, our worries will be minimized. It takes less than ten minutes to load twenty tons. Two trips, two loads and instant cash! Tonight is payday, Crusher!"

"Instant cash from whom?" asked Peter.

"You don't have to know that, Crusher. What do you care as long as you get paid?"

"O.K. Roz, my last two questions: How much do I get paid, and what are my hours?"

"Let me ask you something, Pal. How much does your mother get paid each week?"

Peter didn't like the question. He dropped his head and studied his cleats as he scuffed the turf. Without looking up, he mumbled, almost inaudibly, "About twenty dollars a week."

Alley Oop Rozer put his hand on Peter's shoulder and whispered, "Tonight you'll make triple that amount, Crusher."

Peter took a hard swallow and said, "What time do you want me on the job?"

"Meet me at my car after we get cleaned up. We'll arrange a time."

It was four-thirty in the afternoon as the Model A jounced Rozer and Flanigan down the washboard road to the breaker. Rozer identified the check points that Flanigan would reconnoiter later that night. Then he showed him the hopper from which the coal would be drawn. The young men scurried up a slate hill that divided the truck road from the railroad cars. Shouting to be heard above the din of the breaker, Rozer told Flanigan that he was to position himself on the ridge by eight P.M. At eight fifteen, he was to give the signal.

Several hours later, Peter told Ella Flanigan that he was going downtown to meet some friends. The walk to the hopper was only a half mile from his apartment and in the opposite direction from town. Flanigan arrived at seven forty-five and moved slowly through the maze of railroad coal cars; he was expecting to see a company detective behind each one.

By eight P.M., he was posted on the slag heap. Flashlight in hand and close to the ground, he concentrated on keeping a low silhouette. He wondered what it would be like on a moonlit night. Tonight there was a quarter moon, its light dimmed by low clouds.

Several times Peter took out his heavy steel Waltham pocket watch, covered his head and flashlight with his jacket, and checked the time. At eight fourteen, he began counting while surveying the surrounding terrain. At the count of sixty, he hit two quick flashes in the direction of Alley Oop's truck.

The crushing, rumbling intensity of the breaker was beginning to put a strain on Flanigan's eardrums. He wondered aloud how people could stand to work here eight hours a day, and was relieved when he saw the truck approach. He slid down the bank and got to the bottom just as Rozer got to the hopper.

No greetings were exchanged. Flanigan shimmied up the smooth steel pipe to the hopper chute, took a deep breath, and pulled the long auxiliary lever that lifted the metal plate from the rectangular opening. Coal poured out into the truck with such speed that Flanigan didn't look at the opening but fixed his eye on Rozer for the signal to close the chute.

Rozer threw both arms over his head and Flanigan slammed shut the gate and stopped the flow of coal.

As planned, Flanigan jumped onto the truck bed from his perch above and waited for Rozer to drive the big vehicle away from the coal chute.

Following instructions, he leaped out of the slow moving truck after it had traveled the length of a football field. Since there were no trees or bushes to act as cover, Flanigan sought out the large boulders which were scattered throughout the barren landscape. Crouching low for several minutes, Flanigan imagined himself being grabbed by the shoulders and looking up into the contorted face of a Susquehanna & Hudson bull.

After the truck was out of sight, Peter began once more his reconnaissance of the breaker and hopper areas. By nine P.M. he had again positioned himself on the slag pile. Fifteen minutes later, another smooth operation was underway.

When the truck was loaded, Flanigan jumped down onto the pile of coal in the bed of the truck. Then he vaulted over the side and got into the cab with Alley Oop.

"Nice work, Crusher. Chalk up two victories for Rozer and Flanigan today. Teamwork, Flanigan, that's what it's all about—on the gridiron or on the job. You've got to stick it to your opponent."

Grinning, Flanigan said, "I have to admit that it's a real joy to beat the S & H."

"Yaaaa-whooo," Flanigan let out a victory whoop and drummed his fists on the dashboard.

"Time to light up the road," said Rozer as he switched on the head lights and left the dirt road.

As the truck turned onto Main Street, Flanigan commented, "Oop, you're the boss man, but isn't it a bit chancy to drive twenty tons of hot coal past the police station?"

"Who said that we were going to pass it?" Rozer shifted into low gear. "You gear down a monster like this," he said as he turned into the driveway of the police station. The officer who was on desk duty peered out through the window at Alley Oop, gave a perfunctory wave and looked away.

"See, Flanigan, not to worry. We've got the law on our side. That's almost as good as having God watch over you."

"I can't wait for the next scene," said Flanigan.

"You won't have to wait; the paymaster is on his way."

The headlights picked up a figure that was slowly moving through the gate behind the police station. The man waved Rozer on, and Alley Oop backed the truck up to a small pile of coal. Raising the hydraulic, Rozer tipped the truck bed at an angle and added the second load of the night.

"Forty as ordered, Mr. Walsh."

The man came over to the truck. Flanigan, recognizing the mayor's assistant, slid down in the seat and pulled his jacket hood over his head.

Reaching up to the window of the high cab, the man handed a white envelope to Alley Oop. The compound was well lighted and Flanigan could see Walsh clearly.

"This is a good start, Lad," yelled Walsh over the sound of the idling engine. "You're only one tenth of the way home, young fella. By Christmas, that pile will be a small mountain. See ya next week, Lad, God bless ya."

Rozer gave Walsh a quick wave, drove out of the compound and handed the envelope to Flanigan. "Count it for me, Lad. Just a bit of the green to warm the cockles of yer heart..."

Peter tore open the envelope and counted twenty ten dollar bills. He didn't want Rozer to know that he had never handled that much money before.

"Now peal off six of those pretty bills and put them in your pocket, Crusher."

Flanigan took his share and handed the envelope back to Rozer.

Tucking the money into his jacket, Rozer said, "Crusher, all you have to do is keep your mouth shut and continue your good work, and your mother will have one of her best Christmas holidays ever."

Rozer drove straight to the city motor pool and parked the truck between two rows of garbage trucks, snow plows and assorted highway machinery.

Back in the Model A, Rozer questioned Flanigan. "You were a

trifle surprised about a few of the activities tonight, right, Crusher?"

"Wouldn't you be?" asked Flanigan.

"Hell, yes. You just about shit your pants when we drove into the police compound, but, otherwise, you acted real cool."

"Roz, why don't you cut out the b.s. and give me the story behind these moves. What is going on? Are we selling the coal to the cops?"

"Naw, the cops aren't even aware of the scheme, Crusher."

"What about old man Walsh? He's the mayor's flunkie, and tonight he was the paymaster. What gives?"

"What gives, Peter me boy, is that Mr. Walsh is simply the conveyer of good news. He's the delightful messenger and deliverer of the green from his boss, the mayor, to us hard working lads."

"So the coal is being delivered to the city and Mahoney is turning a good buck on the whole operation," said Flanigan.

"Not quite, dear Watson, but bloody close, old boy," commented Rozer as he slipped out of his badly done Irish brogue and into a lame English accent.

"You see, dear fellow, 'tis simply a case of bringing coals to Newcastle. His excellency, the lord mayor, is in need of some public assistance to maintain his vast real estate holdings. You and I, dear sir, are the public agents."

"So we sell the coal to the mayor; he uses a city vehicle to transport it and public land for storage?"

"Not quite, old boy; 'tis true he borrows a lorry, but the land behind the police station was sold by the city to the mayor many years ago."

"Fill me in on Mahoney's real estate deals. With the store of coal he is hoarding for the winter, he must have a few places about town."

Dropping the accent, Alley Oop related the facts of how Mahoney had acquired over fifty dwellings in the past ten years. Most of the homes and apartment houses had been put up for sale to the public by means of sealed bids because of delinquent taxes. Mahoney found it easy to unseal the bids, find the highest one and put his own a few dollars higher.

"All of the houses owned by the mayor are, of course, heated by anthracite," said Roz. "That means about ten per heating season. Our little verbal contract with Mr. Walsh is to get five hundred tons into that storage lot by Christmas. Figure forty ton per week times twelve weeks and we'll come close. Some Saturday nights we'll make three runs to complete the deal before the snows fly."

"I'm surprised that Mahoney doesn't have us make home deliveries," quipped Flanigan.

"That's a job for the city maintenance men, Crusher. They like the mayor so much that they are willing to give up some of their own time to help the delightful fellow."

It was midnight by the time Flanigan eased the kitchen door open and shut it gently behind him. Before he could take a step, his mother's voice floated out of her bedroom, "My, my that was a long visit with your friends, Peter."

"Yes it was and enjoyable too. We're going to get together every Saturday night. With football and school work, we don't get a chance to see each other very often."

"Well, you better go to bed; we have early mass in the morning."

Autumn weeks passed quickly, and Ella didn't question Peter again on his late night activities.

Flanigan and Rozer made three trips to the hopper on a couple of Saturday nights in November. Their hope was to finish the five hundred ton order by the first week in December.

The football season came to an end on Thanksgiving Day. St. Catherine's had compiled a respectable six wins and three losses by then. Alley Oop Rozer didn't set any school records, but he did manage to put a few of the opposition out for the season with his smashing drives. However, Flanigan's fortitude against grown men, who were masquerading as high school football players, came to a stunning halt at the Thanksgiving Day game against Blakely. Hit by a bruising block from a monster fullback, Flanigan managed to turn his body in an attempt to right himself when he was virtually run over by the ball carrier. The crunching sound and immediate pain let him know that the injury was not a minor one. As bad as the pain was, Flanigan watched and could hardly bear the sight of the Blakely halfback as he stomped into the end zone to make the final score: Blakely, thirteen, St. Catherine's — twelve.

Rozer, the first team member to recover from the shock of losing, helped Flanigan to the locker room. "It doesn't look good for Saturday night, Crusher. We've got our last run of 1941 and you're a Hopalong-Cassidy. We have fifty tons to deliver this Saturday and fifty more next week."

"My frigging ankle is screaming and the only thing on your mind is coal. Roz, forget that scheme for now."

"Forget it, hell, my friend, we take more chances on this gridiron than we do every Saturday night in the truck. The only difference is that here on the gridiron, we bust our humps only to lose, and the silence of the dissatisfied fans is deafening. They couldn't care less about our bruises and bumps. If we don't win, we're shit. At least we get paid for our risks at the hopper, Crusher."

Team trainer, Tony Mancuso, helped Flanigan into his car and drove him to St. Joseph's hospital. Within the hour, a cast was hardening on Peter's broken ankle.

On Saturday, Alley Cop Rozer ran the coal run on his own. The following morning, he told Flanigan how scared he was to drive into the hopper without any reconnaissance.

"Crusher, you've got to help me next Saturday. Three more runs and we've got it. I'll pay you one hundred for the night."

"Roz, how am I going to recon the area with this," snapped Flanigan. He lifted up his huge plaster of Paris foot. "Can't you just picture me as I try to get to the top of the slag heap and then run down that loose slippery mess?"

"Crusher, you won't be on the top of the slag. I'll drive you up the little rise on the north side of the hopper. From that vantage point, you'll be able to see at least half as far as you did from the slag. Simply give me the light signals, and operation-coal-delivery termination will be in effect."

Flanigan, half smiling, shook his head. "O.K. Roz, you have got yourself a crippled partner. Pick me up early and deposit me."

Flanigan was posted on his lookout at seven forty-five. Rozer drove to town, switched vehicles, and was back at the hopper by eight fifteen after receiving the all clear signal from Peter.

Flanigan could see Alley Oop and the whole operation quite easily. It was the final phase of the waxing of the moon, a cold, starry, bright night. It took Rozer longer to complete the job without Flanigan. When the coal chute was slammed shut, Rozer waved to Peter, got into the vehicle and was off toward town.

Sitting on the slag, Flanigan was bored and very cold. It seemed silly to have his crutches up on the huge mound of coal refuse, but he used them periodically to raise himself up from his cold seat. Looking to the southeast, he saw lines of railroad cars loaded with coal. The cars would eventually be pulled to the breaker where the coal would be broken into burnable pieces—pea coal, chestnut and stove coal. Flanigan had worked the coal cars many times. Most cars were filled with large chunks of anthracite double the size of a basketball. To "work the coal" meant to steal it, and adults and kids worked in pairs. One person would stand on top of the car and drop the booty; the partner would load it on a wagon or sledge. It was easier to haul heavy loads after the first snow had fallen because the long wooden runners of the sledge would then glide more smoothly over the terrain. Few people worried about being tracked, and everyone who was engaged in taking the coal had his own standard wooden box built on the sledge. With boxes two feet high built over the runners of an eight foot sledge, it was easy to see why entire families often showed up to help push home the winter's warmth.

There was no action tonight along the cars except for the passing of an occasional railroad cop or bull. Flanigan wasn't concerned about the cop because the slag pile hid the truck from the cop's view, and the breaker would continue to rumble until the end of the evening shift.

Rozer completed his second run by ten thirty. Flanigan picked up his crutches and began to feel his way down the rough road. Rozer, who was still at the hopper, was about to climb up to release the coal chute gate when the breaker came to a halt. Flanigan and Rozer quickly checked their pocket watches. It was only ten thirty-five.

"There should be another twenty five minutes before shut down," whispered Rozer. "Must be a breakdown, Peter."

"What do we do now, Roz?"

"It usually only takes a few minutes to get it back in operation. Let's just wait and see."

"But, if they don't get it going soon, they will probably quit for the night. The breaker is due to shut down in just twenty minutes."

"Yeah, you're right, Crusher, we'll just take the chance and load up. Noise doesn't mean much to those poor bastards working the breaker. Their hearing is usually shot to hell anyway, so a quick roar of twenty tons from the hopper isn't going to faze them any."

"Sure, Roz, but what about the bulls?"

"Fuck the bulls. We'll be out of here before they put their asses in gear. Let's fill up."

Rozer climbed the pipe and released the gate. The initial clatter of coal falling on metal, gave way to a crashing rattle as the truck filled to the brim. As he slid down, Rozer heard Flanigan say, "Hurry up, Roz, bulls!"

Rozer turned and jumped the remaining six feet to the ground and ran for the cab. Flanigan, who had been standing a few yards away from the rear of the truck, swung his crutches in long strides as the railroad cop raced toward them.

Rozer started the engine, kicked open the passenger door and screamed "Hurry up! Goddamn it!"

Flanigan threw in his crutches, and, as he was raising himself up to the metal step, was collared from behind and quickly yanked to the ground.

Rozer gunned the big engine and the huge truck rumbled into the darkness. The bull yanked Flanigan's arms behind him and snapped on handcuffs.

Chapter 6
Dollar Signs Of War

"Officer Kelly, I've arrested this young man. He's to be booked and charged with the theft of a city truck and a load of coal from the S & H hopper at the Coalbrook colliery."

Ned Kelly, a gaunt, dreary-eyed man, had the look of a fellow who was fighting sleep. The only excess weight his skinny frame carried was under his eyes. Sucking the last possible drag of his cigarette butt, he pinched it from his mouth, and without removing his eyes from the two people on the opposite side of the desk, crushed the cigarette in a heaping, butt-laden ashtray.

"Clarkie, what the hell are you doing in that railroad dick uniform?"

"Making a few Christmas bucks, Kelly. Only I didn't think I'd stumble on a heist like this lad was into. This kid is a fuckin' Jesse James. He doesn't steal buckets of coal; do you, kid? No, no, no. This young hop-along robs by the fuckin' truck load. Right, kid?"

"I told you on the way down here that I was just taking a ride with a guy I met this afternoon. He was delivering coal, and he promised me a job if I went along with him."

"How about that line of horseshit, Kelly? This boy kissed the fuckin' blarney stone, didn't he? Look at the likes of him, Kelly, as Irish as Patty's pig, but he tells me his name is Russell Stephens. Stephens, shit; I know the Stephens family, and you're not one of them."

"O.K. Matt, let me talk to him; you go and write out your report."

Kelly gave his saddest Basset-hound look at Flanigan and said very quietly, "What is your full name, Son?"

"Peter Flanigan, Sir."

Flanigan proceeded to give the officer whatever information he wanted, but he stopped short when questioned about the coal incident.

"Is your mother or father aware that you have been taking coal, Peter?"

Peter refused to answer. Officer Kelly smiled and said, "That was a bit unfair. Let me simply ask you how we can contact your father or mother."

Flanigan sat silent for a few seconds. Then he said, "My mother doesn't have a phone, but you can reach my father through my uncle, Pat Walsh."

Kelly looked up quickly. "You're not talking about the mayor's assistant, are you, Peter?"

"Yes, I am, Officer, and if you contact him, I'd like to talk to him in private. Is that O.K.?"

"Sure, Son, I suspect old Pat could be here in no time. Your uncle hasn't lived anywhere other than the fire department ever since I've known him."

Officer Kelly lifted the phone off the hook and asked the operator to ring the sleeping quarters at the fire department. Within a few minutes, Pat Walsh was standing at the door. Officer Kelly left the room and closed the door on Flanigan and Walsh.

"Now, what the hell is all this about, Mr. Flanigan, me being your uncle? Bejesus, you're no more related to me than a monkey's arse."

Flanigan suppressed a chuckle and put on his best serious face. "You're right, Mr. Walsh, you are not my uncle, but the mayor is my father. All I ask of you is that you contact the mayor and have me released. I'm sure he doesn't want people to know about me."

Walsh scratched the stubble of gray beard on his chin, and, with one eye cocked and quivering, he saw that Flanigan's firm stance and resolute voice was credible. Without saying a word, Walsh turned, went out the door and shut it quietly behind him, leaving Flanigan alone.

Within minutes, Walsh returned and said, "Mr. Flanigan, the mayor would like to talk to you but not until tomorrow at noon. He wants to have you over for Sunday dinner and a chat. You'll be there, won't you?"

"Yes, Mr. Walsh, please tell him I'll be there. I know where he lives."

Alley Oop Rozer was waiting around the corner from the police station. Flanigan got into Rozer's car, and on the way home, told him about his relationship to the mayor.

"You gave me a trade secret to keep, Alley Oop, and now I'm asking you to keep my secret under your hat."

"Crusher, having you as a partner couldn't have worked out better. We were nailed tonight, and, if I had someone else with me, I'd probably be behind bars now, and the mayor would have my mouth gagged."

Rozer slapped a bill onto Flanigan's leg. Rays of a streetlight illuminated the one hundred dollar mark on one corner of the bill. Although Peter had never seen a hundred dollar bill before, he displayed no emotion. He simply folded the bill and tucked it into his shirt pocket.

"Thanks, Roz, but these crutches got us into that mess tonight. I would have escaped that railroad dick if my ankle was in one piece."

"The season's over, Flanigan; we won at the hopper and on the gridiron. If that bull didn't nab you, he probably would have set chase in the company car. Chasing down a fifty-ton load wouldn't have taken much. He would have pulled us over before we got to town. Instead, he ended up with the mayor's handicapped son." Slapping Flanigan on the back, he said, "Sleep well, my friend."

Flanigan gently turned the living room door knob and quietly pushed it open with the tip of his crutch. As the door swung open, he faced Ella who was sitting in a large wing back chair, resting a book on her lap, and staring Peter down with a worried look.

"It's one-thirty in the morning, Peter. I've never been so worried about you. What in God's name have you been doing? Where have you been?"

Flanigan had expected that the moment of truth would come with his mother, but now he was too tired to spill out his story. He started for his bedroom and muttered, "Sorry, Mom, but let's wait until morning for the explanation. I just don't feel like going over it tonight."

Seeing Peter in one piece relieved Ella so that she was disarmed. Yet her anxiety about his activities stayed with her throughout her sleepless night.

At breakfast, Flanigan told his mother part of the story. He said that he and Rozer were delivering coal for Mayor Mahoney and that the mayor did not want a lot of people to know about the special price he was getting for the coal.

"Who is giving the mayor the special price?"

"I don't know, Mom; I only know that Rozer was hired by Mahoney and Rozer hired me to help."

"Why didn't you tell me about the job, Peter?"

"Probably because I knew you would only worry about me working on a truck, especially at night."

Flanigan reached into his pocket, took out the hundred dollar bill, and placed it in front of Ella's coffee cup. Then he went into his room and came back with a stack of twenty dollar bills. He counted out ten of them as Ella sat stoically, giving neither rejection nor approval.

While Flanigan beamed, Ella took her eyes off the pile of money and said quietly, "Peter, I'm having a very difficult time believing that this is honest money."

"I worked hard for it, Mom. Rozer and I hauled five hundred tons of coal over the past two months. That money wasn't earned in one night."

"Peter, have you ever met the mayor?"

"Yes, but just briefly."

"Does he know who you are?"

"Yes, I told him who I was and a bit more."

"What was the 'bit more,' Peter?"

"Mom, you never told me directly, but it wasn't necessary. Even if some kids hadn't told me, I would have guessed by now."

"What did kids tell you, Peter?"

Fighting off tears, Flanigan forced a sardonic smile, "I don't think you really want to hear what some kids have said to me, but, in general terms, it seems to be neighborhood gospel that the mayor is my father."

"Peter, I saw no benefit in ever telling you. I lied to you when I told you that your father died shortly after you were born. I lied because I thought that people would forget about Bill Mahoney and me. After you were born, my world centered on being your mother, and I tried to forget the way things should have turned out."

"Why didn't you marry him when you became pregnant with me?"

"He never asked."

"Would you have married him if he did?"

"Yes. Our relationship, by the standards of society and of our religion, was probably wrong, but it was the strongest and most loving thing that ever happened to me. We not only loved each other, but we were living in a world filled with fun and few worries. For my part, I suspected that it would be only a matter of months before we would be married."

"Why did you split?"

"I never fully understood, but it was probably because I was a political liability, and Bill decided he loved politics more than he loved me. He needed someone to help him succeed, someone with financial and social connections. That was not me. He saw it as especially damaging to his career when he returned from a long trip and discovered that I was to be the mother of his child. It didn't take long for our beautiful, blooming romance to wilt: Bill looked upon me as more of an embarrassment than as a wife to be. He simply stopped coming to see me, and now we both try to act civilized whenever we meet in town."

Flanigan leaned back in his chair and studied Ella's face. He wondered if he was reading sorrow and rejection. After pausing for several moments, he said, "Mom, would you be opposed to my being absent from our usual Sunday dinner today?"

"Not if you tell me why, Peter."

"That's the hard part, Mom; the mayor has invited me to dinner at his place at noon today."

Ella's mouth opened and her chin sagged. Staring at Peter, she said, "And what in God's name did he invite you for?"

"He knows that I know who he is — our relationship. Since I am now employed by him, I guess he wants to know me better."

Ella began to clear the dishes from the table. Peter was surprised to see the glow that had come over her face and the change in mood that was reflected in her voice.

"Go ahead, Peter. I am delighted to think that you are able to sit down with your father for the first time. Maybe I shouldn't have been so harsh in my references to Billy. Keep your mind, emotions, and options open, Peter. Mr. Mahoney could do you some good, you know."

After eleven o'clock mass, Flanigan and his mother went their separate ways, Ella back to the apartment and Peter to the mayor's house. Knowing that he had plenty of time, Flanigan methodically extended his crutches and swung his body slowly toward town. He mused about his finances and reflected on how much better things were this Christmas, compared to previous ones. He stopped as he neared the business section. Holding the two crutches in one hand, Peter reached into his pocket and felt the wad of twenties that he had not told Ella about. He took out the small bundle and, turning the corner of each bill, he counted a total of three hundred and forty dollars. Then, gazing into each shop window, he considered possible purchases for his mother for Christmas. Coats, dresses, hats — all seemed like good ideas; but Peter had no idea about size or style.

Shuffling on, he arrived at his favorite spot — Mangan's Buick. Mr. Mangan's son, Freddie, was hosing off a grey '36 Plymouth. As he looked up, Freddie pointed to Flanigan's ankle and hollered, "Hey, Crusher, glad the season is over?"

Peter replied, "Heck, no." Holding up his crutches and waving them in the air, he remarked, "Can you imagine what I could do with these weapons out on the turf?"

Freddy continued to blast the mud off the Plymouth. The outside of the car was a mess. Peering into the back seat, Flanigan could see the remains of chicken bones and swatches of animal hair that was stuck to the seats.

"You know, Freddie, Sunday is supposed to be a day of rest. You're going to be dragging your tail if you expect to finish this car today."

Freddie turned off the hose and said, "You're right, Flanigan, this is the messiest car I've ever seen." Peter examined the car as Freddie continued, "A farmer from Uniondale traded it in yesterday for a new Buick."

Flanigan opened the front door and a gush of manure laden air rushed to his nostrils. He quickly slammed the door and said, "Good luck, Freddie, you should advertise this as shit-kicker special."

Peter was quiet for a moment, and then said, "What are you asking for this heap?"

"I don't know, really; I suspect my old man has a couple of hundred in it."

"I'll give you three hundred after you clean it, do a tune up and change the oil," said Flanigan.

"Let me call my old man; he never comes in on Sunday."

Freddie ran to the office phone while Flanigan continued his inspection of the crusty vehicle. When he had opened the door previously, he had noted that the odometer had only 12,500 miles on it. He gave some consideration to the possibility that it was the second time around on the odometer. However, he found no rust; the tires were good, and even the shocks seemed to be able to withstand his jouncing on the fenders. Lifting the hood, he checked the oil and noted that there were no decayed or split hoses. The area under the hood was amazingly clean.

Freddie, a sad look on his face, approached slowly. "Crusher, my old man said that he had to get three hundred fifty out of this car."

"I don't have three-fifty," said Peter, "so I guess this sale is dead."

"Wait a minute, Crusher. Dad said that if you really want this car and can't come up with the three hundred and fifty, he would take a slight loss on it and give it to you anyway because I know you."

"Freddie, you're a conniving rascal. You were going to pocket the extra fifty bucks, weren't you?"

Smirking, Freddie replied, "Crusher, I'm not out here working on Sunday for the goodness of God and country."

"Do you want your money now, Freddie?"

"Naw, come in tomorrow, Crusher, and this grey mare will be ready for humping."

Flanigan stepped up his pace as he headed toward Chestnut Grove and the dinner that was awaiting him at Mahoney's house. He easily found the large Georgian structure with its slate gray mansard roof and took note of the circular driveway, and the pillared portico with an ornate chandelier. Startled to find that the door opened even as he was ringing the bell, he realized that someone had been watching his approach.

A woman who appeared to be his mother's age, smiled pleasantly and asked, "Peter Flanigan?"

"Yes."

"My name is Sally Caufield, I'm a good friend of the mayor. Won't you please come in?"

Flanigan stepped into the marble foyer and followed her to the parlor. Never having been inside a house like this, he scanned the room immediately and was impressed by the exquisite look. Oriental carpets of deep burgundy, walnut doors, stained-glass windows framed in oak, and tables of teakwood and mahogany caught Flanigan's eye. He gleamed at the polished marble hearth and wondered if the fireplace was ever used.

"The mayor just returned from mass, Peter. He's upstairs and will be down shortly. Have a chair and relax. You must be tired after that long walk, especially with those crutches. What happened?"

"Football. I broke my ankle playing football."

"Oh, poor boy, will you have to keep the cast on for long?"

"Just a few more weeks, Miss Caufield; it will come off some time after Christmas."

"Speaking of Christmas, we're having my Christmas specialty for dinner today. I'd better check." At the doorway she turned and smiled at Peter. "Oh, and please call me Sally. 'Miss Caufield' sounds a bit stodgy."

Flanigan worked his way over to a huge oil portrait of a very proper-looking woman of the nineteenth century. "Why would Mahoney want to have a painting of Queen Victoria in his house?" thought Peter.

"Do you like that painting, Peter?"

Recognizing the mayor's voice, Peter did not turn but simply said, "Interesting."

Then slowly, he turned around, smiled and extended his hand to the mayor.

Mahoney seemed nervous, but he broke into a wide grin. As they shook hands, the mayor laid his left hand over the joined right hands and said, "It's good to see you, Boy."

"I guess you could say that the circumstances under which we previously met were somewhat stressful," Flanigan said dryly..

With a deep belly-laugh, Mahoney replied, "God almighty, you do have a way with language, Peter."

"My mother often says that I didn't get it from the wind," said Flanigan.

"Well, my old Irish mother had another way of expressing it, lad. She said that the apple doesn't fall far from the tree."

Flanigan liked that one, and, for the first time, looked steadily into Mahoney's eyes. Both of them stopped smiling, and Mahoney put his arm around Flanigan and drew him into his shoulder.

Peter suddenly had an indomitable need to pull away and give Mahoney a tongue lashing that would drive him to his knees. He didn't, and, for a moment or two, father and son embraced. Flanigan felt uncomfortable with the sensation of pleasure that flowed through his body. He did not want to feel good about the man who'd rejected his mother, and he was determined not to crack under a wave of sentiment. Easing away from the mayor, Peter nodded toward the dining room and said to Mahoney, "Sally seems to have everything set for dinner."

The mayor and Flanigan moved toward the table as Sally placed a platter in the center of the large oval.

"Sally, that smells great. You do like prime rib, don't you, Peter?"

"Oh, yes. We have it quite often."

"Fine. Fine. We have it rarely, but today seems like a good occasion for prime rib and Yorkshire pudding. Sally likes to show off her Johnny Bull British ways so that Micks like you and me can sit back and appreciate at least one thing the English do right - Yorkshire pudding."

Flanigan had never had prime rib, nor had he ever heard of Yorkshire pudding, but he was not about to declare his ignorance to these two people.

"Peter, your mother won't mind if you have a glass of wine, will she?"

"Well, what she doesn't know won't hurt her, Mayor. Actually, she wouldn't mind; we have had a glass or two together."

Mahoney got up from the table and went down to the cellar. After a moment, he emerged with a dusty bottle of red wine and was already in the process of extricating the cork. As he poured the ruby vintage into Flanigan's glass, he asked the boy to call him 'Bill'. Then without waiting for a reply, he elaborated on the wine.

"What we will enjoy today, we may not see for years to come. This, my friend, is my last bottle of Bordeaux. Since the fall of France last year, no French wines have made it to our shores, and restaurants are getting outrageous payments for anything with a French label. Notice this label, Peter, Chateau Lafitte Rothschild, the crème de la crème of Bordeaux."

Flanigan sipped the wine once again, but didn't find anything special about it. It tasted pretty much like wine to him.

"Smooth, isn't it, Peter? It's light on tannic acid, but has a perfectly balanced body. Your taste buds are dancing, aren't they, lad?"

Flanigan nodded, "Yes."

Sally, who was busy serving the dinner, finally had a chance to savor the wine. She gave Mahoney the compliments he wanted. Then, quickly, she turned to Flanigan and asked, "Peter, do you plan to go to college?"

"Unless I get a scholarship, I won't be able to."

The mayor pushed himself up straighter in his chair and said, "Peter, don't let money stand in your way to a college education. Start saving now. When the time comes, you'll have a big chunk paid for."

"You mean save the bread and milk money, Bill?"

"No, I'm saying that you should get a job that pays well, and save your earnings at the Miner's Bank. Sally can testify to the importance of that. Right, Sally?"

"Yes, my father is the president of the bank, Peter. He frequently tells success stories of young men who scrimp and save their huckleberry and paper route money. After a few years, they have enough savings to invest in a business or in a college education."

Flanigan looked at Mahoney with a mischievous twinkle in his eye. Then, he shifted his attention to Sally and said, "Yes, I believe you are right there. I've been involved in some private contracting and it does pay handsomely."

"Well, then, stay with it, Peter. Don't think of giving it up. What exactly do you do?"

"I'm in the coal business, Sally. Of course, now it's just a seasonal thing, but I'm hoping to come up with a job that pays well through out the year. Do you have any ideas?"

"No, not at the moment, but surely the mayor of Wurtzville has."

"No, Sally, I don't. But listen, Peter, let me make some contacts this week. Stop by my office on Friday. That will give me time to think and look about for you."

Rising from the table, Sally said, "Let's have our apple pie and coffee in the Florida room, boys. I'll clear away a few dishes and you fellows can listen to some nice music."

Mahoney led the way. He turned on the large Zenith radio. It was an attractive piece of furniture, about three and a half feet high and two feet wide. The honey colored wood curved into a circular window that was set above a large white knob. When the knob under the glass housing was turned, the dial would move three hundred and sixty degrees and pick up stations around the world.

"This wireless is one of the best on the market, Peter. Some nights, while sitting here, I can pick up England or Germany. I don't understand Kraut, but those Huns seem to be as excitable as the Italians on the west side of town. I'm sure I had the Fuehrer on the set last night."

Fascinated by the radio, Flanigan sat closer to it. He listened as Mahoney preached the wonders of the electronic age.

"Peter, do you know that there is a button on the back of this set that's for television?"

"Television?"

"Yes, television. Come around and see it."

"Television hasn't even been designed yet, Bill. There has been a lot of talk about its happening, but don't put me on. There isn't a television anywhere yet, is there?"

"No, Peter, but it's far beyond the talked-about stage! Television has already been sent and received in Schenectady, New York. A fellow from the General Electric corporation has been transmitting pictures for years."

"Transmitting to where?" asked Flanigan.

"Just within their corporation. The company admits that it's far from perfect, but they promise that in just a few years, we'll be able to sit in our living room and watch things happen on a screen."

Mahoney turned the radio on and pushed a number of frequency buttons before he found the station he wanted. He turned up the music, closed his eyes and danced around the room with an imaginary partner as the Glenn Miller orchestra got into the swing of "Moonlight Serenade."

Carrying a tray of pie and coffee, Sally entered the room. "Will Fred Astaire please waltz aside?" As she set the tray on the table, the music stopped. A very serious voice announced, "We interrupt this program to announce that the Japanese have bombed Pearl Harbor. We repeat, the Japanese have bombed Pearl Harbor, the island of Oahu, the city of Honolulu, Hawaii. Casualties appear to be very numerous. A number of American ships have been sunk, and the islands are preparing for possible attack. We will bring you more information as it comes to our studio."

The three listeners sat staring at each other in disbelief before the mayor spoke.

"This is war, folks; no way are those Japs going to get away with this action. Big stuff is coming. Just like I've been telling people, big shit is going to fly. Those sons-of-bitches are going to get their asses kicked."

"What's going to happen, Billy?" asked Sally.

"What's going to happen? What the hell do you think, woman? War! That's what is happening, and, now that we're in it with the Japs, we might as well tangle with their Nazi friends. We should have declared war on the Nazi bastards last month when they sank the Reuben James off Iceland. Over a hundred of our young men killed and what did we do about it? Shit! That's what we did. Well, goddamn it, FDR better get his ass in gear on this one."

Looking at Flanigan, Mahoney took control of his emotions, and in a moderate tone, said, "Peter, my boy, you were just asking about work and college money. Let me tell you, lad, the money that will be made from this war may make college attendance obsolete."

Quickly rebutting Mahoney, Sally snapped, "Billy, don't say such things to the boy. He's interested in doing something more than just making money."

"Oh yeah?" replied the mayor. "Just wait until the big bucks start pouring in. Peter will make his own decision, and my guess is that he won't be running around some campus with a beanie on his head and his finger up his ass."

Chapter 7
Going Abroad To Kill People

The following morning Flanigan did not have to attend school; it was a religious holy day. Over breakfast, Flanigan told his mother most of what had transpired at the Mayor's house. Ella Flanigan seemed interested, especially about Sally Caufield.

Peter struggled to choose his words carefully. The predetermined notions he had formed about Sally Caufield were wiped clean by the generous manner she extended to him. Yet, he knew the hurt in his mother's heart, and thinking that perhaps she would find some satisfaction in hearing about Bill Mahoney's poor choice of mate, he hedged the truth of his real impression of Sally Caufield.

Demeaning Sally was not something he wanted to do, so he simply commented on food and conversation.

"Did the mayor say anything about me?" asked Ellie.

"Yes. He asked how you were. He seemed to light up when I talked about you."

71

"Do you think Sally Caufield is an intelligent woman?"

"I'm not so sure what it means to be intelligent. The nuns at school are supposed to be intelligent, but more than a few of them seem to have little intelligent control over what their mouths say. I sort of expected Sally to act like some mean-spirited nun. Instead, she treated me with respect. She seems to be thoughtful and caring. Guess that doesn't mean 'intelligent'."

"She does sound like a nice person, Peter. Yet I could never understand why a woman of her education and financial status would take up with a small-town mayor like Billy."

"Don't criticize her judgment, Mom. Remember who you selected as my father."

Ellie sat down with that comment. Visibly crushed, her face drained, she sat for several minutes without speaking. Peter Flanigan, just after commenting about nuns letting their mouths run ahead of their brains, sat with his head in a half bowed position. When he looked up, Ellie was staring at him. She looked older and more tired than he had ever seen her before.

"Peter, let's get this straight between you and me. I loved Bill Mahoney and he loved me. But with some men and women, power and status mean more than love. I didn't know that at the time. To me, our love affair was a prelude to marriage. If you need convincing on this point to assure yourself that your mother was not an 'easy woman,' then maybe it's time for you to do a little reading."

Ellie got up from the sofa and went into her bedroom. When she came out, she had several envelopes in her hand.

"These are letters from Bill Mahoney, written 18 years ago. I was pregnant with you at that time, Peter. Bill served during the Great War in 1918 but never got to leave the country. He sat out the war in Camp Dix, New Jersey and the most action he saw was removing bodies of influenza victims in the winter of 1919.

"In 1923, The American Legion sponsored a trip to the French battlefields and a tour of Europe. Bill felt he had to take the trip. His yearning for Europe was motivated by the stories of returning veterans who told marvelous stories about the 'old world.'

"Bill left for Le Havre, France on June 2, 1923. The night before, we made love for the first time. We had loved each other for over a year but our passion of that parting night I will never regret because you are the joy of my life, Peter."

Peter quickly brushed away wetness from his eyes and took one of Bill Mahoney's letters.

Chateau-Thierry
July 15, 1923

Dear Ellie,

After spending a month in Paris and touring small country towns, I guess it is appropriate that we came as a group to Chateau-Thierry. Just five years ago today, inexperienced American troops stood up to the best forces Germany had to offer. Looking up from the words I write to you, I gaze upon fields of red, white and blue American flags flying over a blanket of crosses.

Chateau-Thierry was the last desperate offensive of the Germans and they did manage to cross the Marne river. We not only held them, Ellie, we defeated them and pursued them aggressively. We changed the war from an Allied defensive war to an offensive war. It was the beginning of the end for the Kaiser and his kin.

Ellie, all this historical musing is not the purpose of this letter. Historical recall allows me to transfer my fixation from you to other things. It is not easy. The escape is fleeting. Sweetheart, you are always on my mind. You did not escape me on the rough trip across the Atlantic. You were with me in every little cafe on the Champs Elysees.

The physical expression of our love the night before I sailed for Le Havre is a beautiful reminder of the years we will have together. I will always love you, Ellie.

Love, Bill

Flanigan read only one letter. He softly set the remaining letters on the table. Feeling a bit uncomfortable with his father's love letter, he rose quickly and with a sardonic twist of his lips, said, "Speaking of you, Bill and myself, do you know what day today is?"

"Of course, Peter. It is December 8th, the Feast of the Immaculate Conception."

"Very good, Mom. Now when you and I are canonized maybe there will be two feasts of the Immaculate Conception, December 8th and June 1st."

"Peter! If the good nuns heard you say that they wouldn't be telling me that you should be a priest."

"After yesterday's attack on Pearl Harbor, few people my age will be considering the cloth as a vocation. Come June, I'll probably make a swift change from graduation gown to Army brown. Right as we speak, President Roosevelt is meeting with a joint session of Congress. Did you see the morning paper? It reports that the United States will declare war on both Japan and Germany! This could be bigger than the Great War. I don't feel excited about going, but if my country wants me I'll go."

"Why don't you feel the excitement, Peter? Is it because I would be alone?"

"Maybe. Maybe it's the long talk about government-sponsored violence I had with Mother Rachel a while back. But most of all it's because of Uncle Frank."

"You mean the few times we were able to see him was enough for him to influence you?"

"No doubt about it. You told me about him when I was little, and I was so anxious to see him. What a shock when I did! I'll always remember the first time we went to the Oxford Soldier's Home. Now I understand what you meant when you said there were basket cases there from the Great War of 1914. At least Uncle Frank was able to talk to us. Most of the veterans there didn't seem to blink their eyes. They stared holes through everyone. But Frank, between deep breaths, had a lot to say to me."

"Like?"

"Like saying it wasn't chlorine gas that ruined his life, it was the United States Government."

"You do know that my brother Frank was a conscientious objector, don't you Peter?"

"Yes, but I still can't understand why he was in France fighting if he was a C.O. He did tell me never to volunteer. 'Don't even register for the draft' is what he said."

"Peter, Frank wanted to avoid prison so he registered but claimed C.O. status. He said when pressure of family, church, community and peers became overwhelming, he felt he had no choice but to serve without joining in the killing. Even though he was a medic without a weapon, he said afterwards that it was a huge mistake."

"That's not hard to believe," Peter said, "in bed for most of his life, hacking and gasping and angry. I don't feel I got to know him well in those few visits we made. Now, I guess I understand what he meant when he said if he'd gone to prison he would not have been gassed, and he'd be living here in Wurtzville with us, not among the living dead in Oxford."

"Well, he's gone now, Peter. May he rest in peace."

"I'm not sure he's resting easy. Not if he knows what's happening now. I think of him often. Especially in history class when the Great War is discussed and our teacher gloats about victory and heroism. It's bizarre. My mind flashes to Oxford and all those blank faces and the moaning and crying. Frank told me the Great War wasn't any victory. It was a major loss of young blood, he said. Uncle Frank told me to go to American Legion and Veteran of Foreign Wars parades and see if they wheel basket-cases down Main St. He was very bitter. I still keep a copy of a letter he sent me last year, shortly before he died. He told me to be sure to read All Quiet on the Western Front and see the movie. He read the book but was never able to see the film. In the same letter he had a copy of a speech made by the great U.S, Marine war hero, Major General Smedley Butler. He told me to read and reread the speech of General Butler and to follow his advice."

"Would you read Butler's advice to me, Peter? I'm curious. You never showed me that part of Frank's letter."

Peter pulled the worn pages of the Butler speech from his American History textbook and began reading the General's words:

> War is a racket. A racket is best described, I believe, as something that is not what it seems to the majority of people. Only a small inside group knows what it is about. It is conducted for the benefit of the very few at the expense of the masses.

> I believe in adequate defense at the coastline and nothing else. If a nation comes over here to fight, then we'll fight. The trouble with America is that when the dollar only earns 6 percent over here, then it gets restless and goes overseas to get 100 percent. Then the flag follows the dollar and the soldiers follow the flag.

> I wouldn't go to war again as I have done to protect some lousy investment bankers. There are only two things we should fight for. One is defense of our homes and the other is the Bill of Rights. War for any other reason is simply a racket.

I suspected I was just part of the racket all the time. Now I am sure of it. Like all members of the military profession, I never had a thought of my own until I left the service. My mental faculties remained in suspended animation while I obeyed the orders of higher-ups. This is typical with everyone in the military service.

Looking back at it, I feel that I could have given Al Capone a few hints. The best he could do was to operate his racket in three districts. I operated on three continents.

Peter put the Butler speech back in his text book. "I only wish that this speech was part of my history text book. In our history class, we're told killing is just fine if our government tells people to kill. It's bizarre the way history books lavish praise on our killing deeds. The opposing people are usually depicted as savages or barbarians. Uncle Frank told me about the 'hate German' campaign right before we declared war on Germany in 1917. It got worse when the war started, he said. I think guys like General Butler and Uncle Frank are leaning me to non-action. I'm not afraid to fight. I just can't see myself going into other countries and killing people. In fact, I probably would have gone to Canada in 1861 rather than kill my own countrymen. I'm a bit confused. I don't think I'm a pacifist, but then again I'm pretty sure I'd have a hard time shooting someone. Maybe I'm a bit like General Butler; maybe I'd shoot to kill if we were invaded."

"Easy enough to say, Peter, but twenty-four years ago, that kind of attitude was considered un-American, and those who did protest and refuse to sign for conscription into the services ended up in prison. Few men went that far, and I suspect the same pressures will be on young men today if they refuse to follow government orders. I'm sure you learned about the Socialist, Eugene Debs. Debs gave a speech in opposition to our entry in the Great War and was sentenced to 10 years in prison. The Supreme Court upheld most attacks upon individual rights of dissent even after the war was over. In 1919, Judge Oliver Wendell Holmes ruled that during a time of clear and present danger, free speech was not a constitutional option. Even after the war was over, Debs remained in prison.

"What a waste war is. What an ungodly waste of good manhood. And for what? To prove how powerful we are, or to send our boys to die because Europeans chose death over diplomacy?

"Political slogans are mindless. 'A War to End All Wars!' That was the propaganda the government and press fed us in 1917, and you can see it all happening now in 1941. I think by now you understand this country never really cared about your uncle Frank. He had good reason to detest the Beer Belly Brigade of the Veterans of Foreign Wars and American Legion as they did their Main Street Shuffle every Armistice Day. Do you think people watching really care or even know about the basket cases from the Great War? I'm glad you're beginning to question the tough talk, flag waving and hate making, Peter. We had that during the last war. You don't have to prove your patriotism or your manhood."

"I will next June 1st, when I turn 18."

"Every mother and father knows about the Selective Service Act. You've been the man of this house for many years. Signing away your life to generals and politicians won't make you more of a man. It didn't for my brother Frank. It didn't for those poor forgotten dregs in the Oxford Soldier's Home.

"I know I might sound harsh saying all this, Peter. It's out of character for me to whine. But you're so much a part of my life. I loved my brother Frank and agonized with him and his decision in 1917. Now, another madness is sweeping Europe. Does this mean that after giving up my brother to European violence, I now must give up my son?

"I just hope," continued Ellie, "that we don't become the country of hatred, suspicion and persecution that we were in 1917-18. Above all, I pray that we won't force our young men to give their lives for issues across the seas — issues not our own."

Chapter 8
Meeting Anna Maria

Freddie Mangan had Flanigan's Plymouth road-ready by mid-December. Peter did not want to take the car home. The Plymouth was a Christmas gift to his mother. Besides, not only did she not know how to drive, Peter had to get a permit — the prerequisite to getting a license. So the shiny grey sedan sat idle in Mangan's garage. Anxious to get a licensed driver to take him out, he had Alley Oop Rozer travel the back roads of Wurtzville as his instructor.

"Crusher, you don't need me to tool around town as your instructor, you can drive this baby yourself," said Rozer.

"Sure, and then I can have another confrontation with the law. I think I better wait."

"Look, Peter. You have to put this car to a test right away. You never even drove the heap. Maybe it doesn't have any guts. Mangan's say they'll back up the car for thirty days. Your time on the car is running out before you even take it home as a Christmas present. Maybe it's a shit bucket and you don't even know it. You wanna give that to your mother for Christmas?

"I'll show you one hell of a good test for the old grey mare," Rozer said. "You can crank that car up, goose its rear end over the mountain and when we get to the lake, I'll show you a way to winter check it! If we find a problem, we head into town, park the car at Mangan's door and raise hell until he fixes it."

Flanigan wondered for a moment why he wasn't opposed to the idea. Before he had time to counter, Rozer was behind the wheel of his Model A.

"Peter, it's two days before Christmas," Rozer hollered from his rolled down window. "I've got four days before I'm off to the war. Forget about cops, just follow my little buggy and I'll keep you in my rear view mirror."

Flanigan stayed close to Rozer over the frozen road to Laurel Lake. For the past week, the temperature had plunged and a light snow now glazed the tortured hills ripped apart by strip mining. Tall mounds of slate, rock and dirt gave the valley an alpine village look for a few days. Then, if no new snow came, accumulated particulate matter from coal burning steam engines, coal burning homes, and dust from collieries would blacken the region once again.

Rozer drove to the lake edge and Flanigan parked his Plymouth along side.

"How she handle up the mountain, Crusher?"

"Great. I should have led the way and sucked that Model A up my tail pipe."

"Oh yeah? Well, Mr. Flanigan, let me tell you about this old A. My little black turd will run rings around your pussy Plymouth. You might outrun me and out maneuver me on the gridiron but not on the ice."

"On the ice. You want to drive on the lake?"

"Hell yes, Crusher. We came out here for a winter test. I told you that back in town."

"Oh no you didn't. You said that we were going to winter test my Plymouth. Not drive it on the friggin lake."

"Crusher, driving on the lake is the best test drive you could give your car. Starting, turning, speed driving and stopping — all on slippery stuff."

"Sinking stuff, Roz. The ice is fresh. It can't be thick enough to hold your old A let alone my heavy Plymouth."

"Crusher, the lake has been frozen over for two weeks. I'll get my crow bar and check it for thickness."

Wind had blown the light snow off the lake, letting the sun sparkle dance on the surface. Chopping steadily, Rozer broke through the ice and held his thumb at the water line on the bar. "Six inches, Peter, thick enough to hold a truck."

"Says who?"

"Says me and says the ice cutters down at the north end of the lake. Look over there."

"Holy cow, you're right, Roz. That is a truck."

"Yeah, and the ice is always thicker down there, Crusher. Those guys are cutting first ice. The local restaurants and bars claim that first ice is best for mixed drinks. Laurel Lake is spring fed and its ice is the best. Come out here in January and February and you'll see a dozen ice cutting teams on the lake and trucks lined up to haul ice to storage houses around the county.

"Keep in mind, Crusher, that we're going to have some fun as well as test brakes and steering and stuff. So quit your bellyaching and let's go!"

Rozer ran the old Ford onto the ice. Seeing Peter in his rear view mirror, he accelerated to 40 mph and slammed on his brakes. The Model A went into a spin. Flanigan saw Rozer's left hand extended above the roof of the car and with his own window open, heard Rozer's booming "Yahoo" across the frozen surface.

Rozer came out of the spin after two complete turns, sped out toward the ice cutters, then headed back toward Flanigan at top speed. Coming down hard on the brake pedal and keeping it there, Rozer's old Ford was spinning like a child's top as it headed for Flanigan's Plymouth that now sat idling near the shore. The Ford came to a halt just a few feet from the Plymouth. By now, Peter was excited with the ice demonstration. It looked exhilarating and he wanted in on the fun.

Rozer yelled, "Race you to the south end, Crusher. A couple of hundred yards before the foot bridge, hit your brakes. Be sure to count your spins. Most spins and closest stop to the bridge wins."

Flanigan, in low gear, spun his tires as Rozer smoothly moved ahead. Learning quickly, he slipped the gear shift into second and then third gear as he pushed the pedal to the metal and came within several car lengths of Rozer. The foot bridge was not yet in sight. Peter knew it well. He'd carried many golf bags across it and had dived into the water hole to retrieve balls for hundreds of disgruntled duffers and even good golfers who were psychologically defeated by the presence of water just yards from the 5th tee. It was fun to dive the deep water and find a good ball. Flanigan had learned to plunge where a lot of other kids refused to go. He was able to stay down long enough to come up with several balls. Returning a ball to the owner for 10 cents could net a couple of dollars on a busy Saturday. Extra finds would be sold for a price depending on condition of the ball.

Remembering his days at the Water Hole job he had a flash memory of something that an old resident cottager told him about the water at the hole. Immediately, he began to press the horn to warn Rozer of danger ahead.

"The horn! The horn — blow, dammit, blow!" he screamed. But no sound. As he turned the bend in the lake he first saw Rozer start his braking spin, then the bridge was spotted at the water hole. Pumping the brakes to prevent spinning, Flanigan swayed left and right and saw what he expected. On Rozer's fifth spin, the Model A went out of sight as it skidded off the ice and into the spring fed, iceless water hole.

"Yup, the old cottager had said, 'this here lake is mighty cold water. But that main spring you feel when you dive for balls in the middle of the hole is so powerful that it prevents more than a thin crust of ice to form on this little end of the lake. Hell, some years, not even a crust forms until late January.'"

Flanigan stopped well short of the water hole. He lifted the trunk of the Plymouth, grabbed a tire iron, and ran to the edge of the water hole. Shedding his heavy mackinaw, he dove into the body-shocking water. Summer water vegetation long gone, the water was crystal clear and he instantly saw the Ford, ten feet down, where Rozer was struggling to open the door. Flanigan, holding onto a windshield wiper for balance, began smashing the glass with the tire iron. The water slowed down the force of his movements and he needed to breathe; with all his strength he shot himself to the surface, drew several deep gulps of oxygen and swam down again to the car. Rozer was still in the car but the little Ford filled up quickly and Flanigan saw Rozer with his head to the inside roof sucking in the last available air. Positioning himself in the shaft of light that knifed through the water and illuminated the Model A, Flanigan smashed another large piece of glass, reached in, grabbed Rozer by the hair and pulled him out and upward.

Peter, exhausted by the two dives and the strenuous underwater work, clung to the ice edge, unable to muster the strength to lift himself out of the water. Rozer scrambled out of the water and pulled Peter to his feet. Neither spoke as they stumbled and dragged each other to the Plymouth.

Rozer got behind the wheel and Peter with his eyes closed, and his body in a fetal position on the front seat, made a vain attempt to warm himself.

"Hang on, Crusher, we'll be over at the hotel in a minute."

Rozer drove off the ice and up to the rear entrance of Machelli's Laurel Pines Inn.

"Come on, Crusher, we are going to get old Dante to loan us some dry clothes."

"I ca-ca-can't move, Roz."

Rozer slammed the car door and went into the hotel kitchen.

Mrs. Machelli and her daughter Anna Maria, were cutting pasta on a long flour-dusted wood block.

"Mrs. Machelli, call Dante — quick. I need him outside!"

"Dante, Dante. Come quick," yelled Mrs. Machelli.

"Jesa-ma Cris. I'm a busy. Donna you bother me, I'm a wet like a monkey," hollered Dante.

"It's not me, Dante. It's Ally Oop, he needs your help."

Dante Machelli came into the kitchen in his bath robe and Rozer gripped his arm. "Come quick. Dante. I've got another wet monkey out in the car and he can't move."

"O.K., O.K. boy. I come."

Rozer and Dante carried Flanigan into the dining room and Mrs. Machelli ran for dry clothes as Dante jogged into the bar and came back with a bottle of rum. He slapped heaping spoons of brown sugar into large mugs, poured a large smash of rum into each mug and topped it off with hot water from the stove kettle.

"Hold her in a you hands, boys. She keep you warm out-a-side. Drink her down and she keep you warm in-a-side."

Peter had tried whiskey before and nearly gagged. But the sugared rum and hot water was smoothly delicious and a sensation of warmness enveloped his body.

Mrs. Machelli put two sets of dry clothes in the men's room for Rozer and Flanigan. Shortly after, the young men were beginning to look more lifelike as they sat beside the hotel fireplace, comforted with warm crusty bread and large bowls of minestrone soup while they related their adventure to the Machelli family.

Anna Maria sat close to Peter, talking to him in low tones. Peter and Anna Maria had been school friends since first grade. Peter was well aware of the crush she had on him. Yet, she was a friend, not a 'girl friend'. As she sat close to him, the warmth of hearth, rum, and security began to add a new dimension to his feelings for her. Anna Maria's green eyes danced in the light of the fire and invaded Peter's stare. Was she always this beautiful, he thought? Her long, glossy, black hair fell to her shoulders in a wave and when she parted her ruby lips in a smile, Peter tried to break his fixation on her mouth and high cheek bones. God! he thought. Am I crazy or did I just discover that Anna Maria is shockingly beautiful?

"Peter, I didn't know that you had a car," whispered the girl.

"I don't, Anna Maria. The car is my mother's. Alley Oop and I were on a 'test run'," he laughed.

Demurely, Anna Maria said, "Apparently, your mother's brakes worked."

"Yeah. But her horn needs fixing. Ask Alley Oop about that. I tried to horn signal him before he took a nosedive into the lake."

"Well, now that you are an experienced driver, you can come out to see all of us more often. Right?"

"All of us?"

"Sure. My mother and father have always liked you, Peter."

"Aw, come on, Anna Maria. No nice, old-country Italians would want their daughter to get friendly with a wild Irish lad."

"You'll never know until you try them, Peter."

Looking over at Dante, Peter Flanigan saw him gesturing and raising his voice to Rozer.

"What-a-you, crazy, boy? You wanna go to army? No, no. You no wanna go get killed boy. You stupido? Uh?"

Putting his index finger under his right eye and pulling down his lower eye lid, Dante said, "You know why I'm-a-here? Looka me — healthy like a bear — looka my nice wife and my beautiful Anna Maria. You think-a I have all dis if-a I stay in Italy and shoot-a German in nine-deen and a seven-deen?

"I no shita you boy. My brother Alfredo? Where is Alfredo — huh?

"I tella you where Alfredo is — he's a dead. Why is Alfedo dead? Because Alfredo stupido. Alfredo say — we must-a kill a German. We no kill German, then German come kill us.

"Donna a shita me, Alfredo," I say. "Donna shita me. The German, he no wanna Italia. The German want peace, just-a like you and me.

"Alfredo tella me: You coward.

"You know what I say? I tell him. I say — sure Alfredo, I a coward. You? You big hero? Then you go die. I stay here and live."

Rozer was entranced with Dante's story. He leaned closer to Dante. "You really didn't go to war in 1914, Dante?"

"No boy. No 1914, no 1915, no 1916, no 1917, no 1918. What I just tella you? You thinka me dumb like Alfredo?"

Dante lifted his head, and inhaled deeply through his large hairy nostrils.

"Dante Machelli — he's a smell life — aaah."

He lifted his glass of red wine and took a long draft.

"Dante Machelli—he's a tasta life."

Then he stretched his arm across Flanigan to Anna Maria, pulled her to him, and kissed her cheek.

"Dante Machelli — he makes a beautiful life — look-a my Anna Maria.

"Now you a tell-a me Alli Oopa, who's a crazy? Dante the coward who's a alive or Alfredo the hero who's a dead?"

"But maybe you wouldn't be here if Alfredo didn't die for honor and country and for you," replied Rozer.

"Honor?" said Dante. Holding up his hands, shrugging his shoulders and pursing his lower lip in haughty disgust.

"What-sa honor? Die for bigga shot-a politician? Dat-sa honor? Die for da generals who wanta more stars on a da shoulder?

"You a nice a boy, Alli Oopa. Save-a your ass. Take a boat to Soud America. Pick-a banana. Whena they stop-a killing in Europa, you stop picka banana and come home.

"They always kill in Europa. Let them-a kill. That-sa what I say in nine-deen six-a-deen. The government say: Dante Machelli, we wanta you body to fight for us.

"You know what I tella them?" Dante took his thick left arm and cradled it in the crotch of his raised right elbow. "'Fungu' I tella them. 'Up-a-you ass.'"

Peter found a moment to interrupt Dante's soliloquy.

"How did you manage to stay out of the war, Dante?" he interrupted. "Didn't the government come looking for you?"

"Sure, she's a come for Dante. But Dante too smart for shitasses. My mama she help me. 'Go to Switzerland,' she tella me. She give me a big kiss. God bless Dante, and she-a squeeze my hand with 5,000 lira.

"I take-a a train to Chiasso, little-a town near Swiss-a border. But before we getta there the train, she stop. Police come an dey say, 'All show passaporta and working papers.'

"I open compartamenta window and a jump. Roll and-a roll down mountain. Cuts, torn a shirt, a pants, sore legs and scratch on a my ass. Dats-a my war wounds, Alli Oopa.

"I work. I learn how to cook. Then I go home. I pay back my mama. I give a her much more than money — she-a is happy to see me. Now, she says, go to a place where there is no war.

"'Go to America and live,' she say."

"But don't you feel some pain for not helping your countrymen fight the war?" snapped Rozer.

"I no starta da fight, boy. Dante was not-a mad at German people. Why should I kill? The government, she's crazy. Italian. German. English. All crazy. They make good people a-crazy."

Flanigan and Anna Maria were mesmerized by Mr. Machelli's intense anti-war attitude. Peter wanted to question him further but Rozer stood and grasped Dante's hand and shook it firmly.

"Dante, I don't think our government is crazy. The German government — yes. The Italian government — yes. The Japanese government — definitely. I'm seething over the Japs. I'm anxious to get at them."

Smiling, Rozer quipped, "I'm probably the crazy one, Dante.

Flanigan just saved my life and in a few days I'll turn it over to the United States Army. Thanks for the dry clothes, I'll get them back soon."

Anna Maria bounced up from the hearth. "Peter can bring them back, Roz. He's the fellow with the wheels now."

"I'll do that if you promise to have dinner with me over at that fireside table," Peter said.

"Do I have to be the waitress?" replied Anna Maria.

"Nope. We can prepare the meal together in the kitchen and serve ourselves in the dining room. Let's do it on a quiet night or after the last guests are gone."

Anna Maria tugged at her father's sport coat that hung loosely on Peter. " O.K. chubby," she chided. "But you are going to have to watch that figure."

Chapter 9
God, Flag, Blood, Guts

The following day, Christmas Eve, Peter slept late. He awoke to the sound of his mother's voice and sat up in bed listening to a conversation.

"Oh yes. Sure, I can get him to come to the phone but you will have to wait a bit, I think he's still asleep. He must have had a tiring day yesterday."

Peter jumped up and quickly slipped on his trousers. When Ellie arrived at the door, she said in a teasing tone, "What a lovely way to wake up, Peter. A sweet sounding young woman is on the phone-she would like to speak to you."

Peter grinned broadly. "I think I know who it is — and you do too. That's O.K. with me."

"Hello," he said into the phone.

"Hi, it's me! I was just thinking that we should follow through with our last night's plan. Remember? We talked about having dinner and you said we should have the table near the fireplace and be alone.

How about tonight? I can't promise solitude because on Christmas Eve we invite all our relatives for a huge dinner. But if you're willing to help fix and serve tonight's family dinner at our place, then the table is reserved for just you and me. After that we can go to Midnight Mass. Fair enough?"

"Sounds terrific to me. But you know, I should ask my mother if she minds if I miss the traditional oyster stew we have on Christmas Eve."

"Wait, Peter! My mother wants your mother to come out as our family guest. Would you ask her to come to the phone so that my mother can speak to her?"

"You mean we're having our first formal date and you want my mother to come? Gee — that doesn't sound too romantic-but you know what? I like the idea."

Peter, impishly, bowed to his mother and announced, "an offer of dinner, madam," and handed the phone to Ellie. She and Carmella Machelli talked and Ellie accepted the invitation to dinner. Anna Maria came back on and Ellie handed the phone to Peter.

"You know, Peter, that you should be here much before your mother. We have to prepare a lot of food. Can you get here this afternoon?"

"See you about 2 P.M., Anna Maria."

Peter turned to his mother and told her he had a Christmas present for her but that it was a different kind of present and that it might seem selfish that he give her a present he would often be using.

"Well, let me see now. What could that be? A short wave radio? A snow shovel? Gosh, no again, eh. Then how about a pony or horse or burro to take us to town?"

"Ellie Flanigan, you got it right. A horse it is. In fact, about 150 horses. Come with me and I'll show you."

Peter had kept the car parked about a block away. It had some markings from the previous day's activity but it still looked clean and shiny. He and Ellie walked around the block and the only parked car was the gray Plymouth.

Peter leaned on the left fender, raised his thumb toward the car and said, "Merry Christmas, Mom!"

"You don't really mean that my gift is this car, do you?"

"Yup, I really do mean it."

"This is amazing, Peter! How can you afford it? Where did you get it? How can you drive it and how can I ever drive it?"

"Whoa, Mom. One at a time. First, the car was purchased with money that Roz and I made by selling coal. It was purchased at Mangan's Auto Center down town and yes, I know how to drive and so do you."

"I drove in 1923, Peter. Bill Mahoney taught me how to drive but that was almost two decades ago. I can't just pick up from there."

"Why not?"

"Well, to begin with I don't have a license."

"Oh come on, this is Wurtzville. Just get out your old license and take it to the Motor Vehicle Office and they'll issue you another one. You and Mary Addison are old school mates, right? She's the office manager and will give you a temporary license and tell you a permanent one will be in the mail in no time."

"How do you know all this, Peter?"

"Because she issued my permit last week. When I told her that I'd bought a car and knew how to drive, she said that I could skip the driving test and expect to receive the license in the mail before Christmas."

Holding a small card from his wallet, Peter waved it. "See what relative influence can do in this town, Madam? Just arrived in the mail."

"Peter, this is wonderful. When you had the telephone installed last week, I thought it was my Christmas present. It really was a surprise and I love having it-but a car! Are you sure you didn't rob a bank or something? This car must have cost you hundreds of dollars."

"It cost three hundred and I'm just about broke. Yet, it's worth it.

We're going to have fun with this car. My first request is-may I use it this afternoon? I want to go out to the lake at 2 P.M. to help Anna Maria. Her uncle Angelo will pick you up at 6 P.M. and take you to the dinner that I'm helping Anna Maria prepare."

"I'll go. However, I felt somewhat uncomfortable when Carmella Machelli asked me to come out to the Lake. We've known each other since we were young girls. I don't know her husband, Dante, but I remember when he came to Wurtzville. He couldn't speak a word of English. Carmella and I were in 10th grade. She was a bright girl. Her father arranged for her to marry Dante Machelli. She was upset but seemed to understand her fate. It was not uncommon then to marry off one's daughter to a newly-arrived greenhorn-especially if the greenhorn had some cash and a hint of pedigree. Dante claimed to have both. Apparently, he had the cash part of the deal. Within a few years of his arrival, he bought the old hotel at Laurel Lake and opened up a restaurant. I've seen them in town on occasion but I haven't talked to them in years."

On the way to Laurel Lake, Flanigan turned on the radio. News of the day centered on Winston Churchill's visit to the White House. He and President Franklin Roosevelt were broadcasting live from the White House balcony. Flanigan flipped to another station. He told himself he was not going to think about the war today. Christmas, Anna Maria, new car, his mother's high spirits and visions of good Italian cooking danced in his head. When he found the soft sound of "O Little Town of Bethlehem" he down shifted to slow the short trip and settle his racing mind. Within minutes he was in the Machellis' kitchen, rolling out pasta dough.

"Knead the ball of dough like this before you roll it, Peter."

Anna Maria pressed her palm on the dough in a circular fashion then proceeded to demonstrate how to roll the ravioli pasta, cut it into squares, fill each with a spoon of cheese, crimp and set for cooking.

"How many people do we have to prepare for, Anna Maria?"

"Oh, about twenty. If we cut a half dozen for each person that will be about 120 raviolis."

"Then why did I need to come out so early? We should be able to roll and cut these in an hour."

"This is just one course. We have to bake two kinds of bread, panettone and olive focaccia. Then, we'll have to mix those anise seeds into a cookie batter, prepare the tortellini, baccala, smoked bass and fresh trout."

"Anna Maria, do you realize you're talking in a foreign tongue? I haven't ever heard of this stuff — let alone prepare it."

"That's O.K. I didn't expect a poor Irish fellow to 'capisce' right away. Oh, by the way, we have to go out and catch the trout."

"Oh sure. And I suppose we'll have to cut through the ice and sit around for hours to wait for them to bite?"

"Ice isn't a problem. Come with me, dear friend and I'll show you."

Anna Maria grabbed a pair of rubber hip boots, and handed them to Flanigan. "Put these on. Your feet are about the same size as my father's. I'll get mine on and then we're off to get our brown trout."

Flanigan had caught fish in ponds and lakes but trout were mysterious creatures that he'd heard about but never developed the skill to catch. He followed Anna Maria who had grabbed a large net from the porch and marched out ahead of him.

"Where's your rod, Anna Maria?"

"Don't need one, Peter."

Anna Maria followed the small stream that ran through the hotel lawn and into the lake. The stream was only a few feet wide but ran deep. The Machellis' boathouse covered the little stream and Anna Maria and Peter went into the boat house with the net. Inside, a wooden walk edged the stream on both sides with one plank straddling the water.

"See anything down there, Peter?"

"Hell yes! There are about five huge fish just swimming around. Why don't they swim out to the lake?"

"Check the wire covering the outlet. They can't get out unless you raise that chicken wire frame. If you look over there at the inlet, it also has chicken wire preventing them from running up stream on us."

Anna Maria got into the cold water and motioned Peter to get in near the inlet. A large trout thrashed the water, trying to get by Anna Maria.

"Oh, no, you don't, Mr. Brown Trout," she yelled. "I've got him, Peter! He's a beaut! Here-take the net and haul him outside.

"Watch how I kill him. You shouldn't let a fish suffer."

Anna Maria took a small hatchet from the wall of the boathouse and quickly severed the head of the large fish.

"Now it's your turn, city boy."

Flanigan posted himself near the outlet and Anna Maria moved toward him driving another big trout into his net.

"Heck, and some people say that catching trout is difficult," quipped Flanigan. "Of course, I won't comment on the legality of the catch."

"And don't tell anyone at school. Especially the sisters. They think I'm a little saint. I suppose a little saint wouldn't trap fish — especially out of season. But these two fat fellows will be enjoyed by a lot of good folks tonight."

Anna Maria gave Flanigan a lesson in cleaning fish. She showed him how to make a belly cut on each trout and how to remove the intestines and gills. Back in the kitchen, Anna Maria placed the trout in two large pans filled with ice that Peter had cut from the shore line.

"We'll wait until about an hour before dinner and then salt the trout, squeeze fresh lemon juice in the belly cavity and rub a coat of nice olive oil over the entire fish to prevent it from drying out while baking."

Around 5 P.M., Mrs. Machelli came into the kitchen and prepared the baccala she had soaking since early morning. Anna Maria was just finishing the folding of spinach-filled tortellini and was telling Peter to

mash potatoes for gnocchi. By 6 P.M., Dante appeared from the cellar
with an armful of homemade red wine in long bottles capped with ce-
ramic and rubber-tipped tops. Relatives began to arrive but knew their
place, and at the Machelli Hotel, it was not in the kitchen but in the
dining room. Flanigan carried plates of food to the large table, noting
that his mother had arrived and was engaged in conversation. War, of
course, was the topic.

Back in the kitchen, he nudged Anna Maria and said, "Didn't you
promise we could have our own table tonight?"

"Yes, but it would be nice if we all sat together and talked. Wouldn't
it?"

"No. Not if the topic is what it is now and will probably be all
dinner long. I'm not ready to chat about the war tonight."

"Fair enough. Set the table off to the side for just you and me. We
can fix our plates and retreat to our own place. Make it look like there's
not enough room at the main table."

Flanigan shuffled chairs and moved two plates and settings to a
side table. He and Anna Maria got up often to clear the main table, pour
more wine, serve additional courses and avoid war talk.

"Anna Maria, this is great! I didn't know food preparation could
be so involved and I can't believe I'm enjoying it."

"I've noticed that, Peter but you know, we are missing out on the
main purpose of coming together. We're apart from the family. Aren't
you used to crowds of relatives?"

"Crowds of relatives? There's my crowd," Peter motioned to his
mother. "Ellie Flanigan is it, she's family."

"You're kidding me, Peter! Where's your father?"

"I'll tell you about him some other time. For now, let's just say
he's around but that I rarely see him."

"No brothers or sisters, aunts or uncles?"

"Nope."

"Oh Peter, you've got to get to know some of mine. Let me introduce you."

"Not tonight, Anna Maria. Look at my mother. She already knows most of your family. She can tell me about them. Besides, they're not paying any attention to us at all — and that's great. Let's just you and I chat."

Lifting a glass of red wine, Flanigan looked Anna Maria in the eye. "Merry Christmas, Anna Maria. Invite me here next year and I'll be a better mixer. Why don't you tell me a little about your mom and dad?"

"Well, you're not deaf; you know that my father has a thick Italian accent, and my mother speaks with the same local All-American accent as your mother. My mother came to this county when she was four. Look over at the south wall, Peter. Recognize the place from geography or history texts? My mother is from Naples and she insisted that a mural of her hometown be on the south wall of the restaurant. So there it is — a mural of the Bay of Naples. Now look over at the north end of this dining room. How about those Alpine mountains and that strip of blue that's supposed to be the Po River? My father is from the north. His home was in the rice growing area so my mother gave him the job of cooking the risotto. He makes a big deal out of the difference between Northern Italian cooking and Southern Italian cooking. Did you know there is a difference?"

"All I know is that every Monday we have Chef Boyardee out of the can."

"I thought so. Canned spaghetti is for non-Italians, but tomato base is a southern Italian thing. My father has a fit if his pasta is served with tomato sauce. 'Datsa peasant food!' he says. He wants sauces without a hint of tomato. He's big on basil and tarragon and even dill. Remember in history how we learned that the Austrians controlled much of northern Italy? Well, a lot of Germanic influence, including cuisine, has carried over and my father is living proof.

"You probably didn't notice that this dining room we're in has a lot of tables and the north dining room — my father's section — has only a few tables. My father insists good northern Italian cuisine can't be mixed with inferior foods from the south. He refuses to admit that few local people enjoy northern Italian food more than southern Italian. Take a look at our menu. The first page is northern with all the veal and non-tomato pasta dishes. Notice that it's hardly looked at. Then look at the worn pages of the southern Italian menu. Different huh? Pages torn and soiled. That's the food people order. We're a spaghetti and meatball restaurant. Yet, mother has to maintain what amounts to two kitchens. It's almost as if it was a Kosher kitchen — you know, meat kitchen on one side and a dairy kitchen on the other? We have to have separate pots and pans for northern Italian foods because my father says tomato sauce never goes away. 'tomato-she's a stick to your tongue and she's a stick to my cook-a-pot.' So we humor him and do most of the preparing and cooking away from his sacred pots, pans and prep area."

"What do you like better, Anna Maria, southern or northern?"

"I like them both. But I tire of southern cooking. It's good to see my father get into the cooking mood and whip up a variety of dishes that lets you get beyond the tomato taste. He's right but we don't let him know we think so."

"Why not?"

"Because he's so sure of his beliefs that he doesn't need to be pumped up. I admire him for standing up for what he believes in — even if it's only food. He believes even if good cooking does not draw many people, it does draw some and those are worth cooking for. 'Better we do a some-a-ting good. Lots a people, they need-a-learn. Maybe no today. Maybe no tomorrow. Some day.'"

"So, Anna Maria, what are you learning working here?"

"That I don't want to do it for the rest of my life."

"So what will you do?"

"Go to college. I don't have any brothers or sisters so I'm not a financial burden. They still need me here at the restaurant though. But that's O.K. Ellenwood College is only twenty minutes away and I can

drive there each day and be home in time to help in the kitchen and
wait on tables. What about you, Peter? What are your plans?"

"I really don't have any plans. Not yet, anyway. College is out for
now. I'm the only one at home but dollars aren't there for college —
not this year, at least."

"So what will you do when you graduate in late May? Go to work?"

"Work or war, I guess. I said I wasn't going to talk about the war
tonight but the war is impossible to avoid. I bet those people at the
family table talking Italian are talking about the war. The only thing I
understand is 'Il Duce' and 'Mussolini'."

"We don't have to bring war into our first date, Peter. Let's talk
about how you could go to college next September."

"As I said, Anna Maria, it just ain't possible! And I guess I don't
want to talk about killing Japanese or Germans or Italians. You may
joke about your father's English but what he said yesterday made a lot
more sense than what I normally see in movies, read in books, hear in
school and even in church. I know I'm not a wimp or a coward. Maybe
I'm just not very patriotic. Maybe I should feel more allegiance to my
country."

"Peter, you need to talk to more people about this. Since you
don't have any male relatives, maybe someone like Fr. Goodman, our
history teacher. He might have an idea or two for you to consider."

"Goodman annoys the hell out of me. If I close my eyes in class I
swear I'm listening to a Father Coughlin radio message. They both think
they're hot wired to God. Goodman belongs in the Marines or Infantry.
Have you ever noticed how he drools when he tells those stories of
heroic death in war? Pick your war, pick your country. Goodman rel-
ishes blood and guts for sake of land, flag and God. The God part makes
me want to vomit. Goodman always finds a way to sanctify destruction.
It amazes me that a man who is supposed to represent Jesus Christ
always has a theological and historical excuse for killing during war.
He doesn't have any trouble finding the bad guys. Like the American

Civil War — we're supposed to feel great love and appreciation for the north as they slaughter the people of the south. Or the Graet War. His propaganda makes the Germans look like the personification of Satan.

"No, I won't talk to Goodman unless I challenge him in class, and that will probably happen. But I'm sure to lose. Everybody loves flag wavers. Since Pearl Harbor, just about everybody has made up their mind about what we have to do. When I speak up, I'll take the fire of not only Padre Goodman, but my friends and classmates."

"Peter, you've got me on your side. You know my father's views on war. I've been indoctrinated on that topic for as long as I can remember. Now that I'm 18, I think it's time to formulate my own views, and you know what? I like my father's reasoning more than Father Goodman's and the nuns who seem to click their heels to the national consensus. They seem more determined to make us good little patriotic American Catholics. The're probably more flags flying around St. Catherine's Academy and St. Catherine's Church than around the White House."

"Anna Maria, what time do we leave for Midnight Mass?"

"Oh gosh, It's 10 o'clock now. We have to clean up and leave for church by 11. Let's move."

By now, most people had left the dining table and were gathered around the Christmas tree in the sitting room that looked out on the lake. Anna Maria and Peter cleared the tables, scraped the plates and began to wash the dishes and pots and pans.

Shortly before 11 P.M. they were on their way to St. Anthony's Church. Ellie took a ride home, saying she was too tired to go to Midnight Mass. She told Peter that she would see him in the morning.

Chapter 10
A Touch Of Passion

On the way to St. Anthony's, Peter asked Anna Maria about the new assistant pastor at the church, Father Sampson. He said he had heard that "Sampson was a reject. Isn't it true that he was sent to St. Anthony's by his religious order to keep him from influencing seminarians where he taught theology?"

"I haven't heard that, and St. Anthony's is my church. Where did you get that from, St. Catherine's?"

"No, not at the church, but at school. Just a few days before Christmas vacation, I overheard Fr. Goodman talking to two sisters in the office. I was scooping up some brownie points by doing filing so I heard most of the conversation. Seems that your new assistant pastor is from a Jesuit University somewhere around New York City. According to Goodman, your new guy is dangerous. Or so Goodman claims. Goodman says that this priest, Sampson, is unpatriotic and a disgrace to American Catholicism. Goodman would like to see Sampson thrown out of the church or as he said at one point in his comments, 'Send him to Tokyo.'

"I guess Sampson has a history of being a trouble maker inside and outside of the church. Something about him being a slacker during the Great War."

Flanigan parked his car under a rail trestle near the church and he and Anna Maria walked up two flights of steps to a viaduct and then past Zapia's grocery store on the way to mass. The market was still buzzing. Customers were snapping up last minute purchases of imported Perugia toffee candy from Italy, assorted cookies, capicola, soprasetta, pepperoni and other meats that would be mixed with cheeses and vegetables and served as an antipasto on Christmas Day.

Angelo, the proprietor, dressed in his normal white multi-stained apron, was taking a break in front of the store. He patted his large belly, waved his stogie at Anna Maria and Peter and said, "Napoli girl and Irisha boy. What a beautiful bambinos soma day you maka."

Anna Maria, flushed but was quick witted enough to respond, "Angelo, shouldn't you be counting your daily take and getting ready for Mass?"

Angelo dropped his stogie, snuffed it out with the sole of his pointed black shoe and said, "Palm Sunday, bambina — thatsa when I go to mass."

As they walked past, Anna Maria murmured, "Sure, that's because he gets something free — palm branches."

There was no snow on the ground or in the forecast, but it was cold. Dozens of young couples were huddled around the entrance of the church and a cloud of steam breath rose from the cluster. Peter and Anna Maria made their way through, wishing "Merry Christmas" to friends and strangers.

The church was aglow with every overhead light on in addition to a multitude of candles and colored bulbs, flaming red Poinsettias decked the main altar and huge white and yellow mums encircled the main altar as well as the statues of St. Anthony, St. Joseph and the Virgin Mary. On the side altar, a crèche, said to be hand carved in the Lake Como region of northern Italy, was surrounded with kneeling worshipers; some reaching into the manger to take a strand of straw for good luck.

Every pew was filled, so the young couple made their way up the steps to the choir loft and found a seat off to the side. It was probably the last available place to sit in church. Within minutes, dozens of standing people lined the back and sides of St. Anthony's.

When the priest came onto the altar, Peter leaned to Anna Maria and asked, "Is that Father Sampson?"

"Yes," she whispered.

When the priest turned toward the congregation and began reading the epistle, Peter judged Sampson to be about 45 years old. Tall, lean, and clean shaven, he seemed to be counting heads as his eyes made contact with the late night worshipers after every brief pause that he made in the reading.

The celebrant then turned to the gospel and surprised Peter by not reading the text. Father Sampson liked to commit the gospel to memory each week. He gave the account of the birth of Jesus according to Luke, chapter 2. 1-7.

Sampson took a moment to scan the packed church and again seemed to make eye contact with everyone — at least that was Peter's impression as he felt the priest's eyes meet his.

"At that time Emperor Augustus sent out an order for all citizens of the Empire to register themselves for the census." Father Sampson began the brief nativity story, told each year in most Christian churches around the world.

The story related how Mary and Joseph followed the Roman order and made their way to the little town of Bethlehem because Joseph was a descendant of King David who was born in Bethlehem. Without looking at a word from the text, Father Sampson told how Mary and Joseph were not able to find lodging and had to stay overnight in a manger, sharing the quarters with domestic animals. It was here that Jesus was born.

He told how angels appeared to shepherds nearby and how the angels told the shepherds not to be afraid and to go and see the child, the Savior. The angels sang the song of peace brought by the humble birth of the Divine baby Jesus.

The gospel recitation completed, Father Sampson stood silent for some time, once again looking at every person in the church. Then he began to speak.

"A few years back, our President, Franklin Delano Roosevelt, cautioned American people to not allow fear to govern their lives. He was speaking then of economic problems resulting from the Great Depression and the financial crisis caused by the closing of banks by some state governors. Roosevelt said 'the only thing we have to fear is fear itself—nameless, unreasoning, unjustified, terror'. He then went on to say that he would ask the Congress to give him 'broad executive power to wage a war against the emergency, as great as the power that would be given to me if we were in fact invaded by a foreign foe.'

"We know that Mr. Roosevelt did obtain that power. We know that his actions did reduce the fear and save the banking system in this country.

"In this church tonight and in all churches around the country there is justifiable fear in the minds and hearts of Americans. The war power that Mr. Roosevelt asked for on December 8th was granted to him only hours after the attack upon United States possessions in the Pacific. If a poll were taken in this congregation, most of you would probably say you are in full support of the President and Congress.

"I feel it is my obligation to speak to you otherwise. The pulpit is not supposed to be a platform for political speeches. It is virtually impossible to speak of violence on the horizon without some mention of political actions. In war there is no separation of church and state. Keep in mind that this is a Christian house of worship and we claim to be Christians and followers of Christ. The Peace of Christ is the message of the gospel tonight and I am simply bringing that message into contemporary focus.

"To be filled with fear at times is normal. It is reasonable. It is at times a necessary, a very human, protective reaction to danger. We teach our children to develop fears and rightly so.

"Yet, suppressing fear and eliminating fear is central to living Christian lives. When angels appeared to Mary to tell her that she was to be the mother of God, she was told to 'be not afraid'. When angels appeared to the shepherds and told them of the birth of the Prince of Peace, the angels told them 'be not afraid'. When Jesus rose from the dead, the first words from the angel in Matthew's gospel were, 'Fear not.'

"Jesus cautioned the Apostles about fear. He wanted them to know that God is love, not fear. Fear is what makes man's law function. Fear is man-imposed. God is love. Since He personally and unconditionally loves us, then we need not fear. Our obligation is to react to fear with love, not hate.

"My appeal to you tonight is to be not afraid of punishment or even death because of your faith. The message of the gospel — the message of Jesus Christ — the central message of our faith is love. Unconditional love. There is no approval of violence in Christ's teachings. There is no approval of hate. 'Blessed are the peace makers for they shall see God' is the message of Christ. How can we then support violence and remain Christian?

"We cannot. Everyone of us must have a vocation of peace. If we do not, we cannot claim to be Christian. If we use hate and violence as our guide we follow man's law. We negate love and non violence for hate and violence. We trade God's love for man's law.

"As I look into the congregation tonight, I see a majority of young people, people in teen age years, twenties and thirties. I can categorize your ages but I cannot categorize your minds. Each of you is blessed with a soul. Blessed with a conscience that informs you of right or wrong. Your decisions are not made by God but by the power of free will invested in you by God.

"As a priest I represent Christ. If Jesus Christ was here in my place tonight, would He ask you to leave this house of worship, find an enemy to kill, and kill him?

"The young men here tonight have been conditioned to accept military service since childhood. You have been taught at the kitchen table, on your father and grandfather's knee and in your schools, that the really important heroes are the soldiers and sailors from the many wars our ancestors have fought. Yet, you must give yourself, your own Christian conscience, the opportunity to question the use of your mind and body by government. Should you allow yourself to become a part of a killing machine? Should you allow yourself to register for that killing machine? Should you in any way serve the man made system of laws that negates your Christian faith?

"The core message of Christianity is to 'Love one another.' War is incompatible with Christianity. I am willing to discuss this topic with any one of you or in groups. Please call, write me note, or stop off at the rectory. I will be happy to pursue this further — that is, if I am still here after this talk to you tonight. May God bless you, protect you and keep you from fear. Remember that God loves *all* human kind.

"Merry Christmas!"

The mass was over by 1 A.M., doors swung open and cold incoming air brought an automatic response of turned up coat collars. A light snow was falling, yet, the sermon had been so intense that little groups gathered in the sub-freezing darkness to comment on what Father Sampson had just said.

A call rang out, "Hey Crusher." Flanigan knew immediately that it was Roz.

"Lordie, Lord — I didn't know you went to church, Roz. When did you convert?"

Giving his girl friend Tina a hug he said, "Naw, I'm here with my little Catholic honey. Since I go to a Catholic school, got a Catholic girl friend, and almost all my friends are mackerel snappers, I thought that

. . . well, maybe I should see the inside of a church . . . at least at Christmas."

"What did you and Tina think of the sermon?"

"You really want to know, Crusher?"

"Yeah. I really want to know."

Roz looked at Tina, then at Anna Maria. Getting up close and cupping his hand to Flanigan's ear he said, "He's a friggin asshole."

"Well, I'm not surprised you thought so, Roz. I suspect that a lot of people had the same thought."

"What about you, Crusher?"

"I'm not sure that I support everything that he said tonight but he gave me a lot to think about."

Speaking loudly now, Roz commented, "That guy should be shipped over to the Krauts or Japs. They could love him to death. What baloney! Don't hate, just love, he says. Sure, the Japs bomb us, kill us, destroy our property and this guy says"— Rozer changing his voice to a high feminine pitch – 'fear not, just love your enemies'— kissie kissie. And all that crap."

Tina Valenta moved in front of Roz and looked up into his face. "Come on Rozzie, it's Christmas. Let's go home and open a couple of presents."

Smiling, Anna Maria agreed. "It's late and snowy and Peter has to drive me over the mountain to the Lake. Guess we better go as well."

"How you two getting home, Roz?"

"Shanks pony, Peter. My wheels are being preserved in ice."

The four young people got into the Plymouth. Roz and Tina got off at Tina's house.

"Stop by my house tomorrow, Roz. I want to see you before you leave."

"Got ya, Crush. See you in the afternoon."

The Machellis had gone to bed when Anna Maria and Peter arrived. They went into the Lake Front living room and noticed that the

Christmas tree lights had been left on for them and a dish of cookies with a Merry Christmas greeting was there from Mrs. Machelli.

Peter Flanigan wanted so badly to hold Anna Maria close and kiss her. The thought had saturated his brain for the past forty-eight hours. He dreamed about Anna Maria; he even thought about her when Fr. Sampson was giving his very contemplative homily. He asked himself why the sudden mad crush when he had known her for years. The truth was, he told himself, "I've never kissed a girl before. Well, a real girl — a girl-woman." He quickly remembered the spin the bottle and post-man games where kisses were exchanged. But that was years ago when he was a little twit, he thought. How could he get up the courage to take her in his arms and kiss her now?

Anna Maria reached up to replace a fallen ornament and bumped a light that blinked and went out. "I'll replace it, Anna Maria."

Flanigan reached over to remove the light and found Anna Maria's waist instead. She raised her dark eye brows, smiled, and demurely allowed Peter Flanigan to bring her to him. Flanigan's pulse raced and a new found joy swept his body as his lips met hers. Anxious breathing between long kisses led Anna Maria to say, "Maybe we should say good night, Peter. I could kiss you forever but that probably wouldn't be smart. Will you come out to see me later today or tomorrow?"

"Will brown trout return to spawn?"

"Ooooh, don't let Sister Hildegarde ever hear you say something so suggestive. Shame on you, Mr. Peter Flanigan. You need to be slapped."

"We are on Christmas vacation, Anna Maria — not a word about Hildegarde or the other hoods. Look, it's starting to snow again. Let's do something in the snow Christmas afternoon."

"You're on, Pietro, but let's plan on late afternoon. See you about 4 or so, O.K.?"

Chapter 11
War As An Act Of Love

Flanigan was up by 8 A.M. It was the pleasant aroma of coffee and sausage that awakened him — not Ellie or the early morning beams of light that pierced his eastern window.

Ellie had visited Hoffman's Bakery Christmas Eve and purchased a stollen for Christmas week breakfasts. Laced with citrus fruits and nuts and glazed with powdered sugar over its glossy surface, it was a visual feast. And it remained so for Peter — only a visual feast. He couldn't eat.

Sipping coffee, he and Ellie chatted about the Christmas Eve meal at Machelli's. When Ellie, without asking, slid once over eggs, and a large link of bratwurst onto his plate, Peter's appetite revived.

"Did you get the bratwurst at Hoffmans?" said Peter.

"Yes, right after I came out of his brother Hans' bakery. It's so handy having those shops close together. The Hoffmans are great. Too bad that some people are so dim-witted that they are not patronizing the Hoffmans. Have you heard about that?"

"No. Is it because they're Germans and we're at war with Germany?"

"That's it. I saw Marjorie Flynn yesterday and she said she wouldn't buy a cookie or a hot dog from the Hoffmans. 'No Nazi food in my house,'" she yapped. "Never did like that mouthy one. Now I have a good Christian reason to avoid her.

"By the way, Peter, would you mind going to mass with me this morning?"

"I went to Midnight Mass — remember?"

"Oh, I know. But it would be really nice if you and I went to Christmas Mass together."

Peter wasn't enthusiastic. Ten o'clock Mass was not at St. Anthony's, the "Italian" church that Ellie usually went to except for Christmas and Easter when she went to the "Irish" church downtown, St. Catherine's. Ellie didn't like the walk, especially near the railroad tracks where passing steam locomotives scattered showers of soot. So, they drove to church — for the first time.

St. Catherine's was the largest church in the diocese that extended from south of Scranton north to the New York State border. Its earliest members had been pre-famine Irish who came to Wurtzville in the 1830's to work in the coal mines. It grew rapidly after the Great Irish Famine of the 1840's with many of the people sneaking in from Canada. One of those illegal immigrants was the father of Terence Vincent Powderly. Young T.V. Powderly would later become the driving force of the largest labor union in the United States — The Knights of Labor.

But few church members remembered anything about Powderly and no monuments or plaques in honor of him existed in the city. Powderly was considered a Socialist by many church leaders in the 1880's and was once ushered out of a Catholic Church in Scranton by order of the bishop, who considered Powderly and his views to be a pox on Catholicism.

American Catholicism in the 1940's was still struggling for national acceptance. Support of the capitalist system entrenched in the political-economic fabric of the nation was often preached from the altar of St. Catherine's. This made some people squirm in their pews but most men and women took it in stride. Since the clergy were Christ's emissaries on earth, and since they were well educated, why would one dare challenge their views? People were told to "Render to Caesar what is Caesar's and to God what is God's."

Most folks got the message. Some, like Ellie and Peter Flanigan were a different sort.

Monsignor Golden was the celebrant. He joked about not being able to stay awake long enough to say Midnight Mass. "I leave that to the young fellows, like Father Goodman. Father will comment on the gospel this morning with the same reflections he gave last night." The old priest sat and Father Goodman came to the pulpit.

"Oh no," thought Peter. "I have to put up with this guy in history and theology classes and here he is again on Christmas Day."

Goodman began by making the sign of the cross — as everyone in the church did as well: "The Prince of Peace is born. In the name of the Father and of the Son and Holy Ghost.

"My dear friends. I want to talk to you this morning about honor, duty, love of God and country, and achieving the peace that Our Lord Jesus Christ wishes to bestow on all of us.

"We are engaged in war against an evil so great that our Christian way of life is in danger. The brutal Blitzkrieg of the Nazis and the slaughter tactics of the Japanese in China, southeast Asia and now even in our own territory must be stopped. To walk away from this evil, to refuse to face it and stop it would be not just foolish, not just stupid, it would be an act of utter cowardice.

"Duty is woven to conscience. Duty is an obligation. Duty to stop evil is a moral obligation and one's conscience must decide to either accept evil and its spread or take action against evil, and by so doing, destroy it.

"Every one of us here today has a duty to fight evil, a duty first to God, then to oneself and to one's country. That duty will depend on factors ranging from physical and mental condition, and on age. We are in a contractual agreement with our God and our country. The obligation of that contract to God is to defend the faith. The obligation of that contract to our country is to defend our nation.

"No one here would want an invading army to rush into this church, kill us and destroy this house of God. Nor would any of us want our national capital pillaged and destroyed.

"Of course, we are a people of peace. We do not want to harm other people anywhere. Yet, our very existence is threatened. We have no recourse. In standing firm, in meeting the enemy, some of us shall die. Some of us in this very church will probably give up their lives so that others may live—so that our faith will live—that our nation under God's good guidance will continue to be the light of righteousness and justice that our forefathers made it.

"In the United States Congress, one of our good Catholic congressman, John W. Flannagan Jr. of Virginia, said it all when he stated: 'It is a war of purification in which the forces of Christian peace and freedom and justice and decency and morality are arrayed against the evil pagan forces of strife, injustice, treachery, immorality and slavery.'

"One of the greatest of our Christian scholars, St. Augustine, spoke of a just war some 1700 years ago. St. Augustine noted that a particular war may be an exception to the non violent teaching of the holy gospel. Augustine said that war at times can be an act of love and mercy. He outlined the factors into four clearly understood conditions:

    1. War is permissible only after all other efforts have failed.

    2. The intention of the war must be good.

    3. Non-combatant immunity must be preserved.

    4. The force used in war should be proportionate to the goals sought.

"As a priest and a teacher of history and religion, I can say to you that this conflict meets the Just War Principles of St. Augustine. In fact, if St. Augustine did not exist, these rules would exist. They are clear, they are unequivocal, and one does not have to be a priest or scholar to understand what led our leaders to declare war on the forces of evil. We were attacked, attacked after every effort on our part to keep the peace. Our intention is positive—we intend to save western culture and Christian life. There is no intent to harm non-combatants in this conflict and you can be sure that we will meet our goal of victory with the proportionate force needed to save us. Our cause is just. It is up to all of us to heed the admonitions of St. Augustine, and keep the conflict just.

"Let me end by telling you an event that touched me deeply and made me proud. One of my high school seniors, a young man who expected to graduate in May, a young man who is not Catholic, but an outstanding Christian, came to me the last day before Christmas vacation. He said, "Father, I won't be coming back to school after the holidays. I want very much to finish high school. No one in my family has ever achieved a high school diploma. As much as I hate to disappoint them, I must do as my conscience tells me to do, Father. I have joined the Army and will be leaving for training on the 27th of December. Maybe some day, I can come back an complete my schooling, but for now, I have no choice. Duty calls, Father, and I'm going to meet that obligation."

"God bless that young, courageous man and God bless all of you."

Ellie spoke first on the way home from mass.

"Father Goodman is a very powerful speaker, Peter. I got the impression from you that he was a bit of a bore. He was very dynamic today, I thought."

"I didn't mean to give the impression that he was boring. He's interesting but I can't seem to ever feel good about his manner of expression — his logic, and especially the way he thinks that everything he believes in is gospel truth. If anyone disputes his views, he goes crazy. Its like he is right and no one should dare question his opinion.

In fact, cross out 'opinion' — he doesn't have opinions. He has only the truth."

"Well, I thought his views were to the point and well organized. Some of those rambling sermons we have at St. Anthony's have me counting the mosaic chips on the ceiling angels. I heard about the Just War theory before but it was never spelled out to me. I need to think that one over."

"Oh no! Just when you were beginning to make me think for myself, you get converted to Padre Goodman's line of thinking."

"St. Augustine's line, Peter, not Father Goodman."

"You really do mean that you accept the just war argument?"

"I'm thinking about it, Peter. There is a difference between considering something and accepting it."

"Well, maybe I need to do some more thinking too. Goodman turns me off but what he had to say this morning has my head in a spin."

"Peter, it's Christmas. Let's tone down the war talk and enjoy the day."

"What are you up to today, Mom?"

"Just relaxing. The turkey is in the oven. We will have our dinner at about 1 o'clock. I'm planning on listening to some Christmas music, read—and a couple of friends will be stopping by later this afternoon. They will want to see my Christmas presents. My guess is that I will be telling them that 'it's out and about', right?"

"Well, you do have a couple of small gifts that I won't be taking 'out and about'."

"Just joshing, Peter. I suspected that you would be seeing Anna Maria today and I know you won't be walking out to the lake."

"Right, and when Father Goodman told his student-soldier story this morning, there was no need to guess who he was talking about. I immediately remembered that I told Alley Oop that I would see him this afternoon. His home time is short and I'd like to say good bye today."

After dinner, Peter drove across town to visit with Alley Oop Rozer.

"Crusher, I wish you were coming with me. We're good team-mates and teamwork is the name of the game in the military. Why don't you sign up and meet me in camp?"

"Naw, Oop. I think I'm going let them come and take me."

"Yeah, that's right, you're just a spring chicken. Hell, I'm nine-teen and you're not ever eighteen yet. Yeah, Peter, stay home and grow into the fighting age bracket. By the time you get in I'll be a top sarge and you'll be a piss ant private."

The young men shook hands, said their good byes. Then, as an afterthought, Peter called to Rozer from his Plymouth, "I'll check your Model A next May, Oop. Maybe we can tow her out."

"Don't bother. When I come home from the war, I ain't going to drive no Model A, Crusher. Leave it in the drink."

Flanigan drove up the mountain road to Laurel lake. Anna Maria met him at the door. She was wearing a bright red satiny dress and a Santa Clause hat.

"Come on in, Peter. We have company."

Walking behind Anna Maria, he was mesmerized by her tiny waist. And with high heels on, her port to starboard sway raised his eyebrows. "Wow! Have I been blind or what?" he thought.

"Do you know Marion and Sam?"

Two attractive young people rose. The young man extended his hand before Anna Maria introduced him, "Hi. I'm Sam Cohen."

Anna Maria said, "And this is Marion Rappaport. Marion and Sam have been friends of mine since we were little. They haven't missed a Christmas afternoon here at the lake in years."

"Yeah, but the past two years, we haven't had good ice on the lake. It looks terrific today," commented Sam. "We should be able to get a long run this afternoon."

Peter looked at Anna Maria. "A long run?"

"Oh, I forgot to tell you about our toboggan run, Peter. Well, actually, it isn't the Machelli's but we like to think it's ours because we use it so often. Come here and look out the window. See that rise on the other side of the lake. It doesn't look like much from here but by the time we haul our toboggans up that hill, we'll think it's Mt. McKinley."

Peter glanced at Sam and Marion. They were wearing rugged wool shirts and wool pants bloused at the top of leather boots. Peter, expecting to hike in the snow with Anna Maria had dressed for the occasion but he turned to Anna Maria. "Are you going to wear your dress and high heels tobogganing, Anna Maria?"

Anna Maria gave Flanigan a flirtatious flick of her long black eye lashes, smiled and said, "Gee, Peter, how often do you get to see me in silk satin at St. Catherine's? Isn't this a tad nicer than the navy blue uniform?"

"Oh, yes. Oh yes. Oh yes," said Flanigan.

Everyone laughed as Anna Maria did her wiggle up the steps to change into appropriate clothes.

"You know, I recognize you folks. I know that you're from Wurtzville, but it seems strange that we never met," said Peter.

"I guess we keep a low profile in Wurtzville. Most of our friends are in Scranton," commented Marion.

"We go to school in Scranton," said Sam. "Each day we take the train to school. About a forty minute ride with all the stops. We often stay there until the last train back to Wurtzville. Some nights we don't get home until 8 or 9 o'clock."

"How come you go all the way to Scranton to high school?" said Peter.

"Well, mainly because our parents think it's better for us to go to school there. We didn't like the idea at all at first. Now, we're glad that they made us go to Central," said Marion.

"Don't your parents think that Wurtzville schools are good?" replied Flanigan.

"Oh, they think they are O.K., but not as good as Central. Central offers more courses and I guess they think that the teachers at Central are better. We really don't know if that's true but our parents do," said Sam.

"It just seems like a very long school year for you — all for the sake of maybe having a couple better teachers," responded Flanigan.

Anna Maria returned with a change of clothes and commented, "I heard you guys talking about why you go to Central rather than Wurtzville High or St. Catherine's. Come on now, Sammy and Marion — tell the whole story to Peter."

Marion and Sam both smiled. "You tell it, Marion," said Sam.

"Well. Actually, it's more than just the teachers. They do challenge us and make us analyze. But the point is, we're Jewish and Wurtzville doesn't have many Jewish kids, let alone teachers. It's not an even divide at Scranton, but we get to meet a lot of young people who are Jewish."

Sam jumped in, "Yeah, lots of nice girls and goys."

"Were you serious when you said that you like going there?" said Peter.

"Oh yeah," said Sam, "really, it's a good school but there are a lot of things going on. Not just at school but at the Jewish Community Center. I'm no basketball star. I could never make it in Wurtzville, but I get to play on a team at the Center. We're in an inter-city league with Catholic and Protestant Church teams. That's not possible in Wurtzville."

"And I get to play in the Youth Symphony. That keeps me overnight often but I don't care. I stay with friends. You know Scranton has a Temple but Wurtzville only has a synagogue. A lot of activity develops around a Temple community. I love that," said Marion.

"The funny part is, I think the real reason behind all this is that our parents don't want us to get matched up with a goy. So they went through the expense of sending us off to school away from town, having to pay extra taxes, train and cab, etc.— and what happens? The two of us, who have been saying ga-ga and goo-goo to each other since our diaper days at the Synagogue are now a match. We could have stayed in

Wurtzville and saved our families a lot of time and money," quipped Sam.

"O.K. let's saddle up everyone. It's ride time," Anna Maria said.

A four person toboggan was strapped on the flat bed truck and all four young people got into the cab. Anna Maria drove her vehicle around the lake and up the hill to the chute.

The toboggan chute was a natural trough made by centuries of water flow. It drained quickly after a rainfall and in the cold months, snow and rain froze to the sides and bottom and made it an excellent conveyer.

The toboggan was set to go. Sam sat up front, Marion's legs entwined around his hips and thighs. Anna Maria wrapped her legs over Marion's thighs and Peter shoved off and quickly jumped on wrapping his legs around Anna Maria. There was immediate acceleration as the chute dropped abruptly and the waxed wood slid swiftly down the frozen run.

No one told Peter to expect a bounce on the approach to the lake but when he saw the embankment ahead, he knew they were in for a smash landing. When the toboggan hit, Peter dug his head into Anna Maria and held tightly; Marion did the same with Sam. The toboggan continued across the lake, finally slowed, and ended about 200 yards from the shore.

Everyone was exhilarated. Whoops and shouts, laughs and friendly slaps punctuated the crisp air. Peter grabbed the rope, swung the toboggan around and shouted, "Let's do it again."

"You are going the wrong way, Peter. Into shore," cried Anna Maria.

"No ride that way, Anna Maria. Let's cross the lake and do it again."

"Sure there is a ride. We can all go in your Plymouth, Peter."

Minutes later, all four were packed into the Plymouth for another ride up to the chute. The Plymouth looked more like a vintage aircraft. The back windows of the car were turned down and the toboggan was shoved through one window and out the other.

It was dark after the next run. The girls went into the hotel to fix some hot drinks and food. Peter and Sam walked back up the hill to get the vehicles. When they returned, mugs of hot chocolate and Italian Christmas cookies were by the fireside.

Marion said, "Don't get too comfortable guys. After the sweets we have another treat." She swung open the door to the restaurant. It was closed for the day and the Machelli's were in town having Christmas dinner with relatives. The girls had moved aside tables in the north dining room and rolled the one large rug to the wall.

Anna Maria went over to the juke box, hit a couple of keys and filled the room with Glenn Miller's Band piping out *Tuxedo Junction*. By the time everyone had finished their snacks, Sam and Marion, their heavy shoes off, were jitterbugging to *Pennsylvania Six-Five Thousand*.

"God! Are they ever good, Anna Maria. I'm glad this is not a contest."

"Oh but it is a contest, Mr. Flanigan. The first couple that stops loses. You don't want to be a loser, do you?"

Anna Maria fed the juke box with a mess of nickels and when one selection was played, the next jumped right in. *I've Got A Gal In Kalamazoo* rocked the room. *American Patrol* and *String of Pearls* took their toll on Sam and Marion first. They sat down for a breather and fanned their wool shirts to cool off.

"Losers, losers," called Anna Maria from across the floor.

"All is fair in love and war," said Marion. "And dancing too."

"I just knew we couldn't miss getting in a war plug," said Sam.

Peter and Anna Maria walked over to the resting couple. "Since you brought up the topic, what are your thoughts on the war?" asked Peter.

"Ah, war," started Sam, sardonically, "I think every society should have one annually. Cleans out the trash, you know. Eliminates the weak blood. Just read Oswald Spengler's book, *The Decline of the West*.

Good point he makes. Says that civilizations are like people, they pass from birth to maturity and then death. The Great War is only twenty years behind us and now we have another Great War. Some are now calling it World War II. Spengler said it was going to happen. Just a natural consequence of aging, you might say."

"So what are you saying, Sam, we should join the civilization disintegration?" asked Anna Maria.

"Sure, if we're suicidal. Let's get it over with. Why prolong the misery."

"Come on Sam. Get serious," said Marion.

"I am, sort of. You know the whole thing is madness. How can a person be really serious about something that is insane?"

"The insanity is on the other side, Sam," replied Marion.

"The hell it is, Marion. It's all over. We're as crazy as they are," snapped Sam.

"Whoa, Sam. You know that we have relatives in Europe who aren't just threatened — word is coming out that they're being executed in prison camps."

"Where did you hear that?" Peter asked.

"From Rabbi Orlevsky. Last Saturday, after a Torah reading, we talked about the frequent historical persecution of Jews. He went over what we already knew, the Babylonian Captivity, enslaved in Egypt, the great Diaspora after the Roman conflict of 70 A.D., and the many pogroms from the Inquisition to modern Europe. But then he said that this pogrom of the Nazis may be the most terrible ever; that the saving grace may be our entry into the war. Rabbi Orlevsky said our entry into the war may save our relatives from slaughter — if they haven't already been slaughtered."

"Surprise, surprise," snarled Sam. "Remember when Mr. St. Ledger, the best history teacher in the school, had us read *Mein Kampf*? Remember what Hitler said he was going to do? That book was a bestseller in Deutschland — that was over fifteen years ago before little

Adolph came into power. What do you expect him to do — go around and kiss Jewish babies? I say that any Jew who did not have enough sense to pack his or her bags and get out then, shouldn't complain now."

Peter looked Sam squarely in the eye. "So Sam, tell me. Are you going to be part of the Spenglerian prophecy? Are you going to get into the conflict or sit back and let the conflict get you?"

Sam lost the sarcastic tone and said in a low voice, "Peter, I don't know. I honest to God don't know."

Peter, turning to Marion, asked, "Marion, would you do me one little favor? Would you arrange for me to meet with Rabbi Orlevsky? Would you tell him that I'd like to talk about our involvement in the war — and would he not hold back — would he say exactly what he has in mind. I need to get more information."

"Good as done, Peter."

Sam Cohen grabbed his coat on the way to the door, turned, and said, "This has been great. Hope we don't have to wait until next Christmas to do it again."

Chapter 12
The Rabbi's Logic

The day after Christmas, a Friday, Flanigan walked to town. He reasoned that he needed the exercise but the real reason was twofold. First, he wanted to think about Anna Maria. Secondly, he had to sort out feelings and confusion he had about the United States' entry into the European and Asian conflict.

"Puppy love. That's what high school romances are all about — puppy love. Fall in love when you are mature — when you have some control over your future, when you are emotionally and financially prepared to accept the enormous responsibility that love entails," Sister Dominique had said. "Only then can you seriously say that you are prepared to 'fall in love.' So, if you think you are falling, pinch yourself and ask: Am I mature enough? Do I have some control over my future? Am I emotionally ready for love? Do I have the financial needs to carry through with love? Am I ready for marriage?

"If you can't say yes to each of the above — then suppress the emotion. You are not really in love. You are suffering from a common teenage malady known as 'Puppy Love'. Do yourself, your partner, family and society a big favor — dampen the relationship. Wait until you are ready to turn love into marriage. For all of you, that means years to come."

Maybe Sister Dominique is right, he thought, but I'm not going to question how I felt last night, and how I feel this morning. Why question it when you feel great? Flanigan scuffed through the snow, then jogged, and tightly cupped both ears with the palms of his hands when he came to the Metal Perforation Factory. He wanted to move away quickly from the ear pounding sound of patterns being smashed out by the huge, slam, bang, punching presses. Federal government contracts for metal parts had recently increased dramatically; three shifts were now working. But that meant twenty-four hours of constant pounding mixing with the roar of nearby coal breaking collieries.

The perforated-metal factory was generally known as a place where few Catholics were hired. The word was out that so much work was becoming available that Catholics were getting jobs. "Why don't you get in an application now before you finish high school, Peter," a kindly neighbor had told him.

Flanigan told the man that he was not interested in working in a factory. But he was not able to give any indication of just what his future was going to be.

"Guess I'll just wait and see," said Peter.

He walked past the 109th Infantry Armory that housed the area National Guard. The local newspaper, the *Wurtzville Miner*, reported that many National Guardsmen had already enlisted in the regular army. They were anxious to get into action and didn't want to wait for their home unit to be federalized.

Turning onto Pike street and the small Jewish section of town, Peter headed to the Synagogue. He wanted to talk to Rabbi Orlevsky. The Christmas Day conversation with Marion Rappaport had struck a chord with Flanigan. He was fascinated by what the Rabbi had told Marion about the suffering of Jews at the hand of the Nazis — especially, the

Rabbi's comments about the goodness of our entry into the war. Peter had some questions for the Rabbi.

The Jewish community in Wurtzville melded well into the life of the little city. Several clothing shops were Jewish-owned. The most prosperous plumbing business, and the largest furniture store, were operated by Jewish families. Then, there were the jewelry stores, newsstands, and junkyards. All three junkyards were owned by Jewish people. Several Jewish medical doctors and lawyers had grown up on Pike Street but had since moved to the old English and Welsh side of town — a place of nicer homes — like Sally Caufield's.

Peter had learned to respect Jews. His mother spoke glowingly of Jewish people. During high school years Ellie did house work for the Cantor family on Pike Street. Mr. Abraham Cantor Sr., had come to Wurtzville in the 1880's and was one of the original builders of the synagogue. The Cantor family was generous to Ellie and thought of her as one of the family. When Ellie graduated from high school, the Cantors urged her to go to college. Ellie could not afford it, so the Cantors recommended her to Dr. Silverman, the optometrist and synagogue member. Ellie took the secretarial and receptionist job and stayed with it.

"Don't ever let others say nasty things about the Jews, Peter. I know you are going to hear things but pity those who say them. They are the sad creatures in our society," advised Ellie.

"Oh, I hear stuff, Mom. Like 'Kike Street', Shylocks and shysters, jew-boy, Christ Killers."

"Where did you ever hear such things, Peter?"

"At school, mostly."

"My God, not from the sisters, I hope?"

"Oh, no. The Sisters like to praise Jews. How many times have I heard them say the Jews are the Chosen People?"

"So kids come up with the nasty comments?"

"Well, I don't hang around that much with adults."

"I don't believe that young people invent those bigoted remarks, Peter. Apparently, they bring them to school after hearing them at home. Please don't lower yourself to their level. Jewish people have suffered terribly over the centuries. Bite your tongue if you ever allow such prejudice to flow from it."

Peter assumed that since it was the day before the Sabbath, the Rabbi would probably be in his house rather than in the synagogue. Rapping on the front door, he received no response. Hearing a rooster crowing out back, he walked around the house and saw the Rabbi shoveling manure from the chicken house to a wheelbarrow. Two large chickens hung from the clothes line, their heads off, dripping pools of crimson in the snow.

As he approached the Rabbi to introduce himself, the stench of the chicken manure in the cold, crisp air took Peter's breath away.

"Hello, Rabbi Orlevsky," he started, but found himself gasping for short breaths. "My name is Peter Flanigan. Marion Rappaport and Sam Cohen are friends of mine. Marion said that you would probably answer some questions for me."

The Rabbi smiled. "Maybe we should move away from the manure pile. It's nice to breathe when you talk."

He put down the shovel and motioned Peter to follow him. Walking behind the Rabbi, Peter noted that his yarmulke was shiny and weathered. He wondered if the Rabbi ever took off the little skullcap. He saw the Rabbi in town many times and when the Rabbi wore a fedora, the edge of the yarmulke could be seen under the large hat. Now, Peter observed that the black suit had also seen better days. It had a threadbare glossiness and both pants and coat were soiled.

Never saw a man wearing white shirt and tie and shoveling chicken shit, thought Peter.

As they came to the latticed back porch, the Rabbi turned to Peter. "Would you like a nice cup of tea, Mr. Flanigan?"

"That would be fine."

"Then come into the kitchen and make yourself at home."

Flanigan sat at the large oval oak table and scrutinized what appeared to be a two-foot high, copper pot-bellied stove in the center of the table. The stove had ornate legs and filigreed swirls of silvery metal laced around its fat coppery middle section. Under the stove were red-hot wood coals.

The Rabbi cut chunks of coarse, dark bread, put them in a deep bowl, and set the bowl before Peter. A large saucer of jam was placed next to a small wicker basket of garlic cloves. With one large mug under the samovar spigot, the Rabbi drew hot tea and handed it to Peter.

"Would you like plum jam or garlic on your bread, Peter."

"I guess jam would be fine."

"Good," said Rabbi. "I suspected you would like a sweet. I'll have my morning favorite — fresh garlic on toast."

Rabbi Orlevsky skewered a chunk of bread and toasted it in the stove coals. Then he peeled a clove of garlic and using it like a sanding stone, he rubbed the garlic onto the toast and filled the room with its pungent odor.

"That is an unusual tea pot," remarked Flanigan.

"It's a samovar, Peter. Been in the family for about 100 years. My grandfather carried it with him when the family left Minsk in 1840. They settled in Kiev and then had to leave there around 1880. The samovar came with them to Wurtzville, and hopefully, it will stay here for many years to come."

"Seems like your family has been on the move a lot."

"Yes, for thousands of years, Peter. Probably the only good thing about earlier moves was that the samovar wasn't part of the baggage." With a deep smile and a twinkle in his eye, he said, "This big tea pot is relatively new to my family. We have picked up on a lot of customs. The Russian samovar is just one, but thank God we didn't have to cart it around from the time of the Babylonian Captivity."

Chuckling, Peter asked, "Why is it that Jewish people seem to have such a strong sense of humor?"

"Oh, I don't know about that, Peter. I meet a lot of sour-faced, humorless Jews. Just as I met a lot of the same type in every grouping of human beings.

"But, you're probably right. Jews do joke a lot. Maybe it's because they can't sing and dance," he laughed. "Actually, Peter, it's deeper than that. Do you know what gallows humor is?"

"No."

"Well, it's often reported that when men are about to be executed — to be hanged for example, they often make light of it. They make jokes and laugh. Psychiatrists and psychologists have a lot of fun explaining why, but it appears that when your life in hanging in the balance, so to speak, you might just as well laugh at life as take it too seriously. We have learned to temper the heavy with a lot of light. We have found that our greatest survival mechanism is to remember to smile, to joke, to laugh — even in the face of the hangman."

"So Jews have had to face hangmen more often than other people?"

"Yes. More than any other group of people I know."

"Last night Marion said that you have information about mass executions of Jews by Nazis. I told Marion that I would like to talk to you about this and she said she would arrange a time that we could talk. When I awoke this morning I told myself that I couldn't wait. I felt I had to talk to you now."

"Why is it so urgent to know more, Peter?"

"I come from a Catholic background, Rabbi. In fact, I go to St. Catherine's. Little is ever said about avoiding violence. My school text books, teachers, even the priests usually complain about war but praise most of those on our side who were involved, who were injured, or did some heroic thing, or died. I just wonder about the truth of war. Every battle and every war we have fought is made to look good. I'm just not so sure about that. My view is that I don't want to kill another human being. Maybe I'm too sensitive. Or maybe I'm not sensitive to the pain of others — others who need me to help stop the violence. Maybe stopping violence with violence is what I need to rethink?"

The Rabbi drew another cup of tea for Peter and himself. He sat back and looked pensive. Then with eyes closed, he took thumb and forefinger of each hand, lightly grasped the chin hair of his heavy gray beard, and began to slowly run down the long strands to his chest, where the beard ended. Without speaking he continued to repeat the motion as he sat in contemplation.

Flanigan, a trifle nervous because of the lack of response, leaned forward. "Rabbi, I would like to hear what you know about what is really going on. I'm aware that a lot of lies came out of the Great War. I know about how we treated the German born people in the United States after we declared war against Germany in 1917. All of our information then was coming through Great Britain. They wanted us to join with them to fight the Germans. Our newspapers were full of British propaganda. The English worked hard to make the Germans look like devils."

Rabbi Orlevsky stopped tugging at his beard, opened his eyes and said, "That's true, Peter. Hate did come out of England. I know for I worked in my fathers' grocery store and I heard people commenting every day about the Germans. Most of what they had to say came out of communications from London and Paris. It was stupid, Peter. German as a language was eliminated from the curriculum at high schools throughout the country. German clubs, associations and restaurants were sometimes attacked and burned. German-American people were beaten up by thugs claiming to be patriots.

"I even had a small part in it. The U.S. Federal Government sent new can labels out to grocery stores. Sauerkraut could no longer be called that — now it had to be labeled LIBERTY CABBAGE. We had to tear off the sauerkraut labels and paste on the new approved labels. It got so bad that some Americans began to seek vengeance on all things German — even dogs with German breeding. Dachshunds and German shepherds were stoned — it was all that crazy."

Peter looked puzzled and commented, "So here we are less than twenty five years later and we are getting horror stories about the Germans again. Isn't propaganda just mainly lies? Why should we be so gullible the second time in less than a quarter century?"

"Peter, keep in mind that not all propaganda is untrue. Some of, maybe much of it is. Propaganda is information that may or may not be true. It's purpose is to promote some cause. What I am hearing that concerns me is not an isolated story — something that is coming out of the mouths of Germans, or English or other groups. What I am hearing is coming from people who have escaped the terror of the Nazis."

"You talked to some of these people."

"Just weeks ago I visited relatives in New York City. Like me, they have roots — family in Minsk and Kiev. Some of our people stayed and survived the pogroms, the organized massacre of Jews that seems to follow us wherever we go. Two of those descendents, my cousins, escaped the most recent pogrom of the Ukraine — in Kiev. They told me first hand of what they saw and how they got out. It is a story that is almost too awful to tell.

"If you read the newspapers, Peter, you know that the German army is sweeping through Russia. The blitzkrieg they used against Poland has now pushed into the Ukraine and the objective of the Nazis is to get to the rich oil fields around the Caspian Sea. Last September 29th, the Nazis sent out an order in Kiev for 170,000 Jews to report immediately for resettlement. Most people knew enough not to report, but 34,000 did. My cousins watched from afar as the thousands were marched to a Jewish cemetery in Kiev that borders on a deep ravine called Babi Yar. My cousins watched with binoculars from high ground. They watched until they could take it no longer. Rifle and machine gun fire was poured into children, women, and men, and their bodies bulldozed into the ravine."

"What about those Jews who didn't report?" asked Peter.

"Who knows? I only know my cousins did not wait to be part of the next wave of murders. They made their way south to the Black Sea. American merchant ships just completing a delivery of Lend Lease materials for the Russians, allowed my cousins to come on board as crew. By November, they were in New York."

"So, Hitler is to blame for Babi Yar?"

"No, he's just another of an historical line of brutes. We can't put the blame just on Hitler. When he spoke and when he wrote he was merely stirring up learned attitudes — bitter prejudices, bigoted teachings. A whole society doesn't change overnight or even over the course of a few years. Hitler helped speed up a cancer that has been festering in Germany for centuries."

"What did he do to bring such hatred out?" asked Flanigan.

"Do you know about his book — *Mein Kampf?*"

"I heard about it. It attacks Jews, doesn't it?"

Rabbi Orlevsky reached back to a book shelf and pulled out a tattered brown book. He held up the cover for Flanigan to read.

"Mein Kampf," Flanigan said aloud.

"Let me read just a few lines to illustrate not just propaganda, but vicious hatred." The Rabbi thumbed through the pages of *Mein Kampf* and said to Flanigan, "Here is a brief passage that probably had some effect on people of your age in Germany. Hitler says here, "The blackhaired Jew-boy lurks for hours, his face set in a satanic leer, waiting for the blissfully innocent girl whom he defiles with his blood."

Rabbi Orlevsky turned his lip in disgust as he closed the book and flipped it on the table. "I could read more. But why deal with trash."

"Rabbi, do you have any information about the treatment of Jews in Germany?"

"Mr. Flanigan, I have already related to you the massacre of Jews by Nazis outside of Germany. Do you suspect that Jews are being treated with dignity in Germany?"

"Probably not," said Peter.

Rabbi Orlevsky buried his head in his hands and paused for a moment, then, with a deep seriousness, he continued, "Peter, those of us with contacts know much more than our newspapers are reporting. Notice that our State Department is very quiet on the topic. Virtually nothing is mentioned about Jewish persecution other than removal of Jews to camps and resettlement programs. The fact is, much is happening that we in the Jewish community know about — at least some of us."

"Like what, Rabbi?"

"Like massive incineration of Jewish people."

"Burning people?"

"Yes. Our people are being shot and then burned in crematoriums. We've been aware of this for some time. We understand that shooting and then incinerating our people is not fast enough. The Nazis are looking into new methods of extermination."

"How do you know this?"

"We have our sources. When thousands of people are killed in many different places in Germany, in Poland, in France, in Russia and the Ukraine — then it is only common sense that the truth will get out. The stench of death is neither masked nor forgotten."

"But lies about the Germans came out of the Great War. Isn't it possible that this is propaganda of the Allies?"

"No, Peter. These are not made up stories. I have no pictures to show you. I have no German Jews as first hand witnesses to the terror that we know is going on there now. Truth will have its day. Some of the sources I cannot reveal for they are reporting by short wave from Germany. What they report is unthinkable. A great horror.

"I can appreciate your confused state of mind, Peter. You ask if violence should be answered with violence. You question whether you should be part of violent actions. You feel that you cannot kill another human being. These are all heavy considerations. You must deal with each of them on your own terms, with your own God given-conscience.

"I can only speak for myself, what should I do, what would I do if I were your age? I'm getting old. I'm not physically ready to fight. If I were 18, I would fight violence with violence. The Torah says 'an eye for an eye, a tooth for a tooth.'"

"Yes, but Rabbi, wasn't it Isaiah who advised humankind to 'beat swords into plowshares and spears into pruning hooks and war no more?'"

The Rabbi smiled. "So they actually do teach you some Bible at St. Catherine's. Have you ever read the Prophet Joel, Peter?"

"No."

Rabbi Orlevsky reached back once again and pulling the Old Testament from the shelf, he read from Joel: "Proclaim ye this upon the nations, prepare war, rouse up the strong: let them come, let all men of war come up. Cut your plowshares into swords, and your spades into spears. Let the weak say: I am strong. Break forth and come, all ye nations, from round about, and gather yourselves together: there will the Lord cause all the strong ones to fall down."

"Peter, I'm not trying to counter Isaiah with Joel. What I'm saying is that God's grace and judgment must fit time and circumstance. The time for 'all ye nations, from round about, and gather yourselves together: there will the Lord cause all the strong ones to fall down.'

"The strong ones today, Peter, are the Nazi-Axis Powers. We must prepare war, young man. We must rouse up our strong people. We need to call all to war as the Prophet Joel stated.

"Peter, it's good and just to quote Isaiah at the right time and in the right circumstance. The time and circumstance now is to listen and heed the prophet Joel. Are you listening, Peter? The just nations must fight the evil. The evil of the Nazis is evil personified. God is giving a command to destroy the evil before the evil destroys all of us."

Flanigan sat in silence. How could he counteract the logic and the sheer magnetic personality of this holy man, this Rabbi? What he quotes, what he interprets, what he believes is so powerful that I have no rebuttal, thought Flanigan.

Peter Flanigan stood, extended his hand to Rabbi Orlevsky and said, "Rabbi, in this short exchange, you've given me more to think about than all the history and religion classes of my past year."

"Peter, you must come back to chat. You're the first Christian young person ever to come to me to discuss religion. I am honored. I only hope I've helped you sort out the wonderful God-given conscience that has been bestowed upon you.

"And Peter," chuckled the Rabbi, "Don't try to get a government job to remove the sauerkraut labels from the cans at Gilgannon's Market."

Flanigan beamed a wide smile. "That's a promise, Rabbi."

Chapter 13
Buy Now, Sell Later

Following the attack on Pearl Harbor and the United States' declaration of war, Peter Flanigan and millions of other young men grappled with thoughts of conflict. The patriotic call to duty, the urge for vengeance, the glory of possible heroic deeds, the danger of serious wounds, the thought of dying in combat, became even more intense as the Japanese achieved victory after victory in the Pacific and Southeast Asia. Americans were not over the shock of Pearl Harbor, when daily news releases told of Japanese invasions of Hong Kong, Singapore, Thailand, and of Luzon in the Philippines. By May of 1942, all the Malay Peninsula, the 3,000 islands of the Dutch East Indies and Burma had fallen to the Japanese.

The only lift for Americans in the first six months of the Pacific war was the daring attack on the Japanese homeland by sixteen B-25 Bombers and their crews. President Roosevelt would not reveal how the bombers were able to reach Japan. He told reporters they flew from "Shangri-La." Actually, they flew from the U.S. Hornet, an aircraft carrier that had sailed to within 650 miles of the Japanese coast. Japanese propaganda, stating that the mission had been led by Jimmie Dolittle, called it a "do nothing" raid. However, it did raise the spirits of Americans and cause some loss of face for the Japanese high command who felt guilty for exposing their sacred Emperor to attack.

In the Atlantic, German U-Boats were sinking American and other Allied vessels at will. United States merchant ships were sunk off the coast of Long Island, and the city of Miami Beach was ordered to be in darkness at night. U-Boat periscopes used Miami Beach lights to target silhouetted ships with torpedoes. Axis Power military successes in North Africa and Russia made the Germans and their fellow Axis nations seem invincible.

There was no escape from war news. Radio, newspapers, magazines, and MovieTone News reports blared out the most recent information. Total saturation by the media made it impossible to avoid a daily war-related discussion.

Peter Flanigan was anxious to talk to Father Sampson, the Jesuit priest who'd given the midnight mass sermon that made some people squirm, and caused Peter to sit up straight and listen. Flanigan went to the rectory to talk to him in early January. He was told that the priest had been called to Jesuit headquarters in Maryland, and that he would be back in a week or two.

Anna Maria Machelli and Peter Flanigan became a close pair in their last semester at St. Catherine's. Some of the nuns thought they were a "cute couple." Others, always on the watch for potential religious vocation candidates, were not very pleased by the apparent loving relationship that was developing between Anna Maria and Peter.

Pulling aside the girl, Sister Hildegarde cautioned her: "Be careful with Mr. Peter Flanigan. Remember what I have told you since you first came to this school — you have a career predisposition for the glorification of God. Anna Maria, you have the style, intelligence and grace of a good sister. We need young people like you, but more importantly, the Church needs you.

"Another caution, Anna Maria, be careful in these last months of school. The occasion of sin is most often found among those who think they know best. The young man you have become so friendly with has not had a normative Catholic upbringing. That is a pity, not having a real father. Yet, what would be most distressing would be for you to become infatuated with Mr. Flanigan. It would destroy what many of us believe you are best suited for." Sister Hildegarde held up her ring finger and pushed the gold wedding-type band out with her thumb — "a partnership with Jesus Christ, Our Lord and Savior."

Anna Maria was uncomfortable with Sister Hildegarde, but she simply thanked the nun for her concern. When Anna Maria told Flanigan about the most recent vocation discussion, he was not at all disturbed.

"Sister Hildegarde and I have had an understanding for some time — it's called mutual avoidance," said Peter. "I try not to dwell on her. I wouldn't want to tell you what I sometimes think of her. It's my occasion of sin — and I'm trying hard to be a real Christian."

"Let's cut class and go to the Caraneeda for one of those sloppy burgers and coke," said Anna Maria, "I'd like to make you a proposition."

"Zowie! One talk with the dragon lady and you want to reverse your course of decency. A proposition! My, my, Miss Machelli how the nuns will cry."

"Cool down, Peter, not that kind of proposition."

The young couple had to wait for a seat in the crowded, bowling alley-wide restaurant. The wait was worth it when hamburgers, topped with ground beef sauce and onions, long, crispy, French fries, and coke arrived at their tiny booth.

"So, what's up, Anna Maria?"

"How would you like to come and work for us out at the lake?"

"Work for the Machelli family? Doing what?"

"Oh, a lot of things, but mainly waiting on table. Most of the time, I work alone and sometimes, I'm needed in the kitchen. It's a bit too much. You could come out on the busy days — Wednesday through Sunday. It's not easy work but we could have a lot of fun together and my family likes you and the money is good, and...."

"And you need say no more. Sure. But what a way to break up our budding romance. I can just see us hating each other forever after one day together on the job."

"Maybe. But I don't think so. Do you realize we have known each other for about 12 years now?" Using a little girl inflection she continued, "You never pulled my hair or tripped me in the aisle or wrestled me into the ground . . . dada, dada, huh?"

"Not yet, but I'm not promising anything. When do I start?"

"You mean you aren't going to ask how much you will be paid?"

"Naw. I know it isn't going to be much. But with my talent, my charisma, my good looks — salary is meaningless. People will be spilling their purses over me — dripping coins and snapping dollar bills my way. Anna Maria, you are going to become so jealous of my skills that you will probably stay in the kitchen and chop celery."

"Golly, Mr. Flanigan. You do catch on fast. That is exactly what my mother would love — someone like me to assist her in the kitchen. You can wait on table and my father can continue to be the entertainer — host, Maitre d' and bartender."

"When do I start?"

"Today is Monday, a very slow day. Why don't you come out and I'll teach you the trade."

Sunday dinner was the best money maker of the week for the Machellis. It was the only time that reservations were necessary. The last Sunday in February, Peter scanned the dinner reservations for the afternoon meal. "Party of six. Mayor Mahoney."

"Anna Maria, did you take the reservation for the Mayor?"

"Yes, his secretary called several days ago."

"I thought he was in Florida."

"No, I have seen him around Judge Barrett's new home this past week. Did you know that we have a new neighbor — Judge Barrett and his wife?"

"You mean that new place just completed on the cove?"

"Yep, probably the nicest addition to the lake in years. The property was owned by the Susquehanna & Hudson Company. My mother said that she didn't know that judges made so much money."

"Who exactly is in the party of six?"

"The mayor and his friend Sally Caufield, Judge and Mrs. Barrett and Mr. Chaddock and his wife."

"Is there anything I should know about their needs or special orders?"

"Sure. Judge Barrett likes to start off with an extra dry Beefeater martini, Mahoney has White Horse Scotch, and Chaddock drinks Manhattans with sweet vermouth. Niagara white wine for the ladies. Remember the Sunday Blue Laws, serve all liquor in coffee cups."

"What about food? Do they actually eat?"

"Barrett and Chaddock will probably order the Sunday lasagna. The mayor likes to think he's a European connoisseur. He'll go for the non-tomato dishes — probably the Lemon Veal Milano and risotto with wine sauce. My mother always starts the risotto when their drinks are served. It takes about 30 minutes to get it the way he likes it best."

By 1 P.M. both the north and south dining areas were filled. Anna Maria had to help Peter by dividing her time between kitchen work and serving dinners. Dante stayed behind the bar greeting everyone as they came. He knew most men by first names or professional titles but all women were greeted with "hello Honeybunch-a". Trays of cups lined the bar. Overhead a sign read 'No alcoholic beverages served after 12 midnight or on Sunday'.

Mahoney gave Peter a big hug when he saw him and seemed genuinely enthusiastic about his working at the restaurant. When Peter took the drink and dinner order, he did it with ease, feeling comfortable with his foreknowledge of their drink and food habits. When they were

served, no errors were made. He knew exactly who wanted what —
and they got it.

"Isn't this young fellow one terrific waiter? Hey Dante, did you
steal this young professional away from the Ritz?"

Dante, busy with his cocktail making, just waved to the table and
said, "He's a good-a boy, huh?"

After desserts were served, Mahoney rose and went over to Peter.
"Peter, I need to talk to you soon. Could you see me tomorrow?"

"Sure. Give me a time and place."

"Just come to my office in the City Building around 3 P.M."

"Will do, see you then."

Sally Caufield had only acknowledged Peter with a kindly smile
but when they were leaving, she tugged at Peter's sleeve and said, "So
good seeing you again, Peter. You must stop by and see us."

The following day, Mayor Mahoney was jolly when Peter came
into his office.

"Peter, I'm so excited about the possibility of your working with
me on this project that I could stand on that desk and tap-dance. Before I explain, let me ask you a couple of questions. To start, are you
planning on college?"

"Yeah, but not for a few years."

"Few years? In a few years you could be married, or already tied
to some dead-end job. Don't you think that you should start college
next fall?"

"That seems unlikely. Next fall I may be in the Army or navy or
Marines. I may be working in a factory or on a farm or maybe in jail."

"In jail!"

"Yes. In jail. I haven't yet made up my mind about military service. In fact, I haven't even decided if I am going to register for the
draft."

"But you have to register for the draft when you are eighteen.
When will you be draft age?"

"June 1st, this year. And, I don't have to do anything if I don't want to. I may decide to tell the draft board that my body and mind is not for them to register and use."

"Peter, that's not the route you should take. Listen to me carefully. You don't have to go into the military. You're the only son of a single mother, you can get a deferment."

Peter glared at Mahoney. "Deferment, huh? Well, maybe I'm comfortable not having a father around. I've learned to do planning on my own, instead of having my old man say that I had to do this or had to do that."

Flanigan waited. Mahoney looked away and stood silent.

Flanigan, sounding more sober, said, "I can get a deferment only if I register for the draft?"

"Right. And if there's a question about a deferment as the only surviving son, then I can get you a job at the Fredricks Perforation Plant. Workers there are draft exempt. Their work is now 100% war oriented."

"Great. Now they can hire Catholics. Catholics seem to love war as much or more than the Protestants."

"Well, let's be diplomatic about it, Peter, let's just say the factory owners have given up their old ways. You would fit in just fine there. I could work something out so that you would report to work just a few hours a week and still keep the deferment."

"Yeah, I heard more than one person call the plant 'Ebbets Field, Home of the Dodgers'. Draft dodgers have been flocking to that place for months."

"Peter, let me ask you two more questions. First, would you like to make enough money to complete college? And secondly, would you like to make your mother's life more comfortable?"

"Mr. Mayor, in English class we learned about rhetorical questions. Those are two examples. Of course, I would like to make money and of course I would like to make my mother more comfortable."

"Peter, come with me for an hour or so. I want to show you

something and give you an opportunity that may only fall your way once in your lifetime. But before we go, take a look at this map of the United States. Point out the states where oil is pumped from the ground."

"What is this, Bill, a geography test?"

"Yup."

"How about Texas, Louisiana, Oklahoma, California?"

"Good enough, you have the picture. Now take a look at this page in the Atlas that I have earmarked. What do you see?"

"Southeast Asia — Thailand, Burma, Malay, the Dutch East Indies and other places."

"O.K. Peter, now what resource do you associate in that area?"

"Beats me. I don't lay any claim to geography knowledge."

"Rubber, Peter. Thousands of tons of rubber come out of those countries each month. That is, it used to come out. Just like the oil used to come out of Sumatra until the Japanese jumped in there a couple of months ago. The Japanese have no oil at home, nor do they have rubber. But now that they control the Dutch Far East Empire, the ball game has changed."

The mayor continued his quiz with Peter. "What is needed to sail ships, fly planes, tanks, trucks and every other damn vehicle used in war."

"Gasoline."

"Right. And to get any kind of moving vehicle going, you need what kind of wheels."

"I guess you want me to say rubber."

"You're damn right I want you to say it, because that, my lad, is the key to your future. Let's get in the car and drive over to Coal Brook."

Flanigan and Mahoney drove to a place very familiar to Peter. It was the #5 mine shaft, better known as Coalbrook. It was well named. Some years before, Peter and his playmates followed the brook and made a discovery that netted them cash. There was a surface vein of coal exposed by this little tributary of the Lackawanna River. The boys ran home, got picks, shovels and wagons and began digging in the stream. They smashed the large chunks into burnable pieces, bagged the coal, and went door to door. It was hard work, but at 25 cents a hundred pound bag, it was a bargain for buyers and profitable for the boys.

Mahoney parked the big black Cadillac just yards from the tunnel opening to Shaft #5. The shaft had not been worked for years. One of the problems was water. A lot of coal was still down there but pumps couldn't manage the flow of water that varied with the season. Besides, it was now cheaper to dig these relatively shallow veins with draglines.

Mahoney took two large flashlights from the trunk of the car, gave one to Peter and said, "Let's take a look."

They began walking down the gradual slope. The old track was still in good condition but ceiling wires were dangling everywhere and large chunks of slate, rock and coal lined the abandoned coal car tracks.

"Watch your step, Peter. We're going down just far enough to show you what this looks like. Stop here for a moment."

Mahoney shone his light off to the side where a second track descended into another tunnel. About 100 yards farther a third tunnel veered off to the left.

"We don't have to go any farther. You have a feel for the size of this place. Let's go back up and I'll talk to you about its use."

The mayor led the way to his car. Leaning back on the fender, he pointed to a number of large rusting water tanks that stood above the horizon.

"Notice those welders up on the scaffolds and how they are torching those old seams, Peter? They are sealing leaks in those old water tender tanks. Do you know what the tanks were used for?"

"Not really."

"Well, until about ten years ago, all the trains up and down the line filled their boilers with water pumped from the river to the tanks. Can't make steam without water and can't run trains without steam, right?"

Peter didn't answer. He was getting annoyed with the question and answer session.

"Right, Peter?"

"Right, Bill. But would you do me a favor and tell me just what this is all leading to?"

"Fair enough, Peter. I can sum it up pretty quickly. You see, this country is primed for the biggest spending spree in its history. We are at war with a European power and at war with an Asian power. We need gasoline and rubber and a hell of a lot of it. So much of it that both items are going to be as scarce as tits on a boar hog.

"Rationing hasn't happened yet, Peter, but mark my word, next year at this time, tires will be selling for triple the price—that is if you can get them. Gasoline is selling for only 18 cents a gallon now but watch the price skyrocket when the military starts using up the stock. Besides, we have to supply the British and others who are in this bloody mess with us. Pulling up to the pump and saying 'fill 'er up' just ain't going to happen by the end of this year.

"But it's rubber that has to be conserved, Peter. We can probably get along with the gas being refined from our own oil fields. But one way to cut down on rubber consumption in this country is to have people drive less. So FDR will probably call for gasoline rationing, that will keep cars off the road and conserve rubber — we don't have rubber trees around here and we sure as hell aren't going to get any out of Southeast Asia for some time.

"Now, that's where you and I come into the picture. We can work as a team, Peter. You and me."

"The picture is still pretty dim, Bill."

"O.K. let me lay it out. See that set of old tracks coming out of #5? See how it still connects to the main line of the S&H?

"Now imagine a train load of tires arriving here at 10 or 11 o'clock at night. A few farm boys from over in South Cannan will do the heavy work. The farm boys know how to keep their mouths shut, especially when they have their hands greased with greenbacks. Besides, they are husky, hard working lads used to tossing bales of hay around. They can unload the tires from the boxcars, toss them into the old coal cars and cable wench them down to storage in the tunnels. You and I will supervise."

"And the gasoline?"

"Right up there," said the mayor, pointing to the old water tanks. "Those tanks are in much better shape than I had expected. They will be sealed tight in just a few days and waiting for the first shipment of gasoline. Each tank will hold hundreds of thousands of gallons of petroleum—refined stuff, right out of New Jersey. By the end of next month, we should have all the tanks filled to the brim."

"Mind if I ask where and how you get all the cash to pay for tires and gas?" asked Flanigan.

"I would mind if anyone else asked. I don't mind telling my own boy."

Mahoney swung his big arm around Flanigan and pulled him close as he began to walk slowly toward the tanks.

"I don't have what people call 'family', Peter. Other than you — whom I feel I have seriously neglected, there is only Sally. Obviously, Sally has financial connections that have benefited me and even some of my friends. I would like to share with you the opportunity to reap the benefits of this relationship."

Peter stopped walking. He turned to Mahoney and asked, "So you are saying that Sally's father's bank is footing the bill?"

"No. Mr. Caufield is not part of this scheme. Only in the sense that he is holding the paper on the loan."

"Sorry. I don't understand what 'holding the paper' means."

"It simply means that the bank will be paid off with interest for the money they loan me. The bank doesn't give, it loans. It is all part of the American system. Wealth is accumulated in proportion to man's ability to think. You and I can become thinking capitalists, Peter."

"Is your plan legal?"

"What is wrong with buying now and selling later? If we have ten gallons of gas to sell or ten tires, then we sell them for the best price, right? It's part of the economic system we live in.

"You can have money too, Peter. The wealth of this valley is changing. The old line Protestant money is not what it used to be. The good old boys still control most of the financial institutions and manufacturing but the handwriting is on the wall. New names and new faces are already appearing, and this war could even out the score.

"What do you say, Peter? Will you be my silent partner?"

Peter and Mahoney walked back to the car before Peter responded. "Maybe, Bill. I've got to think it over some."

"I understand, Peter. I don't want to push you. Take your time and come in and see me anytime. My secretary has been told to give you the Open Door Policy. Just make me one promise, will you?"

"That I won't mention this to anyone?" Extending his hand to Mahoney, Peter said, "My promise."

Chapter 14
Radical Jesuit

Flanigan walked a lot the following week. Much was happening in his young life; so he hiked the hills around town and thought. He wondered about the scheme that his father proposed, but as promised, did not discuss it with anyone. On the surface it didn't sound all that bad. Buy now. Sell later. It seemed to make sense. The fact that the mayor planned to use the Susquehanna and Hudson mining shaft to store tires, and the abandoned water tanks to store gasoline, didn't seem to be a problem. This was Wurtzville and that was how things are done, he thought.

He daydreamed about how he would spend the money to improve the quality of his mothers life. He'd see she had a house of her own and clothing she always denied herself. He thought of her going off on vacation with friends. She always talked about going to the theatre in New York City but said it was too costly. He could change all that, he mused. Plus, he could stash away money for college.

On the next ridge above town, he shifted his thoughts to Mahoney's advice. Maybe he should just register for the draft, take a job at Fredrick's

Perforation and get an exemption. Then his mind switched to St. Thomas's College, seeing Anna Maria every day. Traveling to college together, dropping her off each morning at Ellenwood College, and picking her up and driving her home every afternoon.

When Peter Flanigan thought through all the possible avenues he could take, one overriding problem was on his mind and would not go away. It was a thought that was beginning to possess him. He didn't know why he was so focused on this issue but he did know that if he followed through with his conviction, there was a lot of trouble ahead for him.

Flanigan was moving closer to a decision to not register for the draft. He knew of no one his age who even considered the rejection of the federal government order to register on one's eighteenth birthday. He had only a few months to go before that day would come. He asked himself why he was thinking differently than other people. Flanigan could not put his reasons together. He just knew that there was something terribly wrong with being told that he must ready his total being to do something that seemed so morally wrong — killing another human being.

"You're the only son of a single mother, I can get you a deferment at Fredricks Perforation," Mahoney had told him.

Flanigan cancelled that option. Working in a war production plant, or even claiming conscientious objection would still require going to the draft board and signing their register. Flanigan thought it would be like saying, "Here is my body for you to use. Just tell me what I should do."

He feared that this dilemma — to register or not to register — was becoming myopic. Even his powerful new feelings for Anna Maria were being pushed aside by the thought of surrender to a pressure that he believed was wrong.

He talked to Ellie about his quandary. She told him, "You can go to college part time, Peter. If Bill told you he can get you into Fredricks

Perforation, then why not? You won't have to kill anyone and as far as I'm concerned, you will be here, God willing, when the war is over — not in some distant land, never to return."

The thought of cooperating with the war by making weapons, or doing work that would contribute to the kind of mental and physical misery experienced by his Uncle Frank was becoming a repulsive consideration for Flanigan.

Anna Maria agreed with Ellie Flanigan. She was thrilled with the prospect of Peter not going off to war. The fact that her father had evaded the Great War played a part in her thinking but she saw some fairness in a system that would allow some men to stay home and work in industry. She tried to convince Peter of the reasonableness of the governmental compromise.

"It isn't a compromise," Peter told her. "It's a need, the government isn't being considerate, it's being efficient. They need bodies to make the tools of war. I would just be one of those bodies that simply does what he's told."

Anna Maria found Peter's position incomprehensible but she thought he would benefit from a sympathetic viewpoint. She suggested he speak to Father Sampson who was back from Maryland and once again in residence at St. Anthony's.

"But Peter, if you want to talk to Father Sampson, you'd better do it soon. The word is that he won't be in Wurtzville for much longer."

"Why? Where is he going?"

"He said at Mass last Sunday that he was being transferred to a Jesuit Mission in Central America."

"Why?"

"He didn't say."

The following day, Flanigan knocked on the rectory door of St. Anthony's. Father Sampson's familiar face greeted Flanigan with a smile.

"What can I do for you, young man?"

"Father, my name is Peter Flanigan. I heard your Midnight Mass sermon and decided that I wanted to take you up on the invitation to stop by and chat about what you had to say. I thought your comments were very powerful but I have a lot on my mind, a lot of questions."

"Come on in, Peter. I'm delighted that you have been thinking about my remarks. Have a chair. What are your concerns?"

"Registration for the draft, Father. I don't feel that I can do it."

"What is your conscience telling you, Peter?"

"That I shouldn't cooperate in any way with the war machine. That registration is the first and biggest acceptance of the governmental notion that they can control my mind, my body, my life. Right now, I can't accept that. I just thought that you might be able to help me sort it all out."

"Do you think that you have a unique attitude?"

"Well, most people — probably just about everyone in this country — would disagree with me on this one."

"How do you know that?"

"I just know from every conversation that I have with friends and acquaintances. Almost every guy that I know is talking about when they will join up or when they expect to get drafted. I have never heard any mention of not cooperating with the draft board."

"Why don't you test your best friends? See what they have to say about it."

"Actually, the closest male friend I have left for the army right after Christmas. I would not dare tell him. It would probably end the friendship. But I have told two good friends — my mother and my girl friend."

"What did they say?"

"Both think that I could get a deferment by working at Fredrick's Perforation. I won't do that. If I've decided to not kill another person, why should I make weapons so someone else can kill?"

"Peter, your decision is yours to make. Are you aware of what is in store for you if you decide not to register?"

"Not really. I have heard that people sometimes go to federal prison if they don't register."

"Peter, there is no question in my mind — you will go to prison if you refuse to register. There are some options, Peter. You could claim C.O. status."

"Conscientious Objector?"

"Right. C.O.s refuse to kill another human. They reject war on grounds of moral or religious beliefs. But to claim it, you must register."

"Any other options?"

"You could leave the country. Go to Mexico or Central America or South America."

"When would I be able to come back?"

"Without going to prison? Maybe never. Most likely you would be arrested as soon as you were discovered after you return."

"Even if the war is over?"

"Yes. Peter, you really should give some serious thought to C.O. status. You will have to sign a paper but you can refuse to cooperate with any work that is war-related."

"So, I sign the draft paper and admit that I belong to the government? No, Father that is not the sort of option that I would support. If you were in my place, would you sign?"

Father Sampson leaned back in his chair and folded his hands behind his head.

"Twenty-five years ago, I was in your place, Peter. However, I was about seven years older than you are now. I am amazed at your conviction. How did you come to your decision?"

"I'm not sure. When I was in 7th grade, I began to read a lot of books on war. By the time I was in 10th grade, I had read all of Altscheler's books on the French and Indian Wars, and the Civil War, and the Winning of the West. I began to feel pretty confused with the Civil War books. Altscheler wrote about Civil War battles from the viewpoint of a young Union soldier and a young Confederate soldier. As a northerner, I was confused because I understood the pain, suffering, and the reasoning of the Confederate soldier as well as the Union soldier.

"By the time I read the Winning of the West I was really disturbed by the treatment of the American Indian. Even though Altscheler sometimes seemed to sympathize with the Indians, the only really important consideration was the fulfillment of the white man's greed for land and power. So, the winning of the west was O.K., according to Altscheler.

"Most kids around here go to the cheapest movie on Saturday afternoon — cowboys and Indians. I got sick of seeing the U.S. Calvary charging Indians and cowboys killing Indians. After reading *The Winning of the West*, I stopped going to that kind of movie. Everyone cheered when Indians were killed on film, but I no longer saw the Indian as evil.

"Last year, I read *All Quiet on the Western Front*. Then, I went to the Irving Theatre and saw the film with Lew Ayers. I really think that that did it. I decided that I would not become a pawn to be used by the government — especially to be forced into a killing activity."

"Do you mind telling me what you meant, Father, when you said that you were in my place twenty-five years ago?"

"Not at all Peter. It's not a happy story. Maybe you can consider changing your mind after you hear it.

"By 1916, I completed a degree in history from Fordham and a law degree from New York University. The presidential election was in full swing and President Woodrow Wilson was campaigning as the anti-war candidate. Many of us didn't believe Wilson's anti-war stance. The Democrats went about the country telling people that if they want war, then vote for the Republican Charles Evans Hughes.

"Wilson did not have a change of mind when he got us into war. Even before his reelection he had conscription plans in place. The war in Europe had been going on since August of 1914 and economic factors dominated the European war. The struggle for empire among the

British, Germans and French was sure to involve the United States. We'd been on a power quest since the 1840's when President Polk declared his Manifest Destiny program. Polk's policy was carried out by a long series of Presidents. By the end of the century, we had subdued our aboriginal people either by killing them off, spreading disease, putting them into an alcoholic stupor, and then herding them into the worst land left — reservations. By 1890, the Indian tribes were totally subdued and before the end of the century, we also had the Hawaiian Islands, the Philippines, and Puerto Rico under our domination.

"When Wilson came into office in 1912, there was no frontier left to conquer except for us to become the number one economic and military power in the world. All that President Wilson, corporate America, and military America needed was a good excuse to jump in and use our young men to secure that number one power position. The German U-boat action against our ships in the Atlantic was the type of goading that provided the opportunity that Wilson and other power-seekers needed for an excuse to go to war.

"I had for years planned to challenge any attempt by the government to force me to cooperate with war. Like you, I had a strong moral reservation separate from my religious conviction. I had read extensively about Christian involvement in war and it puzzled me and very nearly forced me to forsake my religious beliefs. But the more I read, the more I became convinced that it was not Christianity that was at fault. It was people claiming to be Christians — many of them the major leaders of Catholicism — popes, cardinals and bishops. After Luther, Protestant leaders just joined in the precedent for violence established some three hundreds years after the death of the Prince of Peace.

"Peter, I read and reread the New Testament long before I went into the seminary. I searched for some indication of an approval of violence by Jesus Christ. I found none. Anger, yes. Violence simply was not part of Christ's message — except the violence that was done to him, and he asked forgiveness for the perpetrators. Peter, if we as Christian Catholics cannot know, from the New Testament, that Jesus rejected violence absolutely, then we can know nothing of Jesus' person or message.

"Let me try to help you to understand why and how Christians turned to violent ways.

"For three centuries after Christ, the Bishops of Rome, the popes, the priests and true followers of Christ and his message, stated emphatically that Christians may not participate in war. It was not until the reign of Constantine, that Christians turned away from the prohibition against war. In the year 312 A.D. one could not be a Christian and be in the fighting Roman army. That was three centuries of nonviolence, yet Christians, persecuted as they were, became the largest religious body in the Roman Empire.

"All that was reversed after Constantine was converted to Christianity. By the year 416 A.D., one could not be a member of the fighting Roman army *unless* you were a Christian. From that time until now, Peter, Christians have found it very easy to convert their plows into swords and their pruning hooks into spears. The church almost always gave its blessing to the ruling power, no matter what kind of force was used. One of the great terrors of all time was Charlemagne. In the year 800, Pope Leo III crowned Charlemagne as 'Emperor of the Romans' because Charlemagne had united Europe. Charlemagne read St. Augustine's *City of God* and was so impressed with the message that he often forced people to convert to Christianity or suffer the consequence — death by execution.

"Peter, you said that you did not want to become a 'pawn' of the government. Take this epic poem from around the year 1000, and read it carefully. It is the *Song of Roland.* When you read it, think of the reasons why young men flocked to follow Charlemagne and dozens of other military leaders after him. The lure to serve continued into the Crusades. It seemed that few questioned the contradictory reasoning of 'Christian Soldiers'.

"When young men your age, in the year 1095, gathered to hear Pope Urban II, he told them that they must stop fighting one another and join in a war against the unbelievers. He told the young men that 'God Wills It.' The people he wanted them to kill were Turks. Turks were Moslems who controlled the middle eastern Holy Lands. Over a period of two hundred years, Christian invaders slaughtered hundreds of thousands of people.

"Of course, there was a reward for slitting a Muslim's throat, Peter. What do you think it was? I'll give you a clue — it was a spiritual award."

"Like a reward for doing a good deed but you just get it in heaven?"

"That's right, Peter."

"Then, you must be talking about an indulgence."

"Yes, Peter. But not just a plain old indulgence award, it was a plenary indulgence. Do you remember your religious education on that one?"

"Sure. You go straight to heaven when you are granted a plenary indulgence."

"Exactly. And we could go on and on, Peter. The violation of Christ's Sermon on the Mount, violations of every gospel message — a gospel that taught love and compassion — was tossed to the wind by Popes and priests, ministers and pastors, all claiming to be Christians.

"By the 15th century, the Church was burning heretics at the stake and stretching arms and legs on 'The Rack' — a torture device for people who would not convert to Catholicism. And after Luther's Reformation in 1520, Christians turned on one another with a vengeance and have been at it ever since. It must be very confusing for opposing soldiers as they pray to the same God to help them kill their enemy of the day.

"So, you see Peter, my decision was made in a moral and religious context. I knew before the Great War started in 1914 that I would not cooperate with president or king, pope or bishop in the business of war."

"So what did you do?" asked Flanigan.

"I refused to sign anything for the draft board."

"Did you claim Conscientious Objection?"

"No. I would have had to register to do that. I simply refused to cooperate."

"What happened? Did you go to jail?"

"No. Federal Agents came to my apartment in New York City and arrested me. I was given a military police escort and taken to Camp Upton, an army training camp on Long Island. I was told that whether I signed or not I was in the army and would serve my country. They tried to issue me a uniform and I refused. When I refused to line up for reveille and retreat, a captain and two corporals came into the barracks. They walked me out on a roof platform and said, 'O.K. coward, join the troops the hard way.' Then they tossed me off the roof. I was sore but not really hurt. But the physical hurt would come and continue for years after."

Flanigan was now on the edge of his chair. He wanted to stop Father Sampson and ask a series of questions that flashed through his mind. But the priest continued.

"Within a few days, I was joined by a number of conscientious objectors. We were assigned the second floor of the barracks and had to move our beds frequently because the soldiers below us would 'accidentally' fire a round through the ceiling. One day, a sergeant came and marched a dozen or so of us out to a group of soldiers who told us to take shovels and dig graves. We all refused and were beaten unconscious with rifle butts. When we came to, we were pushed into the graves and poked with bayonets. They made us stay in the holes for two days. It was below freezing at night and water in the holes froze to our shoes.

"Before I was sent to the Federal Prison at Leavenworth, Kansas, a Polish fellow whom I got to talk with and know quite well, was beaten senseless with a hoe. When I saw him in Leavenworth some months later, he didn't know me and I had a difficult time remembering exactly how he used to look because his face was all scarred and brown welts ran from his forehead to his chin.

"The trip to Leavenworth prison from New York took three days. Before we got on the train, military police marched us before crowds of people in the train station. Shouts of 'cowards' and 'slackers' were enjoyed by the military police because it gave them an opportunity to show how they treated us — beating us with clubs to speed up our transfer. There were about forty of us in one railroad car and we were chained, in pairs, to our seats. The only time we were released was to go to the bathroom and we had to go as two people, shuffling along the aisle in leg irons.

"After a few months of brutal treatment at Leavenworth, I was transferred to Ft. Riley, about 140 miles away. A large number of C.O.s were already there and the hope was that conditions there would be less severe than at our previous place. However, five of us went on a hunger strike after we witnessed the application of what soldiers jokingly called the 'water cure.' A conscientious objector who refused to scrub a latrine was subjected to a torture that was learned by General Wood's soldiers in the Philippines during the Spanish-American war. The young man was tied around one arm, then around his neck and hung until he passed out. Then, they quickly removed the ropes and shoved a water hose in his mouth and pounded on his stomach. The man was in such bad shape that the army transferred him out to Fort Douglas. We learned later that he died there.

"After witnessing that, we went on a hunger strike. The army got worried that word would get out about the torture. When we refused to eat, they insisted we stay alive by force feeding us. We were sent to a medical ward and twice a day, we were held down and force fed with a tube pushed down our throats. We were in more pain from esophageal bruises and bleeding than from lack of solid food.

"The army finally decided to court martial us. Even though all of us never accepted military status, we were tried in a military court.

Some people were given light sentences. About twenty people got fifty years in prison. Another large group got twenty-five years and three other men and myself got the death sentence."

"Death sentence!"

"Yes. Our behavior of total non-cooperation was judged to be most dangerous to the security of the country. Not having ever signed any document, we were not just conscientious objectors, we were total slackers, unfit to be called Americans."

"Well, you are here today, Father. What happened?"

"I was the last person to be released from federal prison. Most C.O.s were released by 1919. I was finally released in 1921. I had decided to become a priest shortly after getting to Leavenworth Prison. That helped sustain me. My belief in God began to strengthen, and the suffering of Christ was on my mind and in my prayers almost constantly. I began to appreciate the psychological torment that he must have suffered, as well as the bodily punishment he endured. With that in mind, I was able to face up to and accept the torment. Indispensable was a copy of St. Ignatius of Loyola's *Spiritual Exercises.* I read them daily and learned to discipline my mind and set my heart on planning to direct myself toward good actions.

"The Jesuits appealed to me for a variety of reasons. St. Ignatius of Loyola was once a soldier. He put down his sword to become a peacemaker, a priest who established the Society of Jesuits. Unfortunately, many Jesuits simply mimicked the philosophy of Counter-Reformation popes and the long string of Catholic Church leaders who bowed to the whims of political and military dictators. For myself, I was determined to be a Jesuit but not so subservient a Jesuit that I would become more of the Society and less of Jesus."

Flanigan had to raise his hand to stop Father Sampson. "But isn't the Society of Jesus organized in a military fashion. At least that is what Father Goodman told us in theology class."

"He was speaking metaphorically, Peter. 'Soldiers of Christ' does not refer to anything in the military except for discipline and willingness to follow orders. But you do raise a fair point. I am struggling with it right now."

"What is that, Father?"

"I've been silenced by my Jesuit superiors. You'll hear me speak only Latin in the future. No sermons allowed."

"Why is that?"

"Why do you think?"

"Your sermon at Midnight Mass?"

"Right. Of course, I'm only the assistant at this church so Father Damian will give all the homilies."

"Doesn't that upset you a lot?"

"Sure. But I'm not discouraged. The reason I'm here is because I was saying too much at Fordham Prep. My Jesuit superiors sent me to St. Anthony's to separate me from students who were beginning to ask too many questions about the position of the Catholic Church and the war. The first semester at Fordham was just ending when the war started so they had me pack my bags two weeks before Christmas and move up here to Pennsylvania."

"But I just learned that you are leaving here for Central America. Is that true?"

"Yes. San Jose, Costa Rica."

"How do you feel about that?"

"Awful."

"You said that you weren't subservient to superiors. So why don't you just tell them no?"

"Peter, Jesuits since Loyola, believe that educating and disciplining children is the best way to prepare them for life. I haven't been able to achieve my goal to do that here in the United States so I'll try in Costa Rica."

"What do you think I should do, Father Sampson?"

"That's for Peter Flanigan to decide, not Bill Sampson. It's your conscience Peter, not mine. I've outlined my experience for you to let you know that if non-cooperation is your choice, then you need to be prepared for it. Think long and hard about it, Peter. In the final analysis, we are never really alone if we live in the Spirit."

The priest then wrote on a slip of paper and gave it to Flanigan.

"Hold onto this address, Peter. I'll be off to Costa Rica in a few weeks. I know of no one around here willing to counsel you on the sensitive decision you are trying to make. Have you ever been to New York City?"

"No."

"Have you ever heard of the *Catholic Worker* or Dorothy Day?"

"No, I haven't."

"Well, a trip to New York City and a visit with Dorothy Day at the *Catholic Worker* would be a good way to spend a day. You can take a bus to the city, get off at 8th Avenue and 42nd and take the subway or city bus downtown to 15 Mott Street. Ask to speak to Dorothy or Peter Maurin. One of them will be there and either person would be able to help you with your personal struggle. They're close friends of mine and I know of no other people I would want to direct you to."

Father Sampson led Peter to the door then as an after thought, he asked Peter to wait for a minute. He went upstairs and returned with a wad of brown paper wrapped tightly like a child's lunch bag. He gave it to Peter and said, "Just in case you take the route I took in World War I, this might come in handy. It was great meeting you, Peter. Go in peace to love and serve the Lord."

Flanigan had never hugged a priest before but he did freely and felt Father Sampson's light slap on his back as they embraced. Outside of the church rectory and around the corner, he opened up the bag and read the title of the small book: *Spiritual Exercises* by Ignatius Loyola.

Chapter 15
Meeting Dorothy Day

As the long dismal winter of '42 dragged on, the American public bristled. Daily headlines blared negative news to a public anxious for a taste of victory. Even America's new ally, the Russians, were being pushed eastward and southward. The threat of Nazi control of vital oil lines out of the Caspian Sea and the possible termination of the supply link provided by the Lend Lease program of the United States, was now real. Would a final push by the German armies do it?

Americans knew that Jews were being badly mistreated in Germany, but had not yet learned about the Nazi "Final Solution" of the "Jewish Problem" — the planned annihilation of the entire Jewish population of Europe. Nazi advances into Poland made it possible to transfer Jews to places doomed to become holocaust history — Auschwitz and Treblinka. It would be over a year before the American Jewish Congress would pressure the United States State Department to release documented information of Jewish annihilation by the Nazis.

Peter Flanigan was fighting his own battle. It was a lonely fight but he did have some support in his corner. If Flanigan was marching to the beat of a different drummer, the lead drummer was Ellie, with the lead ghost of his uncle Frank by her side. His thinking was developed more by her and Frank than anyone else. After meeting with the very likable veteran of non-cooperation in World War I, Jesuit Father Bill Sampson, Flanigan had more grist for his mind mill. The Jesuit made sense to Flanigan; Father Sampson's philosophy and his actions seemed to strengthen Peter's uncertain views. Flanigan assured himself that he could take punishment similar to Father Sampson's in the Great War. He worried about the spiritual side of the plan that was growing in his brain. His thinking on non-violence seemed to be more of a mysterious, deep-seated repulsion against killing rather than a spiritual desire to be Christ-like. He prayed, he went to mass, he studied his religion — but he was aware that he did not have the spiritual conviction of Father Sampson. Peter began to silently repeat "Please God, make me strong." It was to become a mantra for him in years to come.

Flanigan smiled as he thought of another influence in his decision — Dante Machelli. Dante's loss of family, friends and country in the Great War had to be painful but Dante not only saved his integrity, he avoided ever having to engage himself in a killing machine. Peter fantasized about he and Anna Maria driving into Mexico and finding their way to Costa Rica. They would find Father Sampson, who would marry them. They could learn Spanish and work with the poor of Central America.

Peter liked that idea and developed it. When he daydreamed about finances, his mind flashed to the money offer made by his father, Bill Mahoney. The chance to get rich quick from the hoarding and selling of rubber and gasoline would give him plenty of cash to settle in Latin America.

But what about Anna Maria? Would she leave her family to bound off with him to some distant land? Even if she would, should he even consider such a cut-off from people who loved her? And Ellie? Of course, she is an independent woman, he thought. Yet, considering leaving her, perhaps never to see her again, helped Peter to erase the fantasy of flight.

I'll face the consequences on my own, he decided. Reaching into his pocket, he fished out the note with the *Catholic Worker* address — 115 Mott St. New York, New York. Dorothy Day? Peter Maurin? Guess they have something to say to me, or Father Sampson would not have encouraged me to go there, he mused.

Flanigan was right. Few Catholics in the winter of 1942 would be willing to speak out against conscription as Day and Maurin did in their newspaper, the *Catholic Worker*. Flanigan and most other folks in and around Wurtzville knew little about the publication. The bishop of the Diocese of which Wurtzville was a part had admonished a couple of pastors for allowing the newspaper to be offered in church vestibules. It was quickly taken off the racks and if the *Catholic Worker* was mentioned at all, it was not favorable. In fact, its founder, editor and publisher, Dorothy Day, was not allowed to speak at most Catholic colleges in the 1930's. Although she would eventually become the leading Catholic women's liberation advocate of the 20th century, she was bad news to Catholic Church leaders. The Catholic Church had worked hard to maintain a status of acceptability by the entrenched Protestant leadership in the United States. People like Day threatened to throw a monkey wrench into the relatively smooth running accommodation between the two powerful church institutions. Catholic Church leaders considered Dorothy Day a trouble-maker, probably a socialist, and quite likely a communist sympathizer. They did not read coincidence into the fact that her *Catholic Worker* paper was sold side by side with the communist *Communist Daily Worker*.

Dorothy Day had been raised in a caring family, daughter of a newspaper writer and a loving mother. She attended her Episcopal Church, read the Bible and endured a college and post-college struggle with religious belief. She became involved in the Women's Rights movement. Jailed in Washington, DC for suffrage protesting, she and other women went on a long hunger strike that became front-page news throughout the United States in 1919.

Embittered by what she was seeing happening in America — growing violence, increasing poverty, corrupt police and political machines, she began to call it all a "filthy rotten system." She had studied Christianity and saw that the message of Jesus Christ had little relationship to the belief system of people who called themselves "Christians." Day looked around her and found that radicals, communists and socialists seemed to have deep concern for the poor, who in a "Christian" society, had been deprived of good jobs, living wages and safe workplaces.

However, she broke from her socialist and communist friends in the late 1920's, converted to Catholicism and was able to obtain survival money for her child and herself by writing for the journal *Commonweal* and other publications. After the stock market crash of 1929, her attention became more and more focused on the poor. A former French peasant, Peter Maurin, became friends with Day. Maurin's basic Christian philosophy of work, prayer and assisting the poor struck Dorothy Day and invigorated her determination to help those on the very bottom of the social-economic stratum.

Her connection with Peter Maurin gave rise to the *Catholic Worker* hospitality houses and community farms. By the end of the 1930's the *Catholic Worker's* circulation was around 50,000 and Peter Maurin was publishing a number of essays in support of Jews. Deeply concerned about the ugly news creeping out of Europe, Maurin wrote under the theme, "Let's Save the Jews For Christ's Sake." Bluntly, consistently, he pushed for a return to the simple ways of the earth. It was Maurin who encouraged Dorothy Day to foster close communal relationships through farming. He envisioned a richness of the human spirit through communal work on farms around the nation.

Peter Flanigan told Anna Maria and Ellie about his talk with Father Sampson and the priest's suggestion to meet Dorothy Day and

Peter Maurin. Both women were supportive, and Ellie chimed in, "I'd love to go with you, Peter. Train, bus or car?"

Flanigan smiled. "I didn't plan on having company. It's my thing."

"Oh, I won't get in the way, Peter. But I'd love to have an opportunity to go to Radio City Music Hall and catch a stage show and movie at the Roxy or Paramount. You could go downtown to Mott Street and I could meet you later in the day."

Flanigan and his mother drove to Manhattan and parked on 38th Street. Peter walked up as far as 42nd street with Ellie, and then took the downtown bus on Broadway to the Bowery, and went past Chatham Square onto Mott Street. When he saw men standing in line, he assumed he was at the Catholic Worker. Flanigan noted that the men didn't differ much in dress than the fellows he saw in the Bowery. Yet, they were more animated, some smiling and chuckling, as they shuffled into the house at 15 Mott Street. Flanigan walked around the men, fearing that he might be dragged by the collar for bucking the line. No one said a word to him, but he thought he felt stares at his shined shoes, new sweater, and light spring jacket.

Flanigan rubbed shoulders with the men on the steps and squeezed through the crowded doorway overhearing one fellow remark "looka that kid just march right in, he must be Dorothy or Peter's son."

Inside, he asked one of the men for Dorothy Day or Peter Maurin.

"Sometimes they're on the line serving but I don't see them today. Go through the swinging doors and ask one of the servers."

Flanigan approached a young man ladling out chunky soup into a bowl held by an old man with a shaking hand. Soup drained over the side of the bowl and onto the floor. The man grinned and winked at Peter. "Would you wager that I'll have a spoonful left by the time I get to my table."

The server recognized that Flanigan was looking for someone and called out, "Who do you need?"

"Miss Day and Mr. Maurin."

"Go through those swinging doors and ask for them."

Dorothy Day and Peter Maurin were sitting in the kitchen apparently doing bookwork — Dorothy hitting a small adding machine and Peter Maurin reading out numbers to her. They didn't look up at Flanigan when he approached them. It seemed like a long time until Dorothy raised her chin and smiled at Flanigan.

"Can we help you with something?"

"Yes. My name is Peter Flanigan and I drove down from upstate Pennsylvania this morning just to talk to you and Mr. Maurin. You're Miss Day, and you're Mr. Maurin?"

"That's us, Peter. What did you want to talk to us about?"

"I'll turn eighteen in just a couple of months and I don't plan on registering for the draft. Father Sampson told me that if I were to discuss my situation with anyone, then you two would be the best choice."

"Father Sampson! We just heard about his transfer to Central America. Come with us, Peter."

Dorothy and Peter Maurin led Flanigan into a room off the kitchen. "You must be hungry, Peter." Motioning to Maurin, Dorothy said, "Peter, why don't you get your namesake some soup for lunch?"

Peter Maurin returned with soup, bread and tea for all three and the discussion began over lunch.

"Tell us first about Father Sampson, Peter. Is it true that he was exiled to Latin America or did he go because he wanted to leave?"

"Father Sampson told me that his transfer to Costa Rica resulted from his anti-war sermons advising young people to follow their conscience."

"And you heard some of these sermons?" asked Peter Maurin.

"Only one."

"Wow. Only one! I knew Father Sampson was good, but you heard him once and he convinced you to become a non-cooperator?"

"Not really. I had been examining my conscience for some time.

What Father Sampson did was help me confirm what I had already believed."

"Which is?" asked Dorothy.

"That I don't believe any government has a right to tell me that I should cooperate in any way with death and destruction. Just by signing into their system, I surrender my mind and body to political-military leaders and give them permission to use me in whatever way they deem best? I can't let them do that."

Dorothy Day and Peter Maurin turned their gaze away from Flanigan, looked at one another, and grinned..

Maurin said in his distinct French accent, "Are you sure you're only seventeen years old? Are you hiding a decade or two on us?"

Dorothy Day broke in quickly. "Do you mind, Peter, if we call you Flanigan? That way, my friend Peter won't be confused when I address you two fellows. And just call me Dorothy and Mr. Maurin is Peter.

"Now, let's continue," Dorothy said. "As I understand it, you would like our advice, Flanigan. Well, first, don't think that we will deviate far from what I'm sure Father Sampson told you — study the issue, pray for guidance and listen to your conscience. Right?"

"Yes."

"So where can we go from there?" asked Peter Maurin. "Are you aware of the penalty for doing what you plan to do?"

"Yes. I had a chat with Father Sampson about that. I know about prison."

"And you know that you may undergo intense mental and physical pain?" asked Dorothy.

"Yes."

"Mr. Flanigan, you are planning to do what I have been preaching to every young man that I come into contact with. The truth is, though, that I have failed in almost every case. Only a handful of young men that I have known have refused to register. Most of our *Catholic Worker* young men are going off to the army, navy and marines. For Peter and myself, this is at times devastating, totally contradictory to our beliefs. I'm glad you haven't worked here at the *Catholic Worker*. You would probably be getting ready to suit up. It's disappointing to us but people like you prevent us from becoming discouraged."

Looking first at Dorothy and then at Peter Maurin, Flanigan asked: "Do people have to be pacifists to work at the *Catholic Worker*?"

"Not at all, Flanigan," said Dorothy. "My position has always been to use one's conscience as one's guide. However, I have a very difficult time conceiving Christianity as a belief that allows acts that are in absolute conflict with its teaching. I've been severely criticized for my pacifism by press, friends and even members of the *Catholic Worker*. That's painful.

"Fifteen of our hospitality houses have been closed around the country because our young men are being drafted, enlisting in one of the military services or in Conscientious Objector camps. Only a few are in prison. Look at the server line. We used to have five people on the line. The numbers we serve has dropped because people are working again. Two years ago, we sometimes served 1,000 people a day. Now the number is down to 100. War does create jobs.

"Flanigan, are you planning a case to present to your draft board?"

"No. I don't plan on visiting the draft board in my town. I plan to refuse to sign anything that gives up my right to decide my own future. I'm a person, not a thing."

"Just one piece of advice, Flanigan, hang onto your faith. It will nourish you in the hard times ahead. I envy you for your courage to go one major step ahead of those who chose to semi-cooperate with the government. Deciding to be a conscientious objector is a major step away from the mainstream, but those who denied cooperation by refusing to follow orders to work suffered much more."

Maurin turned to Flanigan and said: "Peter Flanigan, I admire your élan and your esprit. Are you familiar with those French words?"

"Oui! High School French and the United States Marine Corps."

"Mais oui! And an esprit of a totally different kind. You have a spirit that I believe we could use at the Catholic Worker. Would you consider being one of our family?"

Looking to Dorothy, Maurin asked if she agreed.

"Yes, Peter Flanigan, you do fit. However, you wouldn't last long here. If you don't register and you work and live here, the FBI will snap you up quickly. They make periodic checks on our people and agents have marched right into the kitchen to make arrests. They have a way of finding people like you. If you want to stay and work here that's fine with me. But consider the consequences."

"You're always looking for recruits for your agronomic university, aren't you, Peter?"

"I think he'd rather work with a plow than a sword, Dorothy."

"Can I tell you something about the farm and how you could stay there, maybe ride out the war and contribute to our program of communal living?"

"I have never worked on a farm. I don't know a thing about growing stuff or taking care of animals. It probably would not be a good idea."

"Flanigan, why don't you come over to the farm and give it try. I'm going to be there at planting season starting in May. Would you come and just look at what we have?"

"I suppose it would be worth a look."

Dorothy spoke up. "When do you finish high school?"

"Mid-May. I could go down to Easton anytime after that to look the place over."

"Flanigan, Peter Maurin is right. The farm is isolated, and so far, agents have not been poking around there. That doesn't mean that it is safe haven. But Peter would be able to teach you some meaningful work and maybe keep you out of prison — for a time at least. My daughter, Tamar, is learning homemaking crafts in Canada. She will be returning from her school in Montreal this April and plans to stay at Maryfarm in

Easton. She has learned a lot in the past couple of years and would be glad to assist you.

"Peter, why don't you write directions to the farm for Mr. Flanigan? Easton is a long way from Wurtzville," said Dorothy.

Maurin gave Flanigan directions to the Easton, Pennsylvania *Catholic Worker* farm. "Try to get to the farm as soon after graduation as possible, Mr. Flanigan. We could use your help at planting time and after. Just take clothes and some spending money for incidentals when you go to town. I think you will be satisfied with the money de-emphasis on the farm. Give us a try."

"I'll think about it, Peter; no promises," replied Flanigan.

Frank Paulson, one of the kitchen workers, told Flanigan that he and a friend were going up to the Village and asked if he wanted to spend some time with them before his return to Pennsylvania. Peter joined Paulson and his friend, Colin Witterby and took the subway to Bleeker Street.

Paulson and Witterby knew a place where large schooners of beer could be had for 10 cents. They ordered three. Peter paid and was not surprised that he was served because he knew the drinking age was 18 in New York at that time. They found a booth in the busy beer garden, with a sawdust-covered floor. Within minutes the young men were deeply engaged in war talk and their individual forthcoming roles.

Flanigan explained his position and was somewhat shocked to learn that Paulson and Witterby were not in agreement with his decision.

"Bloody daft you are, mate. As daffy as me when I came here two years ago. Fresh off me Aussie freighter, the Gay Grouper, I was. Ah ya, full of dreamy stuff that you're spouting Flanigan. I get bloody crook when I think of what a dumb galah I was."

Paulson jumped in on the young Australian. "I didn't jump ship like this Down Under derelict Peter. Yet, we do have a lot in common. We both work at a pacifist house and we both are converts to war —

win it or die. We don't want to die and we don't want our families to suffer and die. That's what's going to happen if we sit on our asses and drink beer for the duration. We need to act and act soon. I leave for the Marines next week."

Peter broke in and spoke to Colin Witterby. "And you, Colin. What are your plans?"

"Leaving for Ottawa tomorrow, mate. Train out of Grand Central Station. Joining the Canadian Army and asking for duty in the South Pacific."

"What made you have a change of heart, Colin?"

"The nips, mate. I gave up on pacifism when they took Singapore just a couple of weeks ago. School mates of mine were part of the force that surrendered to the Japs. Before you know it, Japanese troops will be invading my home country. Now if you talk to Dorothy Day and Peter Maurin, they shrug it all off. Well, mate, I'm not about to shrug off this one. Me da is in the Australian Army in New Guinea, me mum is at home in Wollongong — waiting for the Nips to come ashore. And me? Here I am like so much vegamite on me plate. I figure eight weeks training, a few weeks travel and I'll have me crack at Mr. Nip."

Frank Paulson took three more schooners from the bar and began to caution Peter.

"Peter, consider this. Colin and I thought a lot like you until the attack on Pearl Harbor and Singapore hit home. It's no longer a war just for the Europeans to fight. We're threatened on both sides of the continent. If Russia falls to the Nazis, the Germans will have the petroleum and the troops to turn full force on England. Meanwhile, as we try to come to the aid of the English, the Japanese execute a full scale invasion of Hawaii, Alaska, and California. Next comes the Nazis. They'll post themselves in Iceland, Ireland, Greenland and finally Canada and the United States.

"It's totally ridiculous to be a pacifist in light of the horror going on in Europe and Asia. Sure, it's nice to turn the other cheek but not when the other cheek will be torn to shreds. Pearl Harbor was only a slap on the wrist, but it woke up people like Colin and me. My idealism ended with Pearl Harbor. Colin's ended when Australian blood was drawn in Singapore and Hong Kong.

"Peter, you may not want my advice, but I'm going to give it to you anyway. You're not Jesus Christ. He would probably turn the other cheek. But He's God — or so we believe; and you're simply a man. Don't let the Days and Maurins of the world turn your young mind as they did mine. Their tunnel vision philosophy of non-violence is nice, but they're not seeing the world as it is today anymore than that cop's horse out there on Bleeker Street. The peripheral vision of the horse is blocked. So is the pacifist philosophy. Don't be trapped by their well intended reasoning. Peter, if ever there was a time to do something to counter act evil, it's now. You may like your freedom to do what you want to do. You may think it's your right to decide what should be done with your mind and body. I agree with you. But if anything in life is true it's that exceptions to the rule always exist. Find an exception to the rule that you've made for yourself, Peter. Look at the suffering of mankind at the hands of fascism around the world. If good people choose to do nothing, then evil wins and mankind is doomed."

Colin Wetterby had the third round on the table before Peter tried to excuse himself.

"It's after 3 o'clock, fellows, you have my pacifism nailed to the wall and beer has my mind and tongue in a twist. Can I make it to 38th and 8th in an hour from here?"

"Not a problem, mate. Drink up, I see you're behind."

"My behind," said Peter, "is sore from all the sitting I've been doing since 6 A.M. this morning. A good walk will sober me up, help me rethink my non-violent philosophy, and stretch out my butt. Thanks for the company, the beer and the advice. Good luck, fellows."

Flanigan made it uptown before 5 P.M. and snoozed in the passenger seat of his mother's car. He awoke to her knock on the windshield and her comment, "Do you want me to drive?"

"Sure."

Ellie got into the car and turned the ignition.

"Oh, what is that odor? Not gasoline, but sort of an alcohol smell."

Ellie paid the man at the gate and turned west toward the Hudson River and the Lincoln Tunnel.

"Were you drinking, Peter?"

"Just a couple of beers."

"Is that the beverage of choice at the *Catholic Worker?*"

"No. But it's the drink of the workers. At least the workers I was with!"

"Dorothy Day and Peter Maurin?"

"No. Just two guys that had a lot to say — and a lot for me to think about. It's funny. I had a long conversation with Dorothy Day and Peter Maurin but it was a bit stiff and they seem so old. Then I had a long talk with the two beer drinking Catholic Worker guys and it was great. Maybe their words flowed with the beer. But they were so sincere and so decisive in their views. Nice fellows."

"Was the trip worth the long drive?"

"Oh yah. But if I had another beer, I'd probably be joining the Marines or the Canadian Army."

"What?"

"I'll tell you when we get well into New Jersey. You know the way better than me. When you get to Route 46 give me a nudge and I'll tell you about my day and you can tell me about *Gone With The Wind* at the Roxy."

Chapter 16
Slimeball Maggot

When Ellie Flanigan stopped the car to pay the ten-cent toll at the Delaware Water Gap bridge, Peter awoke from an hour and a half snooze. Ellie did not seem disturbed by Peter's beer-drinking but chatted like a school girl.

"Peter, I didn't go to the Roxy but you won't believe what a great show I saw at the Paramount — Al Jolson. I have heard his voice on radio hundreds of times but to see and hear him in person was marvelous. The pit orchestra was superb and Jolson had dancers that you would have popped your eyeballs over — what gorgeous women!"

Ellie continued to gush about her day. Brentano's Book Store, St. Pat's Cathedral, people watching, Lord & Taylor. Peter felt great that she so enjoyed herself. He hadn't been thrilled having his mother accompany him to NYC but she proved she wasn't a meddler.

"So tell me about your day," said Ellie.

"Before I fell asleep near the tunnel, I was having serious doubts about my decision not to register for the draft. What a great pair of guys — Colin and Frank. It was like being with big brothers. They weren't preachy about their new-found convictions but they were firm. They used to think like I think now and then the war changed all that. As they talked, I kept asking myself if I was ready for a change. If maybe what they are saying is what I really believe."

"What was so remarkable about what they said?"

"I guess their belief that this conflict is a threat to all societies, including our own. That a brutal menace is on its way to our land and people from both sides of the continent and if it's not stopped, our existence as a free people may end."

"Does that belief change your conviction?"

"No. But it does make me want to think it out more. Suppose they're right? Suppose the Nazis invade our east coast and the Japanese our west coast — should I continue to say that I refuse to cooperate with the government?"

"I don't know, Peter. That's for you to decide."

"What would you do if you were me?"

"I'm not you."

"But I've got a lot of my thinking from you."

"Probably. But how much have you taken from school, from teachers and books and magazines and newspapers? From Church, from friends, from radio and movies that you go to?"

"Quite a bit, I guess. How come I'm not thinking like the rest of my friends — like most Americans?"

"Peter, I refuse to take responsibility for a decision that you made through your own free will. If there is anything in which I've come to believe it's my personal freedom to think and act as I choose. Didn't you once tell me about one of the sisters at St. Catherine's telling you that you can think anything you want to think but you can't act on just anything that you do think?"

"Right. She emphasized that man is known by his actions. And that's where I'm at. I think that I'm doing the right thing by refusing to register for the military. But maybe it's a stupid act of disobedience —

like some of the crazy things I've done in the past. You've never really said how you feel about my plan."

"Not so, Peter. When I say that you should follow your conscience, I'm giving my approval to your decision. If you change your mind and go into the service, then I support that decision. I may not like it, but I support it."

"Well, I have less than three months to commit to a final decision."

"Then try to enjoy the time. Don't put yourself in such a mental mess that you ruin your remaining days in school."

Back in Wurtzville, March and April passed uneventfully for Flanigan. He and Anna Maria continued to work together at the Laurel Lake Inn, go to dances and movies together, and search meadows and woods for the first signs of spring. On slow nights in March, Anna Maria taught Peter how to tie trout flies, a skill she'd learned from her father. Peter watched as Anna Maria tied colorful thin thread around snips of grouse feathers that her father had saved from the fall hunt. By the time the lake ice broke, Peter had mastered the art, but needed fly casting lessons. He was disappointed when the first day opened and Anna Maria told him that it was too early to use the flies they had tied.

"We haven't had a hatch yet, Peter. Wait until the May flies start. We can pack a lunch and go up to Starrucca Creek and I'll show you how to fool the browns and rainbows. What we have to do here is to just feed those hungry fellows in the lake. Get a shovel and hoe from the shed and I'll meet you at Robinson's sheep barn."

Robinson's barn and shed were on a rise across the road from the Inn. The Machellis bought the sheep and the Robinsons cared for them. Peter got the tools and met Anna Maria at the barn. The sheep were released to the hill for browsing in late March and Anna Maria showed Peter the treasure they left behind in the barn — manure and worms.

Anna Maria led the way up the hill and Peter carried the tools. "Dig here and I'll hoe," said Anna Maria.

In a matter of minutes they had a can of red worms and were on their way to the lake.

"Worms work best early in the season, Peter. Don't expect to catch a big fish like the browns we netted in December."

They worked the shore and Anna Maria demonstrated the spin casting technique. Peter became frustrated when his line got tangled but Anna Maria patiently showed him how to set his thumb on the line when his bait and sinker got far enough from shore. Maria caught several nice rainbows and Peter looked on in awe. On each strike, the brilliant fish fought the lady angler, jumping high above the water, its tail doing a dance on the surface. When Anna Maria had caught four fish and Peter said he hadn't had a bite, she stood next to him like a father, coaching him to watch the line and wait for just a slight movement.

"They're not hitting hard, Peter. When you see the line going out slowly, raise your rod and set the hook with a tug of the rod tip."

Within minutes, Flanigan was giving a hoot and a holler. He didn't have a big fish, but he hooked it!

"Let it swim about, Peter. Don't horse the fish in. Just keep your rod tip up and you'll have a keeper."

Peter was too excited to listen to that advice and shortly after hooking the fish, he yanked it out of the water and onto the shore.

"Peter Flanigan, congratulation on your first trout caught as they are supposed to be caught — on a hook. But don't catch fish like Huckleberry Finn. Give the fish a sporting chance."

"I've been giving them a lot of chances Miss Machelli and they have been winning every time."

Anna Maria gave Peter a second demonstration of gutting and filleting and let Peter finish the job. Later, in the kitchen, Anna Maria showed Peter how to prepare trout amandine, one of her father's favorite recipes. Then, she set two plates and wine glasses on the kitchen table, took crusty bread from the oven and quickly tossed a salad of endive, parsley and lettuce laced with pine nuts, olive oil and vinegar.

"Now, Peter Flanigan, enjoy. This is what my father calls 'specialita della casa.' Capisce?"

"Si. Specialty of the house."

"Mama mia, you really are catching on, Mr. Irishman."

"Yup. And this casa is becoming my house of skills and you're my maestro."

"No, no, Signor. Maestra!"

"Enough of this language session, let's eat, Anna Maria, mia maestra."

"Do you mind having wine for lunch."

"Why not? Never had it before for lunch so I may as well learn how to really live."

"Well, my mother and I don't always have it for lunch. My father has his red wine every day — lunch and dinner. But this is a special occasion."

"Oh yeah? What's so special?"

"You and me. I think we're becoming a pair."

"Oh yeah. A pair of what?"

"A pair of love birds, that's what!" Anna Maria got up from her chair and went around to Peter and gave him a hug. As they kissed, Peter sitting, and Anna Maria standing; Dante came into the kitchen.

"Wha sa goin on a here? You serve a this a boy kiss or a food."

Anna Maria laughed, winked at her father so that Peter could see her and said, "Papa, I bet you served a lot of kisses when you worked kitchens in Switzerland."

Dante gave a big grin that showed his shiny gold molar.

"Ohhhh so many nice-a girls in Lucerne. Sweet and a juicy, like gold a grape-a, you two I like a together. You stay that a way. You hear?"

Dante left and Anna Maria said, "So now you got it from your boss, Mr. Flanigan." She raised her wine glass: "Here's to my father's good sense."

Peter raised his glass and touched Anna Maria's.

"And here is to many more trout and kisses," toasted Peter.

"Peter, have you heard anything from Roz?"

"Yes. He finished advanced infantry training and went airborne. He expects to be home in early May."

"Have you talked to Tina recently?"

"No. After she finished school last year and started working, I saw her only when she was with Roz."

"Well, I do see her occasionally, and talking to her yesterday was a bit weird."

"Why?"

"Usually she's effervescent. You know, Tina, the bubbly cheerleader. Nothing can go wrong. Father Goodman used to call her Pollyanna. Remember? Well, she wasn't any Pollyanna yesterday."

"She is probably just lonesome. Roz and her are pretty tight and it's been months since they have been together."

"No. That attitude would have surfaced weeks or months ago. She was gloomy. Knowing her, it was kind of spooky seeing the change."

"From what I have read and heard, isn't it a monthly problem?"

"No, Mr. Flanigan, it wasn't her monthly problem. I've know her for years. She didn't just get her monthly problem. Or do you really think that 'monthly problems' start after high school."

"I don't know. I used to think that babies came out of ladies' belly-buttons."

"So when did you graduate from the school of belly-button birth?"

"Naw. Just kidding. My mother is very forward-thinking. She instructed me on the birds and bees years ago. Good thing. I wouldn't get much out of the nuns. And I think Father Goodman still believes in belly-button birth. He's smart, but one of those naive types. Probably went into the seminary when he was ten.

"You know, Anna Maria, maybe you should go and see Tina if you think she is hurting."

"Good idea. I'll drive down to the dress factory where Tina's works and talk to her. But first, let's have some biscotti and coffee."

Flanigan and Anna Maria talked on the phone later that night and Anna Maria told Peter a little of the conversation she and Tina had. She confirmed that Tina Maria was upset but promised to tell Peter more about it some time later. She said that Roz was coming home May 5th and that all four should get together and do something. "Don't call him Alley Oop — call him Charlie or Roz. Those Wurtzville nicknames sound so phony now that he's out of school," said Anna Maria.

***

Private Charles Rozer, tailored khakis bloused at the top of shiny boots, blue infantry braid on his shoulder, a small medal of an open parachute with "Airborne" underneath, and a shoulder patch with a bald eagle — the "screaming eagle" of the 101st Airborne Division, was met at the train station in Wurtzville by Tina, Anna Maria and Flanigan. Everyone agreed that he looked "just great", although Tina asked, "Why did they cut off all your nice hair?"

Rozer seemed to have lost his rough edge after the military training. His tone of voice was different and Flanigan noticed a hint of the south in his often used "Ya'll."

"Ya'll look great yourselves. Now ya'll come with me and I'm treating everyone to one of the super sloppy hamburgers at the Wurtzville greasy spoon."

"Throw your duffle bag in the trunk, Roz. The girls can get in the back seat."

Roz told his adventures from basic training through airborne. "I hadn't planned on airborne when I went in but I began to think: What the hell, if you're going to experience the greatest adventure that a man could ever dream of — why not float into the action. So I signed up and I'm damn glad I did. It was tough but I'm with an elite group of guys — fantastic morale. Let the Marines talk about their esprit de corp. Those jarheads can't compare to airborne."

When the girls had a chance to speak, Anna Maria said, "You know, there are only days left before graduation and the prom is tomorrow night?"

"Yes," said Tina. "And you can count us out. We aren't going."

"Why not?" Anna Maria and Peter said in unison.

Roz spoke up. "For one, it was nice to get the invitation but I didn't finish with the class. Besides, I'd much rather be with Tina away from the high school crowd. Go somewhere. Or, have you guys come along. I just don't feel it's my thing."

"You must have something in mind," asked Peter.

"Oh, I guess anywhere but that uppity country club — everybody decked out in fancy clothes and most guys acting like little kiddies. Fact is, I've seen a lot of nice places since I left Wurtzville. Traveling from the south through pretty little towns, green grass farms and mountains of pine and hardwood forests, I got to thinking about what we have here in Wurtzville. When the train got me back into the coal country it was depressing. I don't have to tell you why. But this ugly, narrow little valley is not the place I want to call home when the war is over and Tina and I settle down."

"You have a prom gown ready to go, don't you, Anna Maria?" said Flanigan.

Anna Maria gave a knowing glance at Tina, and quickly said, "Sure. But that doesn't mean I have to go to the dance." Winking at Roz and Tina and flashing a big smile, she hugged Flanigan, teasing him with her own lilting imitation of southern country talk, "It don't matter none. So long as I'm with my honey."

"It's fine with me," said Peter, "but let's consider some good place to have a great day."

"Have you ever been to Endicott?" asked Tina.

"Somewhere north of here, isn't it?" said Peter.

"Right. New York State. It's only about a hour or so drive from here. Up through Binghamton and then a short drive along the Susquehanna River to Johnson City and Endicott."

"So what so interesting about those places?" asked Roz.

"My aunt and uncle live there and they called to say they have four tickets to the Tommy Dorsey Band at the Pavilion in Johnson City. We can have them if we stop by tomorrow. Tomorrow is Workers Day at the Endicott-Johnson Company. We can join in on their picnic by the river in the afternoon and go to the dance at night."

"Is that the shoe and boot company?" asked Anna Maria.

"Yes," said Tina. "The army boots that Roz is wearing were probably made by Endicott-Johnson. I'm moving to Endicott next month and taking a job at E-J. Wait until you see this area, I can't wait to get out of Wurtzville. I want Roz to see the place so that he can think about joining me there when he gets out of the army. I've been there several times to visit my relatives."

"Sounds good to me," said Peter.

"Let's do it," said Anna Maria. "I'll take the food and drinks."

Tina turned to Roz. "So, Mr. Paratrooper, anything from you?"

"Yes, Ma'am. Mr. Flanigan supplies the car and I supply gas. We leave at 9 A.M. tomorrow morning. In Endicott before 11 A.M., get those precious tickets and find ourselves a good spot to relax. Eat, drink, and knock about until Dorsey Time. Then come back in the wee, wee hours of the morning."

"Just in time to see the Prommies tip-toeing in their back doors all about town," said Tina.

By 11 A.M. the next morning, the two couples were at Tina's aunt's house in Endicott, collected the tickets and were given directions to En Joie Park, just one of many employee recreation facilities provided by the Endicott-Johnson Company.

The four young Pennsylvanians were delighted with the surroundings. From Binghamton west through Johnson City and into Endicott, they saw a model experiment in welfare capitalism. Aware of the lack of concern for workers by the S&H Railroad, they were not prepared for what they would learn. Coming from a place just sixty miles to the south where company owned houses were usually the poorest and in bad repair, where mine caves were common, house foundations split, where crooked politics wedded unscrupulous business leaders into tactics and schemes that left many people on the edge of despair; the trip to Endicott opened up young eyes and made them realize that a more hopeful existence was possible outside of the coal country.

The Endicott-Johnson Company built sturdy, comfortable houses, graded and seeded lawns, planted trees and provided sewage facilities for their workers. Five dollars a week was set as a mortgage payment on each house, with only 3% interest. It was cradle to the grave paternalism started by Henry B. Endicott around the turn of the century and continued by his partner George Francis Johnson. By 1920, employees were receiving surplus profits (bonuses) and encouraged to participate in a profit-sharing stock benefit. Workers' babies were given free booties and a gold coin. Medical services, clinics, pharmacies and hospitals were established for workers by 1925. By the 1930's the company had a staff of thirty four medical doctors, four dentists, and dozens of graduate nurses and nurse assistants.

George F. Johnson and his sons urged workers to stay well and to mix play with work. In every company housing development, the Johnsons built recreation facilities. Parks with baseball diamonds, swings and carousels. So many merry-go-rounds were built that the area became known as the Carousel Capital of the World. Golf, the rich man's game in the 1930's became a workers game when Endicott-Johnson built an 18 hole golf course for its employees. For evening entertainment, E-J constructed a huge pavilion, hired dance bands three nights each week, and featured occasional Big Band nights that lured Benny Goodman, Glenn Miller, Tommy Dorsey, Artie Shaw, Woody Herman and others to the pavilion.

Tina, familiar with the area and activities led the two couples to an expansive park with wide lawns called En Joie. Most people gathered at picnic tables with overhead cover. Roz and Peter were spreading out a ground blanket when Anna Maria called to them, "Let's go over to that table. Tina saw her cousins over there. Maybe we can meet some people and find out more about this place."

Flanigan and Rozer went to the table and met Tina's relatives, set up their picnic basket and eagerly got into the food supplied by Anna Maria. Large bottles of Pepsi accompanied the sandwiches, cookies, fruit and snacks. Roz pulled a flask from his pocket and took periodic nips from it.

"What is that, Roz?" asked Flanigan.

"This is good stuff I got in the Carolinas. Called Jim Beam. Want a swig, Crusher?"

"Nah. Not if it's what I think it is."

"What yawl think it is?"

"Well, I don't think it's soda pop."

"Hell buddy, you won't know until you try. Take a nip."

"O.K. but just a swig."

Flanigan took a swallow and couldn't believe how it burned.

"Peter — from that look on your kisser you'd think you inhaled fire. This is smooth bourbon, boy. You better take a couple more to get your tonsils in tune to good stuff."

"No thanks, Roz." Flanigan began to sing and Anna Maria joined in:

> Pepsi Cola hits the spot,
> Twelve full ounces, that's a lot.
> Twice as much for a nickel too,
> Pepsi Cola is the drink for you."

"The hell it is. Those cute little jingles are a thing of the past.

Pepsi is a kid's drink, Peter. Put some hair on your chest and take a crack."

Flanigan waved away the offer and began to wonder if Roz had been nipping on the flask while traveling from Pennsylvania. Tina's cousin Tony came over to the table and joined in the conversation.

"Do you work at Endicott-Johnson, Tony?" asked Anna Maria.

Tony smiled a little apologetically. "I'm a fair-haired member of IBM, Anna Maria. You couldn't work there — not with a name like Anna Maria Machelli! One look at you and your jet black hair and they wouldn't even process your work application."

"So how did you get in there? Your last name is Italian, too."

"My pay check reads James Cerr. It wasn't my idea, and don't ask me what ethnic derivation Cerr is supposed to have. But the interviewer in the Personnel Department was so happy to get someone with experience in tool and die making that he was willing to overlook my Italian background. When he handed me the work acceptance form, he suggested that I drop the 'a' from 'Cerra' and use my middle name of James. So at the Itty Bitty Machine Company, I'm known as Jim. Fine with me. I have no problem with that as long as I keep getting paid."

"What does IBM make?" asked Roz.

"We make a lot of stuff. We used to make meat cutting equipment, scales, and time clocks for punching in and out of work; but now we do calculators and a whole bunch of business machines. I'm an apprentice tool and die maker and my work is 100% military materials."

"Like what?"

"Well, it's supposed to be classified information but everybody in Endicott knows that we're making the receivers for Browning Automatic Rifles and the carbines."

"I know them well, Tony," said Rozer. "I've fired both. The carbines aren't worth a shit. Like a toy compared to the M-1 and the BAR. Maybe better than a boomerang or a sling shot. But give me a Browning Automatic Rifle anytime, those babies will make krauts and Nips dance to hell fire."

Tony smiled. "Wow, that's not saying much for my carbine work. But anyway, next week I'm moving to another machine shop and starting work on 40 millimeter cannons."

"We don't have 40 millimeter cannons in our outfit. Who do you make them for?"

"The Army Air Force. The guns are mounted in the middle of the propeller. We have perfected a way to shoot them without shooting off the propellers of the fighter aircraft."

Flanigan spoke up. "So this area is a booming war industry place. What else is made around here?"

"Again, it's supposed to be classified but that is a lot of bull. Everyone knows that General Electric is making aircraft propellers and over at Link, aircraft trainers are in production."

"Trainers?"

"Yeah. You get into a make-believe cockpit and all the flight controls are right there. Friends of mine work on them, they say it's a blast to use. The simulator gives the impression of flying — from taking off, to in-air maneuvers, to landing. My friends get all the overtime they want and three shifts are working seven days a week."

Tina and Anna Maria stepped into the conversation.

"Are you guys going to talk war all afternoon or are we up here for some fun?" asked Anna Maria.

Tina began walking toward the grandstands off to the left of the picnic grounds. "Come on, the first race at En Joie is at 2 P.M. and it's almost that now. Let's go watch the horse races."

Tina's cousin Tony joined the couples and explained the setup. "Betting isn't supposed to occur but look for a guy with an apron. He takes bets almost up to the last stretch."

"How do you know what to bet on?" asked Peter.

"You don't. Unless you are one of the regulars and saw the horse run before. I wouldn't advise betting unless you are a real gambler. Let's go around to the reviewing area to look at the nags."

The horses were coming into a small fenced-in stable where people could look close up at the horses and jockeys. The girls picked the cute jockeys as the probable winners and the guys pretended they could tell the winning horses by pointing out muscles, leg size, and even color. Only Tony had ever seen a race before, but he was noncommittal.

They stood to watch the races and several times were approached by the apron men holding tickets for betting. All five wagered a dollar on their picks and after five races, Tony had won two and the others had lost every race.

Waving his winnings in his hand Tony commented, "Like I said, unless you have seen the horses before, you will find no joy at En Joie."

After the two couples had their first ever swim in a pool, hunger pangs hit again and Tony suggested they go to a restaurant for tomato pie.

"Tomato pie?" the girls said in unison.

"Yeah, it's like a bread crust with tomato and melted cheese on top. It really is good. Wash it down with some soda or beer and it's a great meal. A pie cost 80 cents and two pies will feed the four of you."

"Are you going to the Tommy Dorsey Band tonight, Tony?" asked Tina.

"Yeah. I'll see you there about 8 o'clock. Save me and my girl a spot at your table."

The four raved over the tomato pie and Anna Maria went into the kitchen and got the recipes from the baker.

"My father is going to moan about this addition to our menu. I can just hear him now, 'Dats a more Siciliana food. Mama mia. Who's a gonna eat a tomato pie!'"

At 8 P.M. they met Tony going into the dance. Tony introduced his girl, Nancy Adams, and they made their way through the hundreds of couples already gliding to *I'm Getting Sentimental Over You* along the polished dance floor. When the band took a break at 9 P.M., Roz had finished the last liquid from his flask and asked about getting a drink of beer or bourbon.

"They don't sell it here," said Tony. "You'll have to wait until after the dance. There are bars nearby. But in the meantime, fellows, while I'm up to my armpits in tool and die making, where are you guys headed?"

"I'll be up to my armpits in Germans or Japs, Mr. Tony. You keep on making those good ole BAR's and my buddies and me will shoot the asses off the Krauts and Japs. I don't know where I'm going but it ain't going to be anything like the picnic we had this afternoon."

"And you, Peter, where are you headed? Are you getting out of Wurtzville like my cousin Tina?"

"It kind of looks like I'm going somewhere but I'm not sure yet."

"Now that is a hell of an answer, Crusher. Why don't you just tell Tony that you're going to be joining me in the great adventure. You have to decide soon and if you want to see some good action, then you better join up soon — and not some pussy group like the navy or the army quartermaster corp. Join the infantry and go to jump school. The longer you wait, the less action is guaranteed. We should have Tojo and Hitler on the run before the end of the year. And don't sign up with the marines, those grunts aren't worth shit."

"Fact is, Roz, I don't plan on going in to any military service."

"Sold on making the big civilian bucks like Tony, here, huh? Work twelve hours a day, seven days a week, stock up tons of cash, go to dances and other little freebies rich corporations throw your way. Get your head in order, Peter. A tough little cookie like you shouldn't be a homebody weasel making blood money."

"I resent that," said Tony. "If somebody didn't make the BAR's you say are so great, how would we ever get enough made to make a difference?"

Tina stood up. "Come on, Anna Maria. My friend here has had

too much of his southern hooch. I'm going to the ladies room."

"Good, Tina. You should take a little hike and cool it. Peter and Tony and I can get some real talk going."

"Come on outside for a smoke, you guys."

Roz and Tony lit up Lucky Strikes.

"O.K. So we need you, Tony. But Flanigan doesn't know a nut from a bolt. He needs the army to teach him how to be part of the fighting team."

"That's O.K. for you to say, Roz. For myself, I've decided differently."

"So what are you going to do? You got to either work in a war plant or go in the service. You don't have a pot to piss in so how can you go to college? Now if you say the Coast Guard or the Merchant Marines, I'm not going to talk to you — I'm out of here."

"I'm not going to register for the draft, Roz. I respect your decision to do what you wanted to do. You weren't drafted, you signed up. That was your business. My business is not to get involved and that includes working in a war plant or even being a conscientious objector."

"What is this shit? I can't believe my ears. You aren't going to do anything? Your ass is in a sling, Mr. Man. Do you think Uncle Sam is going to let you wiggle out of your responsibility?"

"Probably not. But my personal responsibility is to not cooperate. It's pretty complicated, Roz, but let's wait until tomorrow or some other time to explain my reasoning."

"No. I want to hear it now, Peter Flanigan." Throwing his cigarette to the ground, with his left hand, he grabbed Flanigan by the collar and stood eye ball to eye ball with him. "Are you a fucking coward or what? You disgust me, you maggot. To think that guys are dying to save your little ass and you won't even lift a hand to help? You won't even join the fucking Coast Guard. How about the Waves, you cunt."

Rozer pulled his right fist back and roundhoused Flanigan in the nose. Blood shot from his face and he fell to the ground.

"The only way that you can prove you aren't slime is to get up and act like a man. I know you won't get up, Flanigan, because you're slime and slime always stays close to the ground."

Flanigan got up and was about to be smashed again by Rozer when Tony grabbed Roz and held his arms behind his back.

"I wasn't getting up to hit you Roz. I just want to tell you that I understand your disappointment with me. I'm not a coward, Roz."

"You'll always be a slimeball maggot in my mind, Flanigan. I wish I never met you."

Flanigan went to the men's room to wash the blood from his face and saw that his nose was turned to the side. When he returned to the table, Tina, Roz, Tony and his girl friend were gone. Anna Maria said Tony told her what happened.

"My God, Peter. Your nose is smashed."

"Where did everyone go?"

"Roz said he didn't want to go back to Wurtzville with us. Tony felt terrible about it but he said they could stay at his house overnight and he would drive them back to Wurtzville in the morning."

Looking dejected, Peter said, "Well, what can I say?"

Softly patting the red welt surrounding Flanigan's nose she said, "How about — 'Can I have this dance?'"

The couple slipped onto the dance floor as the Tommy Dorsey Band played *Farewell Blues.*

Chapter 17
Saying Love In A Hot Moment

On the way home to Laurel Lake, Anna Maria sat closer to Flanigan than she ever had before. They were silent except to comment on road signs that directed them south, back into the northeastern Pennsylvania hill country. They were almost home when Anna Maria switched on the car light and turned toward Flanigan. "Let me look at that nose again."

Peter grinned.

"Can you tell me if he hit me with a right hook or a left?"

"Hmmm. Now let me see. Your nose is turned to the left. So I guess he hit you with a right."

"So to fix it I need a left hook."

"No. You need tender, loving care. I'll smooch it back into place."

It was midnight when they pulled into the Laurel Lake Inn driveway. The place was in darkness except for the porch light left on for Anna Maria. The couple drove down close to the water and parked near the boat house.

"Why did he hit you?"

"I told him I wasn't going to sign up for the draft."

"Peter, I can't believe you told him. You know how he is. Especially now after completing paratrooper training. Why didn't you avoid the issue?"

"I had planned on doing that. But he pressed me to tell him. And I did. It was that simple."

"You got that right. It was simple. Simple for you to tell him anything about your plans. Don't you realize that most people don't think like you?"

"Sure. But in history class, we learned that this is a free country. In theology class, we learned that each person has the precious gift of free will. So why would people be upset because I elect to think and act differently than the masses?"

"You aren't listening to me, Peter. What I'm saying is that you can't shout it from the roof tops or tell it to people like Alley Oop Rozer unless you want a strong reaction. Sure, some people will say: Yeah, you have a right to say and do what you want to do. But a whole lot more will be ready to string you up for what you say and do."

"Would you be upset if I said something to you?"

"Probably not. Is this a trick, Peter Flanigan? What is it you want to say?"

"That I love you."

Anna Maria sat back in her seat and said nothing.

"Guess I should not have said that, eh?"

"It's not that you shouldn't have said it. I've sensed it for a long time."

Anna Maria moved closer and when she kissed Peter, he could feel the salty tears that streamed down her face. Flanigan felt lost in a rush of emotion, silence broken only by rapid breathing, and lake water lapping at the boat house.

Peter put his hand up Anna Maria's skirt and stroked her thigh.

When Anna Maria continued to hold and kiss him, he slid his hand slowly up to her panties and got an immediate reaction — a slap on his sore face.

"Stop! Peter Flanigan!" Anna Maria pulled away from Peter.

Flanigan slumped back in his seat. "Not my day. Just not my day. My best male friend busts my nose and my best female friend does a follow up. Not my day."

"I love you, Peter. I didn't want to say that in a hot moment. Now that I iced things over, I can say it and mean it. But don't think that means you have a license to handle me like the license to handle your steering wheel. We're not married. We're just beginning our adult lives, the nation is at war, we don't know what's going to happen, and above all, I have my moral code and I thought that you had yours."

"I wasn't trying to hurt you. You make it sound like I was doing something violent."

"Violence isn't the only immoral act, Peter."

"Oh, here we go again. Sister Hildegarde is here with us in the car. Am I ever going to get her out of my life?"

"No. Not Hildegarde. Me. I have my dignity, my respect, my life to live, Peter."

"I wasn't trying to stop your life from going on, Anna Maria. I was expressing how I felt."

"You're right. Too much feeling! For a person that seems so intent on following his conscience, I would assume that you would respect my virginity."

"O.K. O.K., you got me. I was wrong. I apologize. It's not like I didn't think that I would ever try to go that far with you. God, I dream about making love to you all the time."

"Peter, has it occurred to you that I have a life plan — that I don't want to be a young mother waiting around for you to come back to Wurtzville from God knows where?"

"Oh come on, Anna Maria, I wasn't about to make you pregnant."

"Yeah. That's what Roz told Tina over the Christmas holidays."

"Are you telling me something?"

"I'm telling you that Tina is over four months pregnant. She told me just recently and she was going to tell Roz after tonight."

"So what is she going to do?"

"She's afraid to tell her parents. Tina said they would go nuts if they knew. She has to tell them sometime but her aunt knows, and Tony was able to get her a job at Endicott Johnson Shoe Company. Her aunt said that she could live with them and have the baby up there. Endicott Johnson has its own hospital and medical care is free for workers, so she can get benefits before and after the birth."

"I wonder if she told Roz tonight. He wasn't in the best condition for a fatherly kind of talk. My face is evidence of that fact."

"I'll see Tina sometime tomorrow. I suspect the four of us won't be getting together again after last night."

When Ellie saw Peter's face the following morning at breakfast, her shock was not rewarded with the truth from Peter.

"Yes, I was socked by some goofy guy on the dance floor up in Johnson City. He said that I kept bumping into him when we were dancing. He smacked me. I went down and he went away. It was that quick."

"Your nose. My God, Peter. It's swollen and twisted. What kind of a place is that up there anyway?"

"Oh Mom, don't put down the place because some dope nailed me. Goofs are everywhere."

"Well, you're going to have to go to Dr. Martin and get that nose back in place. Maybe it's broken. I'll call his office now."

After, Ellie made an appointment for Peter to see the physician and then calmed down and learned about the more pleasant events of Anna Maria's and Peter's day.

"Peter, before you're off to other things in your busy schedule, would you tell me exactly what you plan to do after graduation?"

"The Sunday after next is graduation. After the graduation mass and commencement, I'll get on the S&H out of Wurtzville, and make a connection in Wilkes-Barre for Easton. The *Catholic Worker* has a place they call Maryfarm outside of town."

"And what will you do there?"

"Farm."

"What does that mean?"

"I won't know till I get there."

"And what do I say when the police or whoever come looking for you?"

"I don't know if they will. I don't plan to announce to the world that I'm not going to register. I'm simply getting out of town."

"Don't you think that they have a cross check of all males who are 18 or over? They do have records, you know."

Smiling, Peter said, "Maybe not on a little bastard like me."

Months before, the comment would have hurt Ellie, but mother and son were through that before, so she chuckled. "Oh yes they do. Your birth certificate is on file in the county court house in Scranton. If they check records, your name will come up some time."

"Until then, I'll keep in contact with you. Maybe I can sneak home occasionally and see you. Or since you have a car, you and Anna Maria can come down and see me. In the meantime, I won't write to you directly, I'll put your letters in an envelope addressed to Anna Maria."

"How long will you stay at Maryfarm?"

"It depends. Maybe I'll become a little ole farm boy."

"Peter, you don't know a furrow from a fence post."

Ellie left for work. Peter was reading the morning paper when the porch door eased open, and Rozer peered around and said, "Mind if I come in?"

"Nope."

"Peter, I'm sorry about last night. I was drunk, you know?"

"I know."

"Are you going to do something about that nose?"

"Yeah, I talked to a blacksmith down at Fredricks Perforation. He said that a good turn with a plumbers wrench would set it straight."

"So really. What are you going to do?"

"I have an appointment with a doctor this morning. How about a cup of coffee?"

"Guess I need something to get the fog from my brain."

"How about some toast or eggs or . . ."

"Just coffee. Thanks."

"How did you get back to Wurtzville so early?"

"Tony had to go into work today, so we got off early. He drove us down and then went right back."

"Tina is O.K?"

"You know, don't you?"

"Yeah. Anna Maria told me last night."

"You probably knew before I did."

"When did she tell you?"

"About twenty minutes ago. Tony dropped us off at Tina's house. Her parents weren't home so she had a good cry and told me the news."

"How do you feel about it?"

"Lousy. The shit will hit the fan when her mother and father find out. She can't hide it much longer."

"I heard some positive news, Roz. Tina's aunt sounds understanding and Tina has a new job with a company that seems to care about its workers."

"Yeah. And what happens if I never come back from wherever the hell the army sends me?"

Flanigan shrugged his shoulders and raised his hands in wonder. "Maybe you should get married."

"I thought of that. A lot of guys are getting married before we ship out. You ask them why and they say 'insurance.' If you're killed, the government sends the widow a big check. It's supposed to compensate her for your not being there for the rest of her days."

"Well, take it from somebody that knows. I would prefer to have my father's name than my mother's. If you don't come back, at least your child will carry your name."

Rozer pushed his cup and saucer aside and rose. "I'm going over to Tina's and talk to her."

At seven o'clock that same evening, Tina Valenta and Charles Rozer were married in a quiet evening ceremony at St. Anthony's rectory. Anna Maria and Peter were at their side. Mrs. Machelli and Dante closed the restaurant for the night and hosted the young couple, their parents, and a few guests. Afterwards, Roz and Tina drove Peter and his mother home in Ellie's car. Ellie had given the newlyweds the use of her car for a week as a wedding gift. She knew they had planned the traditional honeymoon to Niagara Falls.

A few days later, a bishop of the diocese addressed the graduating seniors at St. Catherine's. He urged them to pray for guidance and mixed his blessings with the common tenor of the day — the need to defeat the forces of evil that threatened a free American society. After the ceremony, Anna Maria and Ellie walked with Peter to the train station. He took only a small satchel with light clothing and toiletries. Ellie and Anna Maria joked about him going off to be a farm boy. He gave them the address he would be at and told them not to reveal it to anyone and to write him only after they heard from him.

When he arrived in Easton about four hours later, he hitched a ride to the farm, about three miles from town. The driver pointed to some high ground with a scattering of shacks and small house. "That's the Catholic Worker farm. The steep dirt road should take you up there."

Flanigan climbed the rutted road and heard a voice call out, "Did you lose your horses, young fellow?"

Off to the left stood an old man with baggy pants. Plaid suspenders rode over his bony shoulders and long-john shirt. He was leaning against a broken down buckboard, one large wheel on its side was partly buried in the turf, the three others tilted and rusted. Behind the man was a shack of rough-hewn lumber aged to a pale gray. An open door exposed a rumpled bed and large tin cans on the shack floor.

"I'm looking for Peter Maurin."

"You'll be looking long and hard."

"He's not around?"

"Nope."

"Do you know when he'll be around?"

"Can't say I do. Never know about Peter and Dorothy. Here one day, gone the next."

"Well, I talked to Peter and Dorothy in New York City and they told me that I could come to Maryfarm and stay."

"Just stay. No work?"

"Oh, no. I plan to work for my keep."

"If you do, you'll be a rare beast," said the old man. "Aren't many around here that do enough work to pay for their cornmeal. Lazy bastards. Where you from, young fellow?"

"My name is Peter Flanigan. I'm from the coal country."

"Where in the coal country?"

"Oh, up near Scranton."

"What are you, a jail bird or something? Don't want to tell where yer from?"

Flanigan knew he had bumped into a farm character of sorts. He laughed at the old man's suggestion. "No. Not yet anyway. Who knows? I might be some day."

The old man didn't introduce himself but pointed Flanigan in the direction of the communal dining hall. "Supper is over but tell them Peter is expecting you and they'll give you a bite to eat."

A cleanup crew was busy in the dining hall. A young, seemingly shy woman approached Peter.

"Are you looking for someone?"

"Yes. Peter Maurin or Dorothy Day."

"Neither of them is here now. Peter won't be back until next week and Dorothy won't be here until mid-June. Peter is in New York and Dorothy is out west visiting Catholic Worker Houses. Is there something I can help you with?"

"Yes. My name is Flanigan and I was invited to come here by Dorothy and Peter. They said that I would have work to do and that I could stay here. I talked to them at the Catholic Worker on Mott Street last March."

"Welcome," said the pretty young woman, extending her hand. "I'm Tamar Day, Dorothy's daughter. Would you like something to eat?"

Tamar called over to a young man to fill a supper plate. When he delivered it to the table, Tamar introduced him as David Hennessy. Flanigan ate his supper as Tamar and David told him about Maryfarm.

"This is really Peter Maurin's farm, his idea, his philosophy, his hope for the world, I guess you could say," commented Tamar.

"Yeah. Hope. So far, hope doesn't make a revolution," said David.

"What David is saying, Peter, is that Maryfarm has had its problems."

"Like?"

"Like people who come here saying that they're committed and want to be part of communal living, and believe in sharing, tilling the earth, tending to animals and stuff like that. They get here and then spend most of their time complaining and goofing off."

"Can't you tell them to work or leave?"

"I probably could. David probably could, even my mother. But not Peter. Peter thinks that people have to be self-motivated. He doesn't like to boss people around. Yet, many of the people who come here are escaping the industrial world where bosses give orders, where everyone is told what to do, when to do it, how to do it. In fact, people want to be told. It's almost like little kids who want to be told what to do, to be disciplined and ordered around. Peter Maurin just can't get himself to be that kind of person. The result is that little gets done, we end up with less food for sale, and less for our own consumption. But we seem to have a lot of disgruntled people who suffer from a lack of direction."

"What we need here at Maryfarm is a team of psychologists and psychiatrists. Some people act kind of wacky on the farm," said David.

"Oh, I don't know about that, David," Tamar objected. "Peter Maurin is a firm believer in love — love as in charity, reaching out and helping people. He believes that justice flows out of love. Yet," Tamar added, "there are folks here at Maryfarm who place charity behind justice and make their own justice. In other words, act to suit themselves, to make sure that they get a fair deal. That's their concept of justice. It becomes a selfish motivation and destroys any hope for charity."

Flanigan took his plate and put it in the dish sink, washed his tableware, and found the cupboard for the dishes and the tray for the utensils.

"Looks like you have good work habits, Flanigan. We like to observe how newcomers act after they get a free meal. So many will just push their plate aside and walk away. When that occurs, we don't need a scientific experiment to suspect that we have another freeloader on board." said David.

"I'm not here to freeload. I'm here to work. What do you have going for me tomorrow?"

Tamar pointed out to the dusky hillside. "Lots out there, Flanigan. It's planting time and David can guide you on that one."

"Sure can, Flanigan. Have you ever hitched a team of horses?"

"No."

"I'll show you how in the morning. Let's get you a place to stay for now. When Peter Maurin comes back, he can arrange a more permanent place for you. Since you're eating here we'll need you to help out in the kitchen."

"What time?"

"I'll call you about 6 A.M."

Hennessey took Flanigan to a clapboard bungalow with a single bunk, a pot-bellied stove, a water heater, a small table with a kerosene lantern and two chairs. On the table were several copies of the *Catholic Worker* and a worn and weathered copy of the *New Testament*. Next to the water heater was a large metal tub, a sink, and faucet, a mirror and two water glasses.

"The outhouse is right around the back. There's extra toilet paper in that old Prince Albert tobacco can on the shelf. Be sure to keep it in the can or the mice will eat the paper," warned Hennessey.

Hennessey lit the kerosene lantern. It cast bright light around the table area, then fell off and left the rest of the cabin in an evening shade. When David Hennessey left, Flanigan turned down the lamp to a dim flicker, got into bed, pulled the two wool blankets over his shoulders and fell asleep quickly.

Hennessey didn't have to wake him in the morning. His cabin, high above the meandering Delaware River, took a direct hit from dawn's early light. He made a trip to the outhouse, drew a sink full of water and washed. He smiled as he thought of what his mother would say if she saw him. "That's a bum's bath, Peter. Why don't you draw water for a bath? We have hot running water — this isn't skid row, Peter."

Flanigan had already touched the heater and knew that it was not on. He saw that the boiler was attached to the wood stove and since it was not lit, he knew he would have to have pull on the razor to get a clean shave with cold water. By the time he finished, he had several tiny pieces of toilet paper stuck to his face to stop the bleeding. He looked at his nose. Dr. Martin had given it a crunching turn with his bare hands. Flanigan thought he would pass out. But the soreness subsided, and after a few days, he took off the wide band of tape that straddled his nose. It was almost back in its original shape. "Almost back," he thought, but he knew that he would never forget Roz as long as he had to look in the mirror each morning.

He went outside and inhaled deeply. No coal dust. Just refreshing air. Down along the Delaware, fog rose from the water and wafted through the valley. He walked the ridge behind the cottage and saw unfamiliar birds. Blue bird boxes were scattered along the edge of a meadow, each box only about five feet above the ground. The birds exited and entered their little houses so often that Peter assumed they were feeding chicks. They didn't seem to compete with the brilliant gold finches that swooped around in an undulating flight, quickly losing themselves in the thorn apple thicket on the side hill.

On his return to the cottage, he saw David Hennessey. The two young men walked to the dining hall and Hennessey showed Peter how to prepare oatmeal for forty people, how to precook scrambled eggs and keep them warm, and how to slice bread taken out of the oven only an hour before.

His chores finished, Flanigan joined Tamar and David for breakfast and discussed the work of the day. David seemed eager to have someone who seemed not only to want to work, but to learn and do a good job. Tamar and David told Peter about Clydesdale horses, bred by Scots to be beasts of burden and now used by Maryfarmers to pull the plows.

"We've got to plow that side hill, Flanigan. We'll draw our furrows in horizontal lines so that we don't lose a lot of soil and seed when heavy rains fall. If we plow vertical furrows, we create little run off ditches that erode the soil. The horses don't mind horizontal runs. They expend less energy walking across rather that up and down the fields.

"The soil is not the best here. That's all the more reason for stopping erosion. Over thousands of years, the good top soil has been drained into the valley below and washed down river. We'll need to fertilize the land well before we plow. That's what we'll do this morning. After lunch, we can start to make furrows."

Tamar took Flanigan back to the kitchen. "Notice that we collect all of our vegetable matter in one separate can. Help me carry it to the bin out back.

"Now look down into that bin, Flanigan. Note the rotting fruit and vegetable material. David has added some leaves, grass, bits and pieces of shrubs, coffee grounds, paper, worms, and manure to it. We'll turn this mess a couple of times a week. Now that the days are warm, we should have rich soil in just four to six weeks.

"The large piles over there are a result of almost a year of composting. That's what you and David will be using to enrich the fields for planting. We could buy fertilizer down at the Grange League Feed Store but it's too expensive. Besides, Peter Maurin's philosophy is to try to avoid using money. We do our best and think that compost is better than just manure. Manure sometimes burns the plants. Most of the Grange fertilizer is now manufactured, chemical stuff that we wouldn't use anyway. Why not give back to the earth what it's given us?

"You can start shoveling our fertilizer into that spreader parked next to the pile. David should be out shortly."

Flanigan had the two-wheeler metal bin almost filled with compost when David appeared. "Let's go to the barn and hitch up Bobby and Bertha."

Two very large horses acknowledged the young men with double whinnies. The larger of the two horses danced around in the stall, the other horse stared at the newcomer, Flanigan.

"Be sure to call them by their proper names. The fellow on the left is Bobby. He's bigger and notice the markings that distinguish one horse from the other, such as the narrow white strip on Bobby's head versus the absence of marking on Bertha's head. From the side or back of the horse, you can tell them apart by the color of the feathered hair that hangs on each leg. Talk in a calm voice. Don't holler at them. Treat them with gentleness and friendship and they'll pay you in work well done. Bobby and Bertha had their feed early this morning so they're ready to go to work."

Hennessey calmly brushed the horses down, talking to them constantly. He told them that they were good, that they would be working all day and that he would stop frequently and take them to water. He continued to chat with them in mellow tones, smiled at them, and gave them periodic love slaps. Then, put the leather harness straps over them, tightened the buckles, led the team out of the barn, and hitched them to the spreader.

Flanigan got on the spreader seat and held the reins to Bertha while Hennessey stood by and held the reins for Bobby. Following Hennessey's directions and watching his style, Flanigan had fun learning to call out instructions to the horses pulling the spreader and scattering the compost over the fields.

After lunch, the two young men hitched the Clydesdales to the plow and began to carve furrows along the fertilized patch treated in the morning work. Tamar plotted out the areas to be planted to specific crops and marked each section with signs labeled bush beans, pole beans, corn, chard. Oats, wheat, and barley had already been planted before Flanigan's arrival and Tamar showed him the green shoots of grain beginning to color the west side of the hill.

"We bake all of our breads. Many of the people who come here have a problem getting used to whole grain, home made bread. Peter Maurin says that they don't know good bread because they're used to 'punk,' his word for the bleached grocery store stuff."

"How do you preserve the vegetables when they all come ripe?"

"Take a look at the cellar below the kitchen and you'll see that we still have a lot of vegetables left from last year. Our canned fruit usually runs out by spring. I don't think you'll find anything but applesauce down there now."

                                    ***

Flanigan visited town once each week to mail letters to Anna Maria and Ellie. Ellie warned Peter about using his name freely, so Flanigan wrote in "Thomas Shaw" as his post office box name. No one asked for identification. A simple turn of the key was all that was necessary to get the letters from home.

Anna Maria's letters told about the early summer crowds in the restaurant, about Tina, and fishing with her father, and visiting friends around town. She had registered at Ellenwood for the fall semester. Her mother or father would drive her to the train station in Wurtzville and then pick her up each evening. Commuting would be difficult and she would miss a lot of campus life, she said, but "with our favorite waiter missing from the job, guess I'll have to fill in until he comes home."

Ellie wished Peter a happy birthday and enclosed a package of raisin oatmeal cookies she and Anna Maria had made. They wrapped the cookies in several sheets of brown paper bags. Anna Maria had written a message on the top of the last wrap he unfolded. It said, "Please Note. You do not have to register to eat the enclosed contents."

It was the first day of June, 1942.

Chapter 18
The Absolutist

Bill Mahoney, Wurtzville's keen observer of the insatiable national appetite for materials of war, was working overtime in 1942, not as mayor but as entrepreneur. His plan to hoard materials became an active scheme. Each evening in the summer of '42, hundreds of new and used tires were unloaded by his crew and stored in the Coalbrook mine shafts. Gasoline, not yet rationed, proved even easier for Mahoney to obtain on credit — that is, if credit ran through a reputable source. By the end of August, the Caufield financial connection made it possible for the former water tanks to be filled to the brim with gasoline. Mark Chaddock agreed on a five cent per gallon storage fee to be paid once the fuel was sold.

Mahoney didn't want Sally to run the gas and rubber business. That job was earmarked for Peter Flanigan. Mahoney was sure that Peter would come around and take the lucrative offer awaiting him but when he telephoned Peter it was Ellie who answered.

"Hello, Ellie. I suppose Peter told you about the business offer I gave him."

"Yes. He did mention it."

"Well, let me talk to him, please. I'd like to get him started on the job."

"Peter isn't at home, Bill. I don't know when he expects to be back."

"You mean he's gone for the day?"

"No. I mean that he is gone away for an indefinite time period."

"Ellie, please give me a straight answer. I'm eager to try to make up for the damn poor job I did with Peter. I know money won't heal neglect but I want to do something positive, late as it may seem."

"I'm afraid it's too late for that, Bill. Peter may not be back for years."

"Where did he go?"

"I'm not able to tell you that."

"Why?"

"Just believe me. He's O.K., but he doesn't want anyone to know where he is."

"Ellie, Peter and I talked about his draft status some months ago. If his absence has anything to do with that, then he should contact me. I can arrange for his name to be removed from the rolls. He could then work for me, help his country, and make a very large amount of money."

"I can't help you. Sorry. Please don't ask again."

Ellie hung up first.

Mayor Bill Mahoney had no choice but to go to his common-law wife, his confidante, his trusted lover, his bankroll, Sally Caufield. Sally had the office in control in a matter of days and was efficiently drafting rubber and gasoline sale ads for publication in industrial journals starting in January of 1943.

Flanigan was far removed from these get-rich plans. He was part of a small core of laborers pulling the major portion of the work load at Maryfarm. But he loved the toughness of it and enjoyed the intellectual stimulation provided by his polemical fellow workers.

Peter Maurin was around for mental exercises. Known for his directness, the former French peasant was a delight to Peter.

"You ask about Communism, Capitalism and Fascism, Mr. Flanigan? Well, keep in mind that the three are in a chain. Imperceptibly, one passes into the other. All three are fundamentally materialistic, secularistic, and totalitarian."

Flanigan said he didn't know what 'ism' fit Maryfarm but that he did notice that a lot of men and women weren't pulling their share of the work load.

"Mr. Flanigan, the *Catholic Worker* believes in the establishment of farming communities where each one works according to one's ability and gets according to one's needs."

"Isn't that what Karl Marx preached?" asked Flanigan.

"Yes," said Maurin.

"Then the *Catholic Worker* is communistic?"

"The syllogism doesn't work, Mr. Flanigan. Communism was around long before Karl Marx. Read your New Testament, Mr. Flanigan. Christianity is love, justice and sharing. That is what we're about here."

Flanigan spent hours each week listening and questioning Peter Maurin but it wasn't until mid August that Dorothy Day made it to the farm. She remembered Flanigan from their Mott St. discussion and was quick to ask "So tell me, Flanigan, did you give up your absolutist position yet?"

"My what?"

"You said you weren't going to register for the draft. That's an absolutist position. Quite different from a conscientious objector, one who cooperates with the government."

"Then I guess I'm an absolutist."

"Fine, but have you considered the ramifications? Catholics have traditionally had a difficult time just getting registered as conscientious objectors because our Church as an institution doesn't oppose war. Most of our Catholic C.O.s are in United States government camps and

I've helped them organize into a group called the Association of Catholic Conscientious Objectors. Our camp in New Hampshire is operated by men from our Catholic Worker Houses throughout the country. It may not be too late for you to register as a C.O., if you know what to say to draft board interrogators. Steve Bednarsky, our C.O. expert, and I can advise you on all this. You'd be with people who are Catholic and that would be a form of solidarity. Things have changed on that score. Until recently, only the traditional peace churches were recognized by the United States Government. If you were other than a Mennonite, Friend or Brethren, then you had no excuse to not kill for the government. So you do have an opportunity to object, and I believe going up to New Hampshire camp would be the best thing for you. As much as I'm thrilled with your absolutist position, I think you're a bit young for prison."

"Dorothy, I respect what you're saying. Yet, when you first met me you noted my maturity. Most people do. I can handle myself, mind, body and soul. I don't plan on making myself available for government work and avoiding arrest is the best way that I can do that. I want to stay off the federal government payroll. I'm not one of their hired killers."

"Did you ever read Edna St. Vincent Millay, Peter?"

"Not that I recall."

"Well, as I sit here listening to you I'm reminded of Millay's comment: 'I shall die but that is all I shall do for death. I am not on his payroll.'"

Flanigan smiled. "I like that. Maybe I'll make it one of my prayers."

"Peter, do you have a *New Testament?*"

"At home. It's the old and new in one book."

Dorothy turned over her left hand and revealed a small book that covered her palm. She handed it to Flanigan.

"We're New Testament people, Flanigan. Keep this for nourishment."

Turning to burly Steve Bednarsky, Dorothy said: "Steve, tell Peter Flanigan what you've heard."

Bednarsky snuffed out his stogie, tapped it on the porch steps and stuck the cigar butt in his shirt pocket.

"Flanigan, something happened yesterday when you and Hennessey took grain to town for milling. We had some visitors. Two FBI agents came here only an hour or so after you left. They were asking questions."

"About me?"

"They asked Peter Maurin and me if we knew anyone named Peter Flanigan. They showed us a picture of you with a graduation cap and gown."

"So, what did you tell them?"

"We told them we didn't know the name and didn't recognize the fellow in the cap and gown."

"Weren't you afraid that lying would put you in jail?"

Bednarsky put on a half smile and said, "I used mental reservations, Peter. When I studied Natural Law in college, I paid particular attention to occasional need to conceal the truth. Mental reservations can be especially useful when a subject's safety and welfare is in jeopardy. In this case, that subject was you. But I have to ask you something. Have you ever been to jail?"

"No. But I've talked to someone who was."

"Well, you're talking to one again. My history of incarceration runs back to the Great War. My confinement has always been because of my actions fighting power, not people. From what you say, we have a lot in common.

"Flanigan, if the FBI is on your trail, you probably have little time left on the outside. I suggest you get yourself prepared for arrest. Do you mind if I give you a few pointers?"

"Go ahead."

"Flanigan, loss of freedom is going to be your greatest enemy when you're taken into custody. I heard you say that you don't have a father. Do you have a mother?"

"Yes."

"Girlfriend?"

"Yes."

"Good. Just those two people can help you. But you've got to depend on more than just them. Something could happen to them. Or your girlfriend might find another guy. You'll come into contact with people who seem mighty strange. The fact is, some will be. Quite likely, you'll be rubbing elbows with killers, robbers, thieves, aggressive homosexuals and people abusers of various kinds. You've got to be very careful. Find reliable prison mates. Get to know people like yourself. The New Testament will help but you've got to help yourself."

Dorothy quickly added to Bednarsky's advice, "Peter, I don't agree totally with Steve. He's right that you may soon be arrested but only if you stay here. My suggestion is for you to leave here. Go to our Catholic Worker in Chicago and if things get heated up there we can make arrangements for you to head for one of our farms in California. You can go down to Philadelphia, get a train to Chicago and someone will meet you at the station and set you up in town. What do you think of that plan, Flanigan?"

"I've got to think more about it, Dorothy. Can I come back and talk to you late tomorrow?"

"I'm not going into the city for a few days. I'll be here."

Flanigan knew what he had to do. He went back to his cabin, counted the money he kept in his shoe box and stuffed it into his pocket. He left a note on his table that read, "Expect to return late tomorrow."

He walked down the steep dirt road to hardtop, hitched a ride to Easton, and an hour later was on a train. He had called Anna Maria from the platform of the Jersey Central Train Station in Easton and arranged to have her meet him in Wilkes-Barre at 7 P.M. The hour long ride back to Wurtzville in Anna Maria's truck didn't have a silent minute. Anna Maria was bursting with the latest news and most of it was about Tina and the baby that was due in another week.

"Peter, you won't believe Tina when you see her. Remember how she hid her pregnancy? Remember how skinny she was? Wait until you see her! She's huge! I just hope it isn't twins. God, that would be too much. But she's so happy, Peter. You can't believe what a change has come over her. She can't wait for the baby to be born. She's so sure that it's a boy that she speaks of the baby as Charlie. I hope she doesn't have to change that to Charlene or Charlotte. "

"Why is she in Wurtzville? Didn't she plan to have the baby in Endicott and get all that good stuff from Endicott-Johnson? You know, medical care and other things?"

"Oh sure. She's going back tomorrow. We had a baby shower at your mother's house in Wurtzville this afternoon. Tomorrow, I'm driving her to her aunt's house in Endicott. When you called, we were just going down to your mother's. We can stop there now and pick up Tina and you can see your mom. After we drop her off at my house you and I can have some time to ourselves. How about that?"

"Time is what I came home for, Anna Maria. I have so little to spare."

When Anna Maria and Flanigan arrived, he wolfed down chicken and biscuits and was anxious to get out the door with Anna Maria and Tina. Ellie waited until they were on the porch landing when she said: "Peter, a number of people have been asking about you but just last Wednesday, a man came to the door, introduced himself and showed me his FBI badge. He wants to talk to you and wonders why you haven't registered for the draft."

"I'm not surprised, Mom. I do wonder how they got on my case but as they say — that's their job. I'll tell you my plans when I come home later tonight. Would you drive me to Wilkes-Barre early tomorrow morning? I'm going right back to the farm at Easton and then on to the Midwest. I'll tell you more about it later."

Flanigan had Anna Maria get in first and then helped Tina onto the running board and helped her as she shimmied herself into the truck. As dark as it was on this moonless night, Flanigan knew every twist and turn of the road to Anna Maria's. On the top of the second ridge, he saw a light approaching from a dirt road on the right. Not unusual, he thought, just the short cut road over to Fall Township, an old coal mining village with two beer joints on every block.

As he passed the road, a vehicle to his right came out of the tree lined darkness and hit the truck on the right side of the cab with a thunderous smash. Flanigan grit his teeth as he struggled to keep the truck from spinning around but the sheer force of the crash neutralized the attempt to straighten the wheels. Two complete turns forced the truck to the ditch on the opposite side of the road and the truck flipped wheels up.

"Anna Maria. Are you O.K?"

"I don't know. I'm bleeding a lot. But where's Tina? Oh my God. Where is Tina?"

The young couple crawled out the passenger side door that had swung open and scrambled back to the site of the impact. Two young men in navy uniforms were wandering around and one hollered, "Hey you. Over here! A woman is lying on the road."

Anna Maria got to Tina first and noticed she was unconscious.

Flanigan waved down an approaching car and with assistance from the two sailors, lifted Tina into the back seat of the car. At the hospital emergency room, nurses and assistants took Tina to the delivery room. Peter and Anna Maria were treated by nurses who tended to their wounds caused mostly by broken glass. Afterwards, the young couple sat, exchanging hand squeezes; silence broken only by muffled sobs of Anna Maria. After a time, Flanigan, his head bowed, began to question his part in the accident.

"This wouldn't have happened if I just stayed where I was supposed to be. Why the hell did I have to leave Easton and put Tina and you through all this? The old caretaker at Easton once told me I had 'shit for brains.' I laughed then but I'm not laughing now. I've got shit for brains. Why in God's name did I ever think that I had to come home to see you?"

Anna Maria stopped crying, wiped away the tears and confronted Peter with anger.

"What do you mean, why did you have to come home to see me? Are you serious, Peter? I thought we had an understanding! Do you mean that something has changed? I wasn't worth coming home to?"

"No. No. No. I didn't mean that, Anna Maria. What I'm saying is that this would not have happened if I hadn't come home. I set up the circumstances. My timing, my involvement, made this happen. And I'm the guy that says that he doesn't want to do harm to anyone. Bullshit. Tina might not live and I'm the one responsible."

"Peter, you saw and smelled those two guys that hit us. They couldn't walk a straight line and it wasn't because of any injury. Their speech was a drunken slur and the booze smell was overpowering. Stop taking blame. We were hit by two drunken sailors. Period!"

"Are you relatives of Mrs. Rozer?"

The intern on duty stood over Anna Maria and Peter.

"No. We're best friends. The receptionist called her mother. Her husband is in the army," replied Anna Maria.

"Well. Perhaps you can cushion her mother's shock when she comes in. Tina just passed away. She must have received very severe brain trauma when she was thrown out of the vehicle and onto the hardtop road. We were unable to revive her. Her water probably broke on impact. We were able to remove the baby with no apparent harm. He seems healthy."

Tina's mother, Mrs. Valenta, was consoled by Anna Maria when she got to the hospital. Mrs. Valenta was not able to control her emotions and Anna Maria and Peter took her home in a taxi. Tina's father was working the night shift at the colliery but Mrs. Valenta told how they both would be in agreement on one thing. They simply could not support another child. Tina was the oldest, but there were six other children.

"My husband has to drag himself to work each night. I feel so sorry for him, poor man. Two miles of agonizing walk to work with a deep leg wound that has refused to heal for years. It's torture for him but he says: 'How can I not work? I won't take welfare. I have to work.'

"With so many little ones at home I know how he feels. But he just can't go on in such pain. I don't know what's going to happen. I just know that we can't take another little baby into this house."

Without a pause, Anna Maria said, "I'll take the baby, Mrs. Valenta. My mother told Tina earlier today that when Tina needed help she was to come to our house. We have a big house, two women, and my father would love to have a boy at home. I'm an only child — the boy my father never had. Let us take the baby. When Roz comes home, he can take little Charlie."

Mrs. Valenta took Anna Maria to her bosom and shook with sorrow and joy. Tears flowed down and around her wide smile as she gently pushed Anna Maria away but held her arms tightly as she looked into Anna Maria's eyes. "You and my Tina were so close. I can think of no better solution. God bless you, Anna Maria."

Chapter 19
Proud To Be An American?

The following week, little Charlie was snug in his crib at Laurel Lake, tended to, loved, and cared for by Anna Maria, her mother, and father. Flanigan was snuggled away as well, but not with tender, loving care. He was sitting in an eight by eight foot cell in the West Street jail in Manhattan, awaiting transfer to Danbury Federal Prison in Connecticut.

He had taken an early morning train from Wilkes-Barre to Easton and the two-hour ride seemed like minutes. He was in a trance. The motion of the train rocked his thoughts and made the countryside a blur. Tina. The baby. Anna Maria. His mother. Maryfarm. Chicago Catholic Worker House. Freedom. Prison.

Anna Maria said that she had sent a long letter that he should read when he got to his post office box in Easton. He was sure that it was not negative. At least, Anna Maria didn't seem negative when she'd met him at the train station in Wilkes-Barre. But they had shared so little time in private — just the ride home to Wurtzville. What was in the letter?

He walked from the Easton train station to the post office, went to his mail box and turned his key. Nothing happened. He tried several times and the key turned but the box would not open. He walked over to the post office clerk and asked the man to fetch the mail for Thomas Shaw.

"Be glad to, Mr. Shaw," he said.

Flanigan noticed a red light going on and off behind the barred desk. Another man from the inner office came to the counter and said, "Mr. Shaw, please wait right here. Mr. Johnson is collecting your mail."

Flanigan saw the man go into his office and pick up the phone. The clerk who was to get his mail was not returning and the mail box was only a few feet away.

"It's time to get out of here," Flanigan thought.

He turned with quickened tempo of mind and feet. He didn't know where he was going, but he felt he had to distance himself. Flanigan was only two blocks away from the post office when a Easton police car pulled along side of him, two cops got out and stopped him.

"Are you Peter Flanigan?"

"Yes."

"Mr. Flanigan, by order of the Federal Bureau of Investigation, we place you under arrest. Please get into the back of the car."

Flanigan was brought before the Easton Municipal Justice that afternoon. The job of the judge was to use powers delegated to him by the federal government to charge Peter with draft evasion; hear his plea; and make a decision. It was a very hurried process. Peter was allowed to tell why he refused to register. The judge politely listened to Peter's reasoned argument.

Then, the judge lectured him on patriotism and told him that Catholic Church is in full agreement with the United States declaration of war and that Catholic men around the country have been accepting conscription. "Who will fight the enemy if our young men do not stand up against fascism? Do you want women and children to go to war, Mr. Flanigan? Who will save this country, Mr. Flanigan? Old men and the infirm? It is not too late for you to change your mind, young man. I'm willing to put you in the Easton lockup, let you come to a sane, reasonable decision and volunteer for military service. I don't want to send a young man like you to prison. The FBI can be persuaded to allow you to change your mind."

"Thank you, your honor," said Flanigan. "I made up my mind long ago, sir. I'm afraid I can't take your generous offer."

The bitterness of the judge came quickly to life as he slammed his gavel to a near breaking point. "I hereby sentence you to Danbury Federal Prison until such time as the United States Federal Government decides your fate based on events beyond my deputized authority. Agents from the New York office who have worked with Postal Officials on your case will be here in the morning to transport you to the West Street jail where you will await transfer to Danbury. You may make a statement or request, Mr. Flanigan."

"Thank you, your honor. I have two requests. First, may I have my mail that was supposed to be available to me at my post office box here in Easton? And secondly, would you please allow me to help with the potato harvest at the Catholic Worker farm? We only need a day to harvest."

The judge chuckled. "Mr. Flanigan, do you understand the severity of your offense? Mr. Your mail is already in the hands of the Federal Bureau of Investigation. And pick potatoes?" The judge leaned back and had another good laugh. "You won't be picking potatoes this time tomorrow, my boy. Not even potato bugs. Maybe cockroaches and maggots in your New York City cell. Harvest potatoes!"

The judge stood, his big black robe falling loosely from his shoulders, he pulled up a cuff of one sleeve and stuck his head into it and emitted a false sounding chuckle. Then he looked at Peter.

"Get it, son? It's called ridicule. I'm laughing up my sleeve at you. Have a nice time following your precious conscience, while young men, like my son, are fighting with the 1st Marine Division to regain

Guadalcanal. When you walk safely out of prison in years to come, ask your holy conscience if you should still be proud to be an American."

Two jail deputies took Flanigan by the arms and led him downstairs to the city jail. It would be just an overnight stay. FBI agents arrived at nine o'clock the next morning and Flanigan was in the West Street jail by noon.

Peter was glad to hear that he would get a change of clothing. He'd been wearing the same underwear and outerwear for several days.

"Strip down to buck naked, Mr. Flanigan," ordered the uniformed guard, as he handed Peter a faded blue shirt and used jeans.

"What about underwear?" asked Flanigan.

"No underwear and no socks, young fellow. Your feet and farts will weld into one great cell odor. Enjoy," he said as he slammed the barred door and turned the key.

Flanigan was searched by police in Easton and they confiscated two small books that he kept in his pocket — the New Testament given to him by Dorothy Day and the Spiritual Exercises of Saint Ignatius. Peter asked an FBI agent if he could keep the two. Agent Malone flipped through the pages and, handing the volumes back to Flanigan, said, "I'll see to it that these stay in your possession."

Taking an inventory, Peter decided he had just six possessions to guard: two books, pants, shirt, sneaks, and his body.

He was too late for the noon meal at the West Street jail but he wasn't thinking about food. When he'd signed in, the desk sergeant told him that he might have to wait for a couple of weeks before going to Danbury Prison. The prison was full and when a vacancy occurred, he would be sent there with at least two or more "absolutists" now housed in the Manhattan jail.

He was led to a small room where he was fingerprinted, weighed, examined by a physician and photographed. The medical doctor told him that when he got to Danbury he would have to go through the same procedure plus "quarantine".

Now, as he sat on his bunk, he surveyed the cell. A cot with straw mattress, a toilet (without seat) and a sink without soap or towel. A shabby blanket covered his cot and he wondered how it would be getting used to sleeping without a pillow when he heard a voice from the next cell.

"Settled in yet, fellow?"

Flanigan leaned against the bars and looked to the right. He couldn't see the person but a hand was extended toward Flanigan. Peter reached out and firmly shook the dark hand of his jailed neighbor.

"Welcome to West Street. My name is Randolph Jackson."

"Flanigan here. Peter Flanigan."

"What are you in here for, Flanigan?"

"I refuse to register for the draft. Guess you can say I'm a federal criminal."

The hand extended to Peter once again, and the voice behind it said, "Shake again, partner. We're probably the only two villains in this whole cell block charged with the same dirty deed."

Flanigan again bonded with his neighbor, and asked what most other people in the block were charged with.

"Oh, we have some very famous people here, Flanigan. See that character sleeping across the way from you — that's Louis Lepke, he's proud of his moniker. He's known as the boss man of Murder, Inc. Want a bank robbed? Just ask Louie. Want some one rubbed out? Just ask Louie. Louie and I are both headed for Danbury Prison. Knowing how this democratic system works, I'll probably end up being a cell mate of Louis Lepke — the Murder King of America. He just can't believe that I'm am in jail for refusing to kill. He thinks I'm hiding the truth from him.

"I'll wake him up and introduce him to you. Hey Louie. Hey Louie."

"What the fuck do you want, ya fucking meathead?"

"Wake up, Louie, and meet your new neighbor."

"Fuck the neighbor. Let me sleep, meathead."

"But Louie, this guy is in jail for the same reason I'm in jail."

Lepke rose from his cot and walked over to his cell door.

"Yer shittin' me, Randolph."

Looking at Flanigan, Lepke said, "Tell me the truth, kid. What are yez in here fer?"

"For refusing to go to war or be part of war system," replied Flanigan.

"Holy shit! Another one? You mean they put youse in here fer not killing?"

"Yup. Guess you could say that."

"Jeez, I can't believe dis. Dis fucking government is nuts. You nice boys that don't want to hurt nobody and what do they do to ya. I suppose youse are going to Danbury too, huh kid?"

"That's what I'm told."

"Well, then stay close to old Louie — boata yez, ya hear? Nobodies goin' ta fuck wit yez when old Louie's around. And I mean da fucking prisoners, da fucking guards and da big fuck himself — the warden. They know enough not to fuck around wit Louie Lepke.

"Now if youse two kids want to talk, then do old Louie a favor — talk quietly." Giving a huge grin that exposed two gold teeth, Lepke added, "Or I'll have one of the turnkeys cut your nuts off."

Thoroughly amused with himself, Lepke lay back on his cot, his shoulders shaking with laughter as he mumbled to himself, "Dey send the fucking kids to jail fer *not* killing. Crazy bastards."

Flanigan and Jackson continued their conversation in muffled tones. Jackson was very curious about how Flanigan had come to accept an absolutist position. He was surprised that Flanigan did so without college exposure, and that he had come to terms with the decision at such an early age. Jackson told Peter that he was twenty-two years old, lived most of his life in Baltimore, Maryland, and finished college at Howard University. "You know about Howard, don't you?" he asked Flanigan.

"No. Never heard of it. If you're from Baltimore and Washington, then why did you end up in a New York City jail?"

"Well, did you ever hear of the March on Washington — July, 1941?"

"Oh, yeah. When the colored people were going to march on Washington to protest something but the march was called off?"

"Yes. But not just something. Quite a lot, Flanigan. Sounds like I'm going to have to give you a crash course in discrimination. In school, did you learn about Lincoln's Emancipation Proclamation?"

"Sure. The freeing of the slaves. 1863."

"Right. And you probably learned that this led to citizenship and equality for the black people of America?"

"I guess so. Black people can live anywhere and vote and get jobs and even go into the military if they want to — isn't that so?"

"Yes and no. Mostly no. Flanigan, have you ever lived near Negro people?"

"Yeah. There's a Negro man in my home town."

"*A* Negro man? What does that Negro man do for a living?"

"He has a shoe shine parlor. He actually does very well. He has a nice car, dresses well, and everybody likes him."

"Everybody?"

"Well. A lot of people refer to him as Huey the Nigger. But there is no real discrimination."

"So I'm one of the few black people you have ever talked to?"

"Correct."

"O.K. Flanigan. From the mouth of an authentic Negro, a guy whose great-grandfather was a slave, a guy who has never gone to a school — including college — with white students in the same room, I want to give you some background information.

"The Emancipation Proclamation and the so-called civil freedoms of black people that followed the Civil War have done very little for American Negroes. Let me tell you a little about myself and how I fit into the picture and why I'm here today, behind bars. Got time to listen?"

"Time? Sure. Especially when a sense of humor is involved."

"My first name is Randolph because my father's cousin is J. Philip Randolph, the nationally known Negro labor leader who called the March on Washington for July of last year. I'm still angry at him for calling off the march. I believe he was cajoled, pressured, threatened, hoodwinked and impelled to call off a march that would have made white America listen to our cry. Yet, as angry as I am at him, I understand. I have learned first hand about discrimination, retribution and power.

"J. Philip Randolph was simply asking the President and Congress to end discrimination and use this international crisis as the tool to bring justice to all Americans. Do you know, Peter Flanigan, if you and I were to leave this jail and go to my home town, you would be able to go into any hotel and get a room? To go into any restaurant and get a meal? To take a leak in any public bathroom? To drink from any public fountain?

"But me, Flanigan? Me, in my hometown? No question, I would be firmly told to leave immediately or the police would be called. I would be turned away in the center of American Democracy — Washington, DC. I know this to be true from personal experience, Peter. My father's cousin, J. Philip Randolph, knows it from personal experience also. What he was attempting to do with the Negro March on Washington, I know from rote memory. Do you want to hear a bit of it?"

"Sure. I'm here to learn, and besides, I'm doing 'time.' Shoot."

"Well, I won't give you the whole declaration. But here goes with a few of his lines that will make the point. He spoke these words in March of 1941:

> Let the Negro masses speak!
> Let the Negro masses speak with ten thousand

> Negroes strong, marching down Pennsylvania Avenue in
> the capital of the nation, singing "John Brown's
> Body Lies a Mouldering in the Grave" and "Before
> I'll Be a Slave, I'll Be Buried in My Grave
> Let the Negro masses, as workers, doctors,
> preachers, lawyers, teachers, nurses, women and
> children, march forward with heads erect, holding
> banners aloft, inscribed with slogans, preaching the
> gospel of justice, freedom and democracy, declaring
> their decisive demands for jobs in national defense,
> equal employment and vocational opportunities,
> together with equal privileges for integration in
> all departments of the armed forces.

"I could go on, Flanigan, but at least you know that the march didn't come off."

"I know it didn't occur, but I still don't know why your father's cousin caved in."

"You're right, he did cave in. He buckled under pressure from Roosevelt. F.D.R. said that if Randolph called off the March, and dropped his call for integration of the armed forces, then he, FDR, would issue an executive order creating a Fair Employment Practices Committee to ban racial discrimination in war industries."

"Did Roosevelt do that?"

"Yes. In fact, I understand that now many black people are being hired by federal war industries, but not in private industries."

Flanigan squeezed his face against the cell bars to try to see his new teacher. He was able to observe only the very animated hands of Randolph Jackson, as he gave his discourse on racial discrimination.

"I'm a bit confused by your anger at J. Philip Randolph. If Mr. Randolph wants colored people to be integrated into the armed forces and to get jobs at war plants, isn't that contrary to what you stand for as an anti-war advocate?"

"Oh, I'm not supporting the war industry or the armed forces. The claim of the United States government that this is a war for democracy and freedom is so much crap. I'm angry that he backed down knowing that FDR and the government, and the white population, will continue to support discrimination. Do you know, Peter, that recently fifteen sailors from a U.S. Navy ship, The Philadelphia, sent a letter to a Pittsburgh newspaper telling about on-board discrimination, and that three of the men who signed the letter were put in the brig? And the other twelve men? They were given dishonorable discharges!"

"Were they all colored?"

"Yes. We call ourselves Negroes or Blacks, Peter."

"What was the discrimination?"

"Oh, the usual. All men joined after being told they would have a chance to do jobs other than mess duty — washing dishes and waiting on officers. Yet, every one of them was assigned to the galley. White sailors are given a pay raise of $14 dollars immediately after boot training. Black sailors have to wait for one year after training before getting the $14 raise. But that was just one of the injustices raised in the letter. What angered Admiral Nimitz and the navy brass was the comment in the letter that young blacks should not join the navy. The letter said 'don't make the same mistake we did, don't be a sea-going bellhop, chambermaid, or dishwasher.'

"That's when I began to rethink my position on military service and any contribution to the war. The thought of killing anyone has always repulsed me. When I thought out the blatant hypocrisy of our government and its continued failure to extend basic civil rights and justice to Black people, I put the two together and they added up to 'no way'! No way, shall I support the killing machine. No way, shall I be part of the claim that this is a war to preserve freedom, justice, and equality. There are no blacks in the Marines. No Blacks in the Air Corps. No Blacks in the Coast Guard. No Blacks in the Tank Corps. In the Army, Negro soldiers are made to dig latrines or prepare for suicide squads.

"So much for fairness, for equality and justice. A war against totalitarianism? Hell, I can't even get a hamburger at a Woolworth's counter in Washington. Now how total is that kind of control over one's own citizens?

"I guess I still haven't answered your question — why am I up here in a New York City jail?

"Well, I was arrested by the FBI just yesterday as I made preparations for a major Black protest on the 16th of this month at Madison Square Garden. Back in Washington, I openly declared my refusal to cooperate and sign for the draft. The *Washington Post* reported it and I knew that once it became an issue, the FBI would be on my tail. I've been living up in Harlem for the past couple of weeks as we tighten up demonstration plans at the Garden. Our plan is pretty basic – we're calling for democracy for American Negroes. It is going to be a bash, Peter. Just wish I was more careful. I don't mind going to jail but I do mind missing the June 16, Madison Square action. It's going to be the biggest protest gathering in Black American history. I helped plan it and here I am."

"Maybe the FBI will let you out to attend," Flanigan quipped.

"Sure. And next week, all schools and public places will be integrated. Yep. Yep. Yep."

A sharp call came from the end of the cell block. "Stand up count. Stand up."

Two uniformed men with night sticks and clip boards walked slowly through the block. Flanigan stood along the barred door and watched the guards as they pencil-ticked off names after a prisoner response. Murphy. Miller. Randolph. Flanigan. Lepke.

"Lepke."

"Lepke."

"Where are you, Lepke?"

"I escaped, ya fucking asshole."

"You're supposed to stand at your door, Mr. Lepke. Stand up and be counted."

"Come over a little closer, turnkeys," said Lepke.

The guard moved to the bars and ordered Lepke to stand up.

"Come a little closer, Mr. Screw. I've been holding a nice present for youse since ya woke me up with yer fucking loud mouth. Count this!"

Lepke raised his rear end toward the guard and emitted a loud flatulence.

"Breath deep, Mr. Screws, der's enough fer everyone," giggled Lepke.

The guards, with a look of disgust and disdain, swiftly checked off Lepke's name, and went to the next cell block.

"Did you say Lepke might be your cell mate at Danbury?" whispered Flanigan.

"If it happens, it would be the supreme test of my non-violent Gandhian posture. But I was just joking. The system wouldn't disgrace Mr. Lepke by putting a Negro in his cell."

"Gandhian? Like the guy from India?"

"Right. The guy from India. Have you read Gandhi?"

"I've seen his picture in the paper. He's a skinny little guy in droopy white shorts. Usually carries a stick and hates the British."

"You mean to tell me Flanigan, that you are a non-violent advocate and you don't know Gandhian philosophy? Yeah, he's a skinny guy. He often carries a stick, and no, he doesn't hate anyone. Gandhi operates on a love principle. But he doesn't just write letters to the editor or give speeches, he rattles cages. Something that American Blacks have got to learn to do. Or at least the leadership — if we have any. I can't imagine Gandhi backing down to the British the way Philip Randolph compromised the Black opportunity to turn things around in this country."

"Was the Negro March on Washington an idea of Philip Randolph?"

"Sure. It was his baby and he dropped it."

"Maybe you're too hard on your father's cousin. From what you tell me, Randolph has been the point man taking all the fire. It is easy to criticize when you're sitting on the sidelines."

"Horseshit to you, Peter Flanigan. I've been risking my black ass for the past year to promote the voice of Negro America. How would you feel when you get this close," said Jackson as he shoved his hands toward Flanigan's cell and made his palms come close to contact. He held them tightly and Flanigan noticed the hands quivering.

"This fucking close, my man. This close. We had those high and mighty types in Washington running scared. Real scared and we dropped the ball. We dropped the ball."

"Let's talk about it some more when we can see each other eye to eye," said Flanigan. "I've learned a lot this afternoon. Can we talk at meal time?"

"No. Not really. You see Mr. Flanigan, there are separate eating quarters. Negroes eat together. Whites eat together. But we can have some time in the yard tomorrow during exercise time — eyeball to eyeball."

It was 5 P.M. and the order to line up for chow time rang through the cell block. Flanigan peeled off to the left by order of the guards and got a quick glimpse of Jackson as he joined several other Black prisoners being ushered into a separate dining room.

Chapter 20
Breaking Jim Crow

As Flanigan awaited transfer to Danbury Federal Prison, he met another absolutist, one who would join Flanigan and Jackson in a strong bond of prison friendship. Handsome Lake was a Native American, a tall, stern looking fellow with a round, pudgy face and narrow dark eyes. He quickly became the cement in the bond between Peter Flanigan and Randolph Jackson. Lake and Jackson were sentenced to two year prison terms for not registering, one year less than the sentence imposed on Flanigan by the angry Pennsylvania judge.

Flanigan was just beginning to think of Jackson as the older brother he'd never had when Handsome Lake introduced himself. Randolph Jackson had an immediate fascination with Lake. "I have to ask you, Lake," said Jackson, "don't most men feel uncomfortable calling you Handsome?"

"That's my name."

"Do you mind if I simply call you Lake?"

"Of course, I mind. Don't most people prefer to be addressed by their first name? You just told me your name is Randolph Jackson. I'll call you Randolph. That's your name. If you want to make things simple, as you say, why confuse names at the very start?"

Jackson grinned, then extended his hand to Handsome Lake and said: "Very glad to meet you, Handsome."

Lake, his shiny black hair pulled tightly into a braid that reached far down on his back had been arrested in Syracuse, New York and sentenced there by a judge who was familiar with Lake's native American background including the historical significance of his Iroquois name. Handsome Lake lived in a small Iroquois village called Nedrow, just a few miles away from Syracuse. The Onondagas, as the smallest of Iroquois nations, have always been respected for their political power, and since the time of Hiawatha have been "Keepers of the Fire." Iroquois representatives from the other nations — Mohawks, Cayugas, Senecas, Oneidas and Tuscaroras, continue to gather around the fire each year to discuss issues introduced by their "little brothers" — the Onondagas. During the American Revolution, most of Lake's ancestors fled from their burned houses and villages to escape the terrible path of destruction laid down by Generals Sullivan and Clinton. The Iroquois people blamed George Washington, whom they afterwards referred to as "Town Destroyer." Washington had ordered the search and destroy mission in the summer of 1779, and that initiative was the beginning of a 111 year genocidal war. Handsome Lake's direct ancestors were some of the first to suffer.

In the years following the destruction of their crops, their fruit trees chopped and the burning of their villages and food stocks, some Iroquois families made it back to their sacred grounds and tried to resettle. But loss of morale among the men set them up as victims of the white man's firewater. One Seneca, the original Handsome Lake, saw that he and his brothers were being destroyed more by alcohol than by white man's guns and smallpox. He broke his dependence on alcohol, had a series of visions, and began a campaign of temperance reform. This was largely religious and eventually became the basis of a creed based on Lake's teachings known as *The Code of Handsome Lake*.

Handsome Lake met with George Washington in 1802 and was well known by leading political leaders of the time. In 1842, Handsome Lake, aware of his nearness to death, walked a hundred miles to Onondaga and the Keepers of the Fire. Days later, he died, and was buried in the land of the "Little Brothers."

On November 11, 1918, when a Onondaga woman gave birth to a son in a house just yards away from the tomb of "Handsome Lake" she named him after the great reformer. It was Armistice Day, the end of the Great War; and the young mother pledged that her son would be dedicated to the teachings of *The Code of Handsome Lake*. She pledged to shelter him from white man's ways and white man's wars.

In the spring of 1942, Lake hid from the Syracuse police who'd been dispatched by the draft board to take him in to register. Other Onondaga families who had sons drafted into the military were unhappy with the draft-dodging of Handsome Lake. When the traditional Onondaga Strawberry Festival was held in early June, to celebrate the first fresh fruit of the season, the FBI was alerted and arrested Handsome Lake during the ceremony. By the morning of the 16th of June, Lake was in New York City, walking on the fenced-in jail roof that served as an exercise yard and, like his new found associates, wondering when the transfer to Danbury would take place.

Lake explained to Jackson and Flanigan why he was an absolutist and how *The Code of Handsome Lake* had molded his character and committed him to avoid being "whitemanized."

"You were put in jail because of the white man's culture?" asked Flanigan.

"Correct. Why should any Native American fight the white man's wars? They came to our land, infected our people with disease, raped our women, burned our villages and poisoned us so that we could no longer defend ourselves."

"Poisoned you?"

"Yes. Liquor is the poison of the white man. It destroyed what little was left of our dignity after we were humiliated by his brutality. Our men were so broken, so crushed by white man greed that we took his drug. We have been killing ourselves ever since. Our prophet, the first Handsome Lake, saved our culture from complete destruction when he was visited by angels of God who told him what to do. We do not want the material goods of the white man. Our life can be rich in faith. This world is temporary, our real world is above the sky. The devil will never buy us as long as we follow the Code of Handsome Lake. So you're in jail because you refuse to be a part of the white man's culture?"

"You know, Handsome, everything I'd known about Indians, I learned from text books and movies. This is great — jail house education," said Jackson.

Flanigan agreed. "Handsome, I'm the real winner here. Randolph has been directing me in a course on Negro history. He's the first Negro I've ever had a conversation with and now it's time for Iroquois history. I guess I've read more than Randolph about injustices toward Indian people but you're the first Indian I've ever talked to. You sound more like a college graduate than a paint and feather guy on horseback."

Lake smiled and said: "Let me be your Indian guide." Then quickly turning sober, he said: "I've sat in on anthropology classes at Syracuse University, free of charge at the invitation of a few professors. My people don't have the incentive to go to college. As for horseback, you must be thinking of Plains Indians, not of us. Paint and feathers? Our religion is a thing of the heart — paint and feathers are accidental aspects of our religion, like vestments on Catholic priests.

"Now it's your turn to educate me. I want to hear your reasons for being in here," said Lake. Flanigan and Jackson gave a quick synopsis of their absolutist position before the whistle blew to return to their cells.

"Let's meet here again tomorrow, I have more to ask and more to tell," said Jackson.

However, the trio would have to wait for another time. After evening meal, the three men were told to stand by their cell door at 6 P.M. to await transfer to Danbury Prison. Two Federal Marshals took the three prisoners in leg irons and handcuffs to a car outside the jail entrance. The '39 Packard had a metal cage separating the back seat from the front. The prisoners shuffled and wiggled their way into reasonably comfortable positions in the big car. As the Marshals pulled out of the jail, Jackson leaned forward and asked, "Do you mind driving by Madison Square Garden?"

"Of course, I mind. We're headed out to the East River and driving north to Connecticut. We're not going to a sports spectacle."

"Look, we're going to be doing time for years to come. Would you do us a small favor and just drive by the Garden?"

The Marshal sitting in the passenger seat waved his finger toward the Garden and said, "Give 'em a look, Will."

The driver turned near Grand Central Station and then swung the Packard onto 8th Avenue, where he became part of a gridlock of cars and buses extending to Madison Square Garden.

"Shit. Bad move. What the hell's going on?"

"I don't know," said the Marshal in the passenger seat, "but I've never seen this many colored people in one place before."

Randolph Jackson was beaming. Grasping his fingers on the security cage metal, he told the Marshals what was going on. "Gentlemen, you're looking at the largest Black American protest movement in American history. Right here, guys. Right here."

"What's the gripe? Colored folks never had it so good," commented the driver.

"That's your take, Mr. Marshall. My story is being written right there — right now. This could be the start of something really big for my people. We're all tired of hearing 'we never had it so good'. Those people out there want the lies, the deceit, the prejudice, and the outright injustices to stop. Those are American people out there, Mister

Marshal. And one more thing, my man, would you roll down the window so that I can call over to some of my brothers?"

"Horseshit. I don't care if your mama and papa are over there. Roll up the windows. We're getting the hell off this avenue."

By 10 P.M., the three men were in their cells in Danbury. If prison officials had known that the bond of friendship they'd developed, they would not have been housed in the same cellblock. As chance would have it, the three cells were within communication distance — creative communication. Cell doors had a small window that allowed tunnel vision into the opposite cell window and a three-quarter inch opening at the base of the door. Flanigan and Jackson were able to make eye contact. Lake was to the side of Jackson and all three men quickly learned they could talk to each other by lying on the concrete floor and calling through the narrow opening beneath the door.

Danbury Prison was not considered to be a hardship place. A fairly new facility in 1942, it was declared a correctional institution with a focus on rehabilitation. Shrubs and flowers surrounded the prison. No iron bars were visible from the outside. Westbrook Pegler, a journalist, wrote that same year that it was a "country club." In fact, it was that for some prisoners. One very rich filmmaker who was serving time for income tax evasion was treated like a houseguest by the guards. The warden actually had the man to his house outside of the prison walls on a number of dinner visits. The filmmaker's wife then invited the warden's wife to her house on Long Island as a weekend visit.

It was not a country club for most prisoners — especially people like Flanigan, Jackson and Lake. A war was on and guards and administrators had deep resentment for C.O.s. To many, C.O.s were cowards. The yellow cornmeal bread was known as C.O. Bread and after a time even the C.O.s knew it by that name. Yet, for all the resentment and negative treatment given to them, Danbury C.O.s were to set the tone for far-reaching civil rights actions in the United States.

Like all prisoners, the trio spent several weeks in quarantine. It was a time for medical examination, psychological exams, I.Q. tests, interviews with various prison officials and a lot of waiting in line. Flanigan and his friends were able to discuss every social, economic and political topic they could conceive of and were frequently joined by other C.O.s. One day, a fellow who introduced himself as Buzzard Bentley tapped Handsome Lake on the shoulder and began to question him about his C.O. position.

"I've been listening to you boys for the past several weeks and I've got you a name. Want to hear it?" said Bentley.

"Feel free," said Lake.

"College Boy and Angel Wings."

"That's our name? College Boy and Angel Wings? Sounds pretty stupid, I'd say," said Jackson.

"Nah. The name ain't dumb. Angel Wings. As in those little people who fly around saying sweet things and doing good deeds. You guys don't look like angels but you sure as hell sound like them with those flighty fancy words you like to throw around."

"I don't think we have any idea of what you're talking about, Buzzard."

"Well, I won't lecture. Not much anyways. You see, I'm from a Union background. We talk straight talk and leave out feathery fluff and holier than thou comments. You guys cry about war and poverty and racism and you whine about the lousy food and the screws that push you around. Flap. Flap. Flap."

"You still aren't making a hell of a lot of sense, Bentley. Get to the point," replied Jackson.

Buzzard Bailey stretched his skinny neck forward and his Adam's apple quavered. His long, thin nose formed a perfect crescent hooking to his pursed lips. He collected his thoughts and pointed to Flanigan.

"Let's start with this fellow. Irish lad, aren't you? You need to talk to Sean McGinley. McGinley was a Catholic once — during his innocent days, he says. He'd be interested in hearing your angel wing shit about the New Testament and the Spiritual Exercises of St. Whoever the hell he is. The great magician Jesus you read about is in my book as mythical as your big Indian friends' visions and angels."

Handsome Lake, forgetting his nonviolent posture, reached out and grabbed Bentley's collar. "Watch your talk, Buzzardman, you're stepping on my wings and I might have to crush your tail and horns."

Jackson raised his hands. "Whoa, guys. Let's talk. We can respond to what Buzzard has to say. Maybe he just likes to open up a bit more than most people are willing to. Let him continue."

Handsome Lake released his hold on Bentley, pointed to Jackson and said: "Now this man is making some sense. Too bad he didn't talk more sense these past few weeks. Now here we have an educated young Negro who likes to throw around big words and drop famous names that he claims he is even related to. I'd say that if Randolph were a relative of yours some of his actions would have rubbed off. You'd be talkin' but not Angel Wing shit, you'd be talking organizing prisoners."

Lake looked at Bentley and said, "Guess it's my turn, Buzzard. Go ahead and eat my liver."

"Can't say I ever heard your namesake or his code of conduct. Sounds like Alcoholics Anonymous to me. Sort of a 'stay away from booze religion.' You've said more than once that your people esteem poverty, that lowly surroundings and sickness are a sure indication of a rich heavenly reward. And you say that the white man gets rich by the power of the devil, and blah, blah, blah. You know what, big Indian man? I think your religion and Flanigan's are the same. I bet your religious leaders are no different than Flanigan's priests at the country club, driving fancy cars and drinking fine wines. It's all about economics, Indian man. Fleecing the believers. Passing the basket at every service and telling the poor to give because they are giving to God. What a crock! No wonder they caution the believers to not rock the political-economic system. Hell, the boys with the Roman collars are a part of the system."

Handsome Lake let out a loud laugh. "My leaders living high on the hog? Mr. Buzzardman, it's you who's into myths. Not us."

"What about me, Buzzard. I'm a Baptist," said Jackson.

"I've traveled the Southland, Jackson. I've seen a lot of skinny, emaciated folk but never did see a skinny preacher. Fat as hogs, most of them."

"Buzzard, we've a long wait in line. Since you claim to be so well informed, tell us your great designs on political, economic and social justice. Is there really substance behind your cocky manner?" asked Jackson.

"I was hoping you'd ask. But before I get on my high horse, let me ask you: are you all dyed in the wool, honest to God absolutists?"

All three men nodded their heads.

"O.K. that means that you probably won't be doing any work in here? Right? You don't want to contribute to the war effort. Right?"

The three agreed.

"Well, that's your first snafu."

"Snafu?" questioned Lake.

"Yeah, snafu. Situation normal, all fucked up". That's what you guys are — all fucked up. There are things to change in here and you aren't going to change them by sitting on your collective asses and yakking about being absolutists. You need to activate. You need work so you don't fuck up the system. Understand?"

"No," said Jackson.

Moving his beak-like nose close to Jackson's face, Bentley snarled, "Well, listen closely, mister, because what I'm about to tell you involves not just you but all Negroes and other people who need to fight the power. Ya see this finger? It can create some movement. But put all these together and you have a fist. A fist is power. I can't put one of you out with my finger." Clenching his bony fist and holding it high, Buzzard commented: "But I sure as hell can put you out of commission with this!"

"Planning a prison bust, Buzzard?" asked Jackson.

"You're damn right I am. Not busting out. Busting Jim Crow in prison." Said Bentley.

"Who's Jim Crow?" asked Lake.

"Jim Crow is the name for the white man's system to deny Negroes their rights in this country. Whether it's practiced by law or custom, it denies Black people access to basic rights."

"Like?"

"Like right here in Danbury where guys like Jackson are forced to sit with other Negroes. They can't eat at the same table as whites. Right, college boy?"

"Randolph is my name. Or Jackson. Cut the college boy crap. And no, I'm not allowed to sit at the same table as Flanigan and Lake."

"Would you prefer to sit with them?"

"Of course. They're my friends."

"O.K. Listen to my plan.

"I've got years of union organizing experience and knew I wasn't going to be part of this capitalist war venture that I could smell coming down the pike. War work is being done in here but most jobs are not related to war. You guys need to get on a non-military work detail and get to know people and prepare them for action."

"What kind of action?" asked Flanigan.

"Strike action. Our plan is to stop work until Blacks and Whites are allowed to sit as one at all meals. Did you notice anything different when we got haircuts the day after we came in here?"

"Yeah," said Jackson. "I was told to wait outside until the Negro barber came back from lunch. There was a white barber inside reading a magazine but a Black guy had to wait for the Black barber."

"O.K. We're going to break that kind of Jim Crow crap not just here at Danbury but throughout the federal prison system. We're going to bust balls on this one. You guys sign up for the pick and shovel crew and we'll get you in on the movement."

"If you stop work won't the prison officials say the work wasn't very important anyway — not being for the war effort?"

"There's more than one way to skin a cat, Flanigan. We'll go on a hunger strike. We'll refuse to eat."

"So we starve ourselves and the warden looks the other way. What good will come out of that?" said Jackson.

"Look. Danbury staff like any prison staff doesn't want to look bad in the press. Once our story gets out, everyone is exposed. Especially the Federal Government, right up to old FDR himself. Roosevelt can't afford a second embarrassment after easing out of the Negro March on Washington. Just a few weeks ago the largest Negro protest against Jim crow took place in New York City."

Jackson smiled. "Yes, we know."

"Just remember," said Bentley, "that your babbling with your finger up your ass won't get you a damn thing. Work with us as a team and maybe some kind of justice will result. Just make sure you don't take this plan to anyone. C.O.s aren't the most loved types in here. As the war poster says: Loose Lips Sink Ships. Keep your traps shut."

It was weeks before they saw Bentley again but when they did it was while they were carrying bricks and mortar up a steep construction plank to a prison addition. Bentley's lecture had struck a chord with the trio, even though they gritted their teeth when they heard Buzzard's chant: "Yoo-hoo. College Boy and Angel Wings. Over here."

Chapter 21
Dreaming The Brotherhood Of Man

When Buzzard Bentley saw Flanigan, Lake, and Jackson in their new role as hod carriers, he was not surprised. Bentley had arranged their job through the prison construction foreman. The foreman was delighted to have skilled masons like Bentley and his skilled co-worker Sean McGinley. When they requested their own hod carriers, the foreman obliged.

Bentley gave instructions to the three absolutists. They were to mix mortar, shovel it into a wooden trough, swing the heavy load to their shoulders, and carry it up to the masons. Stacks of bricks on small shoulder pallets were also delivered to the masons by the hod carriers.

"Wouldn't it be easier to hoist the bricks and mortar up with a pulley?" asked Jackson.

"Sure it would. That's why the foreman wants you boys to do it the hard way. You've got to earn the four cents an hour you get on this job," said Bentley.

"I heard it was eight cents an hour," said Flanigan.

"Eight cents if you're doing military piece work. Like making gloves or sewing sleeping bags. But you boys don't want war work, so this should suit you just fine."

"Why the addition, Buzzard?" questioned Lake.

"Not enough room to hold the new prisoners. C.O. numbers are up, and war capitalists who have been too indiscreet with their thievery are being sentenced to Federal Prisons. They get a little slap for bloodsucking the American people: short sentences, special treatment by the screws, early parole, and then back to their home towns to refuck the tax payers. It's the American way."

"How long can we stay on this job?" said Flanigan.

"Oh, you may get pulled off the job occasionally to do other work, but this building won't be finished for another year. When the cold weather comes, we should be working inside doing cement, paint and wood work," said Bentley.

As they talked, another mason, Sean McGinley, a short, thin man, wearing Trotsky-like glasses over sunken cheeks and pockmarked skin, was sizing up the three men. He said nothing, but his glassy gaze told that he wanted to know more about the new men on the job.

McGinley was a former follower of Father Coughlin, the political critic and anti-Semite priest who'd been silenced by the Roman Catholic Church. McGinley had been one of over 30 million radio listeners of Coughlin's weekly diatribe during the Roosevelt New Deal Programs of the early 1930's.

McGinley broke not just with Coughlin but the Church itself. He embraced economic determinism, fought with the Loyalists in the Spanish Civil War until their bitter defeat by Franco's fascist forces, and afterwards returned to the United States to wage war against what he called "corrupt capitalism."

Bentley turned to McGinley and said, "Sean, why don't you tell these lads some of our organizational plans and what they can do to make those plans work."

"Sure. It's break time. Let's go over and have a sit on the brick pile."

Taking a small Bull Durham pouch from his shirt pocket, he tapped a line of tobacco on the cigarette paper, ran his tongue across the paper edge, rolled the paper and tobacco slowly, lit, deeply inhaled, and made eye contact with the young men as smoke billowed from his thin lips and wide nostrils.

"Let me begin, lads, with a quote from a fellow named Thomas Curtis Clark. It goes:

> Let us no more be true
> to boasted race or clan,
> But to our highest dream,
> the brotherhood of man."

"In time, I'll learn more about your individual reasons for being in a United States Federal prison. In weeks and months to come, you'll learn that although we're C.O.s, we're divided in purpose. From what Buzzard tells me, you three have different reasons for being here but you have an overriding commonality in your thinking. I hope that your highest dream is the brotherhood of man. If it is, then you have a lot of work to do here in Danbury.

"First, let's get something straight, I know that Buzzard has tagged you with 'Angel Wings' and 'College Boy.' I really don't care if you have religion or not. My experience in the Spanish Civil War led me to a position of non-violence, but it also destroyed my faith. I'm trying to put all that aside. Personally, my religion is now the brotherhood of man. I saw what religious leaders do when faced with political and military power. The decision of the Vatican and the Roman Catholic Church in Spain to side with the treachery of Franco was the last straw for my back to withstand. When religious leaders have to choose between accepting the status quo of brutal power or to listen to the voice of the people, they inevitably chose fascism. Have you seen or heard Pius XII speak out against Nazism or Fascism? No! And you won't either. Nor will the leadership of the largest Christian Church speak out against English Imperialism or subjugation of Irish, African, and Asian people. Why? Because organized religion is part of the system of subjugation, that's why."

Buzzard Bailey gave one of his rare smiles and stretched his neck toward McGinley and interrupted in a mocking Irish accent, "Sean, me lad. Now don't you suppose these fine byes would like to hear what plans ya have to offer? Your offering is about the Church. Bejesus, don't you have anything else on your mind?"

McGinley took off his glasses and wheezed a laugh. He snubbed out his cigarette and pinched the remaining tobacco back into the Bull Durham poach.

"The old Buzzard is right. I apologize. All I have to do is look into your faces and see that I don't have to preach the brotherhood of man to you. As young as you are, each of you, for sure, has experienced racial and ethnic injustice. There's no escape from injustice anywhere in the world. But here in this country, we live the lie. We feign democracy. We feign justice. We feign the meaning of the flag.

"If we're together in our movement to fight hypocrisy, then we must fight it — not just outside of prison walls — but inside as well. If after you hear what I have to say, and you decide you do not want to be part of it, then go in peace. All we ask is that you swear you'll not go to any authorities nor will you reveal our plan to bootlickers and finks.

"Fair enough?"

Flanigan, Jackson and Lake all agreed.

"O.K. Our plan is very basic but it will take months to put into place. We plan to end Jim Crow practices here at Danbury. Work strikes, hunger strikes — maybe other actions that will force the Federal Government to end segregation — will be planned and executed in coming months. We'll circulate among the C.O. population and try to find people who will join us. Individuals like ourselves. People who are true followers of the brotherhood of man. Some C.O.s are bigots. Some will hate you for your color, your ethnic background, your religious or political beliefs. Engage every C.O. you can locate and report back to Buzzard and myself on your findings. We want to learn whom we can trust. Try to determine loyalty. We have nutcases among the C.O. population. Find out who they are. Ass-kissers, bootlickers, anarchists, wide-eyed Bolsheviks, even some Nazi characters are in here. Keep records of people and bring them to our meetings."

"Sounds like spying on people," said Jackson.

"Maybe it is. But remember this: our secrets are to protect people. Government secrets protect the powerful and very often harm everyone else. We have no reason to retaliate against people — even if they rat on us. All we want to know is whom to trust, whom can we work with in the context of our goals."

"Goals? I thought that an end to Jim Crow was our goal?" commented Handsome Lake.

"That's our number one objective. We also need to address the need for freedom of mail censorship. We need to address parole — why do the fat cats get early parole and C.O.s are here forever? Work and conditions in the hole are other issues."

"The hole?" questioned Jackson.

"Right. You should know that if you're caught in any of the activities we're planning that you'll be put in the hole. The hole is a 5 by 8 foot cell. Isolation is where you go when you violate pokey rules. You can almost count on finding yourself in the hole sometime before we pull off the strike."

"Who among the prison population do we stay away from?" asked Jackson.

"One group to avoid are the Jehovah Witnesses. They're the biggest lot of C.O.s in the place. You guys are probably devils' tails compared to them. They have their noses stuck in the Bible constantly. They look upon themselves as God's chosen people waiting for Armageddon — for the Lord to take them all home after the final war between good and evil. Chesterton says that 'the test of a good religion is that you can make a joke about it.' JWs are humorless. They're no trouble for the Warden, or the screws; they never complain — total cooperation — say shit, and they squat and strain.

"From my experience your most cooperative people will be socialists. They can be Friends, Brethren, Mennonites, Methodists, Baptists, Catholics, Jews, and atheists. Interesting isn't it that atheists are often the most anti-violent people?

"And you, Jackson, be careful. Especially among the general prison population. There are 'nigger haters' out there. Also beware of the Father Divine types as well. They're only one step up from the JWs."

"Father Divine?" said Flanigan.

"Yeah," answered Jackson. "I know about Father Divine. The Black preacher from Chicago who has convinced thousands of followers that he's God. God lives good — Cadillacs, diamonds, women in furs. Owwee. You won't find Father Divine in here."

Buzzard Bentley rose first. "O.K. conspirators. The foreman is coming. Guess we extended our break. Let's get back at it and be here tomorrow for a follow up."

For much of the remaining summer of '42, Flanigan and friends mixed mortar and hod-carried. In late August, they were pulled from their job by a guard who took them to the prison farm to load produce. When Jackson saw that it was an army truck, he refused to do the work. Flanigan and Lake decided to join the work refusal with Jackson. The warden was intent on making an example of the men to other prisoners, most of whom were in full support of the war.

Warden Ripkin was furious with the refusers. He called them into his office, lashed out at their unpatriotic acts, and confined them to two weeks of isolation. He called two guards and ordered them to put the men in leg irons and handcuffs. The man in the middle had both hands cuffed and each man on the outside with one hand free, was to carry a sign that said "We Don't Want to Defeat the Nazis."

Flanigan, Lake and Jackson were made to shuffle through the mess hall at lunch time. When Flanigan and Jackson, both flanking Lake, threw down their signs, guards picked up the signs and held them high as the parade continued through the hall. The prisoners responded with anger.

"Rotten bastards. Don't put 'em in the hole, string the bastards up."

"Put them on a ship and send them to Hitler."

"Naw. Der yellow. Sen 'em to da Japs."

Handsome Lake was hit in the face with a gob of jello, and Jackson and Flanigan, brushing by tables, were smeared with assorted condiments, mostly catsup, mustard and margarine.

At the top floor of the maximum security bloc, the shackles and cuffs were removed and each man was placed in a 5' x 8' cell. The door was solid steel with a tiny opening that allowed a bar of light to shine through. A single low watt light bulb hung from the ceiling. A toilet bowl was the only other object. No bed, just bare concrete floor. Each night, the men received two blankets, one to sleep on and one to sleep under. They were removed each morning.

Flanigan learned to walk himself to sleep the first few days. He couldn't stand the flopping sound of his laceless shoes as he paced the few steps to the wall, turned and paced again. He thought that it was somewhat fortunate that it was still summer and the cells were not nearly as cold as they would be in winter. Since he was not allowed any reading material, he tried to tire himself out with pushups, sit ups, and constant pacing. Food came three times a day. Not bread and water that he expected. But the food was intentionally bland, no salt or pepper, no meat and tiny portions.

Yet, it became a positive time for Peter Flanigan. It was time to review his thinking. Why was he here in prison? Why here in solitary? What benefit does the strike plan have? How much more time will have to be served for strike action and other actions that will erase goodtime from his record and lengthen his stay in prison?

Sitting back against the dark concrete walls, he rested his eyes:

> Peter, when you told me that you loved me,
> I didn't tell you exactly how I feel about you.
> I want to tell you now...

Flanigan's eyes flickered. Then closed slowly.

> Peter, let's paddle along the shore and see if we can spot
> trout rising. Look! Across the lake the sun is dipping
> behind the tree line, that's when the Browns get
> active. Keep your eyes on the water for the feeding
> frenzy. Get ready to cast, Peter, I'll paddle gently so we
> won't spook the trout when we see the first rise.

Then he would picture Anna Maria in her red Christmas dress. He saw her gorgeous figure, vibrant brown eyes and glossy black hair falling to her shoulders. He reached out to her and put his hand around her tiny waist and they danced to the sounds of Glenn Miller. Flanigan drew air through his nostrils, and instead of musty cell odors, he took in sweet smells of Anna Maria's soft hair and skin. He held her tightly.

His eyes flickered and he saw his mother. Ellie was writing a letter telling him that this was the third letter she has sent.

> I know you left the West Street Jail. They told me
> you are in Danbury Prison. Why don't you answer
> my mail?

Flanigan snapped his eyes open and jumped up. His cell door was being unlocked and his tray of greens, bread, potatoes and milk was left on the floor by a white-garbed kitchen attendant with a guard behind him. It was after 5 P.M. and Flanigan toyed with the vegetables. He ate bread, drank milk and shoved the tray aside. Fifteen minutes later, the tray was picked up and the evening blanket delivery was made.

A few hours, he thought, and the first day of my isolation will be over. Only thirteen more to go and back to my bed, eatable food, conversation, reading, and work. Only two years and nine months and I'll be out of here — unless my time is extended, he reflected.

By the end of the first week of isolation, Flanigan actually began to feel stronger. He hadn't walked this much since he was in Wurtzville, and two hundred push ups and two hundred sit ups a day, had already tightened the muscles in his arms and chest. What was a really important discovery, however, were several editions of the *Catholic Worker* that he found the morning of the seventh day in isolation. When he came back from taking his weekly allowed shower, he found the papers taped to the inside cell door. He read them cover-to-cover several times, and then stuffed them in his pants so they would not be observed by the guard.

A note was inside the January-February 1942 edition of the *Catholic Worker*. It read:

> Dear Peter: Thought you might need some more
> nourishment. Ben Salmon's letter in my January
> edition of the *Catholic Worker* should be of special
> interest to you — it might lift your spirits. Note that
> the letter was written to President Wilson during
> the First World War. Salmon was an amazing man.
> Like you, he was a Catholic who rejected conscrip-
> tion on religious grounds. As he told President
> Woodrow Wilson in an earlier letter sent in June of

1917: "Regardless of nationality, all men are my
brothers. God is 'our Father who art in heaven.' The
commandment 'Thou shalt not kill' is unconditional and inexorable."

Ben Salmon was tortured physically and mentally in
United States Federal prisons during and after World
War I. He was sentenced to death because of his
firm belief in Christian unconditional love and the
non-violent teachings of Jesus Christ. Salmon was
the last conscientious objector to be released from
prison after World War I. Salmon stood firm, while
others, including the hierarchy of the Catholic
Church, refused to accept the fact that Jesus Christ
taught unconditional love. Church leaders' support
of violence in WWI, and now in WWII, make a liar
of Christ.

Jesus Christ was a radical. Ben Salmon was a
radical. You have something in common with both
— agape.

        Peace of Christ,
        Dorothy Day

Flanigan had no idea how the papers and Dorothy Day's note got
into his isolation cell. He wondered about the meaning of agape. He
would keep that word in his mind and search it out at another time.
Meanwhile, he was fascinated with the story of Ben Salmon. Bits and
pieces about the man and how he was convicted and sentenced to death
by the United States government because he refused to register for the
draft, were all included in the notes and letters sent to him by Dorothy
Day.

It was as if Salmon had done theological research for Flanigan. As he sifted through the comments of Dorothy Day regarding Salmon and the words of Salmon himself, Flanigan became even more convinced that his own beliefs, convictions, and actions were absolutely correct and part of his persona.

Flanigan looked at one of Salmon's letters that quoted scripture: "You have heard that it hath been said, Thou shalt love thy neighbor, and hate thy enemy. But I say to you, Love your enemies; do good to them that hate you; and pray for them that persecute and calumniate you." Matthew v-43, 44.

Peter lay on the floor with his head and shoulders resting on the wall, the smuggled *Catholic Worker* in his hand, and reflected on the day that he refused to load crops for the army. "As ye sow, so shall ye reap," he said out loud, "and I ain't gonna sow, Lord."

A few days later, Flanigan, Jackson and Lake were hauling mortar and bricks up to the masons, Buzzard Bentley and Sean McGinley.

The masons called an early break and the three young men related the account of their time in the hole.

"I have to tell you guys about the manna from heaven that manifested itself in my cell. In my second week, I somehow got a copy of the *Catholic Worker* and a letter from Dorothy Day. It not only saved me from going stir crazy, but it revitalized my sense of purpose. How do you suppose it got to me?"

"Don't feel like the Lone Ranger, Peter, I got a packet with writings from Tolstoy and Thoreau. Now those white boys had it right. I don't mind that kind of whitemanizing," said Handsome Lake.

"Well, if you fellows would like Professor Jackson to lecture you on Satyagraha and how it can be applied to the American Negro struggle, just let me know. Gandhi was already one of my favorite people before I went into the hole. Now the Mahatma is my number one person, after Jesus Christ. He truly is the Great Soul of the Indian people. Now, I want to be part of making his soul force work for American Blacks."

Buzzard Bentley stood tall, arms folded across his skinny chest. His cheekbones rose up on his face when he smiled and narrowed his eyes.

"Sounds like you boys are getting prime jail house education. Very nice, very nice, don't you think so, Sean?"

McGinley covered his mouth with his hand as he tried to muffle his wheezy chuckle. "Sure sounds that way, Buzzard. Must've ... must've ... must've ... been the Easter Bunny that visited those young fellows."

"O.K." said Jackson. "Tell us what you know."

McGinley explained, "Dorothy Day, the publisher of the *Catholic Worker*, came here last week wanting to visit Peter Flanigan. Apparently, Peter and Dorothy have gotten to know each other somehow. Anyway, she had a packet of reading material for Peter and was very annoyed with the Warden when he told her that Flanigan was in the hole. She asked to talk to someone who knew Flanigan so the Warden contacted me.

"Mrs. Day asked me to hold the reading materials for Flanigan and when I flipped through them, I knew we had to try to get them to you in the hole. That was when the Buzzard came up with an idea that I didn't agree to first."

Bentley pointed his finger at McGinley and said, "Now here is a guy that survived the Spanish Civil War and he doesn't like the idea of using a violent person to achieve positive ends. His mind has been clouded by all that Jesuit philosophy that he got at Fordham. Right, Sean? All that bullshit about rights — Rousseau, Hobbes, Kant and all those old boys who claimed they had a lock on moral and legal concepts of right and wrong acts. Then, the Jebbies pick and choose whatever fits their concept of ethical principles."

McGinley reached for his Bull Durham and began the usual tobacco roll ritual. After he lit up, he said, "Buzzard is right. I know the line about not killing the messenger. But when the messenger is a killer — well, that did bother me. I've changed since Spain."

Buzzard looked at Flanigan and Jackson and said, "Do you fellows remember your cell neighbor at the West Street Jail — Louie Lepke?'

"How could we forget?" said Jackson. "I introduced him to Flanigan."

"Well, I went to old Louie and I said to him, 'Louie, do you remember those young fellows who were across the way from you in the West Street pokey?'

"Louie said, 'Yez mean doze boys in da slammer fer not killin. Sure. What about 'em?'

"So I told Louie about you fellows being in the hole and that you needed reading material and the warden wouldn't allow it.

"Louie said, 'Jes give me da comics and stuff fer those kids and dey'll have it today.'

"So I did. But first I had to get by Sean here. He doesn't trust Louie. Guess I can understand why."

McGinley said, "I wonder what Louie said to the screws to get such fast delivery? Buzzard gave Louie the materials in the exercise yard and you guys got your stuff within hours."

"Maybe he didn't talk to the hacks," said Handsome Lake. "Maybe he went right to the warden. Whatever, I appreciated what you fellows did. Can we expect such good delivery service the next time we are in isolation?"

"We'll do our best," said McGinley. "Let's just hope that the next time you go to the hole, that the prison population won't take it out on the C.O.s."

"Why so?" asked Flanigan.

"After you guys were shackled, paraded and humiliated in the mess hall, the prisoners began to take it out on all C.O.s. A bunch of C.O.s got the crap beaten out of them. The screws left our cell doors open and other prisoners were allowed to tear up our beds, throw them in the shower and piss on our blankets."

"The hacks didn't do a thing to stop them?" asked Jackson.

"Hell no. They helped, and with the blessing of the warden. The warden gave patriotic speeches and lambasted you guys as slackers and cowards. Swell fellow, that warden," said McGinley. "If he was on the outside, he would be arrested for inciting a riot."

"By the way, the mail room hack is holding a packet for Randolph and Peter. None there for you, Handsome."

"Didn't expect any," replied Lake.

At the end of the work day, Flanigan asked one of the guards to get his mail packet. When it came, he snapped off the binding string and quickly fished through several letters, looking for Anna Maria's distinctive handwriting. There were none in the packet.

He opened up the first letter from his mother. It was postmarked June 10th and had been sent to the West Street jail before being forwarded to Danbury. Ellie said that she'd been notified by an Agent Malone that Peter was arrested, tried and sentenced to three years in Danbury. Most of the letter was cautionary advice. She said that Anna Maria was sending letters out as well.

He flipped through letters from Ellie dated late June, two in July and two in August. It was now September and still nothing from Anna Maria. When he got to the last letter dated August 30th, Ellie noted that:

> Anna Maria just received a large packet from
> Danbury prison. In the large manila envelope were
> all the letters she had sent to you over the past
> several months. Each letter was stamped "unauthor-
> ized correspondent." She doesn't know if they were
> opened or not. I know that you must be very upset.
> She has not received any mail from you either.
> Apparently, it is being held by the authorities at
> Danbury. I did get a letter from you after you were
> transferred to Danbury. Why not more?

Flanigan was furious. He threw the letters against the wall and pounded the door. He wasn't aware that he had learned such vile language since his arrest in June. Now, acerbity asserted itself as the profanity flowed like sewage water.

His demand to meet with the warden was, surprisingly, quickly approved. It was too soon after his cell outburst. Flanigan, still seething over what he felt was a serious breach of his personal rights, failed to control his tongue with Warden Ripkin. He was placed back in isolation and the warden ordered that his food ration be cut back again.

Randolph Jackson and Handsome Lake heard about Flanigan being put back in the hole. They refused to leave their cells to work or eat. The following day, both men were back in the hole.

Chapter 22
Fight Fire? Not People?

Censorship of letters was a sore point with not only Flanigan but other prisoners as well. Whole paragraphs would be cut from some letters and others simply not delivered. After release from the hole for actions protesting censorship in early April of 1943, Flanigan had another packet of letters from Wurtzville. Although no letters came from Anna Maria, his mother was able to mention Anna Maria with limited censorship. She told how the girl sometimes shared gasoline with her because Ellie had only an 'A' sticker on the windshield of her Plymouth. An 'A' sticker permitted only three miles of gas each week. Anna Maria usually had extra gasoline since her father was in business and they lived outside of town. Her father had a 'D' sticker that allowed extra gasoline purchases — more than the Machellis needed.

"Speaking of gasoline, Peter, I thought that you might be interested in reading the enclosed articles from the *Wurtzville Courier* and the *Scranton Daily*."

Flanigan picked up the first article, dated April 5, 1943.

WURTZVILLE MAYOR INDICTED AFTER FIRE

Mayor William Mahoney of Wurtzville was released on bail of $10,000 this morning. Mahoney, in United States Federal District Court yesterday, was charged with violations stemming from the massive explosion in Wurtzville last Wednesday. Federal investigators at the scene of the largest conflagration ever in Wurtzville, have connected the explosion and fire to an extensive black market scheme. Mahoney is reported to have broken United States Federal Laws governing rationed materials including rubber and gasoline.

Early reports indicate that an estimated half million gallons of gasoline and as many as 200,000 tires were destroyed in the eruption that occurred. Two juveniles who set off the explosion with tracer and armor piercing .30 caliber projectiles are being held at a local home for wayward boys. The boys have admitted to breaking into a military cargo train parked in the Wurtzville rail yard. The weapon or weapons used to fire the shells is unknown at this time and the matter is under investigation.

Mayor Mahoney would not comment on the charges as he was released from an overnight stay at Lackawanna County Jail in Scranton. Bail was posted by a family friend, George Caufield.

Judge Liam Barrett noted Mr. Mahoney's extensive contributions to the community and the Mayor's "spotless reputation." The

Judge said that he would call for a speedy trial so that this matter can be put behind the good people of Lackawanna County.

In another article from the *Wurtzville Courier*, Flanigan read that the fire may have long- term consequences:

COALBROOK MINE FIRE ROARS

"Thank God that those mine shafts were abandoned," said Gail Rosler. "No person would have survived the roaring fire still raging in the Coalbrook mine shafts."

Anthony Tolerico, a coal truck driver and former miner said, "Those mine tunnels are everywhere under Wurtzville. If the fire is in Coalbrook now it'll be in other connecting tunnels before long. It doesn't look good for this town."

The *Wurtzville Courier* talked to Mike Dermott, mining inspector for Belmont Mines. Dermott said that he didn't know what was going to happen but said, "It doesn't appear that we're going to be able to put the fire out right away."

When asked how long it might take, Dermott said, "Maybe a year. Maybe many years. Remember, anthracite burns slowly. It's not wood or even bituminous coal we have under us. It's hard coal, slow burning coal. I just don't know. This is a disaster for the community."

Another letter from Ellie in May told of the trial of the Mayor.

The Federal District Prosecutor allowed the mayor to elect to have either a trial by jury argued before the judge or to have the case argued before the judge without jury. Mahoney elected to accept the decision of the judge.

With Judge Barrett presiding, the case was argued. The Prosecution had a solid case against the mayor including testimony from men who had stored tires and gasoline in the Coalbrook mine shaft and were paid by Mahoney. A known mobster from Philadelphia, one who acted as the main procurement agent for Mahoney, testified for the prosecution after a plea bargain agreement. He told of tire deliveries to Mahoney from Ohio, and gasoline from Texas.

After two days of testimony, Mahoney had his attorney end the trial by proclaiming nolo contendere.

After a short deliberation, Judge Barrett sentenced Mahoney to three years in a Federal Penitentiary and fined him $15,000. Barrett, however, said he was suspending the sentence but not the fine. The judge said that "Mr. Mahoney's candor in filing nolo contendere is in accord with his usual openness in a long career of service to the people of Wurtzville. The unfortunate circumstances brought about by unsettling world conditions created an aberration in his thinking. Mr. Mahoney assures me that he will pay back his community for the mistakes he has made in the past few months. I have every reason to believe that he will do just that."

Ellie had a short note attached to the articles. It read:

> As you can see, Peter, justice still prevails in this wonderful country of ours. Bill walks the street as if he didn't have a care in the world. That could change. Just yesterday, the bodies of Tom and Anna Culin were found in their bedrooms. Both died during the night of carbon monoxide poisoning from the fire that burns beneath us . Today's

newspaper warns people to keep a window open at all times, even in the coldest weather. Ah, well, at least spring is finally here.

Love, Mom

By 1943, there were an estimated 10,000 men in camps for conscientious objection and about half that number in federal prisons. This number was about eight times greater than the number of conscientious objectors in prison during World War I. C.O. sentences were usually longer than those of most other federal offenders and early parole for C.O.s was rare. The non-cooperation attitude of the C.O.s outside of prison walls was not left at the entrance gate. The principal baggage carried into federal prison by C.O.s was their unique mode of thinking.

During the winter of 1943, Flanigan, Jackson, and Lake were a well-known trio in Danbury. They were migrating jail birds, nesting only for a time in the main cell block until conditions forced them to take up residence in the hole. Virulent feelings against conscientious objectors by fellow prisoners gradually calmed after the summer of '42. But it wasn't because Flanigan and friends tried to convince fellow prisoners of their integrity. It was an evolutionary process. It happened over a period of months as the trio was marched into isolation in the maximum security bloc, and weeks later marched back to their cells: thinner, more resolute, and smilingly confident.

Flanigan, Jackson, and Lake were looked upon as contaminators by prison authorities. The warden thought that the trio was better in isolation — a remission place where he said, "Their cowardly views won't infect other prisoners."

However, among the C.O. prison population, the trio was only a disease of the skin. Unknown to the warden, it was Bentley and McGinley who were infecting the hearts of prison C.O.s with daily verbal contacts. By March of 1943, they had a list of all C.O.s whom they felt

would cooperate when work stoppages and hunger strikes against segregation were called. They learned how to wash ink from old magazines, hand print their own undercover articles, and lampoon prison
officials in cartoons of prison life. Each member of the staff would be
responsible for four or five editions that would then circulate through
the general population. Bentley and McGinley were able to use the
paper to extol their socialist ideas and make pointed attacks on racism
both in and outside of prison.

Two others also deflected attention from Bentley and McGinley.
They were Stanley Murphy and Louis Taylor, men who had walked off a
Civilian Public Service Camp in Big Flats, New York in October of 1942.
Big Flats was one of many camps around the country where conscientious objectors were assigned. Unlike the absolutists who were sent to
prison, Murphy and Taylor elected to work at a camp like thousands of
other C.O.s. After deciding that work at Big Flats was insignificant from
a social point of view, the two men left camp without authorization and
several months later were arrested and sentenced to Danbury Prison.

In February of 1943, Murphy and Taylor went on a hunger strike
in protest of the United States conscription system. Force-fed from their
seventeenth day of fast, they ended their strike after eighty-two days. In
June, they were transferred to Springfield, Missouri because Danbury
prison officials said that they needed medical treatment after their long
fast. Both men were stripped naked and placed in "strip cells." Most
Conscientious Objectors around the country knew about Springfield
and its reputation as a mental hospital. The action of the warden and
the Bureau of Prisons was a signal to the C.O.s that their actions could
land them in a psychiatric institution.

Nevertheless, by June, Bentley and McGinley had over fifty men
who pledged to join the work stoppage. Flanigan, Jackson and Lake
were instrumental in lining up many of the younger C.O.s. Jackson
proved his mettle with people of color. He was not able to move some
Blacks, especially a couple of men who claimed membership in a

Jewish Negro sect and another fellow who recognized Hitler as his true leader. However, many Blacks agreed to cooperate with the work stoppage, and some said that they would try to sit with Whites.

Randolph Jackson had already tried single-handed integration by sitting at a Whites-only table. Yet, each attempt by Jackson failed. He was spotted every time by guards and sent to a Black table to finish his meal.

Jackson usually did not finish his meal. He would wait until the guards repositioned themselves and then he would return to the Whites-only table. From May until August, Randolph Jackson spent as much time in the hole as he did in his assigned cell. Warden Ripkin had Jackson in his office on numerous occasions but was frustrated with Jackson's tenacity.

"If you just try to make a model prisoner of yourself, Jackson," Ripkin said, "I can guarantee you early release."

"How can you do that since I have lost all the goodtime with my time in the hole?" questioned Jackson.

"Don't forget who I am, Mr. Jackson. As warden I can pretty much do what I damn well please. You keep your nose clean, stay away from some of the other trouble makers like Lake and Flanigan, and some of the Negro riffraff, and I'll get you out of here."

Randolph Jackson did not make any promises with the warden but he did keep a low profile. He spent the summer of '43 doing organizational skills-lecturing and recruiting. By early August, the stage was set and Jackson was a leading player. Using binoculars, Warden Ripkin scanned down the exercise yard each day. He looked for Jackson and was pleased to see that he walked with his head down — usually with two older prisoners, not the young hotheads, Flanigan and Lake.

As Bentley, McGinley and Jackson closed final preparations for the work stoppages and hunger strikes, it became apparent that many of those who pledged to strike were now finding excuses to back out.

"Can't do it. I've thought about my wife and children and how they need me. I can't afford to lose my goodtime."

Others had a variety of quick responses: "I'm not feeling well now. Maybe next month." Or, "I don't trust some of the leaders in the group. Now you're O.K., but I don't like that Bentley guy."

One C.O. was very blunt: "I decided that I'm not going to come to the aid of niggers."

Jackson was not able to convince some C.O.s who said striking was an act in opposition to love. As Christians, they argued, they could not participate in actions that could turn violent.

By August 10, the number of strikers was down to twenty-four. Only six considered themselves as religiously and morally motivated like Flanigan, Jackson and Lake. Most of the remainder were experienced Union organizers. When cell doors were opened on the morning of August 11, only 18 men refused to come out for work. The following day another five men also refused.

Warden Ripkin's strategy was to keep the incident out of the national newspapers. The strikers were isolated into a separate cell block, food was delivered to the bloc on trays, and after a brief hunger strike, the prisoners were allowed reading information.

Randolph Jackson developed a method of communicating with other strikers locked in their cells. When some of the hacks were found to be able to hear the strikers talking to each other by calling through the narrow door bottom, Jackson wrote strike plans on tiny pieces of paper and placed them inside of a hollowed-out pencil. Yarn from an already torn blanket was attached to the pencil clip and then skidded under the narrow opening at the bottom of the door.

A delivery to Bentley or McGinley took a lot of practice. First, eye contact had to be made between the men, using the tiny opening near the top of the door. After several tries, the pencil usually slid under the targeted door on the opposite side.

Jackson, in his notes to Bentley and McGinley, stressed the need to make public the actions they were taking. In one note, he petitioned them to use any method possible to get information to the Press:

> The hypocrisy of the United States government must be exposed. We need to inform people around the country of what we are doing and why we are doing it. My suggestion to you is to use whatever influence you have to communicate our strike to national newspapers and radio stations. If you have to use your "delivery man" then do it. The greater good of millions of people must be the consideration. Our nonviolent Gandhian actions will wither if the grapevine is not used. Try to make contact with Harlem Congressman Adam Clayton Powell and labor leader J. Philip Randolph."
>
> P.S. Peter Flanigan and Handsome Lake are several cells away and out of my communication line. As you well know, these two guys are not just my closest friends, they are the most dependable organizers we have. Count on them to work out plans on their side of the cell block.

Bentley read the note and then skidded it several times across the cell block aisle to McGinley. Each skid hit the wall instead of sliding under McGinley's door. Bentley then heard footsteps and a guard's voice: "What the hell do we have here?"

The guard's footsteps then trailed off and Bentley called to Jackson that he had received his note but that the toss to McGinley's was apparently taken by a hack.

Later that afternoon, Jackson's cell door was opened by a guard and Randolph Jackson was taken to Warden Ripkin's office.

"Mr. Jackson, it was my understanding that you and I had an agreement. For several months now, you have been a model prisoner. I had plans to set you free soon. To show other C.O.s that a model prisoner could always have early parole. Then, I am informed that you joined the strike. That was a setback for me, Randolph, Yet, it was the note that you passed around this morning that has forced me to see that you need extra help with your problem.

"Effective immediately, we are terminating your time at Danbury Correctional Facility. Two Federal Marshals are outside of this office right now. You will be transported by train to Springfield, Missouri to undergo psychiatric examinations that are not available here at Danbury. I only wish that you could have kept the agreement that you made to me earlier this summer."

"There was no agreement, Warden. You asked me to be a model prisoner. I have been. I'm proud that I have established myself as a model for justice."

The morning after Jackson had been sent to Springfield for "psychiatric care," Flanigan and Lake were also summoned to Warden Ripkin's office.

Flanigan and Lake had had a number of sessions with Warden Ripkin during the past year. In this meeting, two other men, unfamiliar to Flanigan and Lake, sat beside of the warden. Ripkin had little to say except his opening remark, "You boys lost a close friend yesterday when it became necessary to transfer Randolph Jackson to Missouri for treatment of mental problems. Now, we need to talk to you about your own mental states. The two gentlemen with me today are Wilber Cornwell of the Bureau of Prisons, and FBI Agent, Jeffrey Lambert. Mr. Cornwell will do most of the talking. The only thing that I can assure you is that you will not be staying at Danbury any longer. Mr. Cornwell has reviewed your files with Agent Lambert and has a proposition for you to decide on today."

Cornwell leaned forward in his chair and said, "Mr. Flanigan and Mr. Lake, I am giving you a choice to make. The first choice is the chance to have your strange behavior analyzed by reputable United States government psychiatrists. You may feel that you do not have mental disorders but when young people like you act contrary to the norm of society, there is a strong likelihood that your deviant behavior demands professional treatment.

"However, looking at your records, I feel that your actions, Mr. Flanigan, stem from an overprotective mother and lack of discipline because of an absent father. You need to develop backbone. Courage. Mr. J. Edgar Hoover believes that effeminate traits among C.O.s is largely responsible for their refusal to fight. However, I do not see that in you boys.

"You, Mr. Lake, suffer a deficiency as well. You have lived a sheltered life away from the real America. You need to be tested physically and mentally, and I'm not so sure that the Springfield facility will suit your needs.

"As a good Christian myself, I believe that what you both need is a baptism of fire. Water cleanses but fire purifies. You need to be tested and cleansed, not in water, but as the old Negro spiritual notes: 'And God gave Noah the rainbow sign, no more water, the fire next time.'"

Cornwell handed the men a letter to share. "I want you and Mr. Flanigan to read this over. It offers you men an option."

UNITED STATES FOREST SERVICE
Aerial Fire Depot
Missoula, Montana

5 August, 1943

Mr. Wilber Cornwell
Assistant Director
United States Bureau of Prisons
Connecticut Ave Washington, D.C.
My dear Mr. Cornwell:

The United States Forest Service is in need of several young men to participate in our Smoke Jumping School. Already, we have been able to recruit over fifty conscientious objectors to our training session. Most of our C.O.s are from Civilian Public Service camps around the country.

Our next training session begins August 18th. Would you please come to our assistance by providing several reliable young men? They must be mentally alert, physically strong, and willing to risk their lives to fight fires in very mountainous terrain. If you have such candidates, please wire me at the above address.

Tom Hanson, Instructor
Missoula Parachute Loft

Flanigan raised his eyebrows and bulged his eyes at Lake. He was anxious to get at Cornwell and tell him a thing or two about his own attitudes concerning courage, integrity, ethics and morality. Lake sensed it, and stepped tightly on Flanigan's foot, squeezing the anxiety from the younger man. Cornwell felt he had to lecture some more.

"Have you men ever read William James, the American philosopher?" asked Cornwell.

Lake noted that he had. Flanigan shook his head negatively.

"Well, like you fellows, James was a pacifist. But James knew that a war-like spirit exists in all men. He thought that this spirit should be redirected to redeemable social actions. He was a Social Darwinist, and in the year of the great Rocky Mountain fires, 1910, he wrote an essay he entitled 'On the Moral Equivalent of War.'"

Lake nodded in agreement. He had read the essay in one of the packs smuggled into his isolation cell.

"James wrote," Cornwell said, as he picked up a yellowish anthology of William James writings and opening to an earmarked page:

"'Of now — and this is my idea — if there were, instead of military conscription, a conscription of the whole youthful population to form for a certain number of years, a part of the army enlisted against NATURE, numerous other goods to the commonwealth would follow.'"

Cornwell stopped and stared at Flanigan, and then at Lake. Peter Flanigan stuck his tongue between his teeth and gently pressed down. No one talked.

Finally, after a long silence devoted to digesting James' comment, Cornwell said he had one last thing to say.

"From our FBI reports both of you know fire. Hamilton Lake's people are 'Keepers of the Fire' and Peter Flanigan's mother lives over a fire-started by his absent father.

"The choice is yours to make and you have no time to think it over."

Flanigan smiled and leaned back in his chair and said, "When do I leave for training?"

Lake quickly replied, "Peter means, when do we leave?"

Chapter 23
Smoke Jumpers

FBI Agent Lambert drove Peter Flanigan and Handsome Lake to Grand Central Station in New York City. He gave the men tickets to Butte, Montana and bus fare money for the remaining trip up to the U.S. Forestry Center in Missoula, Montana and gave each man a small gym size bag and an envelope.

"In each envelope is $128.00 for work that you performed in prison. Count it. You would have more if you hadn't spend so much time in the hole.

"Your bag has a kit provided by the United States Bureau of Prisons. In it, you will find a shaving kit, small towel, change of underwear, socks and a white shirt. I suggest that you buy wool sweaters somewhere, perhaps when you change trains in Chicago. You may need them in the mountains. In Missoula you will be issued all the gear you need for your work."

"You mean, you are not going with us?" said Flanigan.

"You fellows are on your own."

"Suppose we get off somewhere and don't make it to Missoula?" said Lake.

"Fair warning, fellows. If you don't show at Missoula, we'll find you and put you in Leavenworth or Springfield. Danbury is a side show compared to Leavenworth and Springfield. I suggest that you appreciate your good fortune and don't do anything stupid — like not showing up. Remember what the warden told you, you still have to complete the sentence given to you by U.S. Federal District Court judges. You have instructions in that envelope about contacting your parole officer in Missoula."

The following day, Flanigan and Lake made their train change for Montana and settled in for the long ride across the prairie. For Peter Flanigan, it was a time to sit back and relax. He had made a call to Anna Maria from the Chicago train station. It was a brief conversation but with his eyes closed, he reviewed every word and the sweet music of her voice muffled the clacking of wheels on iron rails.

"Peter, I can hardly speak. I can't believe it is you. Where are you? Your mother has been feeding me information about you, but I haven't received one of your letters."

Flanigan had to stop Anna Maria and tell her that she would be hearing a lot from him soon. He briefed her on his release, his move to Montana, and the conditions of his freedom — to fight fires for the National Forest Service.

"Anna Maria, I never received the letter you sent to me when I was at Maryfarm in Easton. Was there anything negative in it?"

"No. And that was 15 months ago, Peter."

"I have to catch a train. Can you kind of summarize what you said?"

"Peter Flanigan, I wrote you many letters, none of which you received. How can I remember what was in just one letter?"

"Was there any one thing in all those letters that I should remember?" asked Flanigan.

Anna Maria paused.

"I'd rather tell you in person, Peter. Or in a letter. Let's just say it's how I feel about you."

"Can't you say it over the phone"?

"No."

"This phone isn't censored like my mail was at Danbury. And you know, Anna Maria, in a week or so I am going to be jumping out of planes. It would be."

"O.K. Peter. It's no surprise to you. You know it well, or you should know by now. I just don't like saying things casually but... I love you so much that I could cry. And I do cry when I'm alone and thinking about you. But you know what? I'm not crying now."

"I know. I can hear your smile. You should see the grin that I have on my kisser," said Flanigan.

Peter told Ana Maria that the warden said that his mother would be notified of his departure from Danbury and his new address in Missoula.

"Why don't you call her and tell her. Danbury gave limited information in the past. No telling when or what she will hear from them."

Now, as he gazed out the window, fields of corn flashed by as he and Handsome Lake left behind friends, loved ones, memories, and concerns.

"Why are we here and Randolph Jackson is confined to a mental institution? If I have ever known a guy who had his wits about him it was Jackson," said Flanigan.

"I've thought about that too, Peter. As a Christian, you might have a better fix on that than I. Why did he even have to mention he was a Christian? After observing a lot of holier than thous in prison, I'd say that Croswell, the Bureau of Prisons guy, was a Christian racist. You have met your share of those characters, haven't you?"

"Sure, contradictions in beliefs aren't uncommon, but why let us off the hook and send Jackson to the loony bin? And besides, he had to know your native American background. You don't think of yourself as white, like Croswell, do you Handsome?"

"Croswell isn't lily white, Peter. I have relatives who are whiter than Croswell. One look at him and I knew he was a blood. He is just one of ours who has made it being one of theirs. When he dropped a reference about his home state of Oklahoma, I immediately sized him up. Croswell is a Cherokee. I'd lay my clan wampum on that."

"What do you suppose Randolph Jackson is doing now?" asked Flanigan to Lake who sat by his side.

"From what I heard about Springfield, I don't even want to think about it. Randolph surely did his job to make the strike a reality. I wonder how the guys on strike are doing? Hope they don't cave in to the powers."

"If I have Bentley and McGinley figured out, caving in won't happen," replied Flanigan.

Back in Danbury, twenty three men continued their long strike. The work stoppage continued until December 23, 1943 when the warden called a meeting to announce that beginning in February of 1944, segregation of mess halls would end at Danbury. Inmates would be allowed to sit wherever they wanted during meals.

Danbury was the first Federal prison to end discrimination in mess halls. It was a major victory for the men who refused to work — refused to sit any longer in a racially segregated eating place of the United States Federal Government. Conscientious objectors were beginning to prick the conscience of Americans outside of prison. National publicity about the C.O. strike hit the newsstands by the fall of 1943, and pressured federal officials to act. The C.O.s' victory at Danbury had accomplished what other opponents of segregation only dreamed about. They brought the United States government down on an issue that, in decades to follow, would change this country forever.

Flanigan turning to Lake, asked, "Handsome, do you think you changed any in prison?"

Lake did not have to think long. "Sure. I wasn't constantly aware of the change. But, yeah, I did."

"How?"

"Peter, what Cornwell, my Cherokee kin, said back in Danbury wasn't far off the mark. He said that I was suffering from a cultural deficiency. That I had lived a sheltered life. He was right. Most of my life has been sheltered except for some studies at Syracuse University and limited exposure to a few people outside of my Onondaga clan family. It probably took me longer to adapt because of my lack of exposure to other people before I was jailed."

"Do you mean that prison whitemanized you?"

"No. But I learned about people at Danbury. For the first time in my life I met people from around the country. Each day in the exercise yard, I saw and talked to people from every place imaginable. People with beliefs and practices quite strange to me. I'm glad I listened; and more importantly, I'm glad I began to feel for other people."

Flanigan agreed with Lake. "I'm from a clan too, Handsome. My tribe came to this county during the great Irish famine of the 1840's. I have some friends who are not of my cultural background, but not many. Living back in Wurtzville was like living on a reservation. Most people in my hometown are Christian — divided between Catholics and Protestants. But each group looks upon the other as different as they would look upon Buddhists or Moslems. Marriage between Catholics and Protestants are called 'mixed marriages'.

"At Danbury, I was exposed for the first time to people that I just learned about in school — atheists, agnostics, Moslems, Jehovah's Witnesses, people claiming to be Nazis or Communists, and of course Negroes, Orientals and ..."

"Yeah," said Lake. "Even a real live Indian without feathers."

"That's right. Before I met you I couldn't even pronounce Onondaga. But now I have to ask you this — will you return to your tribe after all this is over?"

"I don't think I'm ready for that right now, Peter. Just a few months ago I wouldn't have said that. But you see, I'm still very much a native American and I haven't lost my religion. I actually gained in religious strength during my time in the hole. I read and reread the *Code of Handsome Lake*. I'm committed but I wonder if my people are beyond help."

"Why? Why do you say that, Handsome?"

"Peter, there is a lake near my home that you can find on any map of New York State. It's a big lake and once was very beautiful. Many of my people still live along this lake but they no longer fish the lake. They no longer take their canoes to the lake to spear and net fish. Instead, they compete for jobs at a battery factory along the lake. The factory spills chemicals into the lake. There are no fish to catch. All life in the lake has been destroyed by acid and other harmful chemicals, but my people do not protest. They've been beaten into submission by the white man. Whitemanized."

"So where would you go to practice your faith?"

"That I've got to figure out. There are people of mine, brothers and sisters in Montana country, who are far removed from outside influences."

"You're talking about the Sioux, or Crow or Blackfeet? Aren't you?"

"No, Peter. I'm talking about the Nez Perce. They're a tribe in Idaho and Montana who have a disposition that would agree with me. Or, so I've studied. They are far removed from the White man and live peacefully with their beautiful Appaloosa horses, fish the Salmon and Snake rivers and their tributaries, and they farm the rich bottom lands in the river valleys. I think I could live with those people and maybe carry on the influence of my namesake.

"But my faith has been expanded, Peter. In prison, I recited the holy book of my creed — the Gai'wiio. The Gai'wiio takes three days to recite. When I finished that, I read about Gandhi and how he, as a devout Hindu, read the Gospels of Matthew, Mark, Luke and John. Gandhi spent much longer in prison than you and I. Yet, he had no problem accepting Christ and remaining a Hindu. I feel the same way after reading the Christian holy gospels. I can accept Christ and continue to follow the teachings of my religion. I don't want to force my beliefs on anyone but I do want to shelter myself and my future family from the apocalyptic fanatics — some of whom claim to be Christian."

"But Gandhi believed in rebirth, that Jesus was one of many reincarnations of God. Do you believe that as well?"

"Maybe. I haven't sorted that out yet. I'm not so sure about reincarnation. What about the book you promised me — the Spiritual Exercises of Igantius of Loyola?"

"Don't have it."

"They took it from you?"

"No. I followed the exercises every time we went into the hole. The hole became a very meditative place for me. It was a retreat. Every day, I had a lot of thinking to do and the exercises got me through each day. When I told McGinley about it, he had a good laugh. Then, shortly before we went on strike, he saw me in the yard and asked me if he could use the *Spiritual Exercises* book. I gave it to him the day before we went on strike."

"Do you think he is reading it now?"

"Actually, I do. I think that he's re-examining his earlier Christian beliefs in light of the violence that has saturated Marxist-Leninist theory. McGinley taught me about the actions of the Soviet system and its destruction of millions of middle class farmers. As he tried to find reasons to accept this perversion, I could see his logic cracking. I think he's ready to mend some fences. It's tough to shake off your roots, right, Handsome?"

Lake grinned. "You're on the mark, Flanigan. There are some really strange folks and beliefs back in Danbury. When I encounter people with goofy thinking, I thank my family for nurturing me in our native value system."

"Well, out in the Rocky Mountains you shouldn't have to worry about straying too far from your values. Fighting fires sounds like positive action in any culture," said Flanigan.

"No. Not really, Peter. Fire to my people is a positive force, not a negative force. We call it Grandfather Fire. If I remember my anthropology right, most native people of the Plains and Mountain tribes also think of fire in positive ways."

"You mean Indians like fire? Think it's good? Don't want to put fires out? Isn't that strange?"

"To the white man it is. But do you try to stop the wind from blowing — the rain or snow from falling — the ocean tides from rolling? Fire to us has meaning beyond spiritual purification. Grandfather fire is practical. Fire is warmth. It is healing. It allows us to cook the 'three sisters' — corn, beans and squash. We use fire to fertilize our land, to chase out deer and rabbits during the hunt and to symbolize our friendship and unity as a people.

"Native Americans do not try to put out fires. Fires make fields for planting. Fires are needed to break open hard shelled seeds that grow new life. To us, fire is regeneration, not disintegration. Knowing that, I question myself in this new venture. Is this what my forefathers wanted me to do — fight fire?

"I may not last long on this detail, Peter."

"But you will do smoke jumping?"

"Oh yes. I gave my word back in Danbury. I just didn't say for how long."

Taking a bus from Butte to Missoula, the two were surprised when a man greeting them as they disembarked. He extended his hand to Flanigan.

"You must be Peter Flanigan," he said, and shaking Lake's hand, added, "and Handsome Lake. Welcome to Missoula. My name is Tom Hanson and I'll be your instructor for the next two weeks. We have been anxiously awaiting you fellows. We had a call this morning to let us know that you would probably be on the afternoon bus from Butte. My truck is over here. It's a short ride to the cabins near the parachute loft."

Flanigan sized up Hanson and thought that he looked more like a grocery clerk than a smoke jumper. Hanson stood only about 5'6". His friendly, lively eyes danced between the two men and made them both comfortable. Although Flanigan guessed his age to be around 40, Hanson had a weathered facial look of a man much older.

Peter was the first to speak up as they rode to the cabin.

"Mr. Hanson, why have you asked C.O.s to work as Smoke Jumpers?"

"Easy answer, Peter, is that we can't get anyone else. Last year, the federal government cancelled the Civilian Conservation Corp, and most of our regular crew of jumpers have gone into the military. The fact is that we probably could get other people but we recognize that you fellows are often a bit brighter than the ordinary bird, and often people who are willing to prove something."

"Prove something?" asked Handsome Lake as he turned to catch Hanson's eye.

"Sure. Like proving that you are not cowards. That you are willing to jump from an aircraft to fight a blazing inferno."

"Maybe that is the case with some people, Mr. Hanson, but I doubt if that is the case with Peter and me."

"Call me Tom, gentlemen. The base point is that I really don't care what your reasons are for coming to the school. If you guys are ready to learn to be smoke jumpers and do your job, that's good enough for me. We don't put out fires with politics or philosophy."

"Sounds good to me," said Lake.

Hanson showed the men their bunk room. Introduced them to their four room mates who had arrived several days before and were waiting for the new class to begin. Three of the men were from Civilian Public Service Camps around the county. Only one was from a federal prison — Lewisburg, Pennsylvania.

Hanson took them to the supply room and issued each man several blue shirts, blue jeans, two pair of boots, a padded jump suit, football helmet, wire mesh mask, 100 feet of rope, a packet of topographical maps, compass and assorted other items — underwear, socks, towels. Then, Hanson took them to the tool shed and issued each man a Pulaski, a small shovel, and a saw.

The following morning, Flanigan and Lake joined the full complement of smoke jumpers and trainees for calisthenics. Their prison time exercises helped both men to keep up with the vigorous early morning regime. The military daily dozen of push ups, sit ups, deep bends, and assorted stretching exercises were followed by jogging, then running several miles. Tom Hanson was pleasantly surprised at the top condition of Flanigan and Lake.

In the mess hall, Flanigan and Lake shook hands with over forty men who had finished training and were on fire call. The two new men were cheerfully greeted with an immediate feeling of inclusion. They would learn more about the men in coming weeks. Most were from the traditional Peace Churches: Quakers, Mennonites and Brethren. There were a couple of Methodists and a Catholic, as well as several fellows who laid claim to no specific group. The conversations in days to come would prove as invigorating as the mountain air and strenuous physical exercises.

Every morning for the next two weeks, the six new recruits met in Instructor Hanson's classroom after breakfast. Hanson informed the men that because of the lateness of the fire season and the small class size, that if all went well, the first test jumps should be made by the 8th day of training. Five jumps in three days, and if satisfactory, candidates would be ready for action.

Hanson outlined the history of the United States Forest Service since it had been established by Theodore Roosevelt and Gifford Pinchot, former governor of Pennsylvania and ardent conservationist.

"Let me make one thing perfectly clear, gentlemen. Our job is not to put out big fires. Our job is to prevent small fires from becoming big fires. We can try to hold a big fire from spreading until mother nature stops the wind from blowing or allows rain or snow to fall."

Hanson taught the basics of fire and fire fighting. He sketched a large triangle on the black board and marked each angle. #1 fuel, #2 heat, #3 oxygen. Then he stacked dry pine needles, sticks and pine cones on the classroom wood stove. Striking a piece of flint, he ignited the fuel, and then gave it shot with a bellows. He showed how eliminating one of the three will put the fire out and started by putting a large lid over the flame to stop oxygen. Then he started the fire over again, only to douse it with water. Finally, he removed the fuel itself.

Then, he moved the class outside and demonstrated heat transfer — conduction, convection and radiation. To show how forest fires often conduct heat slowly, he put large sticks into a small center ring of fire. He allowed the students to test conduction by picking up the warm but not flaming end of the sticks. Then, to teach convection of liquids and gases and how they carry heat away from a fire, Hanson put a small pot of tea on the center ring of fire and waited for it to heat up and steam. He related the manner in which forest fires can preheat surrounding areas with smoke and make it easier for ground winds to rush into the heated areas supplying oxygen and spreading the fire. He told the men how dangerous convection is in hilly and mountainous areas.

"Gasses in the hot smoke sweep up mountains sides, preheat trees and prepare them for quick ignition. I don't have to tell you that this area is extremely mountainous, but I can tell you that this has been a long, hot and dry summer."

Finally, looking at Handsome Lake, Instructor Hanson asked him to explain radiation.

Lake smiled. "I'm glad you asked me. My people often joke about Whitemen's fire, but they would like your fire. It is small. My people like to say that Whitemen build big fires and stand far away. We build a small fire and stand close. Both people know about radiation. We just use less fuel."

Tom Hanson nodded at the response, which also allowed him to explain the key factor in the spread of a forest fire: fuel. He told them that they were in the middle of the largest, richest dry fuel source in the county. A source ready for conduction, convection and radiation.

"But how do most fires start out here?" asked Flanigan.

"Thunder storms. Just since you fellows arrived, we have sent several crews out to contain small fires started by lightning. Almost every forest fire is started that way. There are always a few that begin from camp fires and an occasional fire set intentionally.

"We know the fires are out there because our ground or air spotters contact the fire center here in Missoula on first sighting. Most fires are put out pretty easily if we can catch them early."

As classroom work wound down, the students learned about various types of forest fires. Ground fires that smolder slowly and give off little heat but can lead to surface fires, and surface fires that burn quickly and give off great heat but do limited damage to trees.

"It's crown fires, fires that reach the top of trees and are fanned by winds that are most frightening to smoke jumpers and do the most damage to dense forests," said Hanson.

Hanson told of crown fires that he fought and his friendly and often humorous demeanor turned grim. He spoke as if he had crossed the line to another dimension — a hell fire of terror.

"When you are fighting a fire out there and you hear the roar of a train, you have to stop thinking about containing a fire and immediately think about saving yourself and others. That sound of horror in the forest is a crown fire that has become a fire storm. Winds that are made by the fire itself — so large, so hot, that oxygen is violently sucked into the fire in a deafening roar that sends swirls of tornado-like fire at speeds faster than you can run.

"The text book term is 'fire storm.' We call it a blowup. I pray to God that you will never experience one."

He held up a small combination ax and hoe and asked the men if they knew the proper name for this, the most important tool of smoke jumpers. Hanson told the men the story behind the name of the device: "Pulaski". He told the recruits about the great fire of 1910 in the Rockies. How a dry spell that began in April of that year parched the woodlands and how a series of small fires eventually led to a conflagration that destroyed three million acres of forest and produced one legendary fire fighter — Ranger Edward Pulaski.

"Pulaski was a direct descendent of the Polish General who came to the aid of Americans in the Revolutionary War — Casmir Pulaski. The coolness of Edward Pulaski saved forty men from certain death during the great blowup on August 20th of that year. Pulaski led his crew away from the firestorm to an abandoned mine shaft where he stood at the entrance holding a wet horse blanket as a sheild against the smoke and fire. Pulaski was found unconscious the following morning but he and 39 other men lived. Since that event, the most trust worthy tool of fire fighters has been called a 'Pulaski'.

"We hope you never encounter a blowup, but if you do, we want you to use your wits. You will have to use every bit of mental and physical strength in creative ways that only you will be able to do. We can give you guides but in a blowup, you have to save yourselves."

Hanson reviewed the brief history of smoke jumping to let the men know the unique nature of their job. "You fellows are into something quite new in the story of fire fighting." He told how the Aerial Fire Control Project out of Missoula had been started only two years before, and how the Director of the project, David Godwin, got his idea to fight fires from the air from the Soviets. The Soviets experimented with parachute firemen in the 1930's but gave the project up. Later in the decade, they began using planes to drop chemicals instead of men to fight forest and steppe fires.

"When the first experimental jumps were made just four years ago, we had men jumping out of planes with no previous parachute experience. That is not going to be the case with you fellows. Jumping in the Rockies is not for the timid or untrained. When you fellows fall out, you will be encountering mountain winds. Up drafts, down drafts, cross drafts, all these will push and pull your chutes. Your touch down area can be rock slides, snags and timber territory far different than the Russian steppe lands."

At the end of the week's work of fire study, Hanson knew that the men had learned techniques of creating a fire line to hold back a fire, reading and using maps and compass, survival techniques, and basic instruction in parachutes and how they function, following instruction from the plane spotter, and working as a team under direction of a smoke jumper foreman.

"Parachutes have been around since 1783 when the French physicist, Louis Sebastian Lenormand jumped from a tower. But the design of the chute was improved by one of our own smokejumpers, Frank Derry."

Hanson showed the old standard chute that had no air vents and demonstrated how this caused a rocking motion that spilled air out of one side, then rocked sideways and spilled air out to the other.

Putting the older chute away, Hanson held up the chute they would be using. "Derry cut three openings in his chute, one on top and one on each side of the chute with tails of nylon to act as rudders. You fellows will feel very comfortable guiding yourselves down with the Derry chute.

"O.K., guys, let's have some practice jumps from the Ford Tri Motor mock up. Tomorrow is real-time jumping."

Chapter 24
Hot As A Crown Fire

Flanigan, Lake and their four classmates received additional gear the following morning. Each man was issued a back-pack chute and chest pack reserve chute, a sack that was filled with a sleeping bag, canteens, ration pack, and flashlight. Two five gallon water cans were lashed to the chute pack and a new issue of a cross cut saw bolted between two boards to prevent saw tooth damage. Most of this gear would be dropped by cargo chute.

The Ford TriMotor was revving up when the men lumbered on board and took their bench seats along side of a spotter and Instructor Hanson. This first of five practice jumps would acquaint the men with the job of the pilot and the spotter. The spotter's job was to signal the pilot when a good landing spot for the smoke jumpers was sighted. The first three jumps would be near the airstrip. On actual fire jumps, a jump crew foreman would accompany the men and manage the on-ground fire crew.

The previous day, Hanson had taken them to the airstrip and explained the structure of the TriMotor. "Some folks call the Ford TriMotor a Tin Goose but I have a lot of respect for this old plane," Hanson said with a discernible pride.

Hanson pointed out the wing and nose engines and the corrugated aluminum construction that made the bulky looking plane actually light for its size. "Look at those fat wings, they can lift you out of narrow canyons and glide you to safety if the engines fail. Respect this plane boys. It's guided me to dozens of successful jumps."

Most of the first time jumpers didn't sleep well the night before, and now, as they sat and were inspected by both Hanson and the foreman, they seemed to be calm and reflective. Hanson checked and rechecked the safety catches on the quick release plates and the foreman double checked harnesses, back-packs and reserves.

On the first of three runs around the field, the spotter took his normal kneeling position as he looked out the small window and observed the trial drift chutes for wind currents. On the fourth run, the foreman called out for Flanigan and Lake to stand at the door and prepare to jump. Both men snapped their static lines onto the cable over the door of the Ford TriMotor. Flanigan took a semi-squat position to clear the low door way and placed his left foot out onto the small metal door step to open space.

The spotter hand signaled and called "Cut" to the pilot who slowed the plane speed. Then, tapping Peter Flanigan on the shoulder, Peter left the craft.

Flanigan, his arms wrapped tightly across the reserve chute on his chest, let out a whoop of joy as the chute puffed full. Following the instructions that Hanson had gone over many times on the ground, he managed to drift to a smooth landing.

Before he hit the ground, Flanigan heard Lake calling out above, "Onondaga, Onondaga, Onondaga!"

They landed just 50 yards apart and waved their signal streamers to tell the spotter above that they were O.K.

All six men jumped successfully and assumed that the one jump was it for the day. However, Hanson gathered them around the Tri Motor and had the chute packers take out new chutes for each man and rig them to their harnesses. On board once again, the men repeated their jump and before the afternoon was over, jumped for the third time.

"You fellows did a swell job today," Tom Hanson told them in the late afternoon critique. He pointed out errors, told them how to make corrections and then introduced a type of jump that he said was somewhat unorthodox.

"This is the first group that has not had major problems. You fellows work well together. With that in mind, I'd like a volunteer to try a jump tomorrow that we normally would teach after a couple of weeks of work in the field. We call it the 'Slip Jump.' Let me explain it to you and if you want to wait for a week or two to try it, well that's just fine. Not everyone wants to do this and I suppose not everyone should do it.

"The Slip Jump is used to get a smoke jumper to the targeted fire when there are obstacles or conditions that impede the flight of the jumper. Now these obstacles might be canyons, or mountain lakes, or fast flowing rivers or tall dead trees — 'snags' we call them. Or the condition may be wind that you have to break through to get to the spot you want to hit.

"Now, boys, if you can control the chute by reducing the amount of air that fills the silk bubble, then what happens?"

"You fall faster," said Flanigan.

"Exactly. Falling faster can prevent a jumper from being speared by one of those damn awful snags, or slamming into a rocky side hill or one of our mountain rivers or whatever the hell can cause harm."

Pointing to the parachute hanging from the practice loft, Instructor Hanson explained how to partially collapse the chute and cause it to drop faster and straight down rather than drift with the wind.

"How many suspension lines on a chute?" asked Hanson.

"Twenty eight," said one of the jumpers.

"Right. Now watch as I pull just three of the 28."

Yanking down on the lines, Hanson was able to spill so much air that the chute bubble was pulled almost half over on its side.

"Now, of course this is just a test. In a real drop, you won't have the advantage I have of standing on terra firma."

"So how do you collapse the chute?" asked Flanigan.

"You need to climb against gravity, Mr. Flanigan. You need to reach up as you are falling and climb the three lines to force the bubble to partial collapse."

"Suppose you collapse the whole chute?" said Lake.

"No man is strong enough to do that or defy the laws of physics," commented Hanson.

"You mean the law of physics that tells us that a body in motion will stay in motion unless disturbed by an outside force — like the ground?" said Flanigan.

"Right. You are speeding up the fall to get safely to the outside force that you want, instead of smacking into the outside force you don't want. Better a nice soft grass landing than a snag up your behind.

"Now before I waste my time teaching this technique, do I have a volunteer to try to execute a slip jump tomorrow?"

"Sure. I'd like to give it a try," said Flanigan.

"O.K. but let's have everyone pay attention. You all may be called upon to slip jump someday."

Instructor Hanson had Flanigan practice the maneuver many times and emphasized that Peter would have to remember that fifty pounds of equipment would be added to his body when he did the slip jump. That he would have to literally climb up the strands and look down at the ground so that a miscalculation was not made.

"We do practice slip jumps from higher altitudes so that you have more time to direct yourself to touch down. You must release your lines and allow the chute to fill back up at around 500 feet.

"Flanigan, you seemed to have done well in our aerial distance estimation simulation. Be sure you are alert tomorrow. Sometimes the ground comes up mighty fast when a fellow is tugging on those lines and pulling himself up.

"When we finish our remaining two practice jumps tomorrow morning, only Mr. Flanigan, the pilot and myself will go airborne for the slip jump. The rest of you are to watch from below and critique Flanigan's fall."

The following day, the six jumpers completed the five practice jumps and afterwards, stood near the runway, heads back, as they waited for Peter to make the first slip jump.

The TriMotor climbed not to the 1,000 feet that was the jump altitude used, but up to 2400 feet. The craft circled, and Flanigan could be seen from below as he crouched in the jump door.

Hanson, wearing spotter goggles, looked like a caricature of a hawk in a glide searching for prey. His head stuck out of the window next to the jump door, legs flexed into his backside, he held his left hand high, ready to drop it and call "Cut" to the pilot when it was time. His right arm extended to Flanigan and the moment after he gave the pilot the signal to slow engines, he slapped Flanigan on the back and watched Peter drop and his chute slip open.

Flanigan, getting accustomed to body jolt, gave a quick look up and saw the great mushroom configuration unfold. He immediately seized three lines and thinking of himself as a mountain climber, he began the accent, reaching and pulling himself up to a rock ledge with one hand, hanging on and reaching higher for the next ledge. The chute begin to sag as it swayed beneath Flanigan's wiry strength.

He heard a hissing rush of air as the collapse began — air rushing out as the silk was folded back to a trembling, twirling, half open chute. He felt his body rushing faster downward as the chute took on the movement of a child's play top, spinning with a whirling noise. Looking down, he knew it was time to put air back into the parachute. Dangling slack line surrounded Flanigan as he thought of what Tom Hanson warned: "Don't let the slack get tangled in your boots." But it wasn't his boots that took to the slack, it was his right arm. Two lines became wrapped around his right elbow and he struggled to release them as his eyes bobbed from ground to tangle.

When the lines slipped free, the chute immediately popped back into full bloom and Flanigan guided the rig close to his student audience. Five classmates rushed over, helped Peter out of his harness and congratulated him on his performance.

"If that was a slip jump, let's hope we don't have to do many of them," said Flanigan.

"Why? It looked great, Peter. It came off like clockwork," said Lake.

"Yeah. Like my clock was running out," said Flanigan.

"Let's just say that slip jumps are not easy maneuvers."

With the two week training period officially over, Flanigan and Lake were kept at Missoula and the four other classmates were sent out to a smokejumper base camp at McCall, Idaho.

Blending into the daily routine of smoke jumping was easy. Most days were spent doing chores and keeping fit. Everyone did care and cleaning of equipment. Crews were selected to cut logs and clear brush around camp. Daily refresher classes on a variety of topics such as map reading and fire control kept minds busy and for recreation, a chance to go to town on Saturday afternoon.

Several crews were called to put out minor fires. Flanigan and Lake were getting anxious to be part of the action. Some fellows were saying that maybe the fire season would be over early that year. It was now September 5th and reports of snowfall were coming in from rangers covering the Bitterroot Range south of Missoula and Flatrange to the north of town. However, Tom Hanson noted that humidity had been low for several weeks throughout most of the region and a good rain was needed to reduce fire danger.

On September 7, Flanigan and Lake were sent on their first fire mission. Six men jumped on a grassy slope about forty miles north of Missoula. The spotter complained that the local fire department should be taking care of this fire but as they circled to prepare for a drop, it was evident that no truck could get through to the ridge and fire fighters on foot might take too long to hump it over the high ground separating the tiny village of St. Ignatius from the fire.

Handsome Lake thought it coincidental that their first jump would be onto a place named for Flanigan's favorite saint.

"Naw. It's not coincidental, Handsome, it's just old Iggie looking out for us boys," said Peter.

The drop took place very near the fire because there was no noticeable blaze, but a lot of smoke. It was judged to be a ground fire, smoldering leaf and pine needle duff that needed containment. As it turned out, it was quite small and because a rocky face blocking the forward advance of the fire, the men established a fire line of a few hundred yards to surround and stop its spread. The foreman checked air temperature, humidity and wind and put the men to work with their Pulaskis — digging, chopping and clearing a line as the morning worn on.

By late afternoon, the foreman was satisfied that the job was done and the crew hiked down the mountain to St. Ignatius and awaited their pickup truck for the trip back to Missoula.

By the second week of September, a series of thunder storms struck the region and although little rain fell, lightning strikes kept the whole smoke jumping crew at Missoula busy. Most of the fires were easily contained, but two fires required several days of work and cargo drops to keep the men supplied with water and rations. Flanigan and Lake managed to miss working with the more experienced, larger crews; but on the 14th of September, Tom Hanson cut short breakfast and ordered the twelve remaining men to suit up.

"We're flying over the Montana border to jump a fire near Hungry

Rock Mountain in Idaho. I called McCall and they are sending a dozen jumpers onto the western slope to begin a fire line. We will jump onto the east side of the fire and work a line around to join with the crew from McCall. Take a look at this topo."

Hanson spread out a topographical map and the men gathered around to observe the rugged terrain illustrated by the tightly drawn contour lines.

"We won't know the exact drop zone but I'm making Lake squad leader of the six to drop on the south east side and Flanigan will take charge of the six-man crew dropped on the north east side.

"This is the fire we have feared for the past week. But we can stop it if both crews work their asses off and mother nature calms the wind. Use the buddy system, stay together as a team and sharpen your Pulaskis, a lot of cutting and digging is ahead."

The Ford TriMotor climbed southwest over the Bitterroot Range, and Hanson spotted the fire on the western slope.

"Doesn't look as bad as I had expected. We'll circle the fire a few times to find the best drop."

On the second run, the plane from McCall was seen coming out of the west. Both planes dropped drift chutes to test the wind.

Hanson ordered Flanigan and his buddy on this run to make the first jump onto a narrow strip of meadow land created by a fire years before. When both men were seen to encounter winds that took them away from the meadow and into the tree line, Hanson decided that the rest of the crew would have to slip-jump onto the patch.

The next half dozen men, slip jumping in two's on separate runs, found the mark and avoided tree entanglement. By this time, the wind that pushed Flanigan and his partner into the woods, was fanning the fire and bringing it closer to the grassy knoll.

Flanigan and Lake, both out of their chutes, gathered their men and began cutting a fire line, periodically looking skyward for the remaining four jumpers to join the crews. They worked feverishly to cut a line to prevent the fire from hitting the tall grass. They knew that the grass could explode in a fire ball and ignite the dry Douglas fir and Ponderosa pine at their backs.

Tom Hanson apparently knew that the remaining four could have problems with the slip jump. They had trouble with it in training, and when the next two men landed very near the fire, their chutes filled with hot smoke and the men felt themselves being dragged into the fire until they successfully released their taunt buckle release snaps.

The last pair of jumpers were unable to collapse their chutes on the way down. As a result, they drifted so close to the fire that on landing, the hot chutes dragged them into a smoke cloud.

Flanigan and Lake dropped their Pulaskis and ran into the grey cloud to try to release the men from their ballooned, smoke-filled parachutes. Flanigan managed to snap the release catch from the first man and pull him out of the choking vapor. Lake couldn't hold his man back, so he used his bowie knife to cut the lines free from the jumper. Finding the chutist with head on his chest, Lake saw that he was overcome with smoke. Draping the man over his shoulders, Lake held his breath and ran out of the burning tree line to temporary safety in the little meadow.

Flanigan and Lake saw that the two men would not be able to continue fighting the fire, and delegated a third man to use his topographical map and guide the disabled jumpers to a retreat area near the Selway River Falls.

The remaining nine men continued to remove the fuel for fire by cutting a wide swatch between the slow burning forest and the volatile bunch meadow grass. Lake, facing the forest, stopped cutting and scraping, and threw a handful of grass into the air. It blew back into his face and he knew a wind shift was occurring. He ran across the meadow to Flanigan.

"Peter, we have got to get the men out of here — now! Look!"

He demonstrated the wind direction with the bunch grass.

"O.K. We'll cut for that ridge behind us and check our topos again."

Flanigan and Lake blew their whistles and gave a twirling arm signal for the crew to follow them. Pumping his arm quickly up and down, he yelled, "Double time, guys. Up the ridge and fast."

The heat began to intensify as the wind blew strongly out of the west. As a tall snag snapped and flew into the meadow, the grass, needing much less heat to ignite than the dense woodland, crackled into flame. Within minutes the fire was speeding toward the eastern slope — in the direction of Flanigan and Lake's crews, as they ran up the high ground.

The men found a rocky, saddle-like area behind the ridge top. Below was a small creek sided by a promontory. They filled their canteens and five-gallon water containers and climbed the cliff to distance themselves from the fire that was now burning up the east ridge of the meadow. Looking out from the headland over the creek, Flanigan and Lake told the men to take a break. Then the squad leaders went on reconnaissance to determine where the next fire line should be drawn.

"This is insane, Peter. Absolutely insane," said Handsome Lake as the two men trudged up a deer trail behind the cliff.

"Here I am acting like a total hypocrite. Grandfather Fire will do what he wants to do. Yet, here I am fighting against what I am supposed to believe in — the power of nature. I'm getting to hate myself for it, Peter. I've never been so damn mad at myself. And look at those men, they think that they are doing the right thing by standing up to what is a normal, necessary action of nature. At least they are just ignorant. But me? I'm not ignorant, I'm stupid. I'm getting to hate myself for contradicting my own belief."

"Come on Handsome, stop proselytizing the *Code* to me. I don't try to convert you to Catholicism."

"You don't have to be an adherent of the *Code of Handsome Lake* to understand that the best defense against a forest fire is what we are doing right now — retreating. Let it burn. Nature knows better than my people or Catholics or Jews or anyone who thinks they have a lock on the truth."

"You are making sense, Handsome, but right now, we're in a mess and I can't philosophize. I've got to think of what to do next."

"Well, let me tell you now, Peter. Once the men are safe and secure, don't come looking for me. If you can't find me, not to worry. Only you will have an idea. Just look at your map and keep it under your hat."

"I think I'm deciphering you, Handsome. Enough said."

Although the fire was not an immediate threat, smoke was spreading across the north side of the creek and Peter, noting a flock of hawks gliding over a ridge, questioned Handsome on his impression of the unusual sight.

"They are waiting for the rodents — squirrels, voles and other small animals to run from the fire. Then they will swoop down and have dinner on Grandfather Fire. It's nature, Peter. Look, see that one folding his wings and dropping for the kill."

"Why don't the animals stay in their burrows?"

"They were probably smoked out. They are looking for safety," said Lake.

"Then, if nature knows better than us. Maybe we should see where they are going," commented Flanigan.

"Good idea. Let's go."

The two men changed course and walked up the creek. Using their squad leader binoculars, they saw small creatures running into a hillside. By the time Flanigan and Lake approached the hill, the animals had vanished. Searching a steep rocky slope they found a small opening in the eroded mountainside. Both men tugged one boulder out of the way. Lake then took his flash light and peered into the entrance.

"Take a look, Peter."

Flanigan switched on his flashlight and saw for real what he had only seen in science text books and encyclopedias: stalagmites and stalactites, huge icy looking lime formations pointing up from the cave floor, and icicle looking pieces hanging from the cave ceiling.

They crawled inside and watched as animals scurried away from a new danger. The cave branched off into side passages and the animals found easy refuge from the human intruders.

"This could be useful, Peter. I wonder where it goes to. We don't have time for spelunking."

"Spelunking?"

"Yes. Caving. You Pennsylvania coal miners make your own caves. In upstate New York, we spelunker natural caves. Let's check it out."

"It's almost four o'clock, Handsome. Let's go back and get the crew and make camp for the night. Tomorrow, we can figure out where to carve our fire line."

The crew had moved the cargo drop of sleeping bags, water containers, tools, and rations up to the camp site on the rock ledge above the creek. With darkness, the air cooled, wind subsided, and the forest fire embered instead of flared. Flanigan and Lake discussed working throughout the night on the fire line but reasoned that everyone was exhausted from the trauma of the day. Instead, they made fire watch assignments so that all hours would be covered until dawn.

First light through the smoky haze cast angled beams of shimmering orange and yellow down into the smoldering forest. The fire that was so easily seen during the night was now only a flickering glow through the haze.

Flanigan and Lake decided to divide the crew and clear fire lines. The creek was too small to hold back a crown fire but would help to halt a ground fire. So two lines were started 500 yards north and south of the creek to run west toward the McCall crew. Which way the fire would travel if the wind picked up again was anyone's guess after the previous day's experience.

After a quick breakfast, Flanigan's crew started their west moving line from the upper creek area and Lake had his men begin chopping and hoeing their western line down stream from Flanigan. Both crews were instructed to be concerned with fuel easy to ignite — pine needles, cones, small branches and twigs. There was not enough time or equipment to deal with trees or logs and a lot of ground to cover.

"We're back to dealing with a surface fire," said Lake. "Concentrate on stopping fire ladders by cutting dead twigs and branches hanging from the firs and pines. We don't want to fuel a crown fire. If the canopies get torched, we're in big trouble."

Flanigan and Lake had to encourage the men to budget time spent on the line, to avoid making highway size lanes, but rather, to make ten foot or less paths.

"Let's try to get to the McCall crew before dark tonight. If we have to work in the dark, we can do that as well," called out Flanigan.

By 10 o'clock, the heat of the day was setting in. When they saw smoke drifting westward, they wondered how the McCall teams were doing. By noon, the only breaks were to swig water and straighten backs. Flanigan left his crew to jog down the creek and followed the line over to Lake.

"Handsome, you guys look like you have the same problem we have. Just too much fuel to deal with. Maybe we should have selected a different stand."

"Don't expect me to pick another stand, Peter. This is crazy enough. If the fire picks up as it did yesterday, this fire line is worthless and look around you. Just where is there a good line of defense?"

While they talked, one of the crew called out, "Do you guys see what I see?"

He was pointing westward and watching the smoke begin to spin and change direction, they saw the tips of trees aflame and red embers beginning to fly east.

Looking Lake in the eye, Peter said, "Crown fire coming, Handsome. Let's rendezvous at the cave."

Flanigan sped along an animal trail that ran along side the creek and in a few minutes was directing his crew to the hillside cave. Lake's crew followed shortly after. Each man was instructed to fill their canteens, take off their padded jump suits and soak them in water.

As the men hurried up the slope to the cave entrance, Flanigan said to Lake, "What does that roar sound like to you, Handsome?"

"Chicago!"

"Chicago?"

"Yeah. Remember waiting for the train to Butte and about five locomotives came into the terminal at the same time?"

"You're right. But they were only belching steam. Check those flames. Remember what Tom Hanson said about blow-ups?"

Twirls of hot gases were swirling, leaping, and exploding into red tongues of fire that licked dry snags and oily pine tops. The inferno was consuming so much oxygen that the men could feel their bodies being sucked into the blow up.

Flanigan and Lake waited until the seven others got into the cave, then they took wet padded jump suits and sealed them with piled rocks to keep out dangerous fumes. The squad leaders told the men to keep wet kerchiefs over their mouths if smoke came into the cave.

"Be sure to stay close to the cave floor if we get smoke in here. Remember, carbon monoxide doesn't smell. If someone's speech is going off or you feel a bit dizzy, let us know. There are other areas in this cave we could retreat to. Don't burn your batteries out, get used to the dark," cautioned Lake.

As the men wandered about, Flanigan quietly asked Lake about the other areas of the cave.

"I was over here before daybreak this morning, Peter. I found an exit about 150 yards from here. I've got it blocked off, the men won't find it, but if you have to use it just follow the edge of that little water trickle. It leads to a rocky side hill. That's for me to use, Peter. Let's assume that I got lost in the cave, or left the cave and got into the fire.

Whatever the case, when the fire passes us, I won't be with you guys."

"Do you know how to get to where you're going?"

"Got my topos, compass, matches, and some rations. I'm fine."

"Your rations are pretty meager. The Nez Perce Reservation is still a long hike from here."

Padding his pocket, Lake said, "Fishing line and hooks. I'm told that the cutthroats bite like crazy around here. I won't starve, Peter. Actually, the reservation is pretty close."

"Can we shake now?" said Flanigan.

"We can do better than that," said Lake, giving Flanigan a hug. "Forever brothers."

The blowup reverberations were only somewhat muffled by the cave walls. The smoke jumpers sat with their hands over their ears, and their heads into their knees.

When the ear deafening resonance subsided, one of the Mennonite men spoke out, "Let's join hands and thank God we are in here and not out there. All complied, and bowed their heads as the Mennonite prayed.

"Oh God almighty, thank you for saving us from the fires of hell on earth. Thank you for giving us courage to face up to danger. To look fear in the face. To harm no man. To do your will."

In the darkness, Handsome Lake whispered into Flanigan's ear, "I'm off to do His will. God speed, Peter."

To the other men, Lake said aloud, "I'm checking out the cave, fellows."

Flanigan and the other seven men chatted about their close call with death. Then, smelling smoke, speculated about carbon monoxide. They wet the kerchiefs and tied them around their faces, sat back in silence and waited.

Checking watches, the men were surprised that it was now after 8 o'clock and Lake had not returned. Flanigan told them that Lake was an experienced spelunker and could take care of himself even if he was temporarily lost. The crew fell off to sleep for the night.

In the morning, Flanigan pulled aside the rocks and padded jump suits that covered the cave entrance and heard thunder, not of fire but of rain. It had apparently been raining all night and smoldering forest smoke and fog begin to immediately seep into the cave. The men crawled out into the dimness and found themselves in a quagmire. Dozens of rivulets were gushing down the steep slope and oozing mud quickly covered their boots.

Several volunteers said they would search the cave for Lake. Flanigan cautioned that more people could get lost and not to worry about Lake, but to reassure them, he selected two men to inspect the cave. Within minutes, they found the exit that Lake must have taken.

"Hope he didn't get caught in the fire," said one man.

"Or take one of the many other passages away from this underground stream," said the other man.

Flanigan nodded and agreed that both situations could have occurred but urged the men to get back to the crew.

When the men slipped down from the cave and assembled on the opposite slope, Flanigan remembered that he'd left his Pulaski in the cave and slogged back up to retrieve his tool. As he began the decent, he heard a gushing sound and felt mud and rock slip from under him. Turning his head toward the cave area he saw huge boulders, rocks and mud coming at him in an erosive avalanche.

The men watched in horror as Flanigan tried desperately to outrun the rock and mud slide but saw him go under, his arms extended in a diving position.

The slide was over in seconds and the men ran to the spot where they last saw Flanigan and clawed away until they found a hand wiggling through the mud. They swiped away at the mud and stone, and exposing his hairy scalp, two men pushed through the muck and gently lifted Peter up, only to find him pinned by the legs. As several other men joined to roll away a large boulder, Flanigan let out a shout of agony.

When Peter, now unconscious, was removed from the sloppy mess, they saw his crushed right leg. The tibia had snapped and its jagged ends were both sticking through the flesh beneath his knee. They made a stretcher of half burned branches and shirts and carried him to the wait station near Selway Falls.

When they got to there, Tom Hanson had already slip-jumped into the area and was waiting with the three men who were recovering from their smoke exhaustion. The crew assured Hanson that they thought that Lake was O.K. and would probably be along later. Hanson agreed that the priority was to get Flanigan to a hospital. He started the trek to Lowell, about fifteen miles from the Falls. In his heart, Hanson knew they would not make it, but they trudged on until the men, carrying 60 lb. packs, and frequently confused by the darkness of the bush whack trail, forced Hanson to make camp five miles beyond the falls.

Earlier he had injected morphine into Flanigan's thigh back at the falls. Now, he wondered about the fever that was beginning to boil in Peter's body. He tended to him throughout the night, and at daybreak, the long hike to Lowell continued.

The men flagged a logging truck on the dirt road to Lowell and the trucker took on the motley crew. The smoke jumpers lifted Flanigan on top of the truck load of Ponderosa pines and strapped him to the timbers. The smoke jumper crew sat along side of him on the rough ride to St. Patrick's Hospital in Missoula.

Tom Hanson did not have a body thermometer, but he was as worried about Flanigan's fever as he was about his compound fracture and other possible wounds. Every few minutes, he put his hand to Peter's head.

"This fellow is getting as hot as a crown fire."

It was late afternoon of the second day when the hospital emergency crew of St. Patrick's rushed out to take over from the exhausted crew of smoke jumpers.

Chapter 25
Plutonium Pig

St. Patrick's Hospital in Missoula has existed since the pioneer days of the 1890's. Miners, cowboys, ranchers, loggers and hunters with busted heads, arms, and legs came to St. Patrick's.

"Couldn't have picked a better place in all of Montana," commented Tom Hanson as they walked with the hospital staff transporting Peter to the men's ward.

"I was born in this hospital at a time when most babies were born at home. Hell, my daddy probably wouldn't have survived if I had been born at home. When my Mama first looked at me she would have clobbered my poppa, instead of slapping my little ass."

Hanson looked closer at Flanigan, hoping that he would respond to the comment. But Peter was still unconscious and quite obviously, so deeply, there wasn't a flicker of an eyelid.

Tom Hanson and his crew were politely told to leave and call back in the morning.

Peter Flanigan did regain consciousness two days after he was admitted to St. Patrick's. He softy complained of severe pain in his right leg. He said he could feel electric-like impulses shooting down his leg — all the way to his toes.

It was not until the end of the first week of hospital care that the medical staff thought that it was time to tell Flanigan that he did not have a right leg. It had to be removed because the blood supply to the lower leg was cut off by the crushing blow to his femur. The mass of tissue above the knee was so mangled, that it was beyond mending. With blood unable to flow to the lower leg, gangrene was almost a certainty. There was no other choice for the medical staff but amputation. The right leg was cut off at the joint between the hip and femur.

When told of his loss, Peter Flanigan bit his lower lip, closed his eyes and fell silent.

The surgeon delivering the message to Flanigan respected his silence. It was a quarter of an hour later when Peter opened his eyes and tried to force a slight smile when he said, "Guess I'll never get that college football scholarship."

The surgeon looked at the nurses in surprise. "And we thought this was going to be a long and serious discussion with Mr. Flanigan."

"When can I get up and about?"

"Not for a long time. We'll monitor your recovery and decide when you have healed enough to use crutches."

"And a wooden leg?"

"We refer to artificial limbs as prostheses, Peter. What it is made of is of less importance than the good fit and the willingness of the user to establish a gait that is comfortable."

"So I should be up and about by next month?"

"No. Expect a long hospital stay and then perhaps by Christmas you can be 'up and about'."

In the following weeks and months, Flanigan progressed well. The hospital staff got to know him, and by mid-October he was permitted to use crutches in the hospital corridors. Thanksgiving Day, he ventured out to Mass at St. Francis Xavier Church. He arrived early, sat in the last pew, closed his eyes, and continued a simple repetitive prayer of thanks that he'd begun after regaining consciousness:

O God I thank you for allowing me to continue. I pledge my life to fight the powers of injustice and violence. Oh Jesus, I beg your guidance in helping me to continue to search for ways to fulfill your Sermon on the Mount.

However, the following day, Flanigan learned that his hope to continue to fight had another road block. He was informed that he had developed blood complications; his white cell count was reaching dangerous levels.

One of the hospital internists told Flanigan that he would have to be moved to another hospital where specialized care would be available.

"As you know, Peter, you are still under the supervision of the United States Federal Government," the internist told him. "Every effort is being made to treat your problem. The advice of Federal medical officials is that the best care available for you is at the Oak Ridge Army Hospital, in Oak Ridge, Tennessee. We are informed that specialists there can bring you around — get you healthy once again."

"An Army hospital? I'm not in the army. That's why I'm here today — because I refused to register for the army or any other military branch."

"Right. I'll repeat once more, Peter, you are under the jurisdiction of the United States Federal Government. You are not choosing to go to Tennessee, you are being sent. You will not be compelled to assist the military. In fact, an argument could be made that you are taking up time, space and money that would otherwise be directed to the military.

"Look, Peter, we've all grown fond of you here at St. Patrick's. We want you to receive the very best care. There is no reason not to believe the medical personnel at Oak Ridge, nor the urgency of the directive from the U.S. Bureau of Prisons for your transfer to Tennessee.

"I talked to a member of the medical staff at Oak Ridge this morning and he assured me that you will receive the very best care. I'm confident that you'll be in good hands, Peter. Not every medical institution in the United States has such support and strength of staff as the medical facility at Oak Ridge."

Flanigan quickly made up his mind about Anna Maria. He went back to his room and wrote a hurried letter to her.

> Dear Anna Maria,
> Thank you for the letters and your concern about my condition. I am not unhappy that my mother informed you that I am a one-leg guy. I just couldn't get myself totell you.
>
> This morning I was informed about additional problems and it's time that I got the courage to tell you what must be said.
>
> Anna Maria, our relationship has to end. There is no good reason for you to sit at home and school waiting around for a one-legged jail bird with a blood disease to come hopping home to you. Please don't. It's over, Anna Maria. Don't think that I am giving up on myself or demanding pity.
>
> Pity! God, how I detest that thought!
>
> I've always been able to take some punishment, Anna Maria. But I can't take punishing you. That is the only thing that would threaten my determination to get better. I'll be fine if I know that you can begin living a normal life for a college woman.

Tell your mother and father that I think of them
often. I shall always remember you.

The Best,
Peter

Flanigan was escorted to Oak Ridge by two United States Federal
Marshals who then entrusted their charge to the Military Police at the
hospital. For the MP's, it was simply a matter of signing in Peter and
telling him he was restricted to the hospital. For Flanigan, it was another prison. The freedom he had regained in Missoula, Montana was
gone.

Flanigan would soon find out that Oak Ridge was more than just a
military hospital. When World War II began, radiation research was in
high gear. The University of Chicago, the University of Rochester in New
York State, and The University of California at Berkeley were among a
growing number of research centers contracted to become part of the
Manhattan Project. Two key Federal Government Centers for nuclear
studies and experiments were located at Los Alamos, California and
Oak Ridge, Tennessee.

The active ingredient of a atomic explosion — plutonium, had
been discovered in 1941. Plutonium had several code names, sometimes simply called "the product". In January of 1944, it became apparent that people would be working "the product" as production of
plutonium increased. Leaders of the super secret project issued direc-
tives to test plutonium on animals and later on "HPs" — human prod-
ucts, as medical officials referred to unknowing people who were injected with radioactive plutonium. Scientists would eventually target
dozens of subjects who were long-term care patients and people who
did not ask a lot of questions, people who were culturally trained to
acquiesce to authority. Poor people, Blacks, and prisoners were favorite "HPs".

Oak Ridge Army Hospital was the first institution to inject an
"HP" with plutonium. In the same ward as Flanigan was a 53-year-old
civilian construction worker who had broken a leg and an arm while
working at the Oak Ridge Research Laboratory. There was no other
physical problem with Ebb Cade, in fact, records testify that medical
doctors noted that he was "well developed and well nourished."

Peter Flanigan was curious about the attention given to Mr. Cade.
Cade's bed was across the aisle from Flanigan's, who noted a parade of
people in white as they made a pilgrimage to the bed of Mr. Cade.

"The leg and arm are healing marvelously, Mr. Cade. That is a
credit to your good living, right? Not much smoking and drinking and
horsing around, eh, Mr. Cade?" said Dr. Lark, one of several physicians
attending to the man.

"Guess you must be right. I sure enough would like to get out of
here though and horse around. How long do I have to stay here?"

"You have to mend, Ebb. Can't get you messed up like that young
buck over there that just came in from Montana. He had a broken leg
too. But he lost the leg, Ebb. Be patient, and put your trust in the doctors and nurses."

Ebb Cade did trust the medical staff at Oak Ridge Army Hospital.
A Black person, he became the first of many people to be injected with
micrograms of plutonium. Years later, Dr. Joseph Howland, a medical
doctor at Oak Ridge, in 1944, would testify that injections had been
given with "no consent from the patient."

In March of 1944, Ebb Cabe was injected with 4.7 micrograms of
plutonium. After four hours, his blood was tested. After 96 hours, his
bone tissue was sampled for traces of "the product." Every time he
urinated or defecated for the next 50 days, he had to keep specimens
for analysis at the Oak Ridge Manhattan Project. During that same
time, fifteen of his teeth were extracted and checked for plutonium.

Dr. Glenn Seaborg of the University of California had urged a
quick series of experiments on humans so that more could be known

about exposure to plutonium. He wrote a letter to Dr. Robert Stone, Health Director of the Metallurgical Laboratory of the University of Chicago. In the letter, he stressed that "plutonium and its compounds may be very great. Due to its alpha radiation and long life it may be that permanent location in the body of even small amounts — say one milligram or less may be harmful."

Later, in reference to injections of plutonium, the Manhattan Project term became ---- MPBB — Maximum Permissible Body Burden.

As Ebb Cade's broken bones healed and Peter became more dexterous with his crutches, Flanigan received good news. His first prosthesis was ready for use. The wait was longer than normal because of the long list of men who lost limbs in far off places such as North Africa, the Italian Campaign, and the island fighting in the Pacific.

In mid March of '44, Cade told Flanigan about all the tests he was going through.

"I'm ready to go home and those people are still saying, 'O.K. Mr. Cade, we need another urine specimen. O.K. Mr. Cade we need another turd.'

"I tell you Flanigan, peein' and shittin' is almost like a job here and I just want out."

Cade was released when he was no longer useful to the study but he did survive and would be called back again years later for further tests.

Shortly before Ebb Cade was released, Dr. Duane Lark, one of the Oak Ridge Army Hospital pathologists who was treating Flanigan's purported blood disease,+ had a long chat with Peter. It was a very pragmatic talk, filled with questions about his family background, his Catholic education and beliefs, his conscientious objection, jail and prison, and his injury and illness.

After some time, Flanigan asked, "Excuse me, Doctor, but is this a friendly talk or is this an interview?"

Lark smiled. "Both, Mr. Flanigan. You see, I firmly believe something good may come from your being here. We are going to do our best to make you better and it is necessary for people like me to get to know you patients.

"What pleases me is the progress you seem to be making. Even the physical therapists are astounded when they see you doing push-ups in the ward, and we all marvel at the increased agility you have developed with your prosthesis."

"I feel strong and I'm ready to get out of this place."

"Mr. Flanigan, when the Federal Bureau of Prisons notified us that they had a subject for us to work with, we were surprised to learn that you were a paroled prisoner. The Bureau tells us that you still have over a year to complete under their jurisdiction and that if the accident hadn't occurred, you would be doing something else within the authority of the United States government.

"Now, here at Oak Ridge, you have the opportunity to do something very positive — to save lives, to help other people. From what I have gleaned from our conversation, you are a very moral person, a fellow who wants to do the right thing. Would you like to help other folks stay healthy?"

"Well, yes. Of course."

"Then this is a perfect opportunity, Mr. Flanigan. You can be part of test program than will benefit mankind. That is an exciting thought, isn't it?"

"Sure it is."

"Then you will cooperate, won't you? It won't be necessary to write up a lot of paperwork on it. The tests will be mostly injections and periodic checks on your urine and feces."

"Sounds like the same tests that Mr. Cade went through."

"Yes, somewhat. He was very cooperative."

"But he didn't know what the tests were about?"

"Well, the tests are secret. I don't know the whole story either.

Mr. Cade had only a few years of education. It's difficult trying to explain medical testing to someone from the sub-cultures. Do you understand what I mean?"

"What am I going to be injected with and for how long?"

"Good questions. You will be injected with a substance that will be handled by many people in years to come. We want to be sure that this life-saving substance is not in itself harmful. We will give you very small doses and then study your system to determine how quickly you dispose of them through your urinary tract and lower intestine. Orderlies will provide you with the appropriate containers to collect the specimens.

"We can begin immediately, Mr. Flanigan. I want to thank you for your generosity and cooperation."

From April of 1944 through May, Peter Flanigan was injected with a number of doses of plutonium. Like Ebb Cade before him, he was the center of much attention and like Cade, his bodily excretions were treated like liquid gold and tiger-eye nuggets.

"I've forgotten how a flush toilet works," said Flanigan to one of the orderlies.

Meanwhile, Peter was receiving frequent letters from his mother who kept him posted on news of Wurtzville. Little mention was made of Anna Maria except to say that she stopped by often with little Charlie Rozer who was now going on two years old and saying some words.

On June 6, the Allies began the long predicted invasion of Europe. Among the invaders was Master Sergeant Charles Rozer, platoon sergeant of a heavy weapons company of the 101st Airborne. The 101st, 81st and the British 6th Airborne Division combined to secure bridges and beach heads in Normandy, during the main invasion force called "D-Day."

Rozer and his men had an easier time than anticipated. Winston Churchill later told that he had telegraphed Stalin the day after D-Day: "20,000 airborne troops are safely landed behind the flanks of the enemy's lines, and have made contact in each case with American and British sea-borne forces. We got across with small loses. We had expected to lose about 10,000 men."

In early July, Flanigan received a brief letter from Anna Maria and a news clipping from the Wurtzville Courier. It was the first that he'd heard from her since she'd followed his instruction to stop corresponding many months before.

> Dear Peter,
>
> After you read the news item enclosed, will you please reconsider writing to me? You are always on my mind.
>
> > Love,
> > Anna Maria

Before he looked at the clipping, Peter held the note tightly and did what he had learned to do to try to control pain. He pressed his top front teeth over his bottom lip and bit hard into the skin to control his premonition. Then, he read the article.

LOCAL MAN KILLED AFTER D-DAY

> M/Sgt. Charles Rozer of the 101st Airborne Division was killed on June 28th, just three weeks after D-Day. According to a telegram received by his parents, Mr.& Mrs. Frederick Rozer of Wurtzville, M/Sgt. Rozer was mortally wounded in an exchange of fire with Nazi forces in a small village south of Cherbourg, France.

M/Sgt. Rozer is survived by his son, Charles, his mother, Freida, and his father Frederick Rozer.

Flanigan released the bite on his lower lip, crumbled the news clipping in his hand and sobbed for the first time in many years. He sat for hours and reviewed his young, active life. Images of people he met and things that he'd done slowly drifted through his mind. Drenched in summer sweat of a hot Tennessee afternoon, his pensiveness focused on Anna Maria, then his mother, Ally Oop, Bill Mahoney, Mother Rachel, Rabbi Orlevsky, Father Sampson, Dorothy Day and Peter Maurin, Bentley and McGinley, Handsome Lake and Randolph Jackson, Tom Hanson, and the many other people who had influenced him in some way.

After several hours, he went to Dr. Duane Lark's office and asked to talk to him. He was allowed immediate entrance.

"Dr. Lark, I want out of the test program," Flanigan began. "You said over a month ago that my blood count was back to normal. I know that I agreed I would participate in the program but I feel that I have done my share. I'm anxious to get on to other things."

"Peter, I couldn't agree more with you. We all wondered when you were going to say 'enough of this.' You have been one of the best subjects we have had. Last month, I had my secretary send a memo out to the Bureau of Prisons asking for your immediate release from any obligation to serve out the remaining year of your sentence. I asked that you not be transferred to some other detail or action no matter how removed from any contribution to the war of which you so strongly disapprove."

He handed a letter of response he had received the previous week from the Bureau of Prisons that agreed to the conditions suggested by Lark. Flanigan was to be released whenever Lark felt that the testing was completed.

"We had hoped for another week or two from you, Peter, but I think we now know what we wanted to know. I am going to request that you have yearly examinations by people from our staff. The University of Rochester in upstate New York is not too far from your home area. They are now doing most of the testing that we initiated here at Oak Ridge. We will provide transport and lodging for your one-day visit each June for a checkup. Is that agreeable?"

"Sure. When can I learn more about my guinea pigging? Just what is 'the product'?"

"One of these days, I'm sure we will all learn. I'm as anxious as you to see its application, Peter. It's exciting to just contemplate being a part of history, isn't it?"

"Yeah, I guess so."

The following day, Peter received his release from Oak Ridge Army Hospital and copies of the letters from the Bureau of Prisons suspending the remainder of his sentence. Lark had train tickets that would take him to Knoxville, to Washington, Philadelphia and Wilkes-Barre.

In Philadelphia, he called Anna Maria.

"Hi. Would you do me a favor and pick me up at the train station in Wilkes-Barre tomorrow afternoon at two?"

Anna Maria was almost speechless. Though she'd been completely caught off guard, Peter read her voice as somewhat disappointed.

She was ecstatic.

When Flanigan got off the train from Philadelphia, he immediately spotted Anna Maria, but she was on her tip toes — straining to find him in the crowd. Then she saw a head rising and dropping in the middle of the exiting passengers. It was the smiling face of Peter when he caught her eyes and lost them momentarily as he pulled up on his right hip to swing the prosthesis forward. As Flanigan got closer, Anna Maria ran toward him, squeezed through the crowd and kissed him for what seemed to Flanigan the most wonderful minute he had ever lived.

Peter threw his small grey canvas clothes sack in the back of Anna Maria's old Ford pickup and they drove north toward Wurtzville.

"Peter, reach into the glove compartment and take out the packet with the elastic band on it.

"Now lift off the letter that is on the top. The packet came to me just a few days ago. It's from Federal Bureau of Investigation. Some are letters you sent to me. Most are from me to you, but the important one is the Easton letter. Remember? It's the one you almost got but the Easton police picked it up for the FBI. Well, there it is. Never opened, right? I may have forgotten exactly what I said but after your accident, I quickly remembered the essence of the letter. Open it and read it, Peter. Read it out loud."

Dear Peter,

I'll write a long letter tomorrow. Today, I am in the mood to be aggressive with you. I know, I know, a woman shouldn't be so forward with a man. What kind of good upbringing did I have anyway?

Peter, the simple truth is that I love you dearly, madly, muchly, so muchly, that I can't think of spending my life without you.

Is that a proposal or am I going word nuts? Proposals come from the male of the species, right? So, you know what? I'll stop short of a proposal and let my man make it. O.K? And you know what-what?

The what-what is this: I want you no matter what happens to you in your adventures. I shall always love you. I shall always stand by your side.

Love,
Anna Maria

"Good God, don't I express myself well?" asked Anna Maria.

"Now, it's my turn," said Peter. "Can I make my proposal conditional?"

"How conditional?"

"That little Charlie is ours. That we adopt him."

"It's already done, Peter. He's my boy. When you and I become one, you'll be his daddy."

"Now how do we do all this, Anna Maria? You going to college, me wanting to go to college but without a job."

"Whoa, Peter Flanigan. My father can't wait to get you back on the job. We can drive to college together and back to the job. I've been doing it for two years now — why can't you just join me?"

"A one-legged waiter?"

"Hey, I saw you jogging at the train station on your fake leg. Why not at our restaurant? My father is going to ask you to take over the bar, he hates making mixed-drinks. He practically chases away customers. He thinks everyone should drink Chianti."

"O.K., let me map this out," said Peter. "You finish in two years and start your professional job. That means that I have got two more years to go to finish my bachelor's, and three more if I go into law."

"Law?"

"Yeah, law."

Anna Maria giggled. "But Peter, aren't you a law-breaker?"

"There are laws that need to be broken, to be destroyed, to be thrown out. I want to fight the power that hides behind this legal sham — and I won't give up."

"Giving up isn't you, Peter Flanigan," Anna Maria agreed.

"Nope. And it isn't going to be."

The Wisdom Box

Jack Gilroy

After writing *Absolute Flannigan* I was still haunted by the thoughts of the young men who left my classroom in upstate New York to go to Vietnam. Some came back to tell despairing stories of their ventures. Some were hurt in mind and body. Five came back in body bags. A younger sister of one of my students killed in Vietnam told of going to a funreal home to view the frozen body of her brother flown in the previous day. She told of the wounds on her brother's body and the mud of Vietnam caked in his hair and on his neck.

I anguished over how complicit our culture was in indoctrination of our young people. As an ex-infantryman, I learned how to use every killing weapon available but was taught nothing in the military about human rights. It was us, "people of the home and the brave" vs. the enemy. I was not a Vietnam veteran but I could understand the My Lai type massacres. I could understand how young men from our culture would cut off ears of the "enemy" to prove body count results. I began to understand how we teach our kids to accept violence as a normal part of our existence.

Government violence, the license that makes killing legal, finally struck me as the most dangerous license. Our very culture and government giving encouragement and the means to kill became to me a symptom of an ill society.

The Wisdom Box resulted from those thoughts. I imagined a young man who was educated in respect for all living things. I imagined a young man who was encouraged to question authority and not lock step to orders that clashed with his values and his understanding of right and wrong. The main character of The Wisdom Box, Frank Brosnan, is that kind of guy.

The Wisdom Box is a coming of age, historical novel, of a boy adopted by a college professor and a Catholic priest. The couple, secretly married, expose young Frank Brosnan to questions from a strange box that has been in the professor's family for many generations. Frank's value system, molded by his parents and Wisdom Box questions, lead him into dangerous confrontations with powerful forces of injustice. From the Civil Rights movement to the Vietnam conflict, Frank Brosnan pouts his beliefs on the line. He learns that commands to lead an ethical life are within each person, not words carved in stone or gold tablets or commands from government authorities. He also learns that keeping one's integrity comes with a price, a price Brosnan is willing to pay.

Chapter 1
The Carnival Kid

It was late fall when the carnival closed in on Ithaca. I can still picture the men pitching tents along the canal leading out to Cayuga Lake. My momma was always asking the carnival foreman where we were going next. The foreman was a big fat man who always had a stogie stuck between his stained teeth. He never bothered to wipe the drool oozing from the corners of his mouth nor the brown beads clinging to his stubby facial growth. I was just six years old; looking up at him I always seemed to zoom in on his hairy nostrils. I could look right up and into his bushy nose. I imagined that little bugs must be up there — playing and flying around in those giant caves. "Ye'll knows when we gets there," was all he told my momma.

By ten in the morning, carnival tents were set and my momma had pressed her dancing clothes and hung them on a rope behind the stage. We now had time to walk around town and see the sights. She bought me a Milky Way and we started off. I lagged behind until my mother came back to me, bending over to my height so I could see the

By ten in the morning, carnival tents were set and my momma had pressed her dancing clothes and hung them on a rope behind the stage. We now had time to walk around town and see the sights. She bought me a Milky Way and we started off. I lagged behind until my mother came back to me, bending over to my height so I could see the bright blue of her eyes and freckles on her high cheek bones. She pointed up to a hill.

"Frankie, ya see that tall pointy building? Well, that's where we's going."

We set off again and climbed steep hills to wide lawns that rose to a ridge with a clock tower. People with books under their arms seemed to be going in all directions. It was almost noon when my momma and I entered the tower and began walking up the spiral steps.

"I'm tired, momma. Can I sit down?"

"Sits long as you like, Frankie. But we've got to get to the top so's we can talk about your future."

"My future?"

"Uh huh, your future. You ain't no baby nomore!"

She seemed to have something on her mind, so I decided I didn't need to rest. We were about halfway up when we heard the bell chimes, loud as thunder.

"Cover your ears, Frankie, and keep climbing."

At the top, several young men and women were working the chimes with both hands and feet. An older man smiled at us, motioning us in closer to see the chime musicians as they finished the noon rendition of "High Above Cayuga's Waters."

When they left, my momma had me look through the vertical stone openings. I guess I was too little or too tired to remember the view I appreciate so much today. Yet I do recall the blue lake and how it seemed to disappear in the green hills.

"This old lake just keeps agoing and agoing," said my momma. "It can take a body clear out to the ocean. A man told me that you can get on a boat and go straight to New York City and then to China if 'n you want to. All on the same boat. Ain't that sump'n, Frankie?"

"Can we do that, momma?"

"Someday, maybe. Not just yet. But I think this town's a good place for a boy to be growed up in. After what happened to you yesterday, I don't want you to be growed up in a carnival. Carnival living ain't healthy for little people. You need a nice place like this here town. You see how clean the folks are? Look at those young men wearing nice shirts and ties and going to school. Maybe if in you stay in this town, you could go to school too."

"But where would we live, momma?"

"Oh, not me, child. There ain't nothing for me here. I'm a'talkin about you. Just give me a couple of days to work sump'n out, Frankie."

I was too confused to reply. Walking down the hill from Cornell and seeing the carnival tents, I wondered how I was going to stay in Ithaca by myself.

Momma was right, though. Bad things do happen in the carnival. Especially when my mom was working on stage and I was told to stay in our tent and play. That was when one of the men came in and did things but warned me never to tell anyone what he did. I was so scared that I didn't ever tell, not until the day before we got to Ithaca. The man had made teeth marks on my body. When my momma saw them, she forced me to tell the things he did to me.

"So Weasel did that, did he! I'll mush his brains!" said my momma. She started to go out from the tent, but stopped. She frowned and said, "Reckon if 'n I do, there'll be no work and no bread — him being the foreman's son and all. You got to come and stay under the stage during my acts, Frankie. Later, we'll work sump'n out."

I hated being used by Weasel, but staying under the stage while my momma bumped and grinded, and hearing all the whistles and jeers from the men who paid $2 to see my mom bare naked, was no fun either. I could peek through the board that propped up the stage and see the men whooping and hollering at my momma and saying things. Bad things. And throwing silver dollars up on the stage.

"Pick it up with your lips, Lola."

Lola wasn't my momma's real name. It was Gertrude. But she said that it wasn't a good name for her show. So she had a big sign over the door to the side show that said:

"LADY LOLA & HER LOCKING LIPS"

When my mom did her bare naked split onto the floor, the men would holler, "At a way ta snatch it, Lola." I didn't know what they were talking about but my momma always had lots of silver dollars around.

After the afternoon show, momma dressed and took me by the hand. We walked back into town. When she saw a building with a cross on it she said, "This here is the church we got to go into, Frankie. This is a church about Jesus. He died on a cross. You and me are Jesus people." She had me sit in a back pew and she approached a man with a black suit and a white collar. They talked a while and then the man and my momma went off to the side and the man wrote on a paper and gave it to my momma. He came down to me and smiled at me and patted me on the head. Then he took us outside and pointed directions to someplace for my momma and me. He told my momma that he would phone ahead so we would be expected.

"Let's go, Frankie. We have a lady to meet."

We walked along Tioga Street and up several hills. My momma kept referring to the rough map sketch the man in the church had drawn for her.

"There it is, Frankie. Ain't it grand."

"What is it, momma?"

"It's a big, big, house, child. And look over yonder. The lake. And look down there! Did you ever see such a beautiful fall of water? It spills into that gorge like Niagara. Now you be careful around here. One step over the ledge and my little boy's a goner."

My momma knocked on the tall double door. That was when I first saw Loretta. I suppose I thought she was quite old. My momma was only twenty-two at the time and Loretta was probably forty. She was expecting us and ushered us in right away. She didn't pay too much mind to my momma. She had the biggest grin on her face. She made me want to smile back, and I did. Then, she reached down and picked me up and gave me a big kiss. She held me in her arms and said, "Why, isn't Frankie Brosnan just about the handsomest boy you ever saw."

I kind of looked around wondering if there was another Frankie in the house. But she was talking to me.

"My name is Frankie Pickering, ma'am, and this here lady is my momma, Gertrude Pickering."

My momma looked a little sad but she said, "Frankie, now you have two mommas. Miss Brosnan is your new momma and I'm your old momma."

I looked at Loretta and then at my momma. I was totally confused.

"Let's all go into the kitchen and have some cookies and milk. Then we can talk about all the things we can do to make a good life for Frankie Brosnan." said Loretta, as she carried me from the foyer through the dark wooded hallway to the kitchen. The sweet smell of something baking twitched my nose, and then I saw a mound of cookies. Loretta took a quart of milk from the refrigerator and shook the cream at the neck of the bottle until it blended with the rest of the milk. She poured each of us a glass, and served us cookies on plates with cloth napkins off to the side. It was quite strange. Not at all like our tent house that we put up and took down all around the country. I had seen refrigerators before; but of course, we didn't have one. During the real hot months, my momma got ice and kept it in a tub that was all wrapped and covered in canvas and paper. That was our refrigerator.

I scanned the kitchen and fixed my gaze on a large white stove and a counter with a bread box and toaster. This was really a grand place, I hope my momma and I can stay here, I thought.

We were all eating cookies and drinking cold milk when Loretta shifted her full attention to my momma.

"Mrs. Pickering, have you explained our arrangement to Frankie?"

My momma looked scared and sad again. She didn't look at me but fixed her pretty eyes on Loretta's oilcloth table design. The cloth was a print of a giant carousel and my momma's eyes just followed the horses and children all around the table before she kind of caught herself and smiled a bit. Then she looked up.

"No, I reckon I didn't say much to Frankie. Seein' that you was going to talk to him, I figured best to keep my mouth shut for a spell. I'd sure appreciate if you could talk to our boy."

Loretta turned to me, and I recall very well the sweet smile she gave me, and the gentle tone of her voice. She sounded different from my momma. I didn't think I would ever love her like I loved my momma, but Loretta sure did win me over that afternoon. She made things so clear and simple. I was mesmerized with her words and with her mellow voice. Her eyes sparkled and smiled at me so that I couldn't look away. My gaze focused on Loretta's big green eyes, long silky red hair and a smile that showed big teeth. My momma's teeth were brown and always aching her, but Loretta's teeth were as white as store teeth.

Loretta told me that my momma loved me, but that my momma worried that I might get hurt in the carnival life.

"Your momma has to work to survive, Frankie. It's best you stay with me and have your momma come and visit us when the carnival comes by this way again." said Loretta.

I couldn't speak. I tried to say something but I couldn't speak. My mouth trembled. I felt the tears come down my cheek and saw them splash on the carousel oilcloth. I got out of my chair and ran to the window that overlooked the falls and the lake. I pressed my nose and mouth up against the window so that my momma wouldn't hear my sobs.

Momma always told me to not cry like a baby. "You're the man of the house, Frankie. You're not a little boy. You're a little man."

I stayed there a long time and listened to momma and Loretta talk about me staying as Loretta's boy. After a time, my momma came to me and hugged me. She didn't say much. Nothing that Loretta could hear, anyway. She whispered in my ear.

"Frankie, I ain't going away from you. I'm always goin' to be on your little shoulder. Right here where I'm a hugging you now. When you want me to talk to you, just close your eyes and don't make no sound. Just talk to me without making noise, not even a whisper. I'll get back to you. It may take some time, you know. But if you close your eyes and listen — you'll hear a voice, Frankie. It'll be your momma talkin."

She kissed me on top of the head and I never turned to see her leave. In fact, I never saw her again.